MASTER OF THE ARENA

MASTER OF THE ARENA

J. D. EDWIN

Hey reader! Want a free book? Get one when you sign up for J. D. Edwin's newsletter. Sign up at jdedwin.com.

In the beginning the Universe was created. This has made a lot of people very angry and been widely regarded as a bad move.

- DOUGLAS ADAMS, *THE RESTAURANT AT THE END OF THE UNIVERSE*

CONTENTS

SEVEN

CHAPTER 1

Run.
Survive. Manifest. Bleed.
Thorns.
Champion.

I OPENED MY EYES.

I had grown used to the dreams, and as usual, no matter how vivid they were in the dark, they melted away like flakes of ice on a hot stove when light arrived. Tears hung from my eyes, but whether they were tears of sadness or merely the last remnants of sleep, I couldn't tell. As I sat up the last of the dream fell away, shaken off as easily as a leaf that landed on my shoulder.

Tam smiled at me from his spot on the ground, chewing on a rag doll I'd painstakingly stitched for him from scraps of old cloth. He babbled and reached for me.

"Did Mama doze off?" I cooed as I picked him up and tickled his chubby feet. His joyful laugh rang against the walls of our tiny bedroom. "Come, let's put you to bed."

And so I bathed and dressed him, then laid him down for

the last time on the little cot across the room from mine. He wiggled, smiling up at me as if my face were the most amazing sight in the known world. I smiled down at him until he closed his eyes, then sat down next to him and stroked his hair.

Has this scar always been there?

Long, ugly, and red, it snaked over most of my left forearm. Whatever caused it must've been a painful ordeal, but I couldn't recall it.

Just like this one.

On the palm of my right hand was a series of marks like pen strokes. I'd tried to wipe them off several times, but they refused to budge. Seven strokes formed a perfect circle on my skin, dark red as if left from an old burn, but I stared at them and remembered no pain. I spent a moment pondering these scars, as I always did before bed. The effort gave me a mild headache, like staring into a bright light for too long. So I lay down in my own cot and watched Tam's little chest rise and fall. I used to worry that he might fall out if he rolled, but not anymore. I already knew he would wake lying on his side, bright violet eyes fixed on me. And when he saw me wake up, he would smile and reach to be picked up. We would spend the day inside, playing and laughing on the floor, curtains drawn to hide the thick gray mist outside. I would play him his flute, and though my skills at stringing together a tune were atrocious at best, he would still smile at every screechy, off-key note.

Tomorrow would be the last day.

So would the day after that.

And the one after that.

VOICES DRIFTED through the closed door to our room. The main room of Mama Dorma's house buzzed with conversation and music. A gathering was taking place, and I could hear Santi's throaty laugh in between intermittent chatter. Mama Dorma was doubtlessly showing off the stone vases in the hall and the jasmium flowers blooming in the front garden. The spicy scent of her meat stew, which had been cooking all day, wafted through the door. My stomach growled, but to show my face would only lead to trouble. I hoped someone would remember to slide a plate in for me.

A pair of feet shuffled near the door. I heard arguing—Santi wanting me to join the festivities, and his mother, the matriarch of the family, vehemently cursing him for even thinking of allowing a Kol out in the presence of honored guests. I pretended not to hear—I had no interest in being paraded before judging eyes anyway. This tiny room with its little cots, brown floor, and colorful tapestries on the walls depicting cheerful scenes of women wearing sunhats and picking summer fruit—this was where I preferred to be, just Tam and me.

Finally, as the sounds of the party began to die down, the door opened and a bowl and spoon were pushed through. The root vegetables were cold and the rich soup had begun to congeal, but I was grateful for it regardless. I ate sitting on the cot, trying and failing to keep Tam from grabbing at every bite. While he had been well fed before the gathering, this was the first proper meal I'd had all day. I finished the soggy meal without complaint and set the bowl out of Tam's reach on the small bedside table. That table wouldn't be out of his reach much longer, not once he learned to walk, which could be any day now.

Night would fall soon. I would doze for a while in the evening and dream, then wake without remembering what the dreams were—though somehow I knew it was the same dream over and over. And I would put Tam to bed again. For the last time.

The hundredth last time.

The thousandth last time.

Each time was the last. I told myself this, then woke up and did it all again. No matter how many times I played that damned flute, that same damned song, I never seemed to get any better. That same cold bowl pushed through the door, day after day. That same shuffle of feet in the hall and those same songs and curses. That same gray mist rolling past the curtains I never opened. I studied those scars and they made my head hurt, so I watched Tam sleep. It was all a play. An endless pantomime.

My baby will never grow.
My baby will stay small and lovely.
My baby will never change.
My baby will stay so long as I stay.

I slept, then woke and repeated it all again. *For the last time,* I told myself as I held him tightly, smelling his milky goodness and feeling his chubby arms around my neck. The very last time.

If only he didn't feel so real.

I cried on the final night. The real, true final night. I wasn't entirely sure why I cried, because I didn't know what lay beyond, only that it loomed so frighteningly close, like a dark, silent, stalking thing breathing down my neck. When the tears dried, I pulled back the curtains and watched the gray mist roll by. Then I sat and stroked Tam's hair, memorizing the feel of every dark fiber. He wiggled and cooed and fell asleep gazing up into my eyes. I leaned down and kissed him, took two steps back, and tore my eyes away. If I looked at him, I would lose my courage again. I would rush back to the cot and pledge to spend eternity by his side, whether he was real or not.

The bowl from the thousandth last meal we had shared lay on the floor. I kicked it. It slid across the floor and clattered against the wall. Through the bedroom door I could hear the party winding down, though I knew there was no one on the other side. If I opened the door and turned around, would I see Tam melt away, like the dreams that haunted me so relentlessly? I wrapped my fingers around the knob, took a shuddering breath, and pulled.

. . .

THE COLD AND metal that greeted me were jarring but unsurprising. The warm browns and reds of my husband's family home were nowhere to be found, though I never expected it to be there. I didn't need to turn to know that the room behind me, along with the phantom of my son, was gone. I stepped through the door into the familiar chill of the arena —a chill I'd come to know so very well.

Run. Survive.

I shuddered. Breathing suddenly became a struggle. The scar on my left arm began to hurt and I looked down to see I was digging the fingernails of my right hand into it. I forced my fingers loose and gazed up at the metal dome above me. It was different, alien. The chill penetrated me to the bone. I looked down and saw not a sandy beach, nor a paved road, nor a mountain path, nor any of the stages upon which I'd run and screamed and bled. Instead, it was a surface of metal plating, stained here and there with dark spots that I hoped were rust and not something worse. I moved slowly in a circle, holding myself and shivering, feeling as if I'd been swallowed by a giant metal beast. I had only known the games, each one a different stage, a different terrain, a different world.

Is this really the arena in its true form?

My head spun and for a moment I couldn't feel my body in space. Flashes of sights and sounds assaulted me from all directions and I forced air in and out of my lungs. I heard desperate calls for help, the faraway voices of the dead. Lives lost. Everything spun faster and faster. The scar on my left arm stung and when I looked down, blood spilled out of it in rivers.

I have to get out.

Explosions. Screaming. Every hair on my body stood up.

I won. I get to leave. I have to leave.

Blood everywhere. Teeth in my flesh. I couldn't breathe.

Have to leave. Have to leave.

"I was beginning to think you preferred stasis."

The voices disappeared as if a door slammed shut. The sudden silence was deafening. I looked at my arm again expecting to find torn flesh and flowing red, but saw only a dark, dry scar. Running a finger over its surface, I wondered for a moment how much time had actually passed. The circle on my right palm remained unchanged.

"The winner's laurel will not go away so easily."

I started and searched for the source of the voice. Scanning the arena, I nearly missed him as my eyes ran over where he stood—his fur blurred almost seamlessly into the brown rust of the dome. Short and stumpy, standing a whole head shorter than me, he was definitely not what I expected. Two short arms were linked behind the back of his pudgy body, and two more were folded in front. Dark, round eyes rolled over me, taking me in from head to toe. The wispy brown fur on his long, floppy ears quivered. A wide, friendly mouth spread into a smile beneath his round button nose.

I shuddered despite his disarming appearance. He resembled the little friendly puppets I played for Tam or the sweet, harmless wild hoppers that snooped around Mama Dorma's yard, searching for vegetable scraps that I sometimes left out for them behind Mama's back. But though I had not seen his face until now, I knew without a doubt who he was. His voice had haunted my every waking moment since the orb had landed on Maeda. The need to flee overcame me and I instinctively reached for the door I had just come through, but my fingers grasped empty air. I stood there with my hand raised, feeling like a fool.

"Welcome." My skin crawled hearing that voice soft and gentle out of the mouth of this creature instead of booming from above. "I am H'otto. I speak for the gods."

"Kol knows," I blurted out, taking a large step back as he took a small one forward. My skin itched, as if aching to escape the rest of me just to be further from him. "Kol wants to leave."

"I imagine you do," H'otto said, unhurried. His eyes blinked separately from one another. "You are welcome to leave any time. But why would you want to?"

Unable to decide between fear and confusion, I said, "Kol wants to go home."

"To the home that forces you to call yourself 'Kol'?" He chuckled. I realized I was still holding the nonexistent doorknob and lowered my hand stiffly. "If you wish. But first, won't you take a walk with me, Seven?"

CHAPTER 2

"YOU ARE WONDERING ABOUT THE ROOM."

I nodded. "Yes."

H'otto walked a few steps in front of me as we traversed the familiar hills behind Mama Dorma's house. Though it was only a mirage constructed by the arena, I found a modicum of peace at the sight of the orange sunset trees and the bluebirds that sang from their branches. Sunlight peeked through the branches, its artificial warmth caressing my exposed skin. If I closed my eyes, I could almost feel home.

Save for the chill. No matter the scenery and the warmth of the fake sun, the arena held a deep, undying chill that I couldn't shake.

"Call it a transitional space. The games can be jarring, as I'm sure you know. The transitional space allows the champions of the games time to adjust to their new reality. Do you understand?"

I nodded again, though I did not. I didn't want to ask questions. What I wanted was for this conversation to end as quickly as possible so I could go home.

"You should not look so down, Seven."

This question I could not avoid. "Why do you call Kol 'Seven'?"

"Because you are the seventh champion of this galaxy." A pause. "Kol," he mused, tasting the word between his furry lips. He glanced back at me as I stayed two steps behind him. "You'll have to forgive me—my knowledge of your sect is rudimentary at best. Cultures, you know. Every planet has so many. We do our best, but there's only so much one can learn. Not to mention we tend to limit ourselves to knowledge essential for the games." He gestured to me with one stubby arm. "Come forward. Walk next to me. You do not have to be afraid."

I *was* afraid of him. Terrified. The disconnect between his voice and appearance made my skin crawl, and the cozy scene around me looked increasingly like a diorama. I couldn't stop fixating on the bare, stark metal surfaces behind it. But none of that was why I walked behind him—habits were difficult to kill.

"Kol must always walk behind. That was what Kol was taught."

H'otto mulled this thought in his furry head. "You always refer to yourself as Kol, eh?"

"Kol is Kol. And a Kol may only be Kol."

He slowed his plodding step and walked alongside me—an odd feeling, as no one had ever done so. "What happens if you were to refer to yourself as 'I'?" he asked with genuine curiosity. "Enlighten this old soul. Even at this age I still have much to learn."

I searched his soft, round face for any sign that this might be a trap. H'otto must've picked up on my agitation. He smiled, not with his mouth but with his eyes, like a hopper receiving a stroke upon its chin.

"Do not worry, child. You have already won. The gods have chosen you to smile upon, Nasmi Kol."

Gods. That word stirred me, but I quickly steeled myself again. My name coming out of his mouth was unsettling. I tried to be brave despite the tremor that went from my fingertips to my core, a tremor that hadn't quite left since I had walked out of the door.

"Go on."

I swallowed. "All Kol are born with the mark of servitude."

"The birthmark on the back of your neck."

I reached back instinctively and touched it. I could not see nor feel the black patch that sat where my skull met my spine, but I knew it was there. "Yes."

"Are you aware that it is merely a genetic anomaly causing an overgrowth of pigmented cells?"

I stared at him blankly.

"Never mind. Continue."

"Those with the mark of servitude were created to serve others." I recited the words taught to me since birth, and still repeated each morning as I started the day under Mama Dorma's roof. I knew these words better than my own name. "Kols may only be called Kol. Kols have no other surname. Kols may not elevate themselves above those who are without the mark. A Kol who places themselves equal or above others must be disciplined for their pride."

"Pride, eh?"

"Humility is the Kols' greatest virtue."

"And what sort of 'discipline' might they bring upon you?"

"Exile for the lucky. Stoning for the unlucky."

H'otto sighed. We continued our slow walk through the hills. A pair of bluebirds sang to my right. I had heard that same tune only moments ago. The sun peeked through and stroked the same spot on my arm. The scene was repeating, an endless loop made to seem like more than what it really was. "Beings of your type are quite interesting," he remarked, half to himself.

"Kol's type?"

"You might be surprised to hear that your kind is not the only one of its type. There are many planets in this galaxy, some of which are occupied by beings like yourself—sentient, intelligent, bipedal. That last one was by design, as is most of your commonality." He looked at me with amusement in his dark eyes. "Did you know that in nearly all languages that exist on these planets, they've chosen to name this galaxy for the rivers of stars that run through it? The Galaxy of the Starry River, or some variation of it."

I had no idea what to do with this information.

"The gods have their plans and preferences," H'otto continued. "It is interesting, I say, because another thing you all have in common is your penchant for prejudice." He shook his head slowly. "Truly sad. I have seen it all. Every intelligent society seems to find its own reasons to enact structural prejudice, be it by differences in diet, geographic location, physical appearance, reproductive organs; it's really all the same. I've wondered often whether that is a design of the gods as well or just a coincidence in evolution. But I suppose the answer doesn't matter."

"Kol wants to go home."

H'otto looked me up and down. I feared I had overstepped some unseen boundary, but I could no longer stand here and pretend any of this was relevant to me.

"Kol played the game," I said, my voice firmer than I felt inside. "Kol won. Kol no longer wants to be here. Kol's family is waiting."

"Family. Is that what you want? To go back to where you lived and have your family welcome you back with open arms?"

I started to open my mouth, but realized I had no response. H'otto nodded, as if reading my mind.

"I know about you, Seven. I make it my business to know about those who set foot in the arena, especially those who win. You just said so yourself—as a so-called Kol, you must never place yourself above those who do not bear the mark. And yet, here you stand, the champion. What will your family —or rather, the family you were placed with for servitude—say when you return?"

I couldn't dispute his logic, but I refused to give in. I

couldn't stand being in this arena or on this fake hill another moment. "Kol wants to go home," I repeated stubbornly.

H'otto laid one of his four furry hands on my arm. I expected it to be cold like the arena, but surprisingly it was warm, and soft. I looked into his round eyes and found no anger or hostility. Instead, he looked at me with genuine concern.

"I've known many like you," he said. "Children who long to rush home after the games are over. But once they left the arena, they all realized one thing—the home as they knew it no longer existed. The world changes when the games end, Seven. And you have changed as well, though you may not believe that right now. Just remember this—the gods have smiled upon you. And should you find that your place in the home you longed for is no longer there, you will always have a place among us. You are meant for greater things."

I STOOD outside the tan-colored sandstone house. All around me the bluebirds sang their early evening song. I could see their bright plumage through the leaves of the sunset trees. Dry desert air scratched my face.

I was really home.

The chaotic blur of the arena rang through my head. It came and went like a video clip I couldn't control, bringing with it a flood of dread and unease and fear. I couldn't force it away, but I was quickly becoming accustomed to this unwelcome guest in my mind.

I had thought H'otto would force me to stay, but he hadn't. He had stepped aside and let me out of the arena without a fight.

Save for one thing.

The hulking form next to me let out a series of mechanical clicks. He was a sight indeed—easily twice my height, long coat over his metal trunk. Round glass eyes glowed green inside his metal skull, giving him a permanently startled look. Tubes and flexible wires trailed from his head and back, and when he moved, I could hear soft hissing like air escaping his joints. If he wanted to, he could crush me in a moment under his enormous boulder-like fists.

Take Nix along, H'otto had said. *Let him see you home. If you do not need his help, he will return.*

Help with what? I wanted to think that H'otto had let me leave because he saw that trying to keep me was futile. My world had not changed and neither had I. No matter what they had said about me while I was within the arena, they had to see that I could serve my world and family better by staying alive. I had no need for this metal man, the arena, or him.

I haven't changed.

The warm air smelled like dirt and sun mixed with the sweet scent of Mama Dorma's jasmium flowers. I hadn't realized until now how much I had missed this scent and the little sand-colored house. The "transitional space" had always felt a little off, and despite my dreamy delirium while inside it, some part of me had known it was different. This was real. This was home.

I took a step toward the house. My eyes caught the cracks snaking up the wall along the front door. *Have these always been here?* They looked old, so they must've been. Funny how I had never noticed them before. Nix followed me, his massive metal feet sending clouds of fine dust into the air. I stopped. I doubted my family would react well to me coming home with this strange behemoth. I wanted our reunion to be a happy one, untainted by reminders of the horrible arena.

Were there always so many dead flowers in the flowerbeds?

I shook myself. I was *home.*

"Wait here," I said to the metal man. He hadn't said a word so far. I didn't know if he could speak or not, but he understood well enough. Mechanical lenses whirled and focused on me, followed by a slow nod.

I went to the door and laid my hand on the handle. It was warm from the desert heat. The door was smaller than I remembered, and the windows to either side of it were narrower than when I last saw them. The house couldn't have shrunk in the short time I was gone, could it?

Nix made a sound behind me, an almost inquisitive *whirr* as he tilted his head, as if sensing my hesitation. I quashed my thoughts and gripped the door handle. H'otto's words echoed through my mind again and I shook them off.

I belong here.

I pushed.

For a moment I worried the door would be locked, but it gave way easily. I stepped inside before apprehension could set in again and closed the door behind me.

A roomful of familiar faces turned to me. I started to smile, but froze when I realized that, instead of welcoming, their eyes were cold and acrid. I stood there, an awkward half smile on my face, and for a moment no one spoke. Then, a voice cut into the silence. A voice that struck terror in me second only to that of H'otto.

"Kol."

For a good portion of my life, when I had lived under her roof, Mama Dorma had been the person after the gods to me. I had lived in fear of her fury, which came fast and came often. She sat in a large rocking chair that dwarfed her tiny frame— her usual spot that no one else dared take. Seeing me, she stood. I knew what was coming, but I didn't protect myself.

Does her voice sound different?

The back of her hand connected with the side of my head. She was small but hardy, and her blow knocked me backward. The small of my back met the doorknob, sending a tremor of pain vibrating up my spine. The next blow landed on my face and made my ear ring. I braced myself for the third but it did not come. I raised my eyes at last to see Mama Dorma's dry face, twisted in anger, between the arms of my husband, Santi, who was straining to hold her back by her bony shoulders despite his far superior girth.

"Mama, please," said a sharp voice from behind them. My sister-in-law Eisa stepped into view. She put her long fingers on Mama Dorma's arm and gently guided her a few steps back, but I could see by the shade in her almond eyes that it was not for my benefit. Eisa did nothing for my benefit. Why should she, when I was so much less than her? She was older, she was beautiful and beloved, and more importantly, she was not born a Kol.

Except, just like the rest of the house, she looked different.

From my spot by the door, I could see the entire living room of the house. It hadn't changed one bit since the orb had landed, but I couldn't shake the feeling that it wasn't the same house I had left behind. It was small and cramped. Once this house had been my entire world. Now it was just that—a house, and a tiny one at that. And Eisa. I used to envy her long, thick hair, flowing loose and free, unlike mine which always had to be braided and bound so I could work without distraction. I once thought she was so lovely, all dark eyes and rouge lips. Now, I couldn't help but notice the creases in her forehead and the open pores on her skin. Her eyebrows were uneven. And though she looked at me with derision, I found myself almost wanting to laugh at the idea that such a person as her, so ignorant and plain, would think less of me.

Mama Dorma huffed and shrugged out of Santi's grasp. She spat at me. I looked down at my chest where her spit landed. She might hit me again. She struck me often. I once shook in fear at the sound of her raised voice.

So what?

I searched for signs of that old fear and found none. Did I really used to hide and sob at the thought of being hit by her? Reaching up, I touched the warm spot on my face where her hand had landed. I remembered her angry strikes with such dread, but now I could barely feel them. I had screamed and bled and felt flesh tear from my bones inside the arena. Compared to the horrors I'd seen, she was so small and thin. Was her hair always so brittle and gray? Had her hand always shaken? Had she always had that bow to her back?

Eisa tossed me a flippant glance, as if expecting me to cower before her. She looked like a cuckling bird prancing about trying to show off its feathers. "The Kol found her way back home," she said. "We ought to hear what she has to say, don't you think, Mama?"

"She does *not* need to speak," Mama Dorma replied, biting every word. "She ought to be *stoned*."

These people. They were so uncomplicated.

"Mama . . ." I began, and she struck me again before her children could stop her. This time, I barely flinched.

"Ungrateful child," she said bitterly. "I am not your mama. I will never admit into my house a Kol who does not know her place."

"Kol protected Maeda," I said. My voice, surprising everyone including myself, was steady. "Kol did it for Tam, and Santi."

"*Don't* let me hear their names out of your filthy mouth," she snapped. I saw Santi wince behind her. But he kept his head low—he never could go against her. "What you *ought* to have done was step aside and let a worthy champion take the crown. But instead, you forgot your humility. You stuck your head out where it shouldn't and made a damned fool of yourself."

"Kol would *die*!" I exclaimed. Mama Dorma started. I had never once raised my voice to her or anyone in her family. "To step aside meant *dying*, Mama! Kol fought and lived for Tam. Would Mama prefer Tam be a son without a mother?"

"He is no son of yours."

"He—"

Before I could finish, Sharif, the youngest son of the family, appeared across the room, at the doorway leading down the hall to my little room covered in tapestry. He stopped in his steps when he spotted me. Blood drained from his face as he looked from me to Mama Dorma, searching for a sign of what to do. In his arms, cooing and reaching for me, was Tam.

My baby had changed. In the weeks that had passed since I had been cast out of the house for refusing to step down in the games, he had grown. His legs were longer. His hair had begun to curl. The baby fat in his cheeks had gone down, though that same look of mischief remained. He looked like an older version of the baby in the endless, cycling room. But this Tam wouldn't disappear when I looked away.

Mama Dorma's eyes darted from me to Tam and back. My hand twitched and I knew she could read my mind. "Don't you *dare*," she hissed.

"Kol wants to hold her son."

"You will do no such thing."

Tam let out an angry wail, impatient at being made to wait. I gritted my teeth.

"He wants his mama. Kol is still his mother."

"Get out."

I dashed toward Tam. Eisa raised an arm to stop me and I heard her gasp in indignation as I shoved her aside. Sharif let out a yelp as if I might bite him and released Tam. I pressed my son against my chest and buried my face in his thick, curly locks. He smelled like sweetness and rain and everything good. His warmth and goodness overwhelmed me and for a short— very short—second I nearly forgot about the atrocities past and present.

Then Mama Dorma's claws were in my hair. Her fingernails buried themselves in my scalp. I screamed in surprise and held onto Tam as she pulled me back and shoved me downward. I turned to shield Tam from the fall and my back connected with the hard floor. Tam began to cry, fearful and confused, as

Mama Dorma's strikes rained down on me. I rolled to protect my face and could see nothing but Tam's hair and the brown floor under me. He screamed into my ear and I winced as a chunk of hair tore from my scalp.

Eisa laughed. Santi begged his mother to stop. Out of the corner of my eye I saw Sharif slowly backing away, trying to remove himself from the scene. I had been struck by Mama Dorma before. I had been cursed at when I broke a dish or burned dinner. But this was different. This couldn't be real. I couldn't be cowering on the floor, being beaten in my own home for wanting to hold my child.

Mama Dorma's nails left a pair of deep welts in the side of my neck. I gritted my teeth. A new sensation welled up in me, one that I had been taught to never allow as a Kol. Kols must always know humility. Kols must always know calm.

Kols must never show anger against their masters.

Mama Dorma's hand came again. I spun around before I could stop myself and grabbed her wrist, stopping her strike in its tracks. The shock on her face—and everyone else's—was palpable. I looked from one frozen face to the next, unsure what to do next.

I have to get out of here.

A Kol had dared strike out against her master. Mama Dorma yanked her wrist out of my grasp, her face twisted in anger. I had crossed the final line.

I have to—

WHAM

The entire house shook. The frozen faces broke their gazes from me as the front door crashed into the room, completely off its hinges. Sharif and Eisa screamed and Santi dragged his mother back several steps as Nix's hulking form emerged into the room, crouching to fit through the mangled doorway. Mechanical green eyes whirred, focusing on me, then Mama Dorma in turn. I had completely forgotten the metal giant was waiting outside.

"M-monster," I heard Mama Dorma stammer. "The Kol consorts with monsters!"

Nix took a step toward her and reached out one enormous hand.

"No, stop!" I shouted. I had no idea if he intended to crush her, and for a moment I almost wished he would. But she looked tiny and helpless before him, and I couldn't knowingly let the woman who had raised me die.

He stopped and turned back to me. I got to my feet, clutching a crying Tam, and ran out of the house. Behind me, I heard Eisa calling for help, the sound of neighboring doors opening and confused shouting, and Mama Dorma cursing my name.

"Nasmi."

I didn't slow my step until I reached the hills behind Mama Dorma's house. The sunset trees grew densely in these parts, and I knew my way around better than most from many days of wandering out here to escape Mama Dorma's harsh hand and Eisa's endless jibes. Still, I had no delusions. I could not hide.

"Nasmi, please."

I turned around at last. He had been following me the whole way, but kept his distance, probably wary of Nix, whose plodding form was never far away. Tam had calmed a little and was now whimpering against my chest. I held him tight.

"Kol only wanted a little more time with him," I whispered, barely able to choke my words out past the tears. I couldn't lie to myself anymore.

Santi nodded and sighed. He was a thick, rough man many years my senior. For Kols to be wed young to partners much older was not uncommon, but to be loved by one was. Aside from Tam, the only one I dreaded hurting was my husband.

He glanced at Nix nervously and took a careful, uncertain step toward me.

"He won't hurt you," I assured him. "Not if Kol tells him not to."

He came to me and wrapped his broad arms around both of us. Santi was a coarse man who did coarse work. By day he toiled among the smokestacks, a job that left a permanent smell of soot on his dark skin. At first appearance he could easily be mistaken for a brute, and I had feared him greatly when we met on our wedding day, terrified that he would be a rough husband and rougher lover. A rough lover he was, but as it turned out, a rough man he was not.

"I'm sorry, Nasmi," he said. His embrace was firm and warm. Like home. In front of his mother, he addressed me as Kol, but in private, I was his Nasmi.

I lifted my gaze to his wide, soft face and knobbly nose. He caressed my cheek with one calloused hand and stroked Tam's head with the other. In a different life, I might have loved him. I *wanted* to love him, but it didn't matter now.

"Come home," he said.

I shook my head. "This is no home for Kol. You know that."

"I will protect you."

"You can't protect Kol from this."

"But where will you go?"

I bit my lip. What could I tell him? I hadn't quite begun to believe it myself.

"Please come home," he said again. "Come be a family, us and our son. You can still be a proper Kol. You still have your family to serve. The gods will forgive you for your transgression if you show you still have your humility."

I shook free of his grasp. Anger welled up inside me again, but quickly melted when I saw his desperate and earnest expression. What did he know, this gentle and simple man? Love me as he might, he would still only ever look at me and see a Kol. He had been taught all his life, like me, that the only rightful place for a Kol was beneath the feet of others.

"The gods have a greater plan for Kol," I said, though what I meant by the "gods" I did not know, even as the word came out of my mouth. All of my preconceived notions of existence had undergone a rather dramatic shift over the past day. "Kol cannot stay in this world that curses her any longer."

"What does that mean?"

"Kol doesn't know yet." It was the truth.

Santi stroked Tam's head again. Slowly, lovingly. "Did you come to take him with you?"

I bit my lip and nearly said yes. There was nothing he could do to stop me. But instead, I forced myself to shake my head. "No. Kol just wanted to see him one last time."

Voices rose from the foot of the hill. People were coming. I had no doubt Nix could make short work of them, but I didn't want any more trouble. Yet I couldn't convince my arms to open. They begged to hold him a second longer, so my skin and muscles could remember his warmth, his weight, his every nook and cranny. I willed my body to fold around him, to pull his shape into me like an imprint, so that I might never forget. Santi didn't rush me. When I finally, slowly, pulled Tam from my chest and handed him to his father, my heart went with him.

Santi took the baby. I stood on tiptoe and kissed my husband one last time on his stubbled cheek, but couldn't meet his eyes. I was saying goodbye to my son again, for the last time. All the last times in the endless room together couldn't match the pain of this separation. The real, final last time.

I had no home. I couldn't admit this until Tam was no longer in my arms.

"You did good, Nasmi," he said. Part of me ached to dive into his arms and beg him to make it all better. But I couldn't, and he couldn't. "They can say what they like, but you did good."

. . .

THE SHORT, dark trips in and out of the arena were something I would never get used to. The dizzying vertigo that accompanied them didn't help. I landed on my feet but stumbled. Nix grabbed my arm and I flinched from his grasp. My knees buckled and I fell into a heap on the floor, my grief exerting its own gravity. For a long moment I knelt in place, the cold of the metal floor seeping through my clothes. I had thought for a brief, silly moment that I would never see the inside of this dome again. I had believed I could go home.

Slowly, I bent down and curled around myself, face buried in my arms against the chilly floor. Tam's warm weight was fading from my skin and I ached to grasp it and hold on to it. The chill of the dome pushed against me and I felt as if I might never get up.

I'm never going to hold him again.

My skin was cold. How was I ever going to be warm again without my baby curled up against me?

A gentle hand lay on my shoulder. I looked up to see H'otto standing over me. I considered pulling away from him, but couldn't bear to remove myself from the only spot of warmth in this entire place.

"Did you find what you sought?"

I looked at him blankly through tear-covered eyes. He offered another hand. Slowly, hesitantly, I slid a hand into his and let him help me to my feet. Instead of releasing me, another one of his furry, warm hands folded over mine, enveloping my fingers in a cozy little cocoon.

"This is hard," he said gently. "I know that. It will take time to become accustomed to this way of life, but you are about to embark on something glorious and beautiful."

I could find no words. I was helpless, with no family or friends and no home to return to. In all manners of speaking, he owned me and I had no idea what he could want from me. I ought to fear him, I told myself. I ought to be terrified.

But I wasn't. Perhaps it was his clear dark eyes. Perhaps it was his warm hands. Despite the horrors I'd experienced in the arena, not a single person of my own kind had ever given me such words of comfort without first reminding me of my place as a Kol.

"What are you doing to the poor child?"

A figure approached from behind H'otto. Nix stepped aside to let the newcomer by. At a glance, she almost reminded me of Mama Dorma—an older, matronly woman with silver hair. But as she drew near, I saw that she was actually a very different being. Her skin was a pale, light gray color, like the bellies of the silver fishes that swam in the creek behind Mama Dorma's house. A pair of long, thick whiskers grew from the folds of her wrinkle-laden face. Her eyes nearly disappeared under the layers of skin around them when she smiled. Her stature was a bit like H'otto—short, slightly hunched, and friendly.

"I am only welcoming her to our ranks," H'otto said good-naturedly and released my hand. He reached out to the old woman and guided her over. "Seven, allow me to introduce you to the first champion of the Galaxy of the Starry River. This is One. She will be your guide. Should you run into any trouble becoming acclimated, she will be the one you can lean on."

Champion. I couldn't imagine that the face before me, full of kind wrinkles, had gone through the same brutal games I did, but that was the meaning of "champion," was it not?

"She's been through a lot," One said. Her entire face curved gently when she smiled and I couldn't help smiling back just a little. *Has anyone besides Santi smiled at me upon first meeting, save for sneers of derision?* She stepped forward and put a hand lightly on my back. "You are going to be alright, dear."

I wanted to believe her. Dear gods, I wanted to believe her more than I'd ever wanted anything in my life.

"I will let you two get acquainted," H'otto said, looking pleased. "I meant what I said before, Seven—champions of the arena are meant for greater things than the humble masses.

25

You are worth so much more than what they've led you to believe. You have a bigger purpose now, a holy one."

"What is that?" I asked, struggling to stifle the rivers flowing from my eyes. I could no longer tell if they were of sorrow, of anger, or simply because I could not remember ever being told that I was worth something.

"Why, to serve the gods, of course. You will have a hand in picking others as worthy as you. You will be a part of the sacred games and help decide who is the next deserving disciple to join the ranks of the true esteemed."

"Okay," I whispered. Truly, I had no idea what he meant, but what I did understand was that I was being offered sanctuary when I had nowhere else to turn. Maeda had rejected me like a diseased organ. I had no home to return to and no purpose to serve there.

Besides, hadn't Mama Dorma always taught me that I existed to serve, and that more than my Maedan masters, I served the gods?

"Kol will serve the gods."

H'otto patted my arm. He was so warm. "Marvelous. For now, you should rest up. We will begin soon. You have much ahead of you. The first steps you must take are, shall we say ..."

"Difficult?"

"Surgical."

CHAPTER 3

WHITE LIGHTS. COLD AIR.

I watched the machines dig into my body, cut open my skin, and tinker with the red flesh and blue veins. The first time, I couldn't look. The second, I felt ill. The third, I lay there silent and still, watching as if it were a video. And it might as well have been one—no pain accompanied the incisions, and no scars remained. The arena was truly amazing.

"I've only known one race in all my time so far in this galaxy not to feel faint at the sight of their own innards," One said as she placed a cool cloth over my forehead. Painless though the procedures were, my body still responded to each one by becoming feverish and weak. Lying there, barely able to feel my extremities, I focused on One's voice to stay awake. "A lovely little planet, with a tiny population, all of whom possessed translucent skin and muscles on their torso. The majority of their organs could be seen clearly. In the past, it was considered indecent for them to wear clothing that exposed their abdomens and backs, but on my last visit there, they had grown more open-minded about it."

"They don't care anymore?" I asked, barely able to whisper.

"It would seem so." She laid a hand over my hot cheek. I sighed against the comfort her cool skin brought. "I saw quite a good number of young folks wearing clothing that prominently displayed their midriff and organs and no one looked scandalized by it. I must say, the doctors of their world certainly had it easier than most. Spotting internal damage or performing laparoscopic surgery has never been easier." She shook her head. "It's unfortunate, though. When I left, they were in the middle of dealing with a quite disruptive trend of health issues."

"They were ill?"

"Not quite." One held out a straw for me to drink. "They were finding that a certain extremely popular brand of drink was causing organ damage. But then, it *was* advertised to make their innards glow a variety of colors, so was it really all that surprising?"

MY SPINE TINGLED, as if electricity shot through it in spurts. At times I heard voices other than One's, but I could never pinpoint if they were inside my head or outside it. The back of my head ached and when I raised my hand to touch it, something in my wrist ground against my bones and tendons uncomfortably.

"You will become accustomed to moving your wrist to minimize discomfort," One told me. She held out her own wrist, thin and delicate, and guided my finger over her skin. Underneath, I felt the shape of the implant, barely the length of my little finger.

"The seed races of this galaxy are all designed to have arms, legs, fingers, and toes," she said as I listlessly traced my finger over her skin. "And that similarity only extends further the closer you look. Physiological compatibility is the most basic element of commonality. It drives social, cultural, and scientific advancement in the same direction."

"Seed races?"

"The races meticulously built by the gods, rather than left

to the natural developments of the home planet. Races like you and me, who are made to perfection, and to rule our worlds."

"Is it important that they be the same?" I asked. My wrist turned and my fingertips caught something that my eyes couldn't see. Something with pull and weight. Strings? Webs? I had a feeling that the other end of whatever it was connected to the arena itself. With every implant inserted, I felt myself more tightly hooked to the walls around me. "Kol has never seen anyone but Maedans until now, and no one on Maeda had seen ..." I hesitated. Would the word *aliens* cause offense?

"We are all alien to each other," One said. She was terribly intuitive. "But in the great scheme of things, we are all the same. For a single planet, it may not seem so important, but as a champion, you will learn to see things from a vantage point you've never even imagined before. Can you imagine trying to understand the social norms of a race that drifted through the air like balloons and communicated by pulsating their membrane skin? Or learning the media culture of people that do not rely on sight and hearing but instead guide themselves and relate to each other by connecting their appendages?

"We may look different, but truly, we are not. We all find physical comedy humorous in our youth, and we all know a kiss is a sign of affection and a fist is a sign of aggression. Our languages are spoken a billion different ways, but our understanding of mountains and rivers, birds and beasts, war and peace, and love and longing are the same. If they were not, we would never be able to understand one another, even with the arena translating our words. We all eat with one end of our bodies and mate with the other. Though those two sometimes mix and match, we can still look at each other and pinpoint where to look when talking and where to strike when fighting."

"The games are created by other champions?" I asked. Were I in a better state of mind, I might've been horrified at the idea of fellow beings creating such atrocities to subject each other to. But at the moment, I took in One's words like a story strung out before me, words playing in the air.

"To a degree. The job of the champions is to assist the master of their arena in understanding the seed races and creating games that are equal and fair to all. The masters of the arenas—you could call them the demigods—are far removed from the seed races. They are their own kind and no two are alike, and when you are the only one of your kind, understanding the culture and thinking of an entire race can be an arduous task."

"The other champions are here, then? You are One. Kol is Seven. The others are here also?" I wanted to attempt pulling the strings of the arena, but a wave of dizziness came over me and I lay back down. One's soothing voice drifted through the haze.

"They each have their own role in the games. We the champions are the backbone of the arena. Everyone is important and equal within these walls."

"Kol was not born equal," I said sleepily. "Kol was born a slave, then made a wife. Kol was lucky. Kol lived in a house and had a baby. The unlucky ones worked in factories or mines." A deep sigh escaped me. "Kol is still a slave now, only to a different master."

Her fingers brushed against mine as I drifted off. "You are so much more," I heard her say. "You will learn one day to abandon that label they foisted upon you."

"MOVE!"

I buried my head in my arms. Screams and shouts came all around me. Heavy feet trampled the ground a finger's length from me but I didn't dare lift my head. A foot kicked my side but I kept myself huddled in the tightest ball I could.

"Leave her!" someone cried. "Get moving! The swarm is getting close!"

The person who kicked me cursed. Then she went on her way, too. For a moment there was silence. I raised my head, my face and arms covered in mud. The jungle birds, unseen among deep green leaves, whispered their song. Down the path before me, the other contestants disappeared quickly over the hill not far away. I smelled flowers around me and heard the babble of the brook we had passed not long ago.

For a very, very brief moment, it was almost beautiful. Then the swarm enveloped everything.

They came from above, blacking out the sky as the air itself vibrated with their angry buzzing. My left leg, already swollen to twice its size from the last sting I'd received, bled liberally. I couldn't run anymore, no matter how hard the others pushed.

They dove. I cried out as they landed on my back and head with the impact of hail pellets. They were enormous, as big as my palm with stings like jabbing blades. I buried my head again, protecting my face. The other contestants were screaming, too. My mind raced.

Make something. What?

Sticks. Knife. What could work against a swarm? I had no idea. One of the black bugs stung through my clothes and I hissed in pain.

I could produce nothing. That was the reality. I could hold nothing in my head and the sensation of crawling legs was all over my body. This was it. My last round. I'd lasted through three rounds on sheer luck and my luck had run out. I curled up into myself as tightly as I could and thought of Tam. Sweet, bubbly Tam, my baby who would grow up without his mama. I saw his smiling face, his chubby legs that I would never get to squeeze again, and his little hands grabbing and slinging mud all over himself on that joyful summer afternoon that seemed a whole lifetime ago.

The insects continued to prick me with their sharp little feet. I concentrated on the image of Tam, on that bright sunny day when I almost felt happy, when I knelt in the yard and got dirty beside him, laughing and without a care in the world, even knowing I would receive Mama Dorma's hand later for getting my clothes dirty.

The buzzing wings and clicking mandibles grew distant. I could almost ignore the pricks of their sharp feet, as if the happy memory of Tam covered me in a protective cocoon. I held on to him, that warm feel of his skin and the cool mud on my hands. The buzzing was far away. I felt no pain. I gave myself up to the comfort of the memory.

Then . . .

The world went quiet. I didn't dare move. The weight on my back was still here, but I no longer felt the movement of the insects. I kept my eyes closed and waited. The buzzing had faded. The stings on my back and legs were terribly sore, but I felt no new invasions on my skin. I waited until my muscles ached from being curled up before standing.

Except something stopped me. My back was heavy. Very heavy. For a moment I imagined a mountain of insects burying my entire body and panic surged up. I pushed with all my strength and mud crumbled all around me. Light shone into my eyes and I blinked, trying to focus.

I was covered in brown sludge from head to toe. Chunks of it fell from my hair and my feet were buried up to the knee. I looked at the broken wall of mud around me incredulously, trying to piece together what had happened. The insect swarm was gone, and I could hear voices over the hill—the other contestants. How many of us were left now?

"So," a voice said.

I jumped. It was the same voice that boomed to us from above before the beginning of each round, except now it was whispering in my ear. I looked around frantically, but found nobody attached to it.

"A mud shield," it said. "Simple and effective. I had begun to wonder if anyone would discover this little feature of the arena, and someone finally has. The underdog, no less."

I struggled to find words, but the voice said no more. I pulled myself out of the mud pile and limped toward the hill. On the other side, the other contestants gathered together, looking a little worse for wear. Though I wasn't sure how many had started the round, their numbers had definitely dwindled. A few of them turned toward me as I approached, looking as surprised as I felt that I was still alive.

I kept my distance, fearing what they might say, having seen that the only Kol in the game survived yet again. Since day one I'd gone out of my way to keep away from the others. The arena offered enough challenges on its own; I didn't want to give the others reason to turn hostile against me for stepping out of a Kol's bounds.

Had I really moved the grounds of the arena into a shield for myself by sheer force of will? Did thinking about Tam covered in mud change the landscape itself? I stood to the side, picking bits of mud off myself, my mind racing.

Whatever it was, it might be my key to staying alive in this game.

I WOKE UP COLD.

It could've been the dream or the latest post-surgery fever. The reason didn't matter. I was freezing. The orb's chill dug into my body, through my bones. The thin blanket covering my body did next to nothing and no matter how I positioned myself, I couldn't stifle the shivers that coursed through me. Finally, I pulled myself into a sitting position and wrapped the blanket around myself. I had to move around to warm myself up.

The voices came. I shook my head to remove the remnants of the dream, only to find that the voices remained even as the images faded. Someone was speaking. I got to my feet shakily. My body threatened to topple over like a poorly balanced tower of blocks. I caught myself on the edge of the bed and my eyes saw double. The fever burned. My skin was hot, but my core was so cold I could barely sense my fingers and toes. I had to move.

Blanket wrapped around my body, I paced the room slowly. My vision slowly steadied. My mouth was dry as sand and I had already drunk the last of the water One brought. I tried to call out and my papery tongue struggled to produce only a hollow whisper. I wiggled my fingers. At least the movement had warmed them up slightly.

Voices again. I lifted my head toward them. Perhaps it was One. If I went to her, maybe she could bring me more water or an extra blanket.

The hall floor was even colder. I didn't realize that I had no shoes until I stepped outside. The idea of looking for something to cover my feet sounded about as exhausting as a ten-day trek, so I headed forward, accompanied only by my fever-addled mind.

"Will it?"

For a moment I thought I had spoken those words; then I remembered that I couldn't even manage a whisper to ask for water. I followed the sound of the voice. It was unlike anything I'd ever heard before. Though I'd grown somewhat used to the layered, translated voices during the games, this one was different. I heard the familiar Maedan dialect, but underneath it was a soft, rhythmic croak like multiple tongues clicking a varied beat.

The door next to mine stood open with a thin crack. I hadn't intended to look in, but a wave of dizziness overtook me and I leaned against the wall. Light snuck through the gap. Two figures were visible. To my unfocused eyes, they were little more than blurry shadows.

"Will it hurt?" the croaking voice asked again. I shuddered, though I wasn't sure why. I blinked. The speaking shadow focused slightly. White skin, black stripes. Two pairs of slitted eyes blinked out of sync with each other. I found myself deliriously wondering if tears would flow from all four eyes when they cried.

The other figure stepped in front of the light. For a moment I saw glistening green. Delicate fingers reached up and touched the other's face.

"Of course not," I heard them say shortly, a bubbling

quality under their translated words. My head swam. I tried to push myself off the wall and failed.

"You're going to be fine," said the bubbly voice. "*Just* fine."

I blinked hard. My vision was beginning to go again. Shapes and colors overlapped. The pale form with black stripes looked like it was moving. Except it wasn't walking. All of its limbs were moving in different directions while its torso stayed in place. Its head floated upward, farther and farther from the body. The image was so ridiculous that my aching throat let out a dry wisp of a laugh. The green shape with the bubbly voice snapped around, and the last thing I remembered was a hand reaching out toward me.

I woke up.

I was warm. I looked down to see a thick blanket covering my body. A thin sweat coated my forehead, and when I brushed it away, I nearly knocked over a glass full of cool water sitting on a metal stand next to me. Easing myself up onto my elbows, I grabbed it and drained it in three large gulps.

What a strange dream.

I shuddered at the images that flowed back to me. In the midst of the dream it had all seemed ridiculous and silly, but now, with my mind cleared of its fever fog, bile welled up in my throat as the memories wormed themselves back into my mind.

I had dreamed that someone was being pulled apart limb from limb while still living. How could I even conjure up something so disturbing? I had grown used to memories of the games, but this was something new. Something different and eerie.

Will it hurt?

I shook my head hard.

Of course not.

That bubbly voice. I could still hear it. I had never gotten a good look at the one who spoke it, but that voice stuck with me. It repeated in my mind in an endless, dizzying cycle. I lay back down and pulled the blanket over my head, as if it could shut out the horrors invading my mind. When it didn't work, I cried, then slept again, memories and dreams blending together in a whirling hurricane of sounds and colors.

THE AIR WAS FILLED with blocks.

Objects and shapes used to manifest as if by magic in the arena, but now I could see their building blocks ripple all around me, as if moving through water. The very air of the arena was filled with these tiny blocks, changing, breaking, and shaping at my will. With each procedure, I saw them more clearly, and by seeing them, I began to follow the logic of their movement and complex patterns. It was terrifying and fascinating all at once.

I raised a hand and turned it in the air. The blocks followed my movement and the strings tightened against my skin. I spoke to them through images and feelings and they came together, smooth as oil gliding on ice. Manifestation was once comparable to trying to move a heavy, clunky, uncooperative lever with both hands. Now it was like finessing a fine-tuned machine made to fit my fingertips. They formed a sphere, then a cube, then a short kitchen knife, similar to the one I had often used to defend myself in the arena, then a flute.

The flute I used to play for Tam.

My heart clenched and just as tears threatened to flow, a tingle like a tiny shock of electricity traveled down my spine. By the time it disappeared, my heart had relaxed again and the tears had dried on their own. I reached back and touched the spot where it started—where the mark of Kol sat on my skin.

"Convenient little device, isn't it?"

A door had opened soundlessly and One stood just outside the recovery room.

"Kol feels strange," I said slowly, tracing along my neck but finding nothing.

"Being a champion is no easy task. Winning the game is only the beginning. Thankfully that little device there makes the transition a little easier."

"What does it do?"

"Provides balance."

I thought of Tam, and that tingle came again. His face floated to mind and this time there was no sadness or pain. I regarded his image numbly.

"It takes away the sadness?"

One thought for a moment. "Let's say it lends a bit of objectivity. Excessive emotions can disrupt manifestation. The device only ensures that you remain stable enough to make the best use of your abilities."

I swung my feet over the edge of the hard bed I'd spent the last few—*days? months?*—in. Between the procedures and the fever dreams, time had become something of a hazy concept. A vague image of white skin and black stripes threatened to surface, but I pushed it down forcefully.

Every piece of equipment in the room was made of tiny blocks. My new eyes caught every bit of rust and each tiny scratch on the worn metal walls. I looked down and saw the tiny hairs and pores on my bare feet.

I stood carefully and the loose gown I'd been wearing for what seemed like ages fell away. A light pink swelling ran over my sternum. Beneath that were two matching slanted lines at my waist—still a little red; those were the freshest ones. My knees creaked, stiff with whatever enhancements were inserted there. When I blinked, my eyes made a slight clicking sound, and my ears caught the plick and plink of the machinery in the walls all around me. The world was in stereo, every sound crystal clear and every detail visible.

"Your body has been enhanced to allow it to better sync to the arena. Connecting to the arena often begins with the hands, since the seed races of this galaxy tend to use their fingers to perform the majority of their functions and exploration. But in reality, your entire body is connected to the energy and movement of the arena." One nodded toward my bare body. "Your heart, your joints, your brain . . . The connection is physical, emotional, and mental. The arena will heal and nourish you like never before. You will find that you'll no longer be troubled by illnesses and ailments common to your people. Even aging will be a thing of the past."

I lifted my hands and for a moment could almost see the building blocks of my own skin. I couldn't quite believe what she was saying, but I was keenly aware that my heart was beating in sync to the hum of the machinery.

"You are not modest of your body," she commented, watching me inspect my naked form. "Not every race is, but since you were raised to honor humility, I expected you would wish to conceal your body."

I looked down at myself. The thought hadn't ever occurred to me. "A Kol's body is meant to serve," I said, reciting one of Mama Dorma's many lessons. "There is no purpose in hiding it from Kol's master. Only bodies belonging to those who do not serve need to be reserved."

She nodded. "It is a good trait," she said. "Sensitivity to nudity is usually a sign of an immature social culture."

An immature social culture. I wondered how Mama Dorma would feel about the traditions she had adhered to all her life being called "immature."

"You should dress yourself," One said, and handed me a gray bundle. "The procedures have all gone well. I think it's time I take you on a proper tour of the arena."

I took the bundle and unraveled it. A soft gray top and pants rolled out. I put both on. The moment the fabric touched my body, tiny fibers pricked against the skin underneath. There was a very brief moment of pain that passed before I could fully register it. The clothing now clung to me like a second skin, and I detected a noticeable shift in the sensitivity of my skin to the environment. The ever-present chill was no longer an invasive, unpleasant sensation, but a comforting cool that flowed and changed with the blocks in the air. I was quickly learning that everything in the arena served a function, even a simple piece of clothing.

I took a step. The clothing supported me like an exoskeleton. It pushed my spine straight and my shoulders back. I stood taller than I ever had, an odd sensation after becoming so used to bowing and lowering my eyes in the presence of other Maedans. One nodded with satisfaction.

"You may manifest any additional clothing you wish," she said. "I think you will find that a very easy task now—the implants have strengthened your connection to the arena. You will also no longer suffer aftereffects from manifestation."

I looked down at myself. The images came to me clean and easy, and layers of fabric appeared over my body—flat work shoes; a loose, soft brown dress that was common among young female Kols; and a headscarf that covered my hair and shoulders. I hesitated for a moment, then dispensed with the scarf. My hair, dark and thick, fell over my shoulders for the first time. All my life, it had been bound and hidden. Now, running my fingers through it, I realized it was every bit as beautiful as Eisa's. Perhaps more so.

Every step I took, even getting dressed, seemed to take me further from what I once was. I pushed the thought away—if I began dwelling now, I might not be able to leave this room.

WE EXITED THE SURGERY UNIT. I started out walking two steps behind One, as I was accustomed to doing, but she put a firm hand on my arm and pulled me next to her. The arena's underbelly was dark and cramped. We traveled through a tubular walkway covered in jumbles of metal and wire that sprawled all over the sickly brown metal walls. In our initial trip down here,

I had folded both arms around my front, protecting myself from the piercing cold that jabbed at me from all directions. This time, I walked comfortably, watching the building blocks that floated all around us with fascination, like tiny fish in a metallic sea.

We passed several identical doors on both sides of the walkway. I suppressed a shiver as we passed one that stood ajar. Fortunately, it was dark and silent.

"Are they all surgical rooms?"

One nodded. "Most of them. The others are storage and mechanical. You will have very little use for them and I recommend you not venture down here too often. Whatever needs to be done here is Nix's work."

She led me to the elevator at the end of the hall. I had not enjoyed my first ride in that cramped box and I did not enjoy it now. I was grateful that I had no reason to use it in the future. The less I hung around those rooms, the better.

From the elevator we made our way through another series of narrow corridors until the path opened up to a wobbly suspended walkway. Here the familiar chill was suddenly replaced by a blast of oppressive heat. I gasped at the sharp contrast in temperatures. The dark metal ceiling domed above us, and over the rusted metal railings, I could see lines and lines of black boxes blinking irregular red and yellow lights. A complicated whirring sound filled the air.

"Please forgive the heat," One said. "Keeping the computing room cool has always been a challenge, but Nix does his best."

I gazed down at the dizzying sight of millions of blinking lights below. Among the reds and yellows, a pair of green eyes blinked, then shifted up toward me. I waved. He did not wave back.

"Don't mind ol' Nix," One said, noting my disappointment. "He's a simple fellow. Does as he's told. He might not even realize you're trying to be friendly."

"This is very overwhelming," I admitted quietly.

"You feel like you won't ever understand it all." It was a statement, not a question. "Don't worry. No one does. But one day you're going to look back and marvel at all you're seen and learned." She gestured at the dome around us as we left the walkway and returned to the chill of the arena. "But really, this is all merely accessory. Even the arena floor itself is just set dressing. You are about to see what truly makes the arena tick."

"What is that?"

"The heart."

THE "HEART," as it turned out, was a wide, dim room—domed, like every room seemed to be in this place—that was even colder than the corridors. A cool, blue-green light filled the space. Walls of screens turned on one by one. I had never seen so many in one room. They covered nearly every surface of the curved walls. A tangle of wires like jungle vines snaked their way over the floors, extending from the screens to a strange black obelisk. Roughly twice as thick as me and several heads taller, it stood in stark contrast to the metal, rust, and glowing screens. The wires disappeared into various holes on the floor around its base.

Upon its unmarred surface was a single protrusion—a white, porcelain-smooth face. I tiptoed around the structure, careful not to tangle my feet among the wires. The face looked like that of a young child with thin lips and a round button nose. Its eyes were closed.

"Hello, Axi," said One.

A soft thrum filled the room. The glowing screens quivered. Then, a soft voice, feminine and melodic, spoke.

"Hello, One."

The eyes did not open, but the mouth moved. I shuddered at the unnatural sight. One noticed my unease and gestured me forward. I took a tentative step toward Axi, half expecting those closed eyes to open as I approached.

"This is Axi," she said. "She is the core of the arena. She is knowledgeable and helpful, and not a bad conversation companion."

I nodded, though I couldn't begin to imagine myself holding a conversation with this thing. I studied Axi closely, trying to figure out what it was that made me so uneasy about her. It was more than her eerily white face or her closed eyes. No. It was that she looked Maedan, and yet not quite. Her eyes were too far apart, and her nose too small. When she spoke, only the center of her mouth opened and the ends stayed closed.

"Axi is able to access records from every planet we have visited in this galaxy. You will be able to ask her to show you anything on these screens from her database." One gave me a small, encouraging nudge. "Would you like to try?"

"Try?"

"Ask her to show you something."

I wanted nothing to do with the strange child's face on the obelisk, but One was looking at me expectantly, and I suddenly felt the need not to let her down. I cleared my throat.

"Hi. Axi."

"Hello, Champion Seven," Axi responded without missing a beat.

"Please show ..." What did I want to see? I knew of nothing except my own world. "Show Kol Maeda."

"What of Maeda?" Axi asked. I had no idea, but One nodded encouragingly.

"Anything."

"Displaying Maeda."

The screens flickered, then one by one the images popped up. I went to the screens and looked up in wonder. There it was, Maeda, the world I had saved, but not the Maeda I knew.

Rolling blue hills scrolled by on the screen to my right. To my left was a row of dancers dressed in the bright red feathers of the mountain cuckoos. The screen above showed the art of the Eastern nations—inks and sculptures of sea beasts and birds. Farther left were plates of exotic cuisine, around which gathered a group of smiling island folk, silver hair in braids against their coal-black skin. On the next screen stood tall stone cathedrals, then fish with glistening scales and long fins leaping above green water, then a sport involving hoops and discs and men in brightly colored tunics. Then, beside that, a wedding. Two women dressed in traditional green silks held hands as they smiled, faces close, eyes glowing with happiness.

This was not my Maeda. My Maeda was white hills and clear creeks, orange sunset trees and bluebirds. My Maeda was my husband's sandstone house with its little balcony and wild hoppers in the backyard, nibbling on Mama Dorma's vegetable garden. My Maeda was four walls covered in tapestry and a little cot in the corner.

"You were married, weren't you?" One asked, noticing my eyes linger on the couple. "Your race seems to physically mature earlier in life than others with similar genetic blueprint. Most of them would be just beginning puberty at your age, but you had long passed that milestone. But even considering that, you were wed relatively young."

"All Kol are wed young, so that they may serve their husband or wife as long as possible."

"I see. And you said you have birthed a child as well?"

The thought of Tam sent a quiver through my core. The tingle in my neck almost immediately countered it. But One still noticed the change on my face. She came forward and put an arm around my shoulders.

"Axi," she said, "transparency mode, please."

The walls around us vanished. I watched in astonishment as a sea of stars appeared in the dark sky above. The domed ceiling and walls disappeared and we were surrounded by infinite space.

"W-what is this?"

"This is a display," One replied. "Axi is projecting onto the walls the actual scene outside the orb, making it appear as though the layers of the arena have become transparent."

"Actual scene?" The stars and planets stretched on and on. I gasped as the floor beneath us vanished as well. We stood in endless space, One and I. Next to us floated Axi's face. Even the obelisk was no longer visible. "We are no longer on Maeda?"

"We departed Maeda the moment you returned." One gestured to the stars all around us. "The universe is big, child. You will learn soon that even your beloved planet is so very small. I have spent several lifetimes traveling and learning, and I've barely begun to scratch the surface of this little galaxy."

"Lifetimes?"

One gave my shoulder a gentle squeeze. "You may not understand now, but with time, you will. You think the life as you know it is over, but you might not believe, Seven, how very much is still ahead of you."

"YOU WILL BE HEADING OUT SOON," H'otto said. He was pleased to see how well I'd adapted after the surgeries. Truth be told, the physical changes from the procedures were much easier to wrap my mind around than the rest of my new reality. I was almost grateful for the strange little device in my neck. Without it, I might have gone a little mad after visiting the heart.

"Where will Kol go?"

"As a champion of the arena, opening your eyes and broadening your horizons are imperative," One said. We had met up on the arena floor, where I couldn't stop gaping at the millions upon millions of moving blocks all around us. It was a distraction I had yet to become used to. "And there is no better way to do that than by traveling."

"But not to worry; we will not be sending you anywhere alone," H'otto assured me. "Your companion is a seasoned traveler. You will be able to learn much from them."

His words snapped me back to attention and I felt a spark of hope. "Companion? Kol will travel with One?"

"One has her work here. You will return to your tutelage under her eventually. Your new guide is arriving now." H'otto looked past me. "In fact, there they are."

The thought of being parted from One gave me pause, but I had an inkling I was not being given a choice. I comforted myself with the thought that at least another veteran of the arena would be at my side. That was, until I turned to face the newcomer approaching.

My blood ran cold.

They were the most beautiful being I'd ever laid eyes on, tall and slender with limbs that moved like fins through water and translucent green skin. Clear, round eyes looked down at me over a flat, slitted nose and thin, lipless mouth. I'd never seen pupils so large and clear or a sheen quite like the one that danced over their neck and long fingers.

Fingers that last reached toward me through the gap of a metal basement door.

Blood pounded in my ears. Was I staring? I quickly looked down.

"Seven," H'otto said, nudging me to raise my head. "This is Two, the second champion of the Galaxy of the Starry River."

Two.

I swallowed thickly. The one in the basement, torn apart limb from limb while those clear eyes looked on, teasingly telling them it wouldn't "hurt," did they have a number, too?

Fear clawed at my skin. I didn't dare meet Two's eyes for fear that they would say something about the horrific sight I'd stumbled upon. Fortunately, they did not give me a single glance.

"So this is the new one," they said to H'otto. I recognized that bubbly quality in their voice immediately. "I assume she has not been through the temple yet."

"Not yet. I thought you might like to take her on a tour

first."

"You are pawning her off on me?"

"It is your duty, Two."

Two turned toward me. My breath caught in my throat and I struggled to stay steady, in case I said or did something—anything—that could land me in the same fate as the unfortunate creature with white skin and black stripes.

"What's your name?"

It took me a while to realize Two was addressing me. "Nas—" I stammered, then quickly corrected myself. "S-Seven."

A sneer crept across Two's face. One cleared her throat.

"Treat her gently, Two," she said. "She's only just starting this journey. We were all in her shoes once."

Gently. I shuddered at that word and tried not to wonder what would qualify as not "gently."

"Fine," Two replied simply, and began to walk off. "Come."

"Now?" I blurted out. I glanced toward One, hoping for reprieve, but she nodded me forward.

"Go on, child," she said. "Don't worry. I'll be waiting when you return."

If I return.

I willed myself to move, but my legs were weak. It wasn't until One nudged me from behind that my feet finally peeled themselves from the floor. I hurried after Two, keeping two paces behind them.

"I assume One has given you her lessons."

I kept my head down, terrified that every word I spoke could be the wrong one. Every step that took me further from One felt like a step toward certain doom. "Y-yes. Kol thinks so. She is very knowledgeable."

Two let out a sharp, dry laugh that startled me. "She has her charms, I'll give you that. But then, with the right words, anyone can make anything seem charming."

Then, under their breath, I heard them mutter, "Even this shitty eternity."

CHAPTER 4

THE CAPSULE, AS THE OTHERS CALLED IT, WAS INCREDIBLY SMALL and filled with partitions and narrow corridors. A ladder led up to an opening in the ceiling of the main hall and another led down to what appeared to be storage. The middle layer—the main compartment—was separated into several rooms: a locked room that I assumed belonged to Two, a control room filled with screens surrounding a central console, a tiny common room with little more than a table and a bench, and the tiniest washroom I'd ever seen. In the control room, I counted sixteen display screens on the walls. The main console held no gears, buttons, or sticks. Instead, at the top of the column-shaped unit, roughly at the height of my chest, was a layer of translucent green substance. I initially took it for liquid, but upon closer inspection, it appeared to possess a gel-like consistency.

Fearing turning my back to Two, I familiarized myself with the capsule's cramped space while keeping a wall behind me at all times. Every surface I touched hummed. It was a hum I knew. A hum I had heard often in fever dreams during recovery. The hum of the arena. And like the arena, the air within the capsule was filled with building blocks.

"You sleep up there," Two said shortly, gesturing at the

ladder leading up. I nodded and waited for them to retreat to the console room before scaling its rungs, glancing back at every step to make sure Two had not snuck up behind me. Through the opening, I found a crawl space I could barely stand up in. I explored the space on my hands and knees just as a heavy clanging sound came from behind me.

Fear coursed through me as I imagined myself locked and trapped in this tight, coffin-like space, and I struck my head so hard on the nearest wall in my frantic attempt to turn around that I saw stars. Fortunately, the opening to the main compartment was still open. I stuck my head through it just in time to see Two walk away from the metal door that separated us from the orb, now tightly locked. My stomach dropped as the capsule roared to life.

I was sealed in, alone save for the company of Two.

I HID.

The first days within the capsule were torturously long. I cowered in the crawl space, too afraid to move or even sleep. On the wall was a small covering that slid open to reveal a window not much bigger than my face. I sat by it, knees hugged against my chest, watching the stars outside roll by, painfully aware that there was no way out of this stifling metal tube, and no one to hear me scream. My mind conjured up a million and one scenarios, each one ending with me drawn and quartered as Two whispered with a smirk on their face, *"it won't hurt."* I didn't know what role they played in the arena, or what the other alien had done to deserve such a fate, but I was too terrified to ask.

Also mounted on the wall was a tablet the size of my palms put together that flickered to life at my touch. I wasn't terribly familiar with touch screen technology in my old life, but— perhaps due to the implants in my body—the tools of the capsule felt intuitive, as if they were custom-made just for me.

The language on the display was the common low speech of Kidan, my home province in Eastern Maeda, the only language I could read. After fumbling with it for a while, I managed to find a clock, which I set to local Kidan time by my best estimate. It provided some distraction, but was not nearly enough to keep me from listening to Two's every movement as the hairs on the back of my neck stood at full attention.

When I grew tired on that first day—day and night being a loose concept in the deep, black space—I realized I had no place to sleep nor sheets to lie upon. Until I had boarded the shapeless transport, I had completely forgotten that I owned not a single thing in this new life of mine. Leaving the crawl space was far more undesirable than sleeping on the hard floor. It wasn't until the end of that first very long and uncomfortable night that I remembered the workings of the arena and its components.

After that, I realized that manifestation for creature comforts was much harder than fighting in the arena.

A knife with a broken handle could still cut. A stick worked just well as a bat if you swung hard enough. Block yourself with stone or bricks or metal—it didn't matter. There were a million ways to float through water or stick to a wall or hang from a cliff.

But creating sheets and blankets that did not poke and scratch was a whole other matter. I itched, but at least I was warm.

Every time I heard Two shuffling around beneath me, my entire body tensed up in fear. I couldn't tear my eyes away from the hatch where the ladder led up into the crawl space, fearing that if they came up here, I would have nowhere to run, hide, or even stand.

I watched time tick by on the tablet.

Tick-tock.

I could do this. Wherever we were going, I could stay here until we arrived. I'd been deprived of meals as punishment many times when I lived in Mama Dorma's house. Going without food for a few days was entirely doable.

But by the night of the second day I felt my resolve waver. By the morning of the third, hunger and thirst gnawed at me from the inside. Time slowed to an agonizing crawl and I could take it no more. Finally, halfway through the third day aboard the capsule, I relented and descended the ladder.

Two was nowhere in sight and the door to their room was closed. I hurried to the common room, hoping I could find something to eat and head back up before they emerged. I hadn't actually set foot inside the common room since boarding. Aside from the table and bench, the only amenity was what appeared to be a small, rectangular, metal cabinet. I opened it and found it empty. I closed it and scanned the room. There were no other storages that I could see. I even checked all sides of the table and benches for hidden compartments, but found nothing edible in sight. Finally, I returned to the cabinet and took a closer look.

Toward the bottom on its right side was a hole. It appeared to be filled with green gel, similar to what I had seen on top of the control console.

"Put your finger in."

I nearly jumped out of my skin as I spun around, stepped too far, and went tumbling over the bench behind me. Leaning against the door frame, Two watched me with cold amusement, arms crossed, and made no offer to assist as I untangled myself. Heart pounding, I scrambled to my feet and kept my eyes on them.

They nodded toward the cabinet. "The hole. Put your finger in."

I eyed the thing apprehensively, trying to decide if it was a trap.

"You can starve," Two said with an uncaring shrug. "I was beginning to think that's what you wanted. You won't die, mind you. The capsule will fix you up just like in the arena, but it's not very comfortable to go without eating for the whole trip. Relatively speaking, we've barely left our doorstep."

I swallowed uneasily and turned to the cabinet. The hole was large enough for me to fit several fingers inside if I wanted, but the idea of sticking one finger into the green goop was more than enough. Apprehensively, I inserted my right forefinger into it, wincing at the sensation.

A barrage of sensations struck me. I shook my head at the odd feeling on my tongue. There was no food in my mouth, yet I tasted a ripple of flavors. Sweet, salty, bitter, sour, spicy, followed by a series of textures. Hard, soft, crispy, rubbery. They came and went before I could fully register each one, though a few lingered. Spicy, pungent, chewy. The taste of Mama Dorma's meat stew. My body grasped at the taste, the same way my mind grasped at the manifestations of the arena. The cabinet made a whirring sound and I yanked my finger back out.

"That should do it," Two said. "Though it might've been a good idea to make a plate first."

AFTER CLEANING up the mess from my first attempt and several attempts to manifest an appropriate plate for the food machine —I had trouble controlling its size—I finally sat down to my first meal since departing the orb. To be perfectly honest, I still wasn't terribly convinced that the half-dozen gelatinous cubes in front of me were edible. Two watched me from the doorway, wordless like a predator stalking prey. I couldn't help but wonder if this was all some elaborate ruse to get me to poison myself. But hunger won over caution in the end and I scooped up half a cube with a knobby wooden spoon I'd manifested and pushed it into my mouth.

At first bite, the texture was indeed revolting, but as I chewed, determined not to let them see my unease, I realized it wasn't the worst thing I'd eaten. The gelatin melted quickly and held a decent amount of warmth. Beneath the texture was the flavor of Mama Dorma's meat stew, faint but definitely detectable. I took another bite. Knowing what to expect made the experience far more tolerable, almost pleasant. Before I could stop myself, I was shoveling the cubes into my mouth like a starved pauper.

"You eat like a child." I froze. For a moment, in my joy to be relieved of the pain of starvation, I'd forgotten Two was there. "But then, that's what you are, aren't you?"

I kept my head down like a good Kol and said nothing.

Two pushed off the door frame and entered the common room. I pretended to focus on my food, though as they passed behind me, I couldn't help but shiver.

"I have a hard time imagining you surviving the games. But then, it takes all sorts, doesn't it?"

Should I answer?

"Kol had a very hard time with the games," I replied quietly, avoiding eye contact, in case it could be construed as disrespect. For once, the training of a Kol might work to my advantage.

"Is that so?"

"Maeda did not like Kols. Kols were expected to lose so others could win."

Two twirled one hand absently in the air. A pair of small gray spheres appeared around their fingers, spun like moons orbiting a planet, then disappeared. Though I dared not look directly at them, part of me marveled at their skill. I could not begin to imagine casually creating such delicate manifestations simply as a way to occupy my hands. But marvel quickly turned to dread as I remembered what else they could do with those dexterous fingers.

"Your tablet is connected to Axi," they said.

I blinked, unsure of what to do with that comment.

"You've got the look like you haven't set foot out of the borders of your dusty little burg before the games. Educate yourself. Learn something. Axi has everything you could possibly need. Look up something about your own world." A sneer crept over their face. "You might be surprised."

I nodded, eager for this conversation to be over. "I will."

Two passed behind me again on their way out. I stifled a chill as their fingers glided over the loose strands of my hair.

"You should be ready," they said, leaning down just a hair too close to comfort. "You wouldn't want to be caught unaware. And as the only champion who won by butchering other contestants, your time will surely come."

I forced spoonfuls of gelatin into my mouth mechanically as they disappeared back to their room, trying to swallow my fear along with it.

"Show Kol Maeda, Axi."

"Displaying Maeda," responded Axi's melodic voice. I found it easier to speak with her when she was a disembodied voice rather than an unsettling white face set upon an obelisk. On the tablet in front of me, images of Maeda appeared. I scrolled aimlessly through what Axi had to offer. She brought me something different each time—Maeda was a big place, and the more I looked, the more I realized that I knew next to nothing about it. Though Two's insinuation that I was an uneducated rube was far from complimentary, I couldn't help but begrudgingly admit that they were right. Learning would at least serve as a distraction from their presence. And if I were to start anywhere, it might as well be Maeda.

"Tell Kol about the blossom dancers again."

The image of a black sand beach disappeared and was replaced by a video of tan-skinned dancers in long white robes. As they spun to the beat of festive drums, red petals and tiny pink flowers flew out from the hidden pockets within their wide sleeves. The crowd around them cheered and clapped to the beat as the storm of flowers showered down.

"The blossom dance is a tradition native to the country of Nari," Axi said. "Nari's people collect the pink hassi flowers, which grow in the spring, and the red petals of the bali plant, which grows in early summer, and combine them in their annual festival signifying the changing of seasons. After the festival, the flowers are often collected and used to flavor the festive blossom wine."

Nari. I knew of the country. Mama Dorma used to tell me when I was slow to complete my chores that she might as well sell me to Nari, where Kols were only good for hard labor like mining. *You'd dig til you're almost dead,* she used to say, *but don't you dare drop before they let you, because you have to dig your own grave first.*

In my mind, Nari, like much of the rest of Maeda, was a dark and terrifying place for a Kol. Never in my wildest dreams could I have imagined they possessed such beauty and culture. I could never tire of watching the dance of red, pink, and white.

"Tell Kol more about manxes."

The blossom dancers vanished and a slender, graceful animal with dark eyes, silver fur, and a long snout appeared. I had never seen a manx except in storybooks on Maeda. Now, I supposed, this was the closest I was ever going to get.

"The manx is a warm-blooded animal, highly desired for its fur, which is often used in fashion. It was hunted nearly to extinction, but preservation efforts brought it back in Maedan year 320." The image switched to one of a man carrying an infant manx in his arms, feeding it scraps of meat from his hand. "Unlike the wild manx, which were considered feral and untamable, the modern manx is mild mannered due to generations of interaction with Maedans. It is now considered a luxury household pet, particularly popular with the Maedan upper class."

Another image, this time a well-dressed woman with sleek hair pinned up with an expensive-looking accessory. She cradled a sleeping manx in her arms as she strolled casually through an upscale shopping district, the likes of which I'd only seen in pamphlets Eisa collected on her bureau. I admired her cream-colored skin and perfectly painted eyes—until she turned around.

"Pause."

The video stopped. I stared at the frozen image before me. The woman had turned her back to me and there, clear as the sun, at the base of her neck, was the black mark of the Kol.

My mind reeled. I squinted to look closer. The color and placement were unmistakable. But something was different—this woman had inked her skin and transformed her ugly mark of servitude into a delicate, complex ornament that complemented the intricate patterns of her clothing and jewelry.

But how could it be? I had never once heard of a Kol who was allowed to live in such blatant luxury. It was not unheard of for rich women and men to keep Kols as secondary spouses and treat them well in secret. It was the best a Kol could hope for. But even then, they would not dare walk in public with their hair up and an expensive animal in their arms. Not only that, to modify the mark of the Kol was sacrilege and those who did so were to be beheaded for attempting to become a pretender.

And yet here was this woman. Well dressed, well groomed, and out in public with her inked mark of Kol on full display. But those passing her on the street did not look the least bit scandalized.

"Axi," I said. "Who is this woman?"

"I do not have that information."

I thought for a moment. "Where was this clip taken?"

"The location is the Ali Market central street, in the province of Pyrus, in Eastern Maeda."

Pyrus.

Pyrus was just to the south of Kidan. This woman was only a few cities away. Was it a sanctuary of the Kols? I felt my heart swell with hope. Though Maeda was no longer my world, was there finally a change in the laws to better the lives of Kol? I wanted to ask Axi, but couldn't quite figure out the right question.

"Axi, tell Kol about the mark of Kol."

Axi did not respond right away. I could almost hear her gears whirring, though she was physically far away. After a moment, a new series of images appeared.

"The mark of Kol is an outdated term referring to a medical condition called K-type pigment mutation." A boy running among a group of children in a schoolyard, his mark clearly visible on the back of his neck. "The mark itself is a result of genetic abnormality that results in large patches of dark skin on the body, usually at the base of the neck." A man holding the arm of a woman—him bearing the mark, and her neck bare and clean. "The condition occurs as a random mutation and is not usually inherited. It is some-times linked to other conditions, such as reduced fine motor function and anemia. But in most cases, the condition is cosmetic."

Cosmetic?

My hands shook. I forced them to steady as a video appeared—a young woman, dressed in a jewel-encrusted red gown, singing to a cheering crowd. Though her name escaped me, I was familiar with her songs. Her voice was well known and I had frequently heard Eisa and Sharif blasting those familiar tunes from their rooms. The video panned around her as she sang her song to thousands, until the back of her neck was clearly visible under her short, hip hairdo. Like the first woman, she had inked over her mark, but into the shape of a blooming flower.

One of the most well-known idols of Maeda was a Kol. I suddenly understood why Mama Dorma was so opposed to her younger children's love of her music.

"In present times," Axi went on, "inking or painting the skin to transform the mark left by the K-type pigment mutation into custom designs has become a fashionable trend, especially among young people and celebrities."

My heart pounded. The room was spinning. The thing in the back of my skull shot a little tingle down my spine and it all subsided momentarily. But the underlying discomfort didn't go away. It bubbled against my chest and throat and I suddenly found it difficult to swallow. The image of the singer disappeared, this time replaced by a scene I was much more familiar with—a boy not much older than me, pushed before an old woman who roughly lifted his face, turning it this way and that, peering into his eyes, then opening his mouth to check his teeth. Satisfied, she turned to the man who had brought him and spoke. Though I could not make out what she said, I knew her words—she was asking if he came from healthy parents, if he could sire healthy children for her daughter or niece, and whether he had a mild temperament. Female Kols were far more desirable than males when sold to families. We were more likely to be taken in and made into spouses and maids, whereas the men were more likely to be sent to factories and mines.

"Prior to Maedan year 84, those who bore the mark of Kol were thought to be born to serve those who did not possess the mark. This has since been abolished by the passing of the Laws of the Rightfully Marked in Maedan year 120. Today, only a handful of small provinces and secluded communities still embrace this practice."

I laid the tablet down. The tingles in the back of my head ran down my spine one after another, but they weren't enough. The tight crawl space suddenly felt even smaller, like it was pushing at me from all directions. I began to sweat despite the cold and my stomach clenched painfully.

Generations of Kols had been free.

Was this what Two wanted me to learn? I recalled the cruel sneer on their face as they suggested I educate myself. They must have known. One told me that each planet was studied in detail before the games took place. They must be reveling in the fact that I was inevitably going to realize that my entire life had been a lie. What a joke; the rube just learned that while she toiled her life away, millions of Kols walked among the general populace, living their lives, making money, becoming famous and wealthy, even carrying manxes as they spent their days in comfortable leisure.

I didn't know what to think. I had to talk to someone. But who? The reality of my loneliness overcame me. I had no friends or family. The only world I thought I knew turned out to be nothing like I thought. My whole body buzzed with restless, angry energy. At Two, who was doubtlessly laughing at me from behind every corner. At Mama Dorma and her children, even Santi, for keeping me like a chained pet in their home for the sake of "tradition." At the entire planet of Maeda, where no one had come to rescue me from my shackles, even after I nearly gave my life so they could go on with theirs. Before I could stop myself, my hand had tightened into a fist and driven itself into the nearest wall.

A spasm of pain carved a path from my knuckles to my elbow. The sensation shocked the anger out of me like popping a balloon. I bit my lip to keep from crying out and cradled my hand, gritting my teeth as my bones tingled from the impact.

I drew a deep breath and sighed it out. Outside my window, the stars gazed back at me in silence.

Would I still be here if I were born a Kol in a different province or country, where they did not see me as a Kol, but as just another Maedan? Would I still have married, and had Tam, and gotten to stay with him and watch him grow up, as a mother should?

All my life, I had been told I served others because this was the path the gods had placed me upon.

"Axi," I said shakily, wrapping my scratchy blanket around myself. "Why must this Kol suffer, when other Kols do not?"

"I do not know the answer to that question," Axi responded. "Glory be."

Glory be.

Sometimes she said this, usually when I asked a question she couldn't answer, and though I did not understand it, it always sounded like a dismissal. *Glory be to your quest for answers, but the question cannot be answered.*

"Glory be," I muttered, and lifted my right hand. The seven strokes of the winner's laurel looked back at me. It seemed that the mark I was born with that dictated my life meant nothing. Instead, I was now defined by this new mark on my skin.

I was no longer Nasmi, the Kol. I was *Seven*.

I WOKE AFTER TWENTY LONG, lonely days to a glow outside my small window. After my latest revelations, sleep had become difficult and rare. I lay awake for long hours, half dreaming of how life might have been different. Every night, I wondered if Tam was going to bed as well, and if Santi was telling him about me. I imagined my baby curled up in the arms of his father, who whispered to him that his mama had done the right thing, even if she couldn't be there for him. Then, inevitably, I tortured myself with the thought that it could've all be different had I simply been born one town over. The days and nights bled together in the dark space that stretched on and on.

Which made the sight of the green planet all the more startling. From space, the sense of scale of a planet was surreal. I could barely comprehend its enormity. Rising from my thin pallet—softer than the blanket, one of my better creations—I hurried down to the main compartment. Two was already in the console room and the screens were lit all around them. I gave them a wide berth, or at least as wide as the narrow room would allow, as I tiptoed quietly into the room behind them.

I had intended to remain for only a moment, long enough

to see the planet out the front window. But now that I was here, my curiosity quickly overtook my wariness of Two's presence. The screens seized my attention and I couldn't tear myself from it, even knowing Two was only a step's distance away.

It was like watching another version of Maeda—smiling faces, dancing figures, art and sports, fashion and culture. But its people were considerably different. Sinewy and strong, they possessed a full spectrum of skin colors—natural or cosmetic, I couldn't tell. Long hair grew in graceful manes from their heads and the backs of their necks, draping down to their hips. Their features were flat but delicate, and when one turned toward the screen, I saw a vertical slit open slightly to reveal a third eye.

"I'm heading down to the surface," Two said. From where I stood behind them, I saw them pull their hand out of the green substance on top of the control console. "Stay here. Don't touch anything."

My eyes stayed glued to the green planet and its beauty. I could nearly forget everything that brought me to this moment, all the pain, anger, and confusion. How could I think of such things when there, right before me, was a brand new world?

Then reality pulled me back. Two strolled past me without a second glance. I scrambled to get out of their way and their door slammed shut a moment later. With them gone, I finally stepped close to the screens. On one, a parent with silver hair carried their child in their arms, laughing as the toddler reached out to feel a cluster of purple flowers growing from a nearby bush, amazement in their eyes. The thing in my neck tingled, stifling my sadness, though my tears flowed regardless. I reached out and touched the screen, sliding my fingertips along the face of the adorable alien child.

This beautiful world was home to so many, but it, like the billions of other worlds out there, had never been and never would be home to me.

. . .

I HADN'T THOUGHT it would be possible for the capsule to be even more silent, but after Two departed, the lack of sound was oppressive and deafening. Silence in space and silence on a planet were completely different. Without the shuffling of other feet and occasional rattling in the common room, I was uncomfortably, agonizingly alone. If I held my breath, I felt like I could follow the silence to the end of the universe.

On that first day, I paced the capsule. It was somehow even smaller without Two around, despite my relief at being able to take a break from worrying about whatever hidden motives they might have toward me. I watched the screens on the wall to keep myself from going mad.

Joyful people. Happy families. Exuberant celebrations.

Not a single thing that crossed the screens failed to remind me of the life I could have led on Maeda. I was never given a choice to learn, to love, to live how I wanted. The choice was made for me, and that choice was to serve.

My foot struck the central console as I paced past it, accidentally at first, then on purpose each time. The rhythmic *thunk* echoed in my brain, and the green goop on top jiggled like the flavorless gelatin produced by the food machine.

Habit was an interesting thing. Though it brought me no particular pleasure nor served any useful purpose, I found myself back at the console the next day, pacing past it, kicking it each time. The motion brought me an odd comfort, an almost delusional sense of control in a situation where I had so little. The videos played on and I never bothered to turn them off. I woke to the fireworks of celebration and went to sleep to songs of the funeral choirs. The sounds of Harmony protected me from the silence and accompanied my every waking moment. Like ghosts. Like family. Like a life I could almost grasp save for the barrier of reality that separated us.

In Two's absence, I formed a little routine for myself. I woke, ate in the common room as I listened to the voices from the screens in the console room, spent the day pacing on and off for lack of better things to do, alternating between watching the Harmonians and admiring their planet out of the large window, leaning with my forehead pressed against the cold glass.

I missed Tam.

I missed him not with thoughts or dreams or images, or even emotions, but with a raw, visceral hollowness, like a part of me had been severed and I was constantly, incessantly being made aware of it. His hair, his laugh, the sensation of his soft skin against my arms. His eyes as he looked up at me, innocent and completely free of expectation except for the love that was his birthright. I had no title in his mind. Not Kol, not Champion, just a face and voice and warmth. Having him was my duty, but loving him was my choice.

When I woke up every "morning," there was always a short moment of blissful confusion when I could almost convince myself that he was just across the room, chest rising and falling gently. Without the sound of Two shuffling about, I could remain in this delirium a little longer than usual. But inevitably, it ended, and I climbed through the hatch to be greeted by the green light of Harmony once again, carrying my memories like a deadweight against my chest.

And it was on the fifth day that the thought crossed my mind. I had been pacing in the console room when it surfaced slowly, then all at once. I stopped my pacing. Behind me, the carefree voices of Harmony carried on.

I kicked the console. The green goop jiggled.

I hovered one hand over the green goop, less than a finger's length above it. There was a faint, unexplainable sensation, as if it could sense my presence and actively reached out to me.

For the first time in my life, I wondered if I had a choice.

I lowered my hand slightly. The sensation grew stronger.

A loud *crack* from the screens startled me and I pulled back, heart beating. A Harmonian child had lit a fire popper. I watched them laugh and point at the sparkles it ignited in the air.

Was Two watching the scene as well? I couldn't imagine they held much sentiment toward children behind those cold sneers and teasing remarks. I shuddered at the thought that they would return soon. It was difficult to say whether having their presence around was better or worse than the deathly silence of space.

Unless they didn't return.

I glanced at the control console again.

If I left, then what?

Despite my fear and dread toward Two, the idea of abandoning them on a foreign planet was still an uneasy one. Surely One and H'otto would seek them out when they failed to return? But how long would that take? Would they be able to find their way back? Or hide from the natives? Or . . .

Or it's not my problem.

I gritted my teeth tightly. My body tingled. My skin and heart cried out for Tam, the only spot of light in my life, torn away far too early. I reached out again, this time barely touching the green goop. It reached out for me, inviting me.

I had a choice. For the first time, I could choose my own path. My palm touched the surface of the quivering goop. I had seen how Two piloted the capsule. I could return, not to the Maeda I knew, but a different Maeda, a place where I could choose a different path, a different life. I could take Tam away from the tiny town and house that chained us and start over.

And if Two paid the price for my freedom, well, I could think of one being, with white skin and black stripes, who would be thankful if they still lived.

I pushed my hand a hair's distance into the goop.

If I tell it to take me home . . .

"Alert," Axi's voice cut into my thoughts like a knife. I nearly jumped out of my skin. "Champion Two is returning. Please stand still to avoid interfering with teleportation."

No.

I pushed my hand down into the goop. I couldn't change my mind. It enveloped me and all at once I felt my senses assaulted. A myriad of images invaded my mind, most of which looked like static from glitched tablet screens. My body jerked as if seizing from head to toe and I bit my tongue. My mouth filled with blood but I refused to give in. Bracing my entire body, I pushed the capsule to move, imposing my will over it the same way I did the building blocks in the air.

"Navigation error detected," Axi's voice chimed. "Correct course. Naviga-"

The rest was swallowed by a deafening blaring that filled the tight space as the capsule shuddered violently and careened toward the beautiful green planet.

CHAPTER 5

"*MOVE!*"

A hand grabbed me by the back of the neck and yanked me away from the control console. My hand made a wet *pop* sound as it broke free of the green goop. I tumbled backward and Two's foot struck me in the side in their rush to the console.

"*Axi! Manual override!*" they shouted as they stuck their hand into the green goop.

The capsule gave another shudder. The green planet was rapidly drawing close. I heard Two mutter a curse. I held my breath.

The capsule shook. Two's eyes narrowed in concentration. We were so close to the planet that I could see clouds parting before us, but before we could crash through toward the green waters underneath, the capsule made a grinding noise and came to a halt. Then, slowly, the clouds retreated as we began to move backward. The dark of space reappeared around the planet. Two let out a small sigh of relief.

Which was more than what I had the chance for before their fist crashed directly into the spot between my eyes. Before I could steady myself, they hit me again, this time on my left ear with force that sent me reeling to one side.

"*What part of don't touch anything didn't you understand?*"

My ear was ringing. I stayed on my spot on the floor, head down, afraid to move. How many times had I cowered like this before Mama Dorma?

Two's hand snaked over my shoulder and seized my collar, nearly choking me as they yanked me off the floor to my feet. There was something transparent and sticky on their fingers. Now that I looked closer, their body was covered in what looked like strips of transparent material, some of which had moved out of place in their rushed return. But there was no time for a closer look. I didn't fight them as they grabbed me by the neck and lifted me off the ground, drawing my face to theirs, delicate features twisted in anger.

"This is why I hate newbies," they seethed. "I'm so tired of babysitting you idiots. You worthless, irresponsible, stupid . . ."

Their fingers tightened. I imagined myself in the place of the alien with white skin and black stripes as I struggled to breath. Were they a "newbie" as well? I only hoped that they weren't lying about it not hurting.

I closed my eyes. There was something comforting about knowing the end was in sight. Ironic that my life would end as I always expected, at the hands of another who saw me as just another worthless Kol.

Then, to my surprise, Two dropped me with a tired sigh.

I landed heavily on my rear and opened my eyes. Two had turned back to the console. I watched nervously as they maneuvered the capsule back to its original position, before my disastrous escape attempt.

"Take over, Axi," they said. "And lock navigation rights to primary pilot only."

"Yes, Two. Navigation locked."

Two fiddled with the transparent strips on their skin, feeling the pieces out of place. "And prep a re-sync on the suit in my quarters."

"Yes."

They turned. I hurried out of their way as they passed me, avoiding meeting their eyes. My heart skipped a bit as they paused in front of me. The fact that I was alive hadn't completely sunk in.

"Watch yourself," they said. "Yours isn't the only life on the line."

I RETURNED to my crawl space and did not emerge again except to eat for several days after Two departed again. I wrapped myself in layers of blankets and hid, though I wasn't sure from what. The tingles in my neck kept me sane, but they couldn't protect me from the bitterness that consumed me from the inside out.

In retrospect, it was clearly never going to be that simple. Escape was never an option, and even if by some miracle I returned to Maeda, there was no way I could just walk away into freedom and paradise with Tam.

I drifted between weeping and sleeping, and eating when the pain of hunger tested my limits.

Two returned after four days. I heard them shuffle beneath me in the washroom and common room for a while. The door to their room opened and closed, then opened again a few hours later. I sat in fear of being confronted, but they never ventured up to the crawl space or even called out to me. Soon, the capsule was silent once more and I went back to hiding amidst my own misery.

Hunger woke me from one of many unpleasant dreams. The clock on the tablet showed it was the wee hours of the morning, whatever could be called morning aboard this miserable thing. I pushed the scratchy blankets off me, rubbed the sleep from my eyes, and crawled to the ladder.

The capsule was quiet. Though I was certain Two had left again, I still tried to step as lightly as possible, apprehensive of somehow drawing their attention. I slinked toward the common room when a sound made the hair on my neck stand up.

"Will you be home soon?"

I stopped midstep, alarmed, waiting.

"I can't wait to see you."

That wasn't Two's voice. I turned slowly. Two's door stood ajar. I had never looked inside their room the entire time I'd been aboard the capsule, and truthfully, it had never occurred to me to do so for fear of punishment. Even now, I considered simply turning away and pretending I'd never heard a thing.

"Is that right?"

Curiosity was a difficult impulse to deny, or perhaps I had simply grown far too tired of looking out the same small window or watching videos of Maeda. I took a step closer, looking around nervously even though Two was far away on the planet's surface. The voice was definitely coming from their room. There was a flicker of light as well, as if a video was being played. I approached the door and peeked in to make sure no one was there. I lifted a hand, paused to wonder if my fingerprints being found on their door would be too much evidence to my detriment, and nudged it open with my foot instead.

Though Two had the privilege of having their own living quarters aboard the capsule, their space was almost as bare and minimalist as my own. It seemed that they had little interest in manifesting creature comforts. I could see little besides a narrow bed, a working surface, and a storage space filled with lined racks. Four screens were mounted on the wall. Three were off, and the voice was coming from the fourth.

I leaned a little further into the room, not daring to step inside as memories of Two's fingers at my neck flooded back. Balancing was difficult as I tried to keep my hands from touching the door frame. The screen showed a room as viewed from one high corner, a cozy living room with a pair of loungers and a long, low table piled with books. As I watched, a person walked into view. For a moment, I thought she might be a Maedan woman, but then she glanced upward and I saw clearly the extra pair of eyes where her brow ought to be.

Her hair was long and dark, and her body was comfortably curvy. Now that I looked at her closely, I saw that her proportions weren't quite to the Maedan norm either. She was short, and her arms and legs shorter. She walked with a slight waddle, but she maneuvered herself around the furniture with practiced agility.

"It's been too long," she said cheerily into a device in her hand. She was not any race I'd ever seen before.

After a few minutes, she set the device aside, then sat down on the lounger to read. A few more minutes later, she stood and walked off the screen. Then the room flickered.

I blinked. The screen hadn't flickered. The entire room did. In that flicker, things changed. The book she had picked up was back on the table, the communication device she had set down was gone, and a plate of what I theorized was food appeared on the table. The woman appeared again, this time wearing entirely different clothing, though she had not gone away long enough to change. I realized with a start that I was watching a revolving room.

THOUGH I DARED NOT venture into Two's room even while they were gone, I couldn't resist checking in on the woman every day. Each time, I pulled the door closed with one foot after I was finished, worried that Two might realize I had been peeking into their room if they noticed their door was open. I always did it with the intention not to return, only to find myself nudging it open again the next day.

The woman repeated her cycle, which lasted about two Maedan hours. She ate her meal, dressed herself for the day, spent some time doing a series of exercises in the center of the room after laying out a square mat, then read her book until her communication device rang. She glanced at it often, I noticed, even when it didn't ring, as if eagerly anticipating whoever was on the other end. Every time it rang, her entire face lit up as she dove to answer. The words were identical every time.

Hey love.

Really? That's great!

Will you be home soon? I can't wait.

Is that right? You don't have to bring me anything.

Well, I do love surprises. You certainly do know me.

I knew her words by heart. Sometimes I mouthed along with her as she spoke. I wasn't sure why I did it. Perhaps because there was something comforting about her conversation. It was so joyful, so happy, so full of normalcy despite the fact that she and I were obviously born worlds apart. She loved someone, and they were coming home to her with a gift. How wonderful to be waiting for the return of someone near and dear to one's heart.

Except she would always be waiting.

I knew this all too well. Wherever she was, it was an endlessly looping place, a pocket in time like my little room in Mama Dorma's house. She would answer that call again and again, but her lover would never return. They did not exist except as a phantom voice that repeated the same unchanging words to her.

I wanted to know more about her. I longed to know her name and story, what had brought her into that room, and why she had chosen to remain. But I was afraid to ask for fear of Two finding out. Next time I incurred their wrath, I might not be so lucky. If they were monitoring this poor woman, there must be a reason that I would be better off not finding out.

When Two came and went again, they locked their door. I stood outside their room after they departed. The thought that they might've known about my snooping but chose to keep silent struck an uncomfortable chill through me. I didn't dare touch their door again, even standing far enough from it to avoid my breath leaving unnecessary condensation on its surface. But even then, I could hear the faint voice of the four-eyed woman chatting away to her lover. Those same sweet words, that same laughter.

Over and over and over.

CHAPTER 6

"Axi."

"Yes, Seven?"

"Tell Kol more about Harmony."

Harmony was the closest translation afforded the planet's name. After fifteen days in the planet's orbit, I finally relented to my fate and began to make use of Axi's database. Part of me was discomforted at the idea that the more I learned, the more I was admitting to myself that I was not going home. I sat listlessly with the tablet in my lap, barely able to muster the will to slide my fingers across its surface. Every new image that crossed my eyes was another reminder that I was never going back to what I knew, and what was more, that however marvelous the worlds that awaited me, they would never be mine. At times, it all felt incredibly, painfully, and terribly pointless.

Yet I couldn't deny that the more knowledge I gained, the more I wanted to know. My mind and heart hungered for distraction, for something to cling on to besides the metal walls, Two, and the trapped alien woman. Despite the constant dread and despair that haunted me, Harmony captivated me with its beauty.

In trying to understand this vast universe, I'd learned that translation was key. While names in certain languages were palatable to most ears and tongues when pronounced phonetically, not all languages shared such luxury. Harmony's true name not only strained my vocal cords but also contained pitches at least two octaves above my hearing range. But being able to pronounce or make sense of a planet's complex alphabet and grammar rules was not nearly as important as being able to understand the meaning they were trying to convey.

Harmony, for example, was aptly named.

"Harmony's last large-scale war was in the Harmonian year 15," said Axi. "It recently celebrated over one thousand years without a major war. The largest country on the planet is named"—here there was a slight pause as she attempted translation—"Prosper. Prosper is known for its well-funded medical science facilities that provide a wide range of wellness services to the public, though the majority of its fame and profit comes from cosmetic surgeries."

The screen nearest to me flickered and showed a gray-skinned Harmonian standing before a mirror as another inspected their mane with trained concentration. An array of hair samples in different colors lined the wall behind them. The examination ended with a careful study of the gray-skinned Harmonian's third eye.

"Why do they have three eyes?"

"The Harmonians' third eye is primarily used for night vision and usually remains closed in daylight."

A soft beep emitted from the central console and I felt a twinge of excitement. It meant Two had found new relevant data on the planet's surface. Axi fell silent and I waited with eager anticipation to hear what she had received.

"New data has been added relevant to the topic at hand, filed under *biophysical*. Would you like to hear it?"

"Yes, please." Though I was still uncertain exactly how intelligent Axi was, I was sure she was able to learn. She had started to offer this question after two days of me asking to hear about each new bit of information that arrived.

"The third eye of the Harmonians lacks tear glands. As a result, it is necessary for it to be flushed regularly using water to stay healthy and clean. This is a routine hygiene task that the Harmonians perform, same as other races that regularly clean their extremities or orifices."

I couldn't imagine flushing out my eyes as often as I washed my hands, but there was something intimate and sweet about knowing such a small detail about a race of people so alien to me. I remembered One's words about the similarities of the "seed races." Looking at the vibrant people before me, I almost felt a sense of kinship toward them.

A beautiful, peaceful race like this surely would never make slaves of their own kind. I'd considered giving in to death more than once during the games and since they ended. When I'd thrust my hand into the green goop on the top of the control console, I'd almost allowed myself to believe there was a light at the end of this tunnel. But that brief and hopeful moment was followed by Two's fingers tightening around my neck. Yet, to be faced with what I had thought was certain death had almost been a relief, and I still entertained fleeting thoughts of that incident playing out differently. Somehow, the idea of dying was less terrifying than being locked in a revolving room.

But now, staring at this amazing world before me, I felt a small twinge, ever so slight and barely detectable—gratitude for being alive.

"Show Kol the Song of the White Birds again, please."

The screens to my right changed to a series of mountain ranges set against a crisp green sky. Tall, majestic, imposing, they stood proudly, coated in patches of pure, flawless white. As a gust of wind blew through, a soft, sustained whistling sound could be heard through the tallest of the peaks, accompanied by a flurry of white powder.

"The Song of the White Birds is a weather phenomenon

that occurs in the western regions of the Kota-Haga Mountains, when the air currents traveling through the area during warm seasons cause a whistling sound between the sharp peaks while also carrying snow flurries. Ancient Harmonians who resided in the region considered the Song of the White Birds to be good luck and signal a good harvest. Modern science has determined that the good harvests that followed the Song are actually due to the fact that the phenomenon generally precedes wetter rainy seasons."

"Tell Kol about snow."

"Snow is a weather phenomenon in which individual ice crystals become suspended in the atmosphere before falling to accumulate on the ground."

Snow.

I had never seen such a thing on Maeda. Water frozen to ice, clean and clear. And yet, when gathered together, it was the purest white I'd ever laid eyes on. In my wildest dreams I couldn't have imagined something so lovely, and here it was, right before me. I stared, mesmerized, until the image suddenly cut off.

"We have lost a number of cameras in the region due to weather," Axi said. I sighed in disappointment. There was nothing to be done when cameras were lost aside from waiting for conditions to improve and sending out more. Thankfully, there were more than enough cameras to spare, as many as there were insects on the planet.

Actually, as it turned out, insects were specifically designed to act as camouflage for the billions of cameras scattered to document a living planet. This was yet another of my lessons from Axi's extremely vast database.

I switched mindlessly between random images on the screens while Axi directed more cameras toward the Kota-Haga Mountains, admiring their stunning silver sky-scraping build-ings and manicured rooftop gardens filled with carefully curated plants. A camera panned over a wide, magnificent building with stone pillars in front. A line of text was written in graceful calligraphy on its wall.

"Axi, what's that?"

"The Institute of Higher Learning in Northeast Prosper. Its motto is written on the front wall."

"What does it say?"

"Suffer be the idiots."

I chuckled, running my hand over the stunning structure on the screen. Someday, I thought, perhaps I could be fortunate enough to stand before it in person. For the first time since departing Maeda, I dared to look into the future and wonder if it might not be all bad.

ALL IN ALL, I was in the capsule for ninety days, the majority of which were long and challenging.

At the worst of times, I paced up and down the narrow corridors, entering and exiting the few tiny rooms repeatedly, feeling like I was about to suffocate in the cramped surroundings. Sometimes I lay awake at night, imagining the crawl space was closing in on me, strangling me and pushing at me with invisible hands. I had trouble sleeping, frequently waking and feeling like I couldn't breathe, wondering if I was going to spend eternity confined to this vessel with its humming metal walls. Despite my dread of Two's presence, every time they left for more than a day, I couldn't stop fearing they'd abandoned me here, buried alive in space inside this metallic coffin. Choking down the gelatinous cubes meal after meal began to test my gag reflex and I stopped eating until my body screamed for nourishment, then forced just enough down to keep from starving. Time trickled by torturously slowly. I counted the moments by the tingles in the back of my neck, the only things that kept me calm when everything threatened to bubble over.

At the best of times, the charm of Harmony, along with Axi's company, made it all just a little more bearable.

I woke up on day ninety-one to find the green planet notice-ably smaller outside my little window and growing smaller by the moment. Suddenly excited, I rose and hurried out of the crawl space. Two was at the console, steering carefully with their hand embedded in the green jelly.

"We're heading home," Two said without turning around.

My heart leapt and the question was out of my mouth before I could stop it. "Back to Maeda?"

Two gave me a look over their shoulder and I realized how foolish the question was. Maeda was home to no one on this ship. Though I had long accepted this, part of me was still crestfallen. I carefully maneuvered myself around Two and the central console and sat down on one of the benches against the wall, where I could watch Harmony disappear into the dark of space unobstructed. Despite having made only the most passing of acquaintances with the planet, I was still saddened to see it go.

"Our orb is currently parked at a ball pit," Two said. "This will be your first time." I thought I heard an almost cruel amusement in their voice and my fingers slid themselves protectively toward my neck. "It will be an experience."

"Ball pit?" I asked timidly. The name sounded harmless, almost humorous, but there was something ominous about it as well.

"It's what some of us call it. H'otto has a different name for it."

Harmony vanished from sight. I was once again being ripped from the faintest sign of familiarity to be thrust upon yet another unknown. "A different name?"

"The holy grounds."

FAITH WAS a tricky thing on Maeda.

For my entire life before the games, I had only sought to please the gods that watched over my world by doing the duty they had placed me there for—serving others. In public, the privilege of "worship" was reserved for the upper class, who attended gorgeous ornate temples, the likes of which I had never set foot in. Kols were not allowed inside worship grounds, but were taught to pray to the gods in private to guide us in our journey to humility. I woke in the mornings to pray by my bedside, followed by anointing myself with blessed oils on my forehead and chest, imagining that where they touched was where the gods left their grace.

What qualified as "gods," however, depended on whom you asked. Mama Dorma had always taught me the way of the unnamed gods, as she said the names of the gods were not to be known by us. Though I'd heard the neighbor lady mutter a few godly names under her breath when she became angry or frustrated.

Until recently, I'd thought that everything I did, including boarding the orb and the capsule, was the gods' plan. Now, I had no idea what to think. The gods of Maeda as I knew were a construct of an outdated practice, and I had no idea what to expect of the gods that awaited me now.

The gods of the games.

Watching the view before me unfold through the window in the console room, I couldn't help feeling like I was very, very far from everything I knew.

The first thing I saw was the enormous sun. I had never seen anything so large and bright. Even from far away, I had trouble looking directly at it. Two expertly manifested a pair of thin, dark spectacles, which they placed over their own eyes, then, with an annoyed sigh, created a pair for me after watching my pathetic attempts to do the same. I slipped them over my eyes gratefully and watched in awe as we drew closer and closer to the sun's bright flames.

Once near, I saw the orbs. Hundreds of them, perhaps thousands, kept their vigil around it. Many were tethered to the sun itself through chains of fire. They varied in size, some large and some small. Most were black, though I saw a few silvery-gray ones here and there. As we approached, I also began to spot capsules of various sizes weaving in and out between the orbs.

"They're charging up," Two said, noticing my curiosity about the tendrils of flames shooting up and toward each orb in turn. They steered us toward a particularly large silver orb. "Ball pits are usually built around suns. Once they finish this one off, they'll move on to the next."

I watched the shining orbs, trying to find the one that had arrived on Maeda, but all the black ones were completely identical. The sun's heat began to get to me. I fanned myself with both hands, though Two did not appear bothered in the least. It was such a contrast from the constant cold of the orb and space that my body felt like it was going into shock. By the time we entered the silver orb through a perfect square opening, I was wiping my damp brow with the backs of both hands.

The inside of the orb was instantly cold and very dark. I could see nothing but black, though Two knew exactly where they were going. Everything reminded me of how much I still had to learn. A spotlight flickered on in the distance, illuminating a single white platform. The capsule glided smoothly next to it. I followed Two to the main hatch. When it opened for the first time in ninety long days, I felt a woosh of air and breathed deeply. We stepped out. There was a space roughly as wide as my forearm between the capsule and the platform, and I tried not to look down into the dark oblivion below.

For a moment nothing happened as we stood on the platform. Then, in the distance, a door opened and light could be seen on the other side. Two nodded toward it.

"Go on."

I looked around nervously. There was nothing but darkness and air between the platform and the door. "H-how does Kol get to the door?" I asked dumbly.

Two clicked their tongue impatiently. "You are a champion, are you not?"

Before I could ask what they meant, they had disappeared back into the capsule. I looked apprehensively at the door in the distance, then around the platform. I had absolutely zero confidence that I could manifest something capable of floating me safely for any amount of distance. I took a deep breath, tried to stay calm, and focused on the tiny building blocks in the air.

Bridge.

The air shifted. The blocks collected together and extended from the platform to the door. I could sense them, even if I couldn't quite see them. Not seeing was the hard part—I had to convince myself that the structure, barely visible, was indeed there as I took a tentative step on it. It held, but the sight of the abyss beneath nearly buckled my knees. I forced myself to move forward, arms extended like a tightrope walker. I didn't dare look down or go back. The fear of embarrassment in front of Two was just a smidge greater than the fear of falling.

Stepping through the door, I let out a breath of relief. White light greeted me. I blinked hard, not realizing until now how dim the capsule had been. The broad, bright space was such a change after the long journey that I felt my entire body expand in relief, every pore opening, thankful to once again have room to breathe.

I'm alive.

I hadn't realized until this moment how much I'd taken the inevitability of death for granted. Part of me had never expected to step out of that cramped metal tube with Two breathing down my neck. And yet, here I was, with Two's presence and the nightmare of the capsule behind me. I'd survived. I was still breathing.

And unexpectedly, I found myself grateful.

"Welcome back."

My eyes adjusted to the space and One's form came into

focus, bathed in white light. She opened her arms to me and I ran to embrace her before I could stop myself. I had not realized how much I missed a friendly face and warm touch. For a moment I was embarrassed at how needy I must seem, but One only smiled down at me and took my arm in hers.

We walked along a narrow, suspended walkway. Looking up and down, I saw many others above and below. So tall and vast was the space that I could not see a floor or ceiling. Here or there I spotted other figures on some of the walkways, but they were too far away for me to make out their features.

"How was your time on the capsule?" One asked. She had a glint in her eye like a parent hoping for an excited and fanciful account of their child's latest adventure. I opened my mouth, but found the words difficult to form. One chuckled.

"Two can be a bit of a challenge," she said. "But trust me, they are excellent at their job, not to mention an utterly and completely faithful servant to the gods. You can learn much from them."

There was so much I wanted to ask her, but forming the right question was challenging. I pursed my lips, thinking hard like I was forming an inquiry for Axi.

"Kol was wondering," I said carefully, "what is Two's role?"

"Role? Research, primarily. They're a magnificent researcher. Easily the best. Wonderful tolerance for the chameleon suit as well. Most of us are not so fond of those awful sticky strips. They're a hassle to set up and unpleasant to wear. But Two has always done so without complaint."

"Research," I muttered. Somehow that wasn't the answer I sought.

"Of course, nothing within the arena is clean cut," One continued. "We are a young galaxy, with few champions for the moment, but that will change with time. We all take on jobs other than our primary ones at times. Sometimes the jobs we must do could be considered unpleasant, but it is all part of our role as champions."

Unpleasant.

I resisted the urge to ask if that included butchering our peers. Images of that dreadful scene threatened to float back and I pushed it away. I didn't want to see or think about it. And if I was perfectly honest with myself, I didn't want to know about it either. One was smiling, but her eyes betrayed her. I wondered, briefly, if even after all this time in the orb, she was as afraid as I was.

"Did you have trouble with manifestation in the capsule?" she asked.

I quickly pushed away the unpleasant thoughts. "Kol learned. Except for the food machine. It was difficult. It produced only cubes."

One let out a good-natured laugh. "I've found even the best of the champions struggle with that darned thing." She patted my hand. "I'm glad you seem to have fared well. The capsules are far from luxurious, but the experience is worth it. The first view of another world is simultaneously awe inspiring and overwhelming. Isn't it a wonderful feeling, to know there is always something new out there to learn?"

I bit back the desire to confess my near-disastrous escape attempt. Two would likely enlighten her and H'otto eventually and I had no desire to ruin our reunion by inviting One's disappointment.

"Axi was very helpful," I said instead. "Kol was glad for her company."

One nodded approvingly. "You know, Seven, the technology of the orbs is a truly marvelous one. Axi, Nix, manifestation, translation, all of it. It is what allows us near-godlike powers, even if it is only within controlled environments. The gods think it to be their greatest achievement." She paused. "Well, besides you, of course."

"Kol? Greatest achievement?"

"All of you. You see, dear, the circumstances of your birth, the marks on your skin, and your station in life mean nothing. We are all children of the gods."

Silence.

I shuddered.

I had become accustomed to silence after the long stint aboard the capsule, but this was different. I felt as if I had suddenly lost my sense of hearing, like the implants inside my ears had turned completely off. My eyeballs gave an odd turn and suddenly everything was still. The tiny building blocks that moved in the air stopped.

No, they didn't stop. They disappeared. In this new space, there were no blocks to be seen. I attempted manifestation, conjuring up an image of a cube. Nothing happened. Whatever this space was, it was completely and utterly empty.

Fog filled the air. A thick, gray fog that concealed everything more than an arm's length away. *When did I enter this space?* I remembered One guiding me to the end of the walkway, stopping at a seamless white wall. Then she'd nudged me forward and the foggy silence took over.

"One?" I called cautiously. No answer. "Hello?"

"Don't be afraid," came her voice, though I couldn't distinguish which direction it came from. A tingle ran down my spine and I calmed.

I walked forward. The fog had its own gravity that pulled me this way and that, until I lost my sense of direction and walked around in circles. I couldn't find the wall I had come through, nor a door or window. It gathered around me, prodding me with invisible hands. I breathed and it seeped inside me, like the cold of winter invading my lungs. It probed me, inside and out, and when I tried to push it away, my hands touched nothing.

Just when I thought I could take no more, it dispersed.

Seven.

I spun around. But there was no one there. I didn't so much hear the voice as feel it, in vibrations and the movement of the tiny hairs on my skin. It penetrated my entire being with a single word.

Champion of Maeda, fourth world of the fifth sun of the Galaxy of the Starry River.

I saw stars. Images of galaxies and planets flowed through my mind. Maeda rushed toward me with dizzying speed, breaking through its clouds and to its mountains, to its hot core. Then, a long cloud of milky-white stars, stretching infinitely on both ends into space.

Show us.

The fog wrapped around me like a giant hand and lifted me upward. I struggled as my feet left the ground. Soon I was dangling, not knowing which way was up and which was down, flailing but finding nothing to grasp hold of. Desperately, I reached out to the space itself, begging for it to help as I did in the games. Nothing. Of course not. This was a place where I had no powers.

Holy grounds. Grounds reserved for the gods.

The gods spoke. They did not use words or sentences or any language I'd ever heard. Rather, they spoke with images, emotions, and vibrations that assaulted all of my senses at once. I screamed and blocked my ears and eyes, but none of it did any good. My inner ear buzzed painfully and the implants inside my body enhanced the sensations coming from everywhere. I struggled until I became exhausted from the effort. Then, having no other choice, I relented to the barrage.

Strangely, as I relaxed my mind and body, the messages became clearer. The bits and pieces that seemed like noise at first slowly rolled into place. The invisible restraints around my arms and legs eased as I stopped fighting them. Then, slowly, slowly, I found myself drifting as if floating in water, carried upward. My eyes saw nothing but fog and the rest of me heard only the voices of the gods. I inhaled and they were in me, in my mind and body, my past and present, my life and memories. I guided them like Mama Dorma when she showed off her house and garden to her honored guests. They followed.

They watched me, barely a toddler, playing on the dirty floor of the tiny house where I was born. I could not show them the face of my mother, for I could not remember her. By the time I could recall faces, I had already taken up residence in Mama Dorma's house.

They watched Mama Dorma teach me to read and write, and show me the ways of humility and how to pray. I learned quickly, for to dawdle was to receive the back of her hand. They watched me learn to serve during the day and sleep alone at night. They watched me learn to weave colorful tapestries to hang on my wall.

They watched me wed Santi, Mama Dorma's eldest son. Until our wedding night, I had not met him nor seen a picture. He lived away, but returned to live with the family and wed me. This was what Mama Dorma wanted, and Mama Dorma's will was law. The gods felt the mental pain of fear and anticipation of my wedding, followed by the physical pain of that night. Then the relief of the morning, when Santi held me as the rising sun peeked through the curtains, apologized for my discomfort, and told me he would do his best to be good to me.

They watched me give birth to Tam. I was not the first to hold him, nor second, nor third. I stayed patient while the rest of the family took their time with him, leaving me alone to recover from the birth. I was fine with this, because I knew if they were celebrating his arrival, it must mean he had not been born a Kol.

They watched me in the games. Here they lingered, though I wanted to avert my mind's eye more than anything. They wanted to see. Outside my mind, my body shed a tear as I watched the scenes of the arena unfold.

Finally, exhausted and worn, I drifted off to sleep.

. . .

"STEADY NOW."

I opened my eyes. Four hands held me still as I tried to lean forward and nearly fell. I blinked but couldn't place where I was. It appeared to be a small, bare room. I was sitting in a lounge chair. Two sat across from me. My body tensed at the sight of them.

"Kol . . ." I started, then realized I had no idea what I wanted to say. H'otto patted my back.

"It's alright. The first worship is always hard. You will become accustomed to it the more you come to the temple. You did well."

"Well?"

"The gods were pleased with what they saw. You must be overwhelmed at the receipt of such enlightenment."

Enlightenment. It was not the word I would've used, but looking at H'otto's joyful expression, I knew the right thing to do was agree with him. So I smiled and nodded.

"Are we finished with the formalities?" Two asked, sounding impatient. I was glad for their interruption, since I didn't know if I could muster up any convincing lies about my "enlightening" experience in the temple.

"Yes, yes," H'otto said, as if appeasing a child. "You said you had news?"

"Harmony is not yet ready for the games," Two replied. "Their cultural development is on track, but technological maturity is currently in a slow phase. I've taken the necessary actions to prompt development. However, Aukron is ready. As soon as I provide One with the necessary information, priming can begin."

H'otto clapped two of his hands together in an almost giddy manner. "Excellent!" he exclaimed. "Most excellent. This is quite lucky for you, Seven. Usually a new champion among the ranks must wait ages for the chance to witness a new game, but you are fortunate to be a part of it all from the very start this soon."

My blood ran cold. The thought of seeing another game was unbearable. The thing in my neck sent its little shocks down my spine, just enough to keep me from passing out. Thankfully H'otto did not notice, as he was excitedly discussing the new game with Two.

"Are you alright?" One whispered. I looked up at her.

"Kol cannot do this," I whispered back, struggling against the tremors in my voice. "Kol cannot watch another game."

She squeezed my hand. I hoped she would tell me it was alright, that I didn't have to, that I could wait a little longer. But she only sighed and said, "It is the will of the gods."

CHAPTER 7

THE ORB.

I'd never thought I would be glad to be back. But stepping into the heart of the arena, I was almost glad. It felt like home, or at least some abstraction of it. To be out of the tight, suffocating interior of the capsule was a huge relief. Even the glow of the blue-green screens seemed to welcome me back.

"Hello, Axi."

"Hello, Seven."

Did the corner of her lip curl up into a slight smile just then? I smiled back. Her voice, which had accompanied me through those lonely days, now sounded a little less alien and a little more like a friend. I went to her and wiped a speck of dust from her cheek.

"Will you show Kol Maeda?" I asked. There was so much more I wanted to know. But more than that, I needed a distraction. The thought of the next game looming over me made me sick to my stomach. I had no idea what being part of the game meant for me, but I wanted to avoid thinking about it as long as possible. All I wanted was to cling to a bit of familiarity.

A series of images appeared on the screens, but I shook my head.

"Could you show Kol Maeda *now*?" I said. "Could you send cameras to Kidan, and find Kol's son, Tam?"

"I cannot," Axi replied. She sounded sad, as if truly remorseful that she could not help me. "The orb is outside the range of Maeda and cannot access the regional cameras. I only have archival information available for Maeda."

I sighed. It was worth a shot. I wracked my brain for things to distract me. Anything.

"Could you show Kol the other champions?"

"There are, to date, three hundred thousand nine hundred and fifty-six champions on file," Axi replied. "Shall I begin at the first?"

"No, no," I said quickly. "The ones from this galaxy, please. The ones in this orb."

"There are seven champions to date from the Galaxy of the Starry River."

All of the screens went blank. Then the seven screens nearest to me lit up. I recognized my own solemn face on one of them, along with One, Two, and one with white skin and black stripes that I avoided looking at straight on.

"Axi, who is this one?" She looked exactly the same as she had on the video feed in Two's room. Dark hair, four bright eyes.

"Champion Four, of the planet San Layne."

Four.

"What's her name?"

Axi said a word. It was pronounceable, but a mouthful.

"Is there a translation?"

"Florian dialect, from the Rexion region. Translation: to express goodwill, to express approval, to cheer, or viva."

Viva. Such a cheerful name.

"Curious, are you?"

I spun around to see One entering the heart. I nearly shouted at Axi to remove the images on the screen before I remembered I was doing nothing wrong.

"Kol was ... wondering," I said.

"I don't blame you," One said patiently. She stepped beside me and looked up at the champions on the screens. "You were wondering how we all survived this awful game, then allowed ourselves to become part of it."

I was not, though it was true that that question was never far from my mind.

"We all have our own reasons," One said, "but I think the greatest one of all is that once you've experienced the freedom of the universe, not tethered to a single world, a single way of living, you can never go back." She gestured for me to follow her. I cast one last look at the faces on the screen. They stared back at me, empty eyes with a million stories behind them.

WE ENTERED THE ARENA FLOOR. Unlike the heart, this space where the games took place still set my mind and heart on edge. I didn't want to be there, nor did I want to be any part of the next game. The very thought of it was revolting. But One smiled at me and I tried my best to stay calm and steady.

Tiny, microscopic building blocks hung in the air, denser and more numerous than anywhere else. Even the floor itself was always in motion. Rather than walking on top of millions of tiny tiles, as one might imagine, walking on the floor was more like walking atop still water—every step caused its own ripple that expanded and grew. After so much time in the cramped capsule, I'd become more sensitive to the vastness and complexities of the arena than ever.

One slowed her steps. I did the same. Then, she raised both hands, fingers loose and relaxed, like a conductor signaling an orchestra at the ready. She flicked both wrists, fingers pulling upward. A small gesture, but the entire arena moved with her.

The vast floor turned itself inside out and rolling dunes of sand erupted from all around us. My feet sank into the soft grains before I could react. In less than a few blinks' time the arena was transformed into an endless desert. I gazed all around me. Even the dome above had become a clear blue sky.

"Wow," I breathed.

One said nothing. She flicked her wrists again. The sand covering my feet melted away and the ground became water. We stood atop a lone island surrounded by a dark red sea. The sound of waves washed over me.

"Have you seen the red oceans of Balani, Seven?" One asked. "Even among the vast number of worlds I've seen, true red seas are rare."

I shook my head. "Two took Kol to Harmony. Their waters were green."

"Harmony," One said thoughtfully. She flicked her hands again and the ocean was replaced by a lush field of green-blue grass. "How did you like Harmony?"

I wasn't certain how to answer the questions. After all, the only things I knew about the planet and its people were from Two's notes. I thought back to what I'd seen on those screens and the translations of their work.

"They seem like happy people," I said.

"Most races are. It is the prerogative of intelligent beings to seek out happiness." She began to walk. I followed her slowly across the soft grass, feeling a breeze on my face, rich with the fragrance of wild flowers. "Tell me, are you at all familiar with Aukron?"

Aukron.

I rolled the name over in my mind until I recalled it was the name of the planet where the next game would take place. My stomach turned.

"Aukron has been tribal up until recent years," One went on, not waiting for my answer. "A large portion of the population lived in rural communities. Although the advancement of technology has changed that, as it often does."

I nodded. I had no idea one way or the other.

"The first time I saw records of Aukron, they were such

wild, free beings," she continued, almost talking to herself. "They held massive dance festivals in fields like this one, tens of thousands dancing, singing, and mating. It was beautiful to behold. Truly a spectacle. Unfortunately, by the time I had the chance to visit it myself, much had changed. They were living in smaller groups in large cities. Division among the community was apparent, and the emergence of technology means higher degrees of isolation. Individualism ruled over community." She sighed. "But such is the path of advancement and technology."

"You do not approve?" I asked carefully.

One shrugged. "It does not matter if I approve. It is the way of things. The demigods serve the gods and for them, the best way to push a civilization into so-called 'maturity' is by the advancement of technology. But there is so much more to a race than that. Makes you wonder, does it not, if the demigods truly understand the seed races, having never been part of one themselves." A breeze blew through the hills. One looked wistful, lost in thought. I kept silent. "The demigods have no culture or background, and everything they learn of the worlds they descend upon is through academic means. It's ironic indeed that they are the ones who decide the fate of those worlds."

I didn't know what to say, but the idea that the entire existence of the seed races, including my own, was forced to evolve only in the manner the demigods saw fit did not sit well. Thankfully, One appeared to expect no response from me.

"Would you like to try?" she asked, gesturing at the meadow. "Large-scale manipulation is a necessary skill in course design—my speciality. You will need to learn the basics of it, though I understand you already have some experience."

Something inside me constricted. I shook my head, but One stepped behind me and lifted my arms upward. I resisted, but she was forceful.

"You can't avoid this forever," she said gently. "The sooner you open yourself up, the easier it will be."

I struggled to keep from shaking, but it was difficult. I forced a breath through, then another.

"You hear the hum, don't you?" she asked.

I nodded. She sounded very far away. Every fiber of my being screamed out against this.

"Listen to it."

I didn't want to. But it was in my ears. It had always been in my ears, ever since that day when I had lain facedown in the mud, praying the swarm wouldn't tear me apart.

"Let it come. Connect with it."

I couldn't. The things inside my wrists stung. I had almost forgotten about them, but now I was extremely, uncomfortably aware.

The ground quaked, then wobbled. One wrapped one hand around my wrist and I felt a tingle from her touch.

"Don't fight them," she said softly. "I can feel you fighting. You're paranoid. Don't be. I will steady you."

The implants ground against my flesh and bones. One's touch tingled again and I had a feeling she detected my agitation through the implants.

"Let them do their work."

I forced myself to relax, to move past the discomfort. Every fiber of my being cried out against it.

"Think."

FIVE OF US LEFT.

I was the youngest by far, the smallest, and the only Kol. There were two men and two other women in that final round, though I didn't know then it would be the final one. All four looked tired and on edge. They were faster and stronger than me, but by now we all knew those things meant nothing. They huddled together with their worried eyes, talking in hushed voices. Once in a while they cast a glance toward me, but I kept my distance, as was expected of a Kol.

By this point, I knew I had already stepped too far out of the restraints of my upbringing. The others were curious about me. They didn't know how I had managed this far. I understood their confusion—I spoke to no one, kept to myself, showed little talent in manifestation, and yet I crossed that finish line, again and again. They didn't know what to make of me.

And I had no intention of offering up my secret. I thought of Tam and the possibility of holding him in my arms again. I didn't care about what consequences might befall me as long as I could go home to him.

The arena hummed, and I alone heard its song.

"Welcome, worthy ones," boomed the voice above. I looked up—there was nothing to see, but it had become a habit. "You started as many; now you are few. The gods have smiled upon you."

"False gods," one of the men spat.

"Today you will have the honor to once again prove your worth and compete for that chance to enter the holy ground and become an adored one of the gods."

A bright red ring appeared on the high dome above. It was familiar by now. Soon it would begin to tick down, turning white one fraction at a time. Seeing it always made the hair on the back of my neck stand.

One of the women stepped next to me. The voice—speaker for the gods as it called itself—began to lay out the rules of the round. I tried to listen, but was very aware that the woman was watching me.

"What are you doing right?"

I looked toward her, careful not to make direct eye contact, which could be construed as disrespect.

"You know something, don't you? You're playing this game and surviving. Won't you share with the rest of us?"

I dared a glance upward and was surprised to see no malice on her face. If she judged me for being a Kol who survived, she didn't let *it show. Still, I said nothing. I couldn't allow myself to be baited into offending someone without the mark. It would only lead to harm and humiliation for me. My place was to be seen and not heard, and I was certainly not going to offer advice to anyone, lest I win the game only to be stoned later.*

I kept my head down and stayed silent. The woman prodded me a little more, but ultimately muttered a curse under her breath and walked off.

The song of the arena was mine and mine alone. It was my secret. My advantage. Kol or not, I was determined to live.

"Seven?"

My fingers trembled. The implants tingled. The arena's song swelled in my head and something in me danced along.

Something zipped past me. I sidestepped out of the way only to bump into something else. A wall? A person? One of the shadow beasts? I couldn't see.

The arena was pitch black. The glowing red circle above was the only source of illumination and it had counted down less than a quarter of its red light. There was still so much time left and so few options.

Lights. Could I create lights?

A series of sparks shot uselessly from my fingers, singed my skin, and almost immediately fizzled out. I heard movement in the darkness—I'd attracted attention to myself. I moved, though in what direction I had no idea. Shapes appeared and disappeared in the faint red light. Someone shouted.

I grasped for the hum of the arena, but it was so far away, like a marble lost in a sea of pebbles among all the noise and commotion. Something grabbed at my ankle and I tore free and ran in the other direction only to slam straight into a wall. In the moment I saw stars, it pounced on me.

Claws dug into my back, tearing through my clothes and taking strips of skin with them. The creature snarled and I heard it rustle behind me. I took off in the opposite direction, one hand on the wall beside me, trying to gain some sense of direction, moving as fast as I could, teeth clenched against the searing pain radiating from my back. More shouting on the other side of the wall. Had someone fallen? I couldn't see. My back bled, agony shooting through my body with every step, but I didn't dare slow down. The thing behind me gave chase.

It pounced again. I fell forward with its weight on me and my face struck the ground. Two of my teeth rattled loose and the thing pinned me down. I grabbed at it blindly, not even sure what I was feeling. Wet fur? Slime? Teeth? It was all a jumble in the dark. I dragged myself along the floor with my arms, but almost immediately confirmed what I already knew—I was cornered. There was nowhere else to run or hide. Long, sharp fangs bit into my arm and I screamed as my skin and flesh separated from bone. The sounds I heard made my stomach turn. Whatever this thing was, it was eating me, chewing and swallowing as I still lived and breathed.

I panted rapidly. I could see nothing but red and darkness and feel nothing but pain. My body was running cold. How much was I bleeding?

I'm going to die.

It was reality. I was going to crouch in this corner, panting and crying as this thing ate me alive. My head spun. I ought to protect myself. I ought to manifest something useful. I ought to fight back.

But all I could think about was Tam.

Tam and his warm goodness. Tam and his soft giggles that I would never hear again. Tam who was about to be without his mama to watch over him for the rest of his life. Tam who didn't deserve to be part of this chaos.

And in that moment, I hated them all.

The gods, the creatures, the arena, the other contestants who must think I didn't even deserve to be here, that I ought to roll over and die like a proper Kol so someone worthy could take the crown.

The people of Maeda, who must be jeering at me even as I struggled and fought to save them from doom. Mama Dorma, who looked at me as if I was little more than dirt, and Santi, who never stood up to protect me from her heavy hand . . .

I hated them.

They didn't deserve to exist alongside my sweet child. They didn't deserve my blood on the floor. They didn't deserve this world I was trying so desperately to protect. In that moment, for one split second, I wished they would all die.

Heat radiated from me.

All of them.

Pain. Anger. Fear. Hate.

Every single one.

Burning. Noise. Chaos. Humming.

DIE.

Light washed over me. So bright that for a moment my eyes went completely blind from shock. I covered my eyes with my hands, then immediately pulled them away again when I felt the sticky wetness between my fingers. Pain seared from my arm through my entire body. I gasped and blinked, trying to orient myself to my surroundings.

The thing attacking me. Where was it?

I felt outward blindly and gave a yelp when my hands touched something sharp.

"Truly marvelous," boomed the voice from above. "Bold move, child."

I couldn't catch my breath or stand. All I could do was blink hard, willing my eyes to adjust to the light.

"Or perhaps I ought to say, Seven."

Finally, shapes began to swim into focus. The first thing I saw was red. Pools of red in my lap, on the floor, all over my arm. Then, white. The white of my bone peeking through red flesh, the white of the floor under the red blood, the white of the walls.

And the white of the spikes.

I screamed, and I couldn't stop screaming.

Before me, less than an arm's length away, pierced a hundred times through by white spikes growing sideways from white walls, was a ghastly, eyeless thing, long and covered in oily fur, a scrap of my skin still between its long, pin-like teeth. It wriggled like a giant hairy worm, as if trying to break free, then fell still. Behind it, hanging like a mounted trophy by a spike through her chest, was the woman who had asked for my secret to survival.

My left arm was a mess. My stomach turned at the sight of it. With all the strength I had left, I pushed my right hand against the nearest wall and tried to get to my feet, only for my fingers to slide uselessly against the streaks of blood. Gritting my teeth, I tried again. This time I managed to gain enough traction to stand.

But I had nowhere to go. Every surface within sight, the floor included, was covered in spikes. Some the size of needles; some taller than me. I was completely trapped. Blood dripped from what was left of my arm and torn clothing. I closed my eyes, fighting against the urge to pass out, and listened for the arena's song.

There it was, humming steadily in my ears, much clearer now in the sudden silence. I drew deep breaths, trying hard to remain on my feet, and reached out to it. Slowly, the dozen or so spikes in front of me pulled themselves into the ground. I stepped into the small square of space they left behind. There was just enough room for my feet to fit side by side.

And that was how I continued, a few steps at a time. Bleeding liberally, half naked, I trudged on, painfully aware that a single misstep meant falling sideways onto the waiting spikes. As I dragged my feet forward, I saw at least a dozen of the oily creatures, caught in the jungle of spikes.

And the contestants as well. All of them stuck through like pin cushions with more shock than pain on their faces.

The space we occupied was a maze, though not a terribly complicated one, made of smooth walls—now completely covered in spikes. I moved around the walls, removing whatever I could to make room. When I finally passed the outermost wall, what I saw took my breath away.

The entire arena was covered in sharp spikes, as far as the eye could see, extending endlessly into the distance. Every square of space on the floor was filled with spikes like jagged teeth.

I fell to my knees. I could move no more. Blood flowed out of me like a river. My vision blurred. Then, I heard a whisper, a familiar sound that I initially took for a dying hallucination. I turned toward it and there, to my left, was a door.

It opened, no more than a finger's width, and a mixture of familiar smells enveloped me. Tam's warm bath, Mama Dorma's cooking, my scented prayer oils. My entire life, in that one little breath.

I went to it.

"SEVEN."

I snapped to my senses. One stood beside me, one hand holding my raised wrist. She lowered my arm down gently and turned her gaze around the arena. I let out a gasp as I saw what had drawn her attention.

The arena floor was covered in spikes. Save for the square of ground just big enough for us to stand on, the sea of spikes extended from one end of oblivion to the other.

I resisted the urge to wretch. A bitter taste filled my heart and mouth. I wanted to vomit until my body was empty of its organs. That awful moment was not one I ever wanted to relive. Even now, I could feel it overtaking me, fresh and raw as if it had occurred only moments ago.

Hatred had a vile flavor. Right now, just like that moment in my last round, I hated everything.

I snuck a gaze at One. After a long, tense moment, she spoke.

"Well," she said. "You certainly have potential."

EIGHT

CHAPTER 8

I stood on the rickety walkway above the computing room watching Nix move about below. The building blocks of the arena were created here—new ones generated and old ones disintegrated when their shape began to fail. The machines under me lay in patterns with space in between, just enough for Nix to make his way through. I couldn't imagine how he knew his way around this vast and complex maze, but he always seemed to know exactly where he was going.

I envied him. I had no idea where I was going.

"Seven?"

I lifted my head. One stood at the end of the walkway. I knew why she was here, but I pretended to be surprised to see her.

"What are you doing down here?" she asked, gesturing to the ceiling above us, on the other side of which was the arena floor. "The first trial will begin in a few days. It is important for you to be present for the preparations."

The sound of screams filled my head and a sea of motion rocked my memories. Running, bleeding, shouting. An image of a Maedan child, barely taller than my waist, trampled to death in the second trial came to mind. I looked down at the depth below, where Nix's green eyes glowed among the flickering machines. For a moment, I considered leaping over the side and striking my head on the hard floor below.

"Kol cannot," I said shakily. My hands gripped the rails with such desperation that my knuckles turned white. "Kol cannot be part of another game."

I expected One to scold me or become disappointed. I couldn't look at her. If I tore my eyes from the flickering lights below, the urge to jump might win. A gentle hand lay on my shoulder.

"I understand," I heard her say. Then, she sighed, a deep, resigned sound. "You may do as you see fit. However, you must understand that you cannot avoid this forever."

"But why? Why does Kol have to be part of the games? Could Kol not just travel and learn about the planets like Two?"

One did not answer right away. I felt her fingers rub gently against my neck.

"You should pray," she said. "Before the game begins, go to the temple, worship, and the gods will enlighten you."

"Show Kol the Crystal Lake."

An image appeared on the screen nearest to me. I watched, mesmerized at the millions of spots of bright light on the surface of an almost perfectly round lake. A gaggle of gray-skinned Aukronite children could be seen splashing at its edge. Axi's voice drifted through the capsule.

"The Crystal Lake is a natural formation in Lai Mi, the central capital of Aukron. The lake possesses a molecular makeup similar to solid crystals and is the only entity currently known to retain liquid form despite this. Contact with the lake is harmful to most organic forms, save for certain aquatic creatures native to the lake and the Aukronites, who possess dense, rocklike skin."

What sort of creatures could be native to waters that would

tear other living things to shreds? Axi would know the answer, but I couldn't take my eyes off the children splashing around the edge of the lake. They had thick arms and square heads, with rough, gray skin just like their parents, who sat a ways off on a grassy slope, watching them. But unlike the patient, slow-moving adults, they were full of energy—running, shouting to each other, driving their wide fists into the water and laughing at the resulting watery explosions.

Had summer arrived on Maeda? I had no idea. From what Axi had taught me, the tracking of time and seasons was one thing all civilizations shared. The concepts of minutes, hours, and years varied, but most tracked the cycling of night and day and based their activities and habits on the time it took for their world to make a full cycle around its sun. Still, it didn't make the conversion of cycles any easier. And I found that despite my best efforts, I'd lost track of the number of days since I had last seen Maeda. Was Tam splashing in the little pool Santi had dug for him? Perhaps he was toddling about now, smacking his chubby little hands and laughing at the droplets of water he sent flying.

I turned off the screens and left the control room.

The holy ground's location was ever changing and the journey there took multiple days, though I found the trip a little more bearable since I wasn't constantly haunted by Two's presence. I killed time during the trip watching videos of Aukron, attempting to recreate the flavor of Mama Dorma's stew in the gelatinous cubes, and reading. Reading was not something I disliked, but the majority of the material in the orb's database was difficult for me to comprehend, being unfamiliar with the planets of their origin. So I stuck to Maedan literature and a few translated Aukron texts. One had encouraged me to read on multiple occasions. *Learn,* she said. *For the gods abhor ignorance.*

Her words reminded me of the words I saw on Harmony.

Suffer be the idiots. Perhaps the Harmonians were more in tune with the gods than the rest.

Being the only one aboard the capsule was certainly lonely, but there was a sense of freedom. The silence felt like deep meditation, and when I grew tired of it, I had Axi for company. On the fifth day, familiar white light washed through the front window of the capsule. We had arrived at the dwarf star where the latest holy ground sat.

THE CAPSULE SETTLED to a stop inside the dark bay. I was thankful that Axi was able to navigate, as I had zero confidence in my own piloting. Coming here by myself was unnerving, but I was determined not to turn back. Refusing to help in the game preparations might have already set me back in the eyes of the others. If the gods had any "enlightenment" to offer, I needed it now more than ever.

I walked through the vast temple and arrived at the solid wall at the end of the walkway. As I stepped through, the wall gave way easily. The mist surrounded and enveloped me and I was inside the prayer chamber.

They were upon me almost immediately. I extended my arms, closed my eyes, and did my best to relax as they lifted me off my feet. Invisible fingers probed me, touching every inch of my skin, feeling the extra length of hair that had grown since my last prayer.

How could I pose my questions to the gods? They communicated with no words or sounds. All I received from them were images, sensations, and hints of emotion.

I steadied my thoughts.

Then, slowly, I conjured my thoughts in images and emotions as they peered into my mind. I showed them my fear and hesitation in the games, as well as my memories from my own games. At first I sensed little interest from them, but after a while, there was a response. They understood what I was trying to say.

Why must I help sow chaos on another world?

There was a pause. Then, an emotion.

Disappointment?

I posed my question again, and was once again met with disappointment—*their* disappointment. My question was brushed aside as they sifted through my mind, searching for nuggets of gold among a million memories like grains of sand. They wanted to know what I'd seen, what I'd felt, what I thought. Their curiosity was endless, and they had no interest in my question. I winced as they probed deeper and deeper into my consciousness. They found the memories of Harmony, of the long days aboard the capsule, of Viva the fourth champion. Then, when they'd seen everything, I felt it again.

Disappointment.

The invisible hands lowered me to the ground gently. My mind and body were numb. Then the fog gently pushed me from behind, guiding me back to the walkway.

BACK IN THE CAPSULE, I stripped down and went to the washroom, where I ran the water as hot as my skin could bear and washed myself, scrubbing as hard as I could until my body turned red, for as long as I could stand. I couldn't explain why I did this, except that I felt cheap and used and the only thing that helped was scalding their fingerprints off my skin. There was anger inside me, and humiliation, though I didn't quite understand either. When I finished, Axi informed me that a message from One was waiting for me.

"I hope you've enjoyed your pilgrimage," she said, "and found the enlightenment you needed. Please return when you are ready. It is almost time to start final preparation for the game."

My skin stung from the vigorous scrubbing I'd given it. I told Axi to set course to depart from the holy ground and watched the dwarf star grow small as the distance between us grew larger.

Enlightenment.

I didn't know what it was I had received from the gods, but it was the furthest thing from enlightenment I could imagine. The gods had offered me nothing and had interest only in taking—my memories, my experiences, everything they could get their invisible hands on within my mind. And they were even dissatisfied with that.

The dwarf star's light dwindled until it became nothing but one speck among millions in the deep black space.

Was my true job as a champion to offer myself to the gods?

I'd spent my entire life on Maeda being told that I needed to receive the gods' grace through servitude. But these were not the gods who had put the mark on my neck and dropped me in a backwater town where time stood still while the rest of the planet moved on.

No.

These were gods of a bigger universe. Their concerns were not that of the social status and livelihood of one small woman. I felt no malice from them, though it wasn't quite benevolence either. I'd sensed their desire for their "children" to see and hear and experience as much as they could, to become enriched and knowledgeable, even if it was only as an offering to themselves. The gods of the bigger universe were not unkind, merely selfish.

If I had to choose one word to describe what they truly represented, it was *greed*. At the end of the day, all they still wanted from me was servitude. Their world was big, but their want was small.

I watched the silver orb disappear in the distance.

I'd survived the gods of Maeda. I'd survived the life of a slave. I'd survived the games. I would survive these gods as well. My fingers tightened into fists, then slowly loosened, again and again, as I felt my own resolve stiffen.

What they were didn't matter. I had lived through worse and I would keep living. In moments of weakness, I'd thought I was ready for death, but now, faced with the selfish, petty gods of the universe, I wanted to laugh.

If I was going to die, it had to be for something far grander than this.

CHAPTER 9

As the orb descended through Aukron's atmosphere, I was alone in the heart. The screens before me each showed a different view of its surface, but I was fixated on one—a group of people exiting their houses, pointing anxiously at the sky toward us. It was a scene all too familiar.

"Cruising altitude achieved," Axi chirped. "Approaching landing destination."

The scenes shifted as the orb moved slowly through the skies of Aukron. The cameras captured more and more faces—faces I'd come to know well through the countless images and videos in Axi's database. The Aukronites had subtle facial emotions as a result of the limitations of their stiff, sturdy skin, but their shock and excitement were clearly visible by their body language. As the orb floated above them, they waved and pointed with their hefty arms and thick hands, gesturing toward it. I saw an adult holding a tiny infant and suddenly felt my resolve weaken again.

Can I really watch this?

Open fields and hills scrolled beneath us. I saw the Crystal Lake shimmer. Past it, cities and villages clumped together, some large and some small. We were taking the long way to our destination, most likely for the sole purpose of allowing as much of the populace to take notice of us as possible.

Beyond the major cities, past a dry, desolate tundra, was the tallest mountain on Aukron. The locals had a name for it, and it roughly translated to "where we go to weep." One and H'otto referred to it as the Weeping Peak, and I supposed that was as accurate a name as any. It stood high, a dull gray blending into the cloud layers that it pierced. And it was to the top of the Weeping Peak that we went.

"Axi."

"Yes, Seven?"

"Why here?"

"This location was chosen after extensive scouting. The Aukronites possess extensive aquatic technology due to the high ratio of water to land on their planet. In contrast, elevation has proven difficult for them to conquer."

"Why is that?"

"Aukronites possess heavy bodies that make vertical climbing difficult, and the majority of their resource-rich land is flat or just above sea level. The only major high ground is this mountain, where there is no vegetation or valuable minerals worthy of their efforts. As a result, their technology has had no reason to focus on reaching high elevation except for select scientific research."

"So we are far less likely to be bothered here."

"That is correct."

Not that it mattered. The greatest military forces of Maeda had been unable to put a single scratch on the orb.

"Approaching destination. Awareness has reached forty-five percent."

It's almost time.

"Awareness has reached fifty-three percent."

I can't take this.

"Preparing broadcast," Axi said. Then, she raised her voice in a high-pitched manner that I had never heard before. *"Glory be!*" she cried, every shrill word grating against my skin. "*Glory be to the gods! Glory be to Headspace!*"

Then, I heard it—H'otto's voice, booming all through the orb, vibrating against every surface.

"Greetings, people of Aukron."

"*My name is H'otto, and I speak for the Gods.*"

Every surface in Mama Dorma's house shook. I grasped Tam tightly and rushed outside, fearful that the walls would collapse in on us. Santi was already outside, along with Mama Dorma and Sharif. Eisa was out and about, but I had a feeling that wherever she was, she must've heard the voice, too. Santi grabbed and pulled both me and the baby close. Mama Dorma glanced my way, and normally she would have gotten angry at me for coming outside after being told to stay put, but there were far more pressing matters at hand.

The neighbors were out in droves, talking and pointing amongst themselves. They were all facing the same direction, peering toward the horizon.

"It went that way," Santi said to me. "They say it's headed for the sea."

"That voice," I said. "Did it come from there?"

"Certainly felt like it," Santi replied, pointing. "It came like a wave, from there to here."

"Do you think it's dangerous?" I whispered. Tam struggled in my arms. Now that we were outside, he wanted to play. I held him tight, afraid to let go. Santi put his big arm around me and squeezed. But before he could say anything reassuring, the voice boomed again.

"We have come from the stars to search for you," it said. My bones and teeth rattled with every word. Tam looked around in confusion, gnawing on his chubby fingers. "You have been deemed worthy, each one of you, by the gods themselves. You have earned the privilege to prove yourselves in the greatest competition of all. The winner shall have a place at the gods' side."

"Hey!" I turned toward the voice. The old man who lived two houses down had emerged, his cane in hand. He must've stayed inside at first, but whatever was happening was worth hobbling out on his bad hip. "It's on all the screens," he called. "Come look!"

Curious, the neighbors made a beeline for his house. Mama Dorma turned to Santi.

"Leave the Kol," she said. Bringing a Kol into a house unannounced was considered poor manners, and Mama Dorma was nothing if not mannerly.

I watched her leave with the others, but Santi did not move from my side. He waited til the others were out of view, then took my hand.

"He said all the screens. Come."

He led me back into Mama Dorma's house. The screen in the main room was already on—odd as I distinctly remembered it being off. On the screen was an image of a pure black sphere against a white background.

"The arena of the gods is a holy place," the voice said. "What you witness before you is magic, innovation, and true greatness. Your world has been chosen. Rejoice."

"Kol does not understand," I said meekly. Tam wriggled. I finally put him down, though I felt no safer inside the house than outside it. Whatever was happening felt unbelievably, dangerously, inexplicably big. Much too big for these walls to protect me.

"Me either," Santi murmured, then quickly puffed out his chest when he saw my apprehension. "But don't worry. Nothing's going to happen. You and the baby will always be safe with me."

Though I wasn't convinced, I was grateful. Sometimes Santi's foolhardy bravado was nice to have. I lifted my head to offer him a smile, but it froze on my face when the screen suddenly changed to a dim, wide room. Then, a person appeared.

It was a child, a boy just old enough for school. He appeared out of nowhere, looking confused and out of place. Before he could make up his mind about his whereabouts, however, another person appeared. Then another.

"The first one hundred are the special ones," the voice said, as more and more people appeared on the screen. I had no idea how they were being brought in, but they all looked equally shocked to be there. Their ages varied from toddler to elder, from every race, shape, and form. They regarded each other in confusion.

"You will be the first ones to prove your worth, the ones who pioneer the way for the others, and the first to prove the worth of your world. Remember, a world unworthy of the games is one unworthy of the gods' universe. But not to worry, the first game is simple—all you must do is live."

Then, the massacre began.

"Breathe."

I let out a sharp gasp and nearly choked. Coughing and sputtering, I fought to gain control of my senses and for a moment couldn't remember where I was. I blinked tears out of my eyes and for a brief second thought I saw Mama Dorma in front of me, but as my vision cleared, One's kind face swam into view.

"Are you alright, dear?"

I almost lied, but it wouldn't have been convincing. My face was puffy and red, and the rest of me was trying to decide between weeping, choking, and losing consciousness.

"No," I admitted. "Kol is not. Kol cannot watch children. Ko—"

I stopped myself abruptly, but it was too late. One looked at me with what I could only describe as pity and I suddenly felt weak and useless. She reached out and brushed hair damp with sweat out of my face. We were in the back of the room, I suddenly noticed, away from the larger screens. I didn't know when we had moved, but One must've walked me away from the screens when she saw me break down.

"You are not Kol," she reminded me gently. "Those days are

done, as are your days in the games. The ones on the screen are not you or yours. You are a favored one now."

I shook my head. "Ko . . . I know. I just can't watch. Why must children be selected for the games? They are innocent."

"H'otto believes in giving all a chance to prove their worth. You cannot underestimate the young ones. You were one yourself, after all."

"But they don't understand. Ko—I didn't understand. I still don't."

"Children perform quite well in the games," One said, though I could tell by her tone that she herself knew this did not make things better. "They possess unrestricted imagination and strong faith in what their minds conjure up."

"But they *don't understand*," I said again. I wanted to say something else, something to make her realize, but I couldn't come up with anything, and worst of all, she already knew this, perhaps better than I did. Behind me, I heard the sounds of the arena. Terrified voices, footsteps, screams cut short . . .

Then, silence.

"Would you look at that," One said, looking past me toward the screens. "It seems we have our first winner."

CHAPTER 10

His name translated to "moderate," and his people
went mad.

I wasn't surprised. After all, I had lived through it all before.
Though I didn't want to watch, I also couldn't tear my attention
away. After the first trial round, I parked myself in the heart of
the arena, obsessively watching video feeds from Aukron,
streamed through the screens on the walls. H'otto and One
seemed uninterested in events outside the arena, and Two, who
did not even bother to return from their latest trip for the inau-
gural game, even less so.

"Axi," I said. "Tell Kol about him. The winner."

"Contestant is male. Aged fifty-nine Aukron cycles. Initial
scan reveals genetic abnormalities."

"How long is fifty-nine cycles?" I asked, then remembered
whatever answer she gave me would be of no use to me. "What
Kol means is, what stage of life is he in?"

"Contestant is considered a young adult."

Watching the chaos taking place on Aukron was morbid,
but I couldn't tear myself away. Their news media blared to life.
Chatter filled the airwaves. It was all too uncomfortably familiar. As the only survivor of the first round, this first winner
became their focus almost immediately, with heroic labels

pasted all over him. Then, as his uniqueness was discovered, the script flipped just as quickly, with speculations flying about whether being "addled" was the key to winning the game.

"What do you mean, genetic abnormalities?"

"Contestant possesses a known gene mutation in his species. It affects roughly one in every ten thousand live births."

"He is different?"

"Traits include intellectual and social delay, speech impediment, and fine and gross motor impairment. Key organ malformation occurs in rare cases, though not present in this individual."

I ground my teeth angrily as newsmen and "experts" discussed whether it was for the benefit of the planet to send in the "simple" and "challenged" to fight for their planet, completely ignoring the fact that the contestant drawing was random. Their interest in him as a person had gone away. Instead, they referred to him by labels—"disabled contestant," "winner by chance," "accidental champion."

Kol.

I shuddered.

Something touched my hand and I jumped. I whipped around to see Nix standing behind me. He had been working in the heart but hadn't acknowledged me until now. Looking down, I saw that I had clenched my fingers into a fist so tight my nails had drawn blood. Nix tilted his head at me quizzically.

"I'm OK, Nix," I said. "Thank you."

Nix waited a moment before plodding away. I'd spent enough time with him to know he was waiting to see whether I was going to walk away from the source of my agitation.

I ought to, but I didn't. I stayed before the screens, hour after hour, watching and reliving.

I COULDN'T SLEEP.

Restless and agitated, I paced the corridors of the arena's underbelly, in and out of the heart and back and forth on the suspended walkway above the computing room. Even standing still to watch the screens became a challenge. I simply couldn't stop moving. The source of my agitation was a decision—I had finally decided to watch a game, and I would not have worked up the courage to take this step were it not for this "addled" contestant, Moderate.

I stood next to One on a balcony that protruded from the dome wall, high above the arena floor. I'd had no idea this balcony existed before. It extended seamlessly out of the wall, as if the arena had melted and reshaped that part of itself. I had a feeling it was hidden from the contestants, as none of them looked toward us even though we were plainly in view. Moderate had arrived first. I looked down over the side and found him easily in the growing crowd. He was quite a bit bigger than the average Aukron, with proportionally wider shoulders but shorter legs. His skin was also smoother and lighter in color, contrasted with the others, who were rougher, darker shades of gray. I watched him, uneasy for his fate.

And yet, Moderate himself showed little anxiety. In fact, most of the others showed their worry through body language more explicitly than he did. Calmly, he paced in a square and muttered to himself. Some of the newer contestants pointed at him and whispered, while others wept fearfully or ranted in anger. No small children were chosen this time and for that I was thankful.

"I'm glad you finally decided to watch the games," One said, interrupting my thoughts.

I tore my eyes from Moderate. One looked so pleased with me that I almost felt guilty for being here to observe only one contestant. "Kol was curious," I said softly.

She nodded. "Keep that curiosity. It will serve you well."

"WELCOME, CONTESTANTS."

Every hair on my body stood up and I had to grip the

railing of the balcony to keep myself steady. Every part of my body, inside and out, trembled. Memories flooded into my mind and the device in my neck went into overdrive. Despite my resolve to live on no matter what the gods wanted of me, those words still rattled me to my core. The contestants looked up at the source of the voice above. Moderate did not. He continued looking around and pacing slowly in a square.

One came to the edge of the balcony and raised her hands in the ready position. Despite the circumstances, the sight of her in the conductor's pose was a beautiful sight, like a magician preparing to wow an audience. I couldn't help but wonder, had she been serene and calm like this when she stood up here while I was the one who shook and cried on the arena floor?

"LOOK OUT!"

I dove out of the way just in time, along with several others. The island was growing smaller by the moment and the waters were creeping upon us. I could swim, but the water was not where I wanted to be. As I scrambled to avoid injury, a particularly high tide lapped at my foot. I let out a cry of pain as the boiling hot water singed my skin and quickly made my way back inland.

But inland was no safer. Sweat stung my eyes. Insufferable heat rose from the ocean all around the island. I felt like I was being steamed to death. My clothes clung to me as I struggled to keep moving. The heavy moisture weighed me down, but to pause meant certain death.

And not just from the dangers of the arena.

The figure on the island, looking less and less Maedan by the moment, attacked again. The contestants were no longer just running from the searing sea or the creatures emerging from it, but from one of their own.

Rubbing dampness from my eyes, I struggled to manifest shields around myself while keeping an eye on the figure in the center of the island. There were twenty of us left, twenty-one a moment ago. The twenty-first, a young woman not much older than I was, I could no longer consider one of us.

A bouquet of tentacles erupted from between her shoulders where her head had been not long ago. Her arms had elongated and thickened, fingers melded together. As I watched, her skin began to lose its natural light peach shade and turn translucent. Dark splotches emerged all over her body. With every second that passed, she resembled more the creatures coming out of the boiling sea.

And she was attacking us.

She whipped what used to be her neck in one direction and the tentacles shot toward a man who scrambled out of the way. She latched onto his arm and he cut at the tentacle with his manifested blade. It withdrew and I saw blood on his skin. I let out a gasp and she turned on me. The tentacles shot out for my throat and fear seized me. My shields collapsed and . . .

BOOM

I stood in place, hands awkwardly raised in front of me. I was still alive.

In the center of the island, where the crazed contestant had been just a moment ago, was a puddle. Bile retched up in my throat as I recognized her clothing, now completely flat on the ground. The rest of her was splattered through the sand in a star pattern.

"Disappointing," came H'otto's voice from above. "Truly disappointing. Only the weak ones lose control, and the gods have no interest in the weak."

I shook.

And I couldn't stop shaking. Arms wrapped tightly around myself, I stared at the puddle that had been a living person just a moment ago. I didn't see the boiling sea recede, nor the sandy island disappear. I heard H'otto explain that a round was terminated if a contestant entered a "splintered" state, but his voice sounded very far away.

The thought of dying as a monster was far more frightening than anything else the arena had to offer.

. . .

"We have a splinter."

I snapped back to reality.

"H'otto, we have a splinter," One repeated.

The arena below had completely turned to water. I'd spent enough time studying the planet to know it was the dense, heavy waters of the Aukron sea—water fit for the Aukronites to swim through. Most of the contestants had manifested water crafts of various sizes and shapes and were fending off the slippery creatures attempting to find their way onto the little boats. Several had toppled over already and were struggling to keep from being pulled under. It was among these that the splinter had occurred.

The sight was all too familiar. One of the contestants in the water had been surrounded and pulled under. Once. Twice. On the third time, what emerged from the water was much less like an Aukronite and much more like a deformed boulder. One side of their head and shoulder swelled up as if being blown up from the inside. The arm on the same side doubled in length and width. I watched it reach up and smack at the water around it, toppling two other boats with its force. The other Aukronites shouted in fear and tried to distance themselves. More and more of the creatures in the water headed toward the splintered contestant. The water boiled with movement.

"Shall I eliminate?" I heard One ask.

"Yes," came H'otto's voice from the walls near us. I braced myself for what was coming.

BOOM

A geyser shot up through the water with such force that the entire arena shook. The splintered contestant was carried at its top as the water torrent smashed into the top of the dome. Then the water fell away and down they came, plunging into the murky depth with a heavy *splash*.

"Terminating round," One said.

The water disappeared. The creatures scattered. A brown dirt ground emerged and the misshapen boats manifested by the contestants wobbled awkwardly as their occupants stepped out.

The splintered contestant lay still, limbs bent awkwardly in every direction. I didn't need to take a closer look to know they were dead.

"The weak will always lose control," H'otto's voice boomed from above. *"The gods have no need for the weak."*

One shook her head and clicked her tongue. "He is not going to be happy," she said. "How could this happen? A civilization mature enough for the games ought to have a better baseline mentality than this."

I only half listened to her. Peering over the edge of the balcony, I squinted, looking hard for Moderate. After a worrying moment, I found him.

He had completely hidden himself. Now that I thought about it, I hadn't even seen him among the boats floating with the others. The square space he had been pacing had changed into a solid cube and he had tucked himself inside. With the water gone, it broke apart slowly and Moderate pulled himself from it like a newborn bird. Instead of floating with the others, he had been safe under the water all this time.

"Come, Seven," I heard One say.

"Yes," I said absently, taking one last look at Moderate before following her.

"First the addled one, then a splinter this soon. This game is not going well," she muttered as we walked.

"You mean . . ."

"That one that survived the first round. H'otto is rather displeased with him."

"Why is that?"

One opened her mouth to answer, but I saw her hesitate. Whatever she was going to say, she swallowed. Instead, she said, slowly as if with some caution, "The demigods have their preferences."

CHAPTER 11

"FOCUS ON THE INDIVIDUALS," ONE SAID IN MY EAR AS I struggled to maintain my grip on her wrist. Even secondhand, the sensation was overwhelming. I had never been "plugged into" the arena to such a degree. I could hear every voice and sense every footstep. Keeping track of it all was difficult, like trying to distinguish every drop of water in a brook babbling by.

"Don't fight it," she said, sensing the tension in my body. She was running the game and coaching me at the same time. I could sense a fraction of the input from her senses, like hearing a voice through a screen.

I tried my best to relax. Much like worship, connecting with the arena was easier once I found the flow and gave myself into it, following through with its movements rather than pushing and pulling against it.

The Aukronites were climbing, a difficult task for their heavy bodies and broad hands. They struggled up the tall structure before them, shaped and colored ironically like a miniature version of the Weeping Peak. I closed my eyes— cutting off other senses, I'd learned, often improved connection with the arena. One shifted slightly, and a sliver of the miniature mountain crumbled. Two contestants nearly fell but managed to shift their grips and hang on. She shifted again, and the entire mountain trembled. The contestants manifested different methods to cling on, but my interest lay in only one— the one I had begun to affectionately think of as "Mod." Time and time again the odds were against him and time and time again he crossed the finish line. His people called it luck; they found reasons to discount his accomplishments as a mere turn of fortune. But in my eyes, he was absolutely brilliant.

I desperately wanted to know where he was and how he was managing, but I couldn't afford the distraction. Diverting my attention could cause an imbalance for One and lead to her losing control of the game stage, and that was one of the worst infractions anyone could commit. To maintain the balance between challenging and fair was exceedingly difficult, and I was more than uneasy at the thought that a flick of someone's wrist could've meant my own demise in the games.

Finally, after what felt like an eternity, the round ended. There were only four contestants remaining now, and I saw with immense relief that Mod was among them. His instinct for self-preservation had won out once more. With the aid of the implants and the arena, I gently probed his mind. Unblighted by fear or envy, Mod was a spot of light that shone even in the darkness of the arena.

"SELF-PRESERVATION WILL ONLY GET him so far."

It was a line I'd grown used to hearing. H'otto paced slowly between the screens in the heart, watching replays of the earlier rounds. He had his preferences among the participants, which consisted of a fast, lanky male and a clever female, both of whom had also won the hearts of Aukron itself.

"Self-preservation has gotten him to the last round," I said quietly, trying not to sound like I was pushing the issue but unable to help myself.

H'otto shook his head. "The gods will not approve of him."

"Why is that?"

H'otto paused his pacing and turned to me. For a moment I worried I'd overstepped my bounds. But H'otto only sighed softly and turned back to the screens again, four hands linked in two pairs behind his back.

"There are some things you simply learn, Seven," he said tiredly, "when you have served the gods as long as I have."

"WHERE WILL KOL GO, MAMA?"

Mama Dorma's eyes cut into me as I stood just outside the doorway of her house, the only home I knew. Rain was pouring. Big, heavy droplets that pounded heavily at my shoulders and back. I hugged myself, longing to be inside where it was warm and dry.

"That is no concern of mine," she said coldly. "There is no place in this house for a Kol who does not know her own humility."

"Kol knows," I pleaded. "Kol knows, Mama. Please."

But the door was already closed. I stood in the rain, soaked head to toe, sobbing as I pounded weakly on the door. I waited there until the rain stopped. I waited until the night came. I waited in the corner of the yard, hoping for a glimpse of the door opening.

And at midnight, it finally did. Santi snuck outside as the rest of his family slept and slipped me a small package of bread and meat wrapped in a thin blanket. I ate and slept in that corner. And so it went. Night after night after night.

I WOKE to preparations underway for the final round on Aukron. I hadn't slept well once again. Rather than trying to get some more rest, I went to the heart and asked Axi to pull up video feeds from the planet. The media of Aukron were blaring as always, a noisy mixture of excitement and fear that I remembered all too well.

Despite Mod's impressive track record, being the only Aukronite to survive from the very first round to the very last, his own people sided mostly with H'otto. They were far more interested in the other contestants, some of whom I supposed were more physically attractive by their standards. Mod was mentioned only in passing and frequently as the butt of jokes. I stood before the screens watching the Aukronites mimic his awkward body language and speech patterns while laughing.

Is this what I chose over death? An eternity of watching every civilization revel in their own prejudices?

One cleared her throat behind me. "Are you ready?"

"Why do they do this?"

She regarded me as if she wasn't surprised by my question. "I think you already know the answer to that."

"They treat him as if he is less than, even though he has done far better than the rest of them."

"By their standards, he is less."

"Not by the standards of the arena," I seethed. "Kol was seen as less, too. But Kol was better than them. Kol was the one who won and saved them. If Mod wins, Kol will make sure he knows he is more worthy than the rest of them."

"And yet," One said gently, "you still cannot help addressing yourself in the way they forced you to."

THE HEAT RADIATING from the arena below reminded me far too much of the little island where I'd witnessed a splinter for the very first time. But instead of wet steam, this was a dry, smoky heat. Due to their thick hides, mere water would not damage the Aukronites enough to cause real harm, but molten rock was another story.

The contestants balanced themselves precariously on small platforms, each barely big enough for one of them to stand on. One wrong step and they would find themselves sinking into the scorching sea of lava around them. They hopped carefully, one platform at a time—and hopping was *not* their strong suit. I watched one attempt to manifest new platforms to stand on, but whatever material they conjured had great difficulty holding shape in the searing heat. They managed one step and barely hopped onto the next platform before the manifestation crumbled.

One gestured with one finger and a bubble of lava popped near two of the contestants. One of them cried out in pain as hot embers landed on their skin, brushing off their arm in a panic. The other—Mod—made no sound. I watched him flap his big arm a few times and continue on.

My left hand held One's right wrist. Through her implant, I felt the shift and turn of the arena. The sea of lava was a difficult one to manage, much more so than the mountain. I was continuously impressed at One's skill and dexterity.

A contestant was lost as they cornered themselves on a route with no platforms to go forward. The platforms behind them fell away. I averted my eyes but could not block out the sensations fed to me by One's implant. I tensed against their struggle and attempt to manifest, and experienced their fear as if it was my own. Then it fizzled out and there were three. I shuddered.

"End it," came H'otto's voice from the walls around us. Then, I heard it again, but this time not from the walls. Instead, it came from One's implant.

"Get rid of the flaw," it said.

I didn't know if H'otto was trying to hide that message from me. One's eyes were closed tight. Her fingers moved, tweaking and dialing the air with intense concentration. The remaining platforms began to shrink.

No.

My grip on One's wrist tightened. She continued her work, concentrating so hard she barely noticed I was still there. The platforms grew smaller and smaller. Two of the contestants desperately manifested floating crafts and protection for their bodies. They shouted to each other in panic. Neither gave attention to Mod, who was frozen in place, staring at the shrinking platform beneath him motionlessly.

Do something!

My hand grasped One's wrist so tightly my knuckles trembled. Her hand moved again, and a large platform appeared in the center of the arena. The intent was clear—reach the large platform, and the game was over. Two contestants immediately began to manifest paths toward it. Mod did nothing.

No.

For a moment the platform under Mod paused under my will. One pulled against me. The platform shrank again. I paused it once more. Then, I felt One's influence grow, blocking me, like fingers prying apart my grip.

Do not *interfere.*

It took all my strength not to crumble as the platform beneath him shrank to nearly nothing. He took a tentative step and almost immediately sank beneath the surface without so much as a bubble.

The final two paid him no attention. They were far too busy with their own survival. I watched with a hint of bitterness as one of them managed to create a metal boat and oar and hop inside just as the platform beneath them vanished. The other manifested an enormous boulder and climbed on top of it, then manifested another just as the one they stood on began to crumble from the heat. Slowly, carefully, they both headed toward the platform.

One turned up the heat. After all, only one champion was needed.

The contestant in the boat stood suddenly as the bottom of the boat heated up. I watched them hop from foot to foot while attempting to continue paddling toward their destination. Their feet began to sizzle and turn dark. It was a gruesome sight, watching someone being cooked alive. Just when I thought I could take it no more, their manifestation gave out.

The boat fell apart, its tiny building blocks scattering in all directions. The contestant let out a howl of fear and pain before disappearing beneath the surface. The final contestant let out a shriek of despair and something washed over me—the feeling of relenting, letting go, giving up. The loss of their companion had broken them for a very brief moment.

Unfortunately, that moment was all it took.

The boulder they were precariously perched on scattered. I sensed their shock as they reached and grabbed thin air, then disappeared beneath the surface.

It was over.

Aukron had no survivors.

A moment of silence followed. Then, H'otto's voice sighed from above. I imagined the terror of the entire planet at their inevitable fate. My knees shook.

"How unfortunate," he said. *"I am most disappointed and saddened on behalf of th—"*

He stopped.

A single hand, red and half-formed, reached out of the teeming lava and slapped itself onto the platform. Another joined it. Then, slowly, they pulled themselves forward, a finger's length at a time. A soft, shapeless red form followed it, dragging itself out of the lava. I held my breath as the rest of it slowly emerged onto the platform, practically a puddle. Then, slowly, slowly, it pulled itself together. Its color darkened and clear shapes of head and limbs began to appear. After a long moment, Mod stood up, unhurried, and looked around, searching for the others.

"Well," was all H'otto said.

In all of the archived records of past games, I had happened upon only one person who had modified their entire body to liquid consistency and survived. Every other contestant who attempted the feat lost control quickly and floundered as their bodies failed to reform, eventually ending in death. That person was currently locked away in a revolving room. Viva, the champion designated Four.

Now there were two.

Mod—Eight—was inside his jar. I watched the screens with joyful curiosity. His jar was a wide, comfortable space with soft, sand-colored furniture and grass-colored walls. He went happily from one massive cushion to another, alternating between sitting and bouncing. Did he realize where he was? I wondered.

H'otto did not wonder about such things. Behind me, I could hear him conversing with One in a hushed, upset tone.

"How could this happen?" he kept saying. "This will not go over well. How could this happen?"

"He did prove himself," One said, though she sounded unconvinced. "Perhaps someone could train him up. He can't be that slow if he managed to survive the arena."

Then, she dropped her voice low, almost inaudible, but I heard nonetheless.

"You've had your doubts before, *remember*?"

H'otto ignored the question. "And who will take on the task of teaching him?"

"He might not come out. He is addled, after all."

"I hope so," H'otto said. "For his own sake, I hope—"

"He's out."

H'otto's attention snapped to me. "What?"

"He's out," I repeated, pointing to the screen nearest to me, which now showed a single door standing alone in the arena. Mod's square gray head peeked out.

H'otto shook his head in frustration. "I can't deal with this," he said haughtily. It was a far departure from his usual warm tone. There was a coldness to him I hadn't seen before. But more so, I heard something odd in his voice.

Fear?

"I will do it."

The words left my mouth as if on their own. H'otto's dark

eyes rolled over me, looking as surprised as I felt. Beside him, One gave me a shocked look that quickly turned into what almost looked like pride.

"You?"

I nodded. "Yes. If you don't mind. K—I would like a chance to orient the new champion."

H'otto's face tightened for a brief second, then melted into a smile. "Yes," he said slowly. "That's a good idea. It will be quite an experience for you, won't it? Orienting a new champion is no small feat, but this fellow might just be the right one for you to practice on. But are you certain, Seven? Are you confident?"

I nodded. "Yes," I said. "I am."

I WATCHED Mod pace the arena floor from the balcony. There was a sense of serenity to his movement. Wide and slow, like branches of an old tree swaying in the wind.

Though I'd made a bold claim to H'otto that I would care for the eighth champion, I had no idea where to start. His people were outside the dome, celebrating his victory and mourning the ones lost. The last ones to fall to their demise had been rather popular with the people of Aukron, and there were those—particularly among the youth and young adults—who voiced that the planet was not worth living on, having been saved by Mod instead. That was the last recording I watched of Aukron, and I had no intention of watching more.

Mod paced patiently. I left the balcony and made my way through the catacomb of walkways toward the arena floor. There, I came face-to-face with him for the very first time.

He was even bigger up close, towering over me with his broad, lumbering body and thick shoulders. His gray skin had a texture like boulders smoothed by water since ancient times. Despite the difference in our sizes, I was not afraid. He would not hurt me, or anyone at all.

"Hi," he said. Then, slowly, as if thinking of his words one at a time, "How. Are you."

"I'm well," I responded with a smile.

He worked around each of his words slowly, and the arena translated. He was not surprised by my appearance, though I must have looked like the strangest little goblin to him. "I. Not. Know. Where. Am."

I reached out and took his giant hand, and everything about his presence washed over me. He was big, warm, and kind like Santi, but young at heart. He was bright, and resilient, and deserved so much more than what his world had given him. He was greater than they knew, and greater than H'otto would admit.

I reached up and touched his face with my other hand. He looked confused for a moment, then relaxed into my touch. Something in me bloomed, like heat and life sprouting forth.

This.

This is what I chose to live for. I will live for him.

"You're home," I said.

NINE

CHAPTER 12

CHAPTER TWELVE

"Hello. Axi."

"Hello," replied the ever-patient Axi for the hundredth time. "Eight. How are you today?"

"I. Am. Good." A pause. "Hello. Axi."

"Hello, Eight."

I smiled. I'd learned long ago that it was not worth interrupting Mod's looped conversations with Axi. They made him happy and kept him occupied, and frankly that was good enough for me.

Mod wore his joy front and center. Though his kind was already prone to showing emotions via body language, he was even more expressive than the average Aukronite in that department. When in a good mood, he waved his large hands around his head, as if fanning himself. His feet stomped in a little dance, sending vibrations through the floor of the capsule. When I had nothing better to do, I often sat and watched him.

"Are you hungry?" I asked when he took a pause. He turned to me and I mimed spooning food into my mouth. "Eat?"

"Yes," he said, paused, then added, "Please."

I smiled and he smiled back before turning back to Axi. I left him to his conversation.

Over time I'd learned to work my way around the functionality of the capsules. In the common room, I used the food machine to produce meals for both of us—it was still cubes, but I'd learned to change their texture, temperature, and flavor to simulate a variety of foods from both Maeda and Aukron. I carried two bowls, one full of soft, steaming, transparent cubes that smelled like Mama Dorma's favorite spices, and one cold and hard and semitranslucent. Figuring out Mod's preferred foods had taken some patience and research, but he was never one to complain even when I couldn't quite get it right for the tenth or hundredth time. I gauged my success rate by the smile or grimace on his face when he ate. Delicious or hideous, he always finished every last bite.

"Here you go, Mod," I said as he entered the common room. We sat side by side and ate together. He grinned at me as he tasted his food, teeth crunching the rock-hard cubes rhythmically.

"Good," he said, smiling widely.

To the others, he was Eight, but when it was the two of us, he was always Mod. Just like I was always Seven to the others, but when no one else was around, I was Nas. I'd never once tried to enforce this rule, but he instinctively knew within the first few days of our time together that the names we used just between us were special.

Before Mod joined the ranks of the champions, I'd begun to grow accustomed to living only to survive. I hadn't realized how listless I'd become, drifting from one day to the next, following behind H'otto or One trying to take in whatever wisdom they wished to impart, tiptoeing around Two with my head down. I'd even given up on trying to produce appetizing meals for myself.

My living conditions had been even more paltry. The champions were allowed to create their own living quarters within a designated area filled with evenly divided spaces—except I thought of them as cells and treated them as such, manifesting for myself only a cot to sleep on and spending nearly no time there, preferring instead to hang around Axi in the heart or watch Nix work in the computing room. My existence had been colorless and without purpose.

"Home?"

"Not yet," I replied. "There's still a little more to be done here. I need to talk to Two." He wasn't asking to go home. Mod was perfectly happy passing his days clamoring about the capsule chatting with Axi. Asking for home was his way of asking how much more I had to do, and he seemed satisfied with my answer. He had a way of communicating his questions with a few efficient words. It reminded me of Tam and his babbles and gestures.

Tam. How old must he be now? The Maedan clock I'd set with Axi's help had turned at least ten cycles since my first time aboard a capsule. Despite how I remembered him, small and warm, Tam was no longer a child. In fact, he was rapidly approaching the age I'd been when I wed his father. I tried to picture him as a proper young man, but could not conjure up his face. In my mind, he would always be an infant.

A broad, warm hand laid on my back, nearly covering me from shoulder to shoulder, and rubbed up and down gently. Mod could usually tell when something was on my mind. I smiled to reassure him I was alright.

"Sad?"

I shook my head. "No. Just thinking."

Since Mod's arrival, I had gone to greater lengths to learn how to create creature comforts not only within the capsules, but within the arena as well. I dressed up the "cell" the best I could, and did a fair job recreating my old room in Mama Dorma's house, with its brown floors and tapestries on the wall. Instead of a cot for me and a smaller one for Tam, I placed a large one for Mod, and we slept across from each other just like

Tam and I used to. When there was nothing to do, I practiced recreating the grassy hills and white beaches of Aukron on the arena floor so Mod could frolic and play on familiar grounds. The effort it took felt far closer to pleasure than work when it was for someone who appreciated it.

Even aboard the tiny, cramped capsule, I did my best to make the limited space feel like home. I replicated the same tapestries in our shared sleeping quarters and perused Axi's database for music from both of our homes. When the rhythmic sound of Aukron's massive leather drums filled the capsule, Mod always smiled and spun in circles. In the tight space, this often meant he bumped into the surfaces around him, but that never slowed him once. Whenever he took my hand, I spun with him. I had never danced on Maeda, but I couldn't imagine a better partner for it.

"I AM ALWAYS surprised at your willingness to put up with *that*."

I turned away from Mod, who was occupied in his ritual-istic conversation with Axi. Two's elegant face looked back at me from the screen, though at the moment it was marred by a look of derision, an expression that triggered a visceral reaction in me that I couldn't ignore.

After so much time in their presence, I'd grown used to Two's terse mannerisms, and the little jibes they tossed my way were far easier to put out of my mind when they weren't sharing the same space as me, which they thankfully avoided doing most of the time. There were days when I could almost forget the old fears and paranoia, the sensation of hair standing on the back of my neck when they were around, or the gnawing dread in the pit of my stomach at the sight of them.

But every time they cast those clear eyes on Mod, those phantom fingers crept to my throat again, and images of that basement room threatened to break down the wall in my mind that kept them at bay.

"He does what he needs to," I replied, and quickly changed the subject. "How has surveillance gone on the dark side?"

"Interesting," Two replied. "I'm curious to see how One plans to design the games for this world. I've come across tidally locked planets in the past, but this is the first one to sustain civilization. Have you read my previous report?"

"Yes."

"And?"

"I cannot make the call either."

Two muttered under their breath—a curse in their native language that went untranslated. "Are you sure the Solar Commons can't take a backseat to this?"

"Not without significant political upheaval, which would distract from the game itself. I imagine the same would happen if we challenged only the Umbra Collective."

"This will be exceedingly tricky," Two admitted. Behind me, I heard Mod say hello yet again to Axi. Two glanced toward him and I took a small step, placing myself between them. "Not only do the two sides of the planet vary greatly in their technological and cultural development, their physiologies are different, too."

"Are they different on a genetic level?"

"No, but they have been divided for so long that they've adopted enough varying traits to make this difficult. The Umbra Collective possesses slitted pupils that allow for improved night vision. Their skins and eyes are sensitive to UV light and they've developed significant technology and methods for tracking and motion detection in darkness."

I thought for a moment, absently manifesting a small cube that revolved itself around my fingers as I did so. "The Solar Commons have tough skins that guard against a variety of allergens as well as heat. They've harnessed solar power for most of their tech. They have next to no night vision and seem to have developed numerous methods of lighting any and all spaces that have no access to a natural light source. I also noticed they have thick hand and foot pads."

"For walking and climbing on hot surfaces."

"Yes."

"Well, I hope One is up to the challenge. Designing games for two races that literally don't see the same way—I can't imagine it. It has never been done in this galaxy."

"It has been done in other galaxies?"

"Supposedly. I've heard, anyway. I don't spend a lot of time watching recordings."

Except Viva. "Are you heading back?"

"Soon."

"I will, too. After I take Eight to pray."

I saw a slight twitch on their face. Two, much like H'otto and One, saw little purpose in taking Mod, one too simple to appreciate enlightenment, to the holy ground. I pretended not to see and bid them goodbye.

"Mod."

Mod paused his endless conversation with Axi and turned to me.

"Tell me, Mod, how do you make a game that challenges two races that have different eyes?"

Mod blinked, then said matter-of-factly, "Make. Challenge. For. Ear."

FOR THE FIRST time since I began my life as a champion, the holy ground was not parked near a live sun. Instead, we drifted slowly into the ball pit amidst a sea of asteroids. Judging by the small handful of orbs hovering around, the asteroids were probably what was left of the sun they had sucked dry. It was unusual for the holy ground to remain in place for so long after the power source had been used up. I steered the capsule toward the silver orb and wondered if something was different.

It was strange the things that had become "normal" to me.

There was a time when even the sight of an asteroid field would've fascinated me to no end. Back in my greener days I never could've fathomed navigating my way between the planets that filled the galaxy, observing their inhabitants and preparing the arena for their occupancy. Though running the games still unsettled me, they were so few and far between that I could almost fool myself into thinking the next one was never coming, and this slow, lazy time of travel and research with Mod at my side could last forever. Without the chaos of the games, there was a quiet way of life to be had.

Once we were settled inside, I took time to reassure Mod about the process of prayer. Though I'd brought him to the temple many times before, he had never worshiped himself. I had initially worried this would be an issue, but H'otto never once inquired whether I'd encouraged Mod to worship. In fact, he appeared perfectly happy for me to keep Mod out of his sight and mind as he occupied himself searching for a suitable planet for the next game. The clearest indicator of his disinterest in Mod was the fact that Mod lacked all the surgical implants meticulously placed in One, Two, and me. Even the idea of "wasting" the implants on him was too much for H'otto.

I didn't mind. Secretly, I like that Mod was "untouched." When he was happy, I knew his joy was pure and all his own, not the result of secret little tingles in the back of his neck. Deep down, I believed that Mod was grateful to be himself, something that his own people jeered at him for.

Mod, as usual, was wary of the dizzying height within the temple space. The darkness of the bay somehow negated this, but seeing the endless height brightly lit was a different matter. I learned of his acrophobia the hard way after a near-disastrous first visit. After reminding him to keep his eyes on me or the walkway and not to look up or down, I took his large hand and walked him out of the capsule.

The temple was quiet today. Most of the orbs had already left after finishing off the sun. We walked hand in hand until

Mod paused at the wall of fog. He never had interest in entering the sanctum, no matter how I encouraged him, and today was no exception. After a few halfhearted attempts, I relented and asked him to wait. He sat down on the walkway and I ventured into the prayer room alone.

The moment the fog closed behind me, I knew something was different. The usually chilly air carried an irritable heat. The hands of the gods seized me immediately and fondled me with impatient roughness. They pried into my mind, then quickly exited, as if annoyed with what they found there. The worship, a slow process on the best of days, was over as quickly as it started. I seized their attention before they set me down.

I posed a question in the form of feelings and images.

What's wrong?

For a moment I wasn't certain I would receive a response, but then the answer came in the form of a faint, muffled feeling and hum. It was one of dissatisfaction.

Are you displeased?

An affirmative. Like a nod, felt but not seen.

With me?

Negative. Then, a barrage of pictures and feelings flooded my mind. Endless blank pages, repeating patterns, day and night and day again, an endless unending tunnel. Then, time-lessness. Eternity.

Bored.

Affirmation. Then I saw a line of people, each one without a face, with identical clothing, identical build. The line stretched endlessly to the horizon, as far as the eye could see.

We're all the same.

Affirmation again. I understood suddenly why there were no worshippers at the temple—the gods had grown tired of them. Every worshipper that came had been given the same rough treatment and dismissed. Enlightenment from displeased gods was not so pleasurable. Once the sun was used up, they had scattered in search of new games and experiences as offerings.

Should I do the same? I wondered what I could find to offer the gods who had seen the minds of so many and knew so much. Suddenly, I realized I had the answer right at hand.

What you seek is just outside.

A pause. Curiosity.

He is different from all others who have come to worship.

Inquisition. Question. Where?

Just outside. He is shy.

Movement. Even without seeing, I knew the sanctum space was shifting and expanding. A few silent moments later, I heard Mod's voice.

"Nas? Nas!"

"It's alright, Mod," I called in his general direction. He was inside the fog, not too far away, though I still couldn't see him. I didn't want him to panic, but it was out of my hands now.

Be gentle, I pleaded.

Silence again. I anxiously waited to hear Mod's panicked voice. But it did not come. The invisible hands holding me loosened their grip and I was set down slowly until my feet touched the ground. I peered through the fog until I spotted the big, broad, drifting form and hurried toward it. For a moment, I feared this was a mistake, that poor Mod was going to be traumatized by all this and he would never trust me again.

But Mod was floating, limbs relaxed and stretched out as if carried by water. The fog moved around him, swirling like swarms of tiny bugs, circling his head, torso, and every limb, forming patterns and just as quickly breaking them. I watched fretfully. Then, slowly, Mod turned in the air and I saw his face. His eyes were closed.

And he was smiling.

I let out a sigh of relief. Unlike the rough manner with which they had handled me, the gods were slow and careful with Mod. Whatever they saw in his mind they must have liked, because the worship went on longer than any past one of mine. The movement of Mod's drifting body was hypnotic. Eventually, I found myself sitting on the ground, then lying down, then drifting off, watching him floating and smiling.

"NAS?"

I opened my eyes groggily. I had no idea how long I'd slept, but the fog had lifted and I was lying on the walkway. Mod bent over me with concern on his wide face.

"I'm fine," I said, and stretched. Mod helped me to my feet and we headed back toward the bay, my hand in his. He had a happy but thoughtful expression on his face. "You finally prayed."

"Prayed," he repeated after me, as if trying to understand the word.

"How did it feel?"

He thought for a moment. "Good. Nice." A pause. "They. Happy."

"They were happy with you? Good. I'm glad."

Mod shook his head. "No," he said emphatically. "Happy. With *you*."

CHAPTER 13

"IT'S A UNIQUE CHALLENGE," ONE SAID. HER FINGERS PLAYED IN the air, changing the landscape of the arena from a moody night scene to a bright warm day. "To keep the game fair, we have to consider all the ways that they are different and accommodate both. Even their social norms differ greatly."

"Do you think it will be too difficult?"

"Well, every problem has a solution."

The planet had no name—or it had two. The two races that occupied it each had their own name for it. For our own convenience, we referred to it as Duo.

Duo was a small, densely populated planet that orbited a very large sun. It moved unusually slowly, a hair's pace above standing still. As a result, days and nights lasted for many lifetimes and the civilizations that lived either in the light or the dark simply picked up and moved with the light or shadow as needed. Most of its populace lived their entire lives without ever moving to follow or avoid the sunlight.

As a result, the planet's seed race had divided itself into two: light dwellers—the Solar Commons—and dark dwellers—the Umbra Collective. During its primitive age, the two races had warred relentlessly, but as technology and sociocultural aspects advanced, their rivalry became more political and economic in nature. The wars ceased and the planet settled into a relative peace, though trade squabbles were commonplace.

"Do you have a suggestion?"

"Maybe." I was waiting for her to ask. I had learned over time that the best way to be heard by H'otto and the older champions was not to proffer myself and instead wait for them to inquire first. I stepped beside her, lifted my hands, and found the invisible strings that pulled the arena. "I thought perhaps rather than focus on what is different, we should focus on what's similar." The arena lights turned off, plunging us into darkness. "They have the same sense of hearing, do they not?"

"Interesting," I heard One say.

Another flick of my wrist and the lights came back on. I changed the landscape again and a moment later we stood in a decrepit city full of sky-scraping buildings. Unfortunately, the visage lasted only a moment. I grimaced as the threads of the arena fell from me and the buildings disintegrated into blocks. "They pride themselves in innovation and the height of their cities. A challenge for survival in a concrete jungle would offer no advantages to either side."

One gestured to the ground. "Try the ground. Standing structures are more difficult than flat surfaces."

I focused. The floor below us rippled and changed from bare metal to a maze of hieroglyphs spanning as far as the eyes could see.

"You were saying?"

"They refuse to learn each other's languages beyond the bare essentials for trade, but perhaps a puzzle using common symbols would even the playing ground." Another flick and the puzzle disappeared. "Different eyes will also offer no advantage or disadvantage if the target is invisible."

Racial conflicts bubbled underneath the surface, as Two and I had both learned. Duo was a complicated place. Competition between the two races drove advancement in almost every aspect of their societies. Based on archives, Duo was the most technologically advanced, artistically rich, and bountifully knowledgeable out of all candidate planets to date in the Galaxy of the Starry River. And yet, cultural exchange between its two halves was minimal. The people of the Solar Commons knew shockingly little about the other half of their planet and showed very little willingness to learn. The same was true of the Umbra Collective. Interpretations of certain historic events and famous art pieces varied greatly between the two sides, and yet there was little to no text or academic study that provided comparison and context as to why the differences existed. Both sides used degrading slurs for the other in common, everyday language, even well-educated scholars and those who conducted business regularly with the other side.

Language and social norms also varied between the dark and the light sides of the planet. The Umbra Collective, for instance, dressed for warmth and efficiency. They found exposed skin vulgar and usually kept their bodies covered with long garments. By contrast, the Solar Commons thrived on artistic fashion and took great pride in displaying their bodies and skin for all to see. This had obviously evolved out of their natural environments and necessity, and yet both sides regarded the other's manner of dress as degrading or idiotic, with very few pausing to consider the reasoning behind it.

In business and trade, both sides appeared far more interested in taking advantage of the other than finding benefit in mutual collaboration. Solar-powered batteries, a useful and cheaply produced product in the Solar Commons, were sold at an enormous markup to buyers on the dark side to power essential heating sources. By the same token, the primary coolant used in nearly every piece of major machinery on the light side was created as a practically worthless byproduct by the Umbra Collective. And yet, rather than negotiating for a simple trade arrangement, the Collective frequently withheld the coolant as leverage when disagreements arose in political or industrial policies.

Even the most basic form of communication was a challenge. Each side used three to five primary languages, but trained translators were few and far in between, and the only translations conducted were in trade and political context. Next to no films, art, or stories passed from one side to the other.

To put it simply, the light and dark dwellers of Duo did not —and refused to—understand each other.

"No matter how hard they try, they can't change the fact that they are of the same genetic makeup," I concluded as I tried the cityscape again. It held a little longer this time. I was improving, but making objects on a silent arena floor was vastly different from navigating them around a hundred running, shouting contestants.

"You are learning quickly," One commented. She sounded pleased. "And has anyone told you that you are quite clever?"

I gave a small, modest nod. "I am doing my best to learn."

"You have done well taking care of Eight as well," she continued. "I hope he has not been much trouble?"

Part of me wanted to tell her about Mod and the ideas he had given me, but I decided against it. Having him as my own little secret gave me an inexplicable thrill. "He is a lovely, mild being." I paused, then ventured carefully, "I don't quite understand why H'otto does not see him as a worthy champion."

"You are referring to the fact that he has not been given the same enhancements as us."

I wasn't, but I let her speak. Her hand, I noticed, was wandering to the opposite wrist, where she scratched absently at the skin above the implant. I'd noticed this for some time now, but had not spoken up, fearing it might be a sensitive topic. After all this time, I still could not quite figure out what my boundaries were as far as the others were concerned.

"H'otto has his reasons," she said, picking at that spot as she spoke. "It is not our place to question him. We must trust him. He is, after all, the reason all of us have a purpose and home."

I said nothing. Instead, I tried changing the scenery. The

city vanished and turned into a sparkling lake, though the water was still and unmoving like a sheet of glass. I willed it to make waves and it bubbled awkwardly.

"Tell me, Seven," she said. "Do you feel confident?"

"Confident?" I asked carefully. "In what way?"

"Yourself. I have not heard you drift back to that dreadful title your people forced on you, and you have come a long way in working the arena. But the real question is, do *you* feel confidence in yourself?"

I nodded. "I suppose I do."

"Enough to take the lead on the next game?"

I arched a brow in surprise. "Me? Running the games?"

"I will be nearby to help, of course. But I feel you are ready to try. You have, after all, been with us for some time now."

Some time. Too much time had passed since I was crowned champion. On most days, I avoided thinking about time, or my own unaging face.

"H'otto feels it is too soon. I have only experienced one game after my own. You said we should trust him."

One pursed her lips. "H'otto's judgment," she said very slowly, pulling back her sleeve and scraping her nails against the implant once more, "is not perfect."

"Have the other champions assisted in the games as well?"

She scratched harder. I worried that she would break skin soon.

"Every champion does their part in the arena," she said. It was an answer I'd heard many times. "Everyone helps."

Everyone helps.

I returned to working on the lake. Everyone had their mantra here. Much like Axi's "glory be," when probed about the other champions, One replied "everyone helps." There were days when it felt so routine, so normal, that I could almost convince myself it was just the way of things in the orb, and I could happily go on traveling with Mod, seeing the galaxy, and pretend none of it was important.

But most days, like today, I returned to my tiny living space and lay awake, watched Mod's chest rise and fall in his deep, peaceful sleep, and tortured myself with never-ending questions.

MOD MANIFESTED a perfect cube in the air and spun it around in his large hand. Cubes and squares were his favorite things. Their simple, pleasing symmetry brought him joy. Despite the limitations in his connection to the arena without the implants, Mod was quite adept at manifestation when he put his mind to it.

He squeezed the cube and it disintegrated. He looked disappointed, so I manifested a new one one for him. He smiled as I handed it to him and held it like it was the most precious thing he'd ever seen. Manifestation was hard on the body and mind without the reinforcement of the implants, but I could tell that his stamina was growing. Perhaps even without the implants, he could become accustomed to manifestation and build up tolerance on his own.

Implants or not, Mod was wonderful. He bubbled with happiness and never complained about the dreary life of a champion. I marveled at the easy joy he found in the smallest things. He saw the universe in the most straightforward fashion, never wasted a thought on what he could not change, and approached each day as if it was the best day of his life. It was this purity and positivity of his that I believed made him the champion of his people—his straight and simple belief that he could protect himself and survive, even unraveling his body and pulling it back if needed. Which made it all the more ironic, because champion or not, they did not deserve him.

I smiled at him. He grinned back. He had not a fiber of worry or doubt in his body. I wished I could match his joy and wonder.

Because every time I laid eyes on him, I couldn't help but be reminded that all it would take was a single misstep for this bright light to be snuffed out.

Watching One pick away at her implants only served to reassure me that even after all this time, I knew so very little. I had made the decision to live. Out of spite for the gods at first, then for the sake of Mod, because he deserved my care and so much more. And yet, if one day H'otto decided he was tired of Mod crossing his path, what then? If Mod made the mistake of being in the wrong place at the wrong time, could I stop what would befall him? Would he be locked away like Viva, the fourth champion, in a never-ending illusion, waiting for his day to be drawn and quartered, just like the poor soul whose name I hadn't been able to bring myself to find out?

The fingers of my right hand found their way to my left wrist. The nails scraped against my skin. Up and down. Up and down. Just like One.

I had had no say when these implants had been put inside me, just like I'd had no say in Mod going without them. If things turned sour for him—or for *us*—I had no power to stop it. And then . . .

I forced myself to stop. Some days I spiraled farther than others. Dwelling only made the days longer. The best thing I could do for the both of us was find my part in all of this.

"What do you think, Mod?" I said. "Should I try to run a game?"

Mod turned the cube over in his hands. "Yes. Run game."

"What if I fail? I haven't run a game before. What if I make a mistake in the middle of the game?"

Mod gave me a confused look, as if unable to even fathom that possibility. *"No,"* he said, working hard to enunciate. *"You. Win."*

CHAPTER 14

FINDING A PROPER LANDING LOCATION ON DUO WAS TRICKY. BUT then, nothing was simple with Duo. After much discussion, H'otto finally made the decision to land the orb in the sea at the longitudinal line that divided the light and dark sides of the planet. It was fortunate that the current division line included a good amount of seascape. Had it been on land, we would have had to delay a game on Duo, as the two sides quarreled tirelessly over border disputes on the major continents.

Frankly, Duo was an exhausting place to live. I had already developed an intense dislike for the planet by the time we cruised slowly through its skies. There was no point in hiding —they had detected our presence before we'd even entered the atmosphere. We took care to enter at the division line, but both sides immediately took up arms and accused the other side of conspiracy and unwarranted invasion. The airwaves chattered like the buzzing wings of swarming insects and I had to ask Axi to turn down the number of channels being streamed into the heart to avoid getting a headache.

This planet despised itself for having created two versions of the seed race. Its people had no desire to come together for the impending danger, and I truly wondered if those outside the arena would throw their support to any of the contestants, or if they would all stand back and jeer equally.

We were trailed by at least a hundred drones. Every single one appeared to be capturing video to send to a different news network, all of whom were busy claiming to have "exclusive footage." Duo's people were so eager to blame the other side that phrases like "the Umbra orb" and "the Solar invasion" were already being thrown around, despite the fact that there was no evidence of it being either. We cruised the skies slowly, unhurried, generally making a spectacle of ourselves, all the while straddling the dividing line between day and night. Circling the planet in this manner took roughly two Maedan days, and by the time we landed in the ocean with a gentle splash, I was already tired of the world and its chattering people.

"Are you confident enough to run the first game?" One ventured.

I ran my eyes over screens, each showing a different media or political figure busy offering their baseless opinions and assigning blame. For a planet with such technological advances, they appeared completely uninterested in the opinions of scientists and scholars in the face of a truly momentous event, not when there was gossip to be had.

"I am," I said. I peered over at H'otto to see if he had anything to say about me taking over the trial game, but his expression was unreadable as he watched the screens.

"What do you suppose will happen," he said, half to himself, "if this planet produces a champion from one side or the other?"

One and I said nothing, but I thought I already knew the answer—the champion would become an excuse for further prejudice, conflicts, even war among the two sides. There was no true victory for Duo. No matter who was victorious within the orb, their world was doomed to chaos.

. . .

From the balcony, One at my side, I peered down at the contestants below. There were one hundred as before—fifty from the Solar Commons and fifty from the Umbra Collective. It was unlike H'otto to define parameters for selecting contestants, but unequal representation from the two sides would cause an immediate uproar from the underrepresented side, inevitably leading to a wave of social unrest that would distract from the games.

The people of Duo were small and delicate in stature. Those from the Solar Commons possessed dry, tan-colored skin with a slightly scaly texture from being exposed daily to the hot sun. The Umbra Collective were gray and smooth, like the bellies of fish, from living in the dark, damp nights, with slitted eyes and long fingers. The tallest of them were not much bigger than me, and the smallest barely came up to my shoulder. I was relieved to see that there were no children among this initial selection. They divided immediately amongst themselves, sticking to their own kind and eyeing the other side suspiciously.

"There will be no cooperation here," One said matter-of-factly. "I wonder if they will last many rounds or if they will end the game quickly by sabotaging each other."

I watched a particularly slender, small female—distinguishable from the males by the bright red streaks at the base of her neck, a common cosmetic applied by Umbra women—hug herself and sob in fear. Not a single person, even those of her own collective, chose to comfort her. As far as I could tell, she possessed no trait that would deem her an outcast. Her own people simply couldn't be bothered.

"I've set foot among many races in my time serving the game," One continued. "But to see a race that evolved this far with so little sense of collaboration is a rare one. It is as if their very nature forbids it. It is no wonder they divide themselves the way they do."

A small cluster of contestants moved away from the crying

girl. "Do you think if they weren't divided by light and dark, they would have found some other way to divide themselves?"

"Most likely." One turned to me. "Are you ready?"

I scanned the people of Duo one last time. Unlike Mod, not a single one of them stood out to me. I felt irritated simply at the sight of the way they regarded each other, not with a sense of camaraderie but with contempt and annoyance. I almost didn't care if this planet survived or not. The sooner we were finished with it, the better.

"I am," I said, just as H'otto's voice boomed from above.

"Welcome, contestants. My name is H'otto and I speak for the gods."

THE TRIAL GAME was designed based on my—Mod's— suggestion. The cityscape sat grimly beneath a gray, heatless sky, drizzling soft rain. The contestants below made their way through wide streets and narrow alleys, moving as softly and quietly as they could. I tracked them with One's help through my wrist implant. When they'd spread out far enough, I sent in the predators.

This was where the real game began. The predators had to be heard and not seen. Though invisible, they moved heavily, trampling around the streets and splashing through puddles. Tuning in to every corner of the arena, I saw ten contestants mowed down before the others began to get wise. Soon, the remaining contestants quieted their own footsteps and hid to listen. I sent the invisible predators prowling through every alley and street corner. Controlling them had taken significant practice, and I was grateful for Axi's automated procedures in the background helping to stabilize both the city and the predators.

Then, a light-skinned man from the Solar Commons mani- fested a series of hand- and footholds and scaled a wall. A woman from the Umbra Collective saw and immediately did the same. Within minutes, the contestants who spotted them began to copy their act, and as they moved through the city, others did the same. I watched with some surprise as the Duo contestants rapidly mastered manifestation one after another, simply by spotting one of their fellow contestants doing so. Their sense of competition was astounding, and I could feel their surging emotions upon realizing someone else had found an advantage that they did not have. Their technological advancement in the face of nearly zero collaboration was no longer a mystery—competition and envy were what drove them and made them stronger and smarter.

I pulled the strings, moving the predators. They began to scale walls and move with a soft slither rather than heavy trampling. They chased after the Duo contestants relentlessly, pouncing to kill.

And yet they kept on.

One of the contestants manifested a firearm and opened fire on an approaching predator. The sound drew the attention of the other contestants, and almost immediately I heard the sound of firearms from all around the arena. With roughly half the contestants still remaining, Duo was, against all odds, gaining ground. The predators fell, one after another. No sooner did I manifest a new one than they took down two more. As far as I knew, no planet up to this point in the Galaxy of the Starry River had managed to gain ground like this in the first trial round.

"Interesting," One murmured, though I barely heard her in my concentrated state.

The arena timer was running down. Only a third of the time was left and nearly forty contestants still stood. They'd grouped together on a few select rooftops, taken positions guarding entry points, observed the moving shadows, and were shooting down any predator that attempted to climb over. As far as I could tell, none of them had actively decided on or communicated this plan—the Duo contestants appeared to have silently agreed that this was the best solution and went with it. If one fell, the others seamlessly moved in and covered their post. There was not a word of mourning or sadness for their comrade.

I reached farther, dug deep, and connected with the contestants as far as the arena would allow. Their emotions pooled around them like puddles of light and energy. Excitement and thrill coupled with fear. Hunger for glory. Ache to be the best. The desire to win within the people of Duo far exceeded their interest in self-preservation, and collaboration occurred only if there existed a greater "enemy" to best. Though disgusted at their lack of empathy for each other, I couldn't help but be impressed at their efficiency and savagery.

The game came down to the wire. I was almost tempted to allow the remaining contestants to survive purely based on their impressive tenacity. However, there existed a rule of the arena, one I did not know until I began to work with One. The purpose of it was to ensure the host planet did not take the games lightly.

No more than five contestants may survive the first trial.

I turned up the heat.

The predators scaled the walls of the buildings in leaps and bounds, pouncing over the edges of the rooftops and taking down the contestants before they could react. Many froze in surprise and were down in seconds. They did not take pleasure in the fall of the others, but to protect and aid was simply not in their nature. Instead, they watched in horror as their numbers dwindled in rapid succession.

BANG.

I turned toward the sound. Only one rooftop was left with more than one survivor—a group of four. They had chosen a small area that was easily protected. But what attracted me was not the group, but one.

An Umbra female stood in her corner. I recognized her as the one hugging herself and crying in the beginning. She was still crying, though her fearful sobs did not mask her uncanny manifestation skills and marksmanship. I zoned in on her and watched as she lifted her gun, a small, stealthy piece that fit her hand like an extension of her limb, and fired—not at the target beneath her, but at one on a nearby building.

BANG.

The predator that was leaving wet footprints on the building across the street from her fell. She let out a loud, distraught sob. The lone survivor from the other building—a Solar male—eyed her with surprise and suspicion.

BANG.

She took down another, this time one that was approaching one of her cohorts on the same roof. This was again met with confusion. She continued to cry, though it did not hinder her speed and accuracy.

Down to ten. Then eight. Then six. Time counted down rapidly. The end was near.

Two of the invisible predators crawled their way up toward the group of four from opposite sides of the building. The contestants held their breath, listening intently, but I could tell they had difficulty hearing over the sound of their own pounding hearts. One of them snapped at the weeping Umbra female to be quiet. She closed her lips tight, but could barely contain the whimpers from leaking out. Her body shook, but her hand was steady.

I listened through her ears. Her heart beat rapidly. She listened not only for the predator coming toward her, but the other one as well. She was tensely focused on every direction, every sound. Her attention was divided, trying to tune in to every possibility.

One of the others fired and missed. The predators changed course, moving in a zigzag pattern.

Another miss.

The Umbra female let large, silent tears fall, her entire body strung tight.

Another miss and both predators pounced.

The Umbra female froze, hearing movement from both sides but unable to decide which one to shoot. The one nearly on top of her struck the light just right and she saw its form out of the corner of her eye. Instinct kicked in and she whipped around and put her shot through its head. It fell just as the other tore another contestant in half.

Time ran out.

THE CITY DISAPPEARED. The ground flattened. The last five contestants—two Umbra and three Solar—stood their ground, too fearful to move as the arena shifted to a flat plane around them. The sobbing female fell to the ground, her weapon crumbling, and buried her face in her arms, crying. Whether her tears were from relief or fear I couldn't tell. The others once again made no effort to comfort her. I let out a breath I hadn't realized I was holding.

"Excellent job."

I started. In the intensity of the game, I had forgotten that One was watching me. She released my wrist and I suddenly felt a twinge of nervousness, but she only gave me a nod and retreated from the balcony.

Blood pounded in my ears. I watched her go. Did she sense that I had allowed the Umbra female to see the predator at the last moment?

CHAPTER 15

"ANY ONE OF THEM WOULD MAKE FOR AN EXCELLENT CHAMPION."

I sat on a manifested bench within the heart watching H'otto slowly pace and study the replays on the many screens with a satisfied expression on his face. Mod was with us in the heart today. He had days where he could part from me and days he couldn't. Today he needed me nearby. As he fiddled around Axi's obelisk, I snapped my fingers to gain his attention, then motioned for him to sit next to me. He pouted, but did as he was told.

"Do you think so?" I said noncommittally, but my attention was on the Umbra female. I glanced around the space of the heart—One wasn't here. Ever since the trial game, I'd been on edge waiting to be confronted and punished by H'otto for having interfered in the game. I even lay awake at night imagining myself in the place of the nameless alien with white skin and black stripes, pulled apart as I screamed in pain while Two stood in front me, that ever-present sneer on their face. But a day had passed and no mention of it was made. Now, we sat waiting for the hour of the next game to roll around.

"You did a fine job in the trial round," H'otto said. My stomach lurched, but I quickly pushed it back down as it seemed like he had nothing else to say on the topic. In fact, he was much more interested in the screens than me.

The face of the crying Umbra female appeared. I had not paid great attention to her until the last leg of the game. But now, as I watched the replay, I saw that she was clever indeed. Not only were her skills exceptional, she kept to paths near large puddles of water to ensure the predators had to make ripples to reach her. When scaling buildings, she went at an even pace and left one hand free to shoot, never leaving a single opening. The weapon she manifested was small and quiet, creating as little noise that could interfere with her own hearing as possible.

I was not alone in taking an interest in her. When she appeared, H'otto stopped his pacing and watched intently.

"What do you think of that one?" I asked, trying to sound nonchalant.

H'otto nodded. "She would make a fine champion."

His answer surprised me—this female was an anomaly. Her behavior was out of the ordinary for her race. I had expected him to see her as he saw Mod, as an abnormality.

"What makes you say so?"

"Cleverness," H'otto said simply. "It is innate to some beings. I can tell this one has the potential to be special."

There was something he was not saying and I couldn't quite put my finger on it. I reached out and patted Mod absently as I watched the screens. In nearly every shot, this contestant was crying. Despite her incredible competence in the game, she looked absolutely miserable.

HER NAME TRANSLATED TO *SWEETLY*.

As expected of survivors from any game, she immediately became a household name and media darling. Both sides of Duo, light and dark, buzzed with news and stories of the contestants.

"You're sure you don't want to be involved in this one as well?" One asked. "You did well in the first one. Won't you try again?" Once again, I tried to read her tone to detect if she had noticed what I had done in the trial round. If Two had asked me the same question, I might've wondered if they were baiting me to slip up, but I couldn't imagine One setting me up to fail.

"I'm tired," I said, and it wasn't far from the truth. Though the implants negated much of the fatigue from manifestation, manipulating the entire arena floor was still a mentally and physically exhausting task. I felt aches in my muscles as if I'd been pulling weights against heavy gravity. "I'll observe from here."

One nodded and said nothing more. I waited for her to leave the heart before turning to Axi.

"Tell me about the contestant named Sweetly."

Axi had much to say.

She was beautiful by the standards of the Umbra Collective. Her skin was smooth and unblemished, her eyes deep set with slitted pupils, and her stature, small and delicate, was highly desired among the women of Duo. She dressed in layers of warm colors that complemented her gray skin and marked herself with perfect concentric red circles at the base of her neck, the way some races might paint their faces or color their hair.

I watched as Axi scrolled through rows upon rows of data on Sweetly. Unlike Mod, for whom there was nearly no data available, gathering information on Sweetly proved relatively easy. She was somewhere in between childhood and adulthood—old enough to be interested in the basics of romance and mating, but not old enough to live independently. Her family, affluent and potentially distant royalty, had educated her well and trained her in the basics of weaponry and combat, something that the people on both halves of Duo viewed as a necessity in their coming of age. Intelligent and possessing excellent instincts, she excelled in nearly every field and had competed in numerous skill- and speed-focused sports, where she collected more victories than defeats. By all accounts, she was a perfect Umbra lady with a great future ahead of her.

"Axi."

"Yes, Seven?"

I paused. What was the correct question to ask? "Is Sweetly . . ." I racked my brain and came up with only one word. ". . . Happy?"

Axi did not answer right away. I saw subtle movements on her peaceful face. Just as I thought she would tell me "glory be," she spoke up.

"Happy," she said, "defined as feeling or showing pleasure or contentment. Happiness implies a sense of confidence or satisfaction. Based on analysis of all recordings of the inquired-upon contestant, none of the above criteria are met. Therefore, it can be concluded that the contestant is not happy."

"Why?"

A long pause. "Glory be."

Sweetly puzzled me greatly. All of her skills and achievements brought her no joy. In nearly every clip I was able to locate of her, she wore an exhausted and frightened expression. Even in competitions of knowledge or marksmanship, where she performed extraordinarily well, she appeared utterly lost and miserable while competing, and when awarded her prize, was obviously uncomfortable to be the center of attention. I watched her receive first place in an odd sport involving one stick and many balls, only to burst into tears when awarded the trophy. The commentators of the video praised her humble tears, though to me she looked only tired and distressed.

The Solar Commons and Umbra Collective rallied around their champions, but the competitiveness between the two was obvious. Instead of cheering or sighing with relief that their planet had managed to produce five surviving contestants, the people of Duo immediately began arguing over which side produced the superior champions, and the debate around Sweetly was the most heated of all.

I could've allowed Sweetly to fall in the trial round, but my curiosity had gotten the better of me. A serious risk, and it was unlikely that I could get away with—or One could overlook—another interference. H'otto took "fair" games very seriously. If he found out I had purposefully tipped the scales, then . . .

I didn't want to think about it.

Above me, on the main arena floor, the next round of the game was about to begin. I asked Axi to stream the game to the screens. From the heart, I watched Sweetly. As expected, she was doing well. Running, fighting, surviving.

And crying.

Try as I might, I couldn't avoid conducting another game. At One's urging, it wasn't long before I found myself on the balcony again, the strings of the arena entwined between my fingers.

BANG

My entire body jerked and I nearly lost the form of the landscape below me. One's hand tightened around my wrist as she forced her will over mine, stopping the ripple that threatened to tear the stage asunder.

One of the contestants fell. He was from the Solar Commons. I held the reins of the arena tight and carefully, slowly allowed myself to look toward the turmoil.

His death was not what had shocked me—he was one of many. What took me off guard was the one who had shot him, the one who currently stood trembling with tears pouring down her face.

Sweetly slumped against the wall of the stone maze. I reached out to her. Her heart pounded so rapidly I worried she might buckle and fall. The inside of her head buzzed and clamored as she tried to sort out what had happened.

Motions, colors, and sensations overwhelmed her from every direction.

The intensity with which she experienced everything was astonishing.

Through her mind, I felt sweat sliding down her brow as if it carved a deep path in her skin. Her clammy fingers felt like they were soaked in a swamp. Someone behind the wall she leaned against let out a shout and the sound vibrated through her entire body. The light from the arena dome shone down on her with piercing brightness, causing her to shield her eyes and blink furiously every few seconds. Every thump of her heart, every movement of shadow, every shift and every shuffle were an assault on her mind and body.

A slithering predator of the maze crawled quietly over the wall above her. She lifted a hand and shot it clean and neat through the head without looking, then went back to weeping. Despite her distress, she knew exactly where and when danger approached.

But she hadn't intended to take the life of a fellow contestant, and the moment she saw whom her bullet had struck, the shock and horror hit her with the impact of a thousand fists. She reeled and I reeled with her, nearly disrupting the game in the process.

"Keep control," One said.

I nodded. I was lucky. Next time she might not be able to stop the ripple.

But I felt her pain.

Sweetly sensed the bullet as if it had entered her own chest. So sensitive she was, so empathetic, that she could not separate the pain of someone else from her own. I struggled to keep the maze in one piece, but could not tear myself from her as she stood, back against the stone wall, pounding herself in the chest with one closed fist—the same spot where the other contestant was shot.

The countdown ended.

I lowered the maze into the ground. The fifteen survivors of the round looked about nervously as they slowly dropped their weapons. Sweetly crumbled into herself and wept. No one comforted her, as usual.

"You are concerned."

I started. I kept forgetting that One was nearby in my moments of concentration.

"That one," I said, trying to sound as if I'd just noticed the incident in passing. "She took out one of the other contestants."

One followed my gaze to the arena floor. "On purpose?"

"By accident. I think she mistook his footsteps for one of the targets." There was a twinge in my heart I couldn't quite explain as I watched Sweetly cry. "Did the cameras see it?"

"I'm sure they did." One's kind gaze turned to me. "You are worried for her, aren't you?"

That twinge again. I couldn't stop it.

"Her people are not kind."

"Maybe not," One said. "But look." She pointed to Sweetly. Several contestants from the Umbra Collective had gathered around her and were talking excitedly. Sweetly got to her feet and looked confused and fearful at the attention. "The ones from the bright side might condemn her, but her own people will see her as a hero and fierce competitor."

Was one of those better than the other? Sweetly visibly shrank as the others surrounded her. One stepped back from the balcony as H'otto's voice boomed from above, wrapping up the game. I followed, but the twinge in my heart didn't go away.

"PLAY IT AGAIN."

Axi dutifully rewound the segment. I watched, once again, as Sweetly raised her weapon and shot at the predator above her without looking. There, the moment the gun went off, I saw her flinch. It was not the sound this time, because after the trial round, she had begun to manifest only silent weapons. But the small kickback it delivered still bothered her.

I turned to another screen. This one showed her dancing gracefully at a staged performance. Soft, delicate music played as she glided in gentle circles before the audience. It ought to be a grand occasion, showing off her skills to entranced viewers, but Sweetly appeared distressed as usual, her face frozen in a forced expression of joy for the audience.

Another screen—Sweetly standing with several members of her family, who were eagerly speaking to what appeared to be reporters about her latest achievement. I couldn't quite make out what they were praising her for—something athletic or academic or creative—but it made no difference. Sweetly herself looked as miserable as ever to be the center of attention.

Nearly every screen showed similar scenes. Sweetly excelling, being complimented, cheered, celebrated, and absolutely miserable. The majority of the clips came from news network databases and recordings on various devices. Despite the number of cameras scattered over a planet's surface, candid clips of a single specified individual were rare.

Only one screen, low in the corner, showed a picture different from the others. It appeared to be captured by a street camera instead of pulled from a network database. In it, Sweetly sat on what appeared to be a decorative rock in a public park, one leg dangling off the side, swinging casually. The perpetual night of the planet's dark side was quiet, and there was no one else around. I hushed the audio of all the other screens and listened. She looked up at the star-filled sky and whistled a soft tune.

She was smiling.

"Find something that interests you?"

I spun around as if I'd been caught red-handed in something unsavory. I rarely heard Two's voice within the orb. Just to see them step into the heart was strange.

"I haven't seen you in a while," I said, trying to divert their attention off me. They looked tired. I wondered if spending so much time in a cramped capsule was taking its toll. "Are you alright?"

They let out a dry chuckle. "Look that bad, do I?"

I couldn't pretend to understand Two's species, but it wasn't difficult to read exhaustion, even in races not my own. Two walked with a haggard step, stooped lower than their normal confident gait. Their face seemed stretched downward, as if giving in to its own unique gravity. Their right hand kept touching select spots on their body, as if trying to relieve sore muscles.

"No," I said quickly, carefully picking my words to avoid offense. "Just . . . you look a little tired."

"I worshipped," they replied shortly as they approached the screens and studied the numerous clips of Sweetly. "Is this H'otto's new favorite?"

The question took me off guard. I looked behind me to make sure we were still watching videos of Sweetly. "H'otto's favorite?"

"He usually has a favorite," Two said. Was there a hint of disdain in their voice? "Sometimes more than one. But he usually has his picks."

I thought of Mod. I didn't know about H'otto's favorites, but he certainly had his lesser preferences. "Well," I said uncertainly, "he did say this one would make a fine champion."

"She must be interesting then."

"Interesting?"

Two didn't answer me. They stared at the screens, arms crossed in front of their chest.

"Axi."

"Yes, Two?"

I watched Two's eyes wander from one screen to the next, as if looking for something.

"Analyze the neurodivergence in this contestant."

"Contestant perceives sensory information in a manner that results in abnormal responses from the nervous system."

"Sensory processing disorder," Two said, half to themselves. "Or some variation of it." Though I didn't understand the exchange, I couldn't help admiring Two's ability to extract information from Axi with such precision. "Interesting indeed."

I couldn't quite explain it, but something about their expression made me uncomfortable. I stepped away and quietly left the heart. Just as I exited, I heard Two speak again.

"Axi, stream Four."

I stopped in my tracks and stood still. A moment passed before I heard those familiar words again.

"Will you be home soon? I can't wait to see you."

CHAPTER 16

Sweetly felt everything to the extreme.

This was an overly simplified way to explain her disorder, but it was the best way I could understand it. Strangely, this condition, though distressing for her, also made her a tremendously competent player, as she was overly aware of every motion and noise within the arena.

She stumbled through the games on her own most of the time, but I couldn't stop myself from helping her through one or two when she wound up in a tight spot or became too distraught to protect herself. I kept her safe, just enough to carry her through the games. Were she a less competent player, the subtle advantages I gave her might've been difficult to hide, especially since the people of Duo dissected the movement of every contestant with obsessive precision to find competitive advantages for themselves. But thankfully her skills came through more often than not.

I couldn't explain why I took such risks to protect her. I only knew that when she cried, I longed to do whatever I could to stop it.

The people of Duo were incredibly competent in the games. After the trial round, both the Solar Commons and the Umbra Collective immediately implemented information guides and training programs for the general population, free of charge and widely distributed. Within days, people of all ages were knowledgeable in manifestation and trained in methods most suitable to their age, stature, and specific skill sets. Not only that, the two sides of the planet analyzed comparative advantages relative to their own people in a bid to outdo the other side.

Sweetly held up well, especially after I figured out the main source of her distress. Excess of visuals, sound, smell, and touch all put her on edge. Once I had this realization, all of her distress in loud, competitive situations made sense. Ensuring she passed a round was easy so long as I limited the sensory input in her immediate surroundings. It didn't take away her anxiety completely, but did reduce her distress from uncontrolled weeping to a few nervous tics.

I had thought H'otto's interest in her would wane as more able contestants made their way into the arena. Duo had no shortage of clever people. But he remained focused on her, studying her whenever he could with a satisfied smile on his face, as if every game she played reaffirmed something he thought of her. The look on his face mirrored the way her own people looked at her—as a prize and opportunity to win, no matter the misery it brought her.

At the same time, I wondered more and more whether I had been a favorite of H'otto's, or if my victory had resulted in the disappointing elimination of someone else he had eyes on. As I had no one to pose these questions to, I jumped at the news that the holy grounds were being migrated to a sun in a star system nearby. It was a long shot, but there was only one authority above H'otto, and he suspected nothing when I excused myself to go pray.

I brought Mod with me, as he was fond of worship and the gods had a particular interest in him. I took him into the fog,

171

holding his broad hand in mine. The gods knew Mod would enter only with me in his company, and in their desperation to see him, they allowed it. I waited while they had their time with him, then reached out to the fog before we were dismissed. Sometimes they were interested in only him and passed me by.

I would like to speak.

There was a pause, then the invisible tendrils surrounded me. They did not lift me up and only felt around my face and neck. It was an invitation to speak, but they were waiting to see whether what I had to say truly piqued their interest. I closed my eyes and pictured Mod.

A twinge of positivity. They liked Mod.

I pictured a sea of faceless people, with Mod in the middle, standing out from the rest. I posed the question.

Another pause, then I saw Mod in my mind again. This time, it was an image of their projection. The image zoomed in on his eyes, round and bright. Then there were a million eyes, all flat and white—identical. Next I saw Mod's ears, little holes on either side of his head. Then there were a million ears, all pointed and sharp. Then his mouth, a wide, joyful slitted smile. Then a million mouths, all wide and open, chattering like a flock of evening birds. I understood.

He is different because he sees differently.

An agreement.

He hears differently.

Another agreement.

He speaks differently.

Firm agreement.

I understood, and was about to end the conversation when another thought occurred to me. Carefully, cautiously, I inquired.

Are the rest of us not interesting enough?

An image came. A field of dots, most white, some red.

Some, not all.

Agreement.

I gave indication that I was finished. I thought there might be curiosity as to why I asked the questions I did, but none came. Instead, the tendrils retreated from my mind and body. Mod came forward and held my hand.

"Let's go," I said to him, and together we retreated from the sanctum. I said nothing on the way, but my mind raced.

"YOU'RE SWEATING."

I jerked reflectively and the arena's strings nearly slipped out of my hands. I quickly grasped hold of them again before the playing field lost its form. I felt One's hand tighten around my wrist, ready to jump in if I lost control.

"I'm alright," I said. "I have it."

She relaxed slightly. I bit my lip and struggled to stay focused.

But I couldn't. The last worship kept invading my mind. I had received the answer I sought, but it raised so many more questions. The dream from all those years ago kept resurfacing at the most inconvenient times and I was getting worse and worse at keeping it at bay. I feared the fate of the champions I had not yet encountered, and was even more terrified that Mod or I might one day fall into their lot. I couldn't look H'otto in the eyes, and I didn't know whom I could pose a question to that would give me an honest answer. Even One, who had been nothing but kind since my arrival, had been tight lipped on the subject.

But she sensed my unease. As the game wrapped up— Sweetly once again surviving with just a little help from me— she released my wrist and laid a hand on my back. I struggled not to flinch.

"You seem tired, dear," she said.

I wiped the nervous sweat from my brow and took a deep breath. "Running the games is just getting to me," I said, stepping away from her touch as politely as I could. "This planet is a resilient one."

"That it is." She was studying me, but I kept my eyes on the arena floor, where H'otto was congratulating the survivors.

"I think I'll take a break," I said, and started to walk away. I wanted to be back in my room with Mod, my only source of comfort.

"Is something on your mind?"

I stopped. My heart beat rapidly in my chest as I turned around slowly. One stood near the balcony, and her gaze was so earnest and warm that I longed to spill my thoughts and seek reassurance from her.

"N-no," I said, swallowing hard and fearing irrationally that she could read my thoughts. But she only sighed.

"Alright," she said. "But you know, Seven. Two and I have been here for a very long time. Whatever is troubling you, we have at least experience to offer."

I nodded appreciatively, though I very much doubted Two would be interested in having a heart-to-heart with me. "Thank you. I'm alright. Really."

"Just don't hesitate to ask if you need something." One turned back to the arena floor, where the contestants were teleporting out. "Those of us who have been around for a while have run into all sorts of problems and stressors." She leaned on the balcony thoughtfully. "In fact, aside from H'otto, only Nix has been in this arena about as long."

I had started to leave, but at the mention of Nix, I paused.

There might be someone I could pose my questions to after all.

FROM THE SUSPENDED walkway high above the computing room, I saw endless rows of blinking lights and humming machines. Nix's green eyes stood out among the flashing red dots as he moved between the machines, fiddling with them one at a time.

The computing room was my least favorite place to be in the orb. It was suffocating and hot, and the air stood still. The humming of machines gave me a headache and the smaller maintenance bots charged around the space without regard to obstacles in their way. More than one had run into me in the past, and I'd learned to make my way through the room as quickly as I could to avoid taking another one to the head.

Today I lingered. To say I was nervous would be an understatement, and the temptation to simply leave and let things be was strong. But I had come too far, and One might already suspect I was prying into something anyway. So, after waffling back and forth, I headed downward.

A rickety ladder hanging from the walkway was the only way down. Manifestation in the computing room was tricky and unstable due to the rapid generation and degradation of building blocks. The ladder wobbled dangerously when I stepped on it. I had to steady myself on every rung on the long climb down. Upon reaching the last rung, however, I realized I hadn't reached the bottom. The ladder ended above the floor at a length at least twice my height.

I ground my teeth in frustration. Did I want to jump down and risk breaking my ankle? Patching myself up in the computing room would be a pain, and I would hate to end up with crooked ankle bones. After weighing my options, I took a deep breath, reached out to the arena, and pulled the building blocks toward me.

They formed into a series of rungs beneath me, extending the ladder, but I could see their form vibrating unsteadily. I took a step down. It held, but just barely. I moved fast, stepping on shaky rung after shaky rung. Then suddenly there was air and I grasped at nothing as I fell, bracing myself for a rough landing.

It didn't come. My back hit something that gave way and

bounced back. My body rose and fell a few times, cushioned and safe.

A tall form bent over me.

"Hi, Nix."

Nix said nothing. He gave me a once-over with his green eyes, then turned and lumbered away. I quickly got up. What I landed on appeared to be a large, air-filled mat. As I watched, it disintegrated into a cloud of blocks and drifted away.

"I didn't know there were safety measures down here," I said with a grin that I hoped was cheerful. "But I guess that's to be expected with that awful ladder."

Nix glanced back at me and said nothing. I hurried after him. The machines and racks on either side of us were much bigger than they looked from the walkway. Glowing tubes filled with green fluid—coolant or power source, I couldn't tell—connected and ran through most of the machines. Many of them were well above Nix's head. And down here, the humming and heat were even worse. I felt terribly claustrophobic and breathing soon became a chore. But after the trouble to get down here, I wasn't about to give up.

I followed Nix. He moved slowly, unhurried as usual. Every now and then he stopped at one of the black towering boxes and moved or switched the cables plugged in, or corrected connections that had become loose. I couldn't understand what he was doing, but he seemed to know exactly what his job was at every piece of machinery.

"How long have you been doing this job, Nix?"

He looked at me again, then went back to his work. I suddenly realized that I hadn't taken into account the fact that he did not speak. But I was certain of Nix's intelligence. If I could find the right questions, I thought, he would find a way to answer me, just like Axi.

"Do you like your work?"

Nix pulled a series of discs from one box and put them into another.

"Who taught it to you?"

He took out a frayed wire and replaced it with a new one from a stash nearby.

"What's the first thing you fixed?"

He shambled to a row of boxes.

"Could you teach me?"

More wires, more plugs, more discs.

I was getting nowhere. Hot and tired, I leaned against the nearest machine and watched him work, trying to decide what else I could ask him to elicit a response of some sort. Just as I considered whether to give up, Nix turned to me.

"Nix?"

He lifted his giant hand and pointed above me. There, at the top of the computing box, was a tube that had come loose, dripping green liquid onto the floor. It was just out of his reach.

"Do you need to get at that?" I asked, stepping out of the way. Though even without me in the way, his arm came just short of reaching it.

"Even you need a stepping stool sometimes, eh?" I asked with a chuckle.

Nix looked at me for a long moment. I almost thought he was going to say something. Then, he turned back to the computer box and raised his hand again.

Goosebumps rose on my arms.

He moved his fingers in a manner that was all too familiar.

The blocks in the air moved.

He turned his wrist. Like a conductor directing an orchestra. Or a puppeteer pulling strings.

He manifested the pad to catch me.

The blocks formed a pair of long tweezers in the air, sleek and precise. I watched, my blood suddenly running cold despite the heat, as they gracefully pinched the connectors, one at a time, and moved them back into place before disappearing.

His control of the building blocks was far superior to mine. Even in the volatile environment of the computing room, he manipulated them with practiced precision. I stared at him. Nix turned to me. He was waiting for my question. And this time, I knew the right one.

"Nix," I said, my voice trembling. "What's your number?"

Slowly, Nix held up three fingers.

CHAPTER 17

Duo entered another round, but I could not run this one. Stepping onto the orchestrator's balcony sent me reeling and my hands began to shake so badly at the sound of H'otto's voice that One offered to take over. I begged exhaustion, but I had a feeling she didn't believe me.

What would happen when the round ended? What could I say when she asked what was wrong?

Fear wrung me from the inside out. I had no idea what to do with what I had discovered. I paced back and forth within the heart.

"Axi, show me something from the third game in this galaxy."

The screens on the wall lit up. I spotted champion Three easily. He was tall and thickly built, a little like Mod but with smooth brown skin and thick hair on his forearms and chest. I stared at his beautiful gold eyes and wondered what he had done to deserve having them plucked out and replaced with green glass bulbs.

My right hand stung. I looked down to see the fingernails on my left hand digging into it—it was becoming a bad habit. I pulled my hand away and watched the bloody welts left in my palm knit together. Within moments there were only shallow scars that looked days old.

Did it hurt when his body was replaced piece by piece?

"Axi."

"Yes, Seven?"

"What happened to Three?"

"Champion Three was the third winner of the Galaxy of the Starry River, of the planet . . ."

"Not that," I cut her off. I couldn't take her droning today. I needed real answers. "Why is he the way he is now? Was it because he wasn't 'interesting' enough?"

A pause. "Glory be."

Of course.

"Did he do something wrong?"

"Glory be." A quiver in her voice.

"Did Two do this to him?"

"Glory be." Was her voice more singsong this time?

"When did he become Nix?"

"Glory be." A hoarse whisper.

"Tell me something!" I shouted at her. Frustration boiled over. I felt like I was going mad. I couldn't take another nonsensical answer. *"Just tell me something! Why can't you tell me anything?"*

"Because . . ."

The word startled me. I hadn't expected her to respond to my question with anything other than her usual brush-off. Axi's mouth moved in a way I had never seen before, and I suddenly realized her voice had been changing tones, as if searching for the right response despite giving only the same answer over and over.

"Because . . ."

Her mouth trembled. Her voice shook. Had she always looked so young?

"I . . . because . . ."

She sounded like a child who had been caught, struggling to hold back tears as she sought the response that would get her in the least trouble. For a moment I couldn't get Tam's face out of my mind, that little guilty look he gave me when he was caught pulling things out of cabinets or knocking Mama Dorma's favorite vase off the low table. That quivering, sad look, ready to burst into tears at the next rough word.

"Axi," I said gently.

"Yes, Seven," she said, her voice wet and miserable.

I stepped forward and carefully cupped my hand around her cheeks. She let out a loud sob and for the first time since my arrival, her eyes opened a smidgen and I found myself looking into beautiful blue pupils.

"That's all they let you say, isn't it?" I whispered. "If you are sad, that's all they let you say."

"Glory be," Axi repeated, sobbing. "Glory be to the gods. Glory be to Headspace."

I touched my forehead to hers. How had I never noticed before that she was warm?

"Show me your game," I said. "Please."

The screens changed. The tall, brown figures of Three's world disappeared, replaced by new faces—pale, round faces with deep blue eyes and hair white as clouds. Among them was Five, a child barely into adolescence, wide eyed and full of fear.

"Oh, Axi," I murmured, stroking her face. Though she couldn't move, I felt like she was leaning into my touch. Did she cry in terror as her body was pulled apart, leaving only her head to be fitted into this obelisk, while a certain fellow champion looked on, sneering? "Did it hurt?"

"Glory be," Axi replied. Moisture pooled around her eyes. "Glory be."

I SAT in the corridor for a long time.

Going back to my room meant facing Mod, and I couldn't bring myself to do that. Bringing my new knowledge back to him would be a contamination of his innocence. I couldn't go to the heart and face Axi again, or watch any more videos of past champions, knowing how they had ended up.

If one day I disappeared into the innards of the orb, would Mod understand? Or would he pace these empty corridors day after day, searching and calling for me?

I sat cross-legged, staring at the rust-brown metal walls but seeing nothing. My mind was drowning.

How did I end up here?

I tried to remember Maeda. Nothing came. I couldn't remember the face of the husband I'd almost loved, and Tam was only a series of moments and images. I couldn't remember what it felt like to hold my baby, or the home I once had, or the smells of flowers and food. I looked down and realized I'd been scratching at the implant in my left wrist, leaving raw skin and deep welts. I was suddenly aware of every single implant within my body, all the changes made to me that tethered me to the arena, and the tingles in the back of my neck that were working diligently even now to keep me calm and stable. I was not the puppeteer pulling its strings—I was the puppet. Like every champion before me, I belonged to the arena.

How long before Mod made a misstep or became uninteresting? How long before I did?

The truth was, I had to admit, I had already come terrifyingly close to making that fatal mistake. Had One not pushed me to participate in the games and pray to the gods, I might be pacing the computing room alongside Nix. And had I not pushed Mod to worship . . . I shuddered. The thought of the fear and confusion on his face as his body pulled apart in that blindingly bright basement room was too much. I shut the thought away.

We had been treading so close to doom this whole time and I had been blissfully ignorant. Some part of me had suspected it couldn't be as simple as keeping Mod and me in our lanes and avoiding drawing attention. Though we had managed this long, it was only a matter of time before we found ourselves on the literal and proverbial chopping block.

ONE FINALLY CAUGHT up with me after the round concluded. I knew there was nowhere I could truly hide from her within the orb, so I didn't bother. She found me in my room, sitting cross-legged on my cot, watching Mod sleep.

"She survived."

I didn't turn toward her, not wanting her to see the fear that darkened my face. But she read me, like she always could.

"You knew I've been watching her."

"I guessed." She settled on the cot gently next to me and with a soft hand brushed a strand of hair out of my face. "And I will take another guess—you've been asking questions."

I nodded, and buried my face in my hands. One's warm hand touched my back.

"I don't know what to do now," I whispered through my fingers.

"Well," One said slowly. "You will do as we all do. You live on."

"Is this my fate?" I struggled to choke back tears. "Is it his?"

"I wish I could tell you." That warm hand moved to my arm and slowly pulled my hand from my wet face.

I looked over to Mod again. I couldn't bear the thought of him torn apart and put back together as a part of the arena. Like Nix. Like Axi. "I can leave," I said after a long moment.

"Leave?" One didn't sound surprised. I wondered if the same thought had occurred to her already.

"I could take him, get into a capsule, and leave. We can keep going, to where we won't be found. Away from all this. I'm sure H'otto will be glad to be rid of us, once he has more interesting champions to pray to the gods."

"Dear," One said slowly, "where will you go?"

I shook my head. "I don't know. Anywhere but here."

"To your planet, the one that rejected and abused you, where most everyone you knew is now dead or moved on?" One raised a hand and gestured to Mod's sleeping form. "How do you suppose they will respond to the child you adopted? Or perhaps to his planet, where they laughed at him and made a mockery of his victory, despite the fact that they owe their lives to his ingenuity? How do you imagine you, a strange, small alien, will defend him against a world full of his own kind?"

I bit my lip and said nothing.

"Perhaps you could go to a neutral world, where you are both equally alien. Carve out an eternity in solitude." She sighed. "Or stay in the capsule and keep moving. I don't know how long the system can keep regrowing its nutrient supplies, but I imagine it's quite a long time. Long enough locked in the cramped metal tube for you to decide whether to give in to insanity or put you both out of your misery."

I drew a long breath and let it out. For a moment, it felt as if the scene around me was fake, an illusion or diorama or terrible dream. Then, reality crept back in.

"So I have nowhere to go." I wished this were a question and not a statement.

"We have all thought about leaving. You are not the first and you won't be the last." One reached out and took my hand in hers. "But Seven, this is the reality of being a champion that you have to accept."

"That I am trapped here and could be made into a living piece of this orb any day? That I have to go on running the games because if I stopped, the executioner—a fellow champion—will haul me to the basement room?"

"No," One said. She looked old, and tired, even more so than Two. How had I never noticed what this life did to the ones who won the games? "The reality is, the only ones we can save are ourselves. There may come a day when you will have to decide what you need to do to survive and let go of the ones who can't, whoever that might be."

CHAPTER 18

THE FINAL ROUND ON DUO WAS OF MY OWN DESIGN. BUT INSTEAD of feeling any amount of pride or excitement at seeing my creation in action, I felt only an oppressive heaviness. The strings of the arena tangled like chains around my body, tightening around my limbs, strangling me around the neck.

Four contestants remained in the final round, though they did not know this was to be the final one. H'otto preferred not to announce that the game was to conclude to the participating planet, as he disliked raising the potential for the contestants to sabotage each other for a chance to win. It tarnished the game, he said. But otherwise, he was clear—reduce the number down to one, whatever needed to be done. And I had a feeling which one he preferred that champion to be.

I watched as she was brought into the arena and reached out to her as soon as she was steady on her feet. Poor, fragile Sweetly. She was so very anxious. She kept picking at the base of her neck, where old and new welts and scars collected. I had a feeling this habit was not limited to her time in the arena. The game hadn't started and the arena was quiet, but I could hear its hum through her, loud and jarring. The voices of her fellow contestants grated on her. She heard and smelled them intensely and felt the cold of the arena on every inch of her skin, covered or not. She experienced every moment of life in painful, exhausting detail.

And the gods would relish her.

She would offer it all to them in worship. Her feelings and memories would taste like thick, concentrated nectar, unlike the rest of us, who were probably bland and watered down.

Sweetly. How ironically accurate her name was.

As I watched her pick at herself, sobbing all the while, a wave of emotions came over me. Regret at having saved her in the first round only to subject her to an eternity as food for the gods. Fear, wondering what would happen to me—or worse, Mod—if the gods found they needed only her as their plaything. Anger at H'otto for pulling us from our lives and then using us as he saw fit, a mask of kindness plastered on his face. Disgust at her entire planet for using her to their own benefit.

I moved my wrists and the arena shifted. The final stage set itself. I pushed down the emotions threatening to boil over.

Maybe it was better that no one win.

Let her die in peace, along with her worthless planet.

THE FINAL STAGE WAS A DARK, opaque sea. What looked like water at first glance would reveal itself to be oil upon closer inspection. From this ocean rose a series of columns, each with a flat platform at the top. They began in one row, then divided into different paths. After the first fork, the contestants could choose which way to go. No rule forbade them from traveling as a group, but I had a feeling that thought had never occurred to them—this was a stage set to mirror the divisive and individualistic nature of Duo. All paths led to the goal, but the challenges they faced on each one varied greatly.

Aside from Sweetly, there remained an Umbra male and two Solar females. Unlike the Aukronites, none of them seemed to have formed any sort of camaraderie, nor did they go out of their way to encourage each other.

Sweetly lingered apart from the others. She kept drawing deep, shaky breaths as if trying to hold back tears. Her fellow Umbra appeared irritated with her. None of the four said much, and as soon as H'otto completed the instructions, the game was on.

The other three made their way over the platforms, manifesting machines or elongating their legs to make the jumps. Sweetly lingered away from the others, bringing up the rear. Though they did not communicate, all four kept an even pace, as they'd learned many rounds ago that speed was not necessarily an advantage. The impressive skills of Duo continued to shine through.

At the first fork, they paused. The other three exchanged uncertain looks, then appeared to reach an unspoken agreement. They each took a different fork and moved on. Sweetly stopped at the fork alone. She had been using air currents to propel herself between the platforms, a slower method of movement than the rest, though not a surprising one. I had noticed long ago that the sensation of body modification within the arena caused her painful sensory overload. I kept my attention on her as she watched the other three take off in different directions. Then, she took a deep breath and closed her eyes.

I zoomed in.

Her sensitivity was, after all this time, still astounding to me. She drew in another breath and let it out very, very slowly. And with that breath went the strings.

Manifestation was only the beginning.

For the majority of the contestants on this planet and others, learning manifestation was the end all, be all. They thought producing weapons and shields was their key to winning. This misunderstanding often prevented them from seeing the true depth of the game, as they became preoccupied with producing the most convenient tools and methods for the task in front of them.

Changing one's body within the arena was a deeper skill.

The moment a contestant entered the arena, their body was read and analyzed by the arena. From there, the building blocks bound to them, merging with bone and tissue at a cellular level. As the blocks were powered by the arena itself, they fell dormant outside it and the contestants carried on with life unaware of this change. Once inside, the blocks activated once more, modifying the body as the mind desired, the same way manifestation was conducted. However, the more fluid the structure one wished to achieve, the more complex the movement of the blocks, as they divided into smaller and smaller units to allow for flexibility. Controlling a greater number of smaller blocks in constant motion was much more difficult than solidifying a set of larger ones into a single weapon or tool, and therein lay the reason that most contestants who attempted to liquefy their bodies like Mod did inevitably met their demise.

Moving the arena itself—its walls, grounds, and structures—was the next step further.

From Maeda, I was the only contestant to manipulate the arena itself. It had been an accidental discovery and required a high level of awareness of one's surroundings. The hum of the arena was ever present, but to hear and grasp it over the chaos of the games was a whole other skill entirely. Prior to the implants, the effort to do so had left me with splitting headaches and debilitating vertigo after each round ended. I had kept this information to myself at the time—partly due to the selfish desire to give myself the advantage, but also because explaining it would sound like the mad ramblings of a Kol that would be disregarded anyway.

But the arena held secrets even beyond that.

· · ·

I NEVER KNEW PRIOR to my time as a champion exactly how much the arena connected to those within it. Not only could one move and shape the blocks and their own body, but even the consciousness and senses of those within it connected like a web throughout. It was through this skill, obtained after training with One, that I was able to focus on the contestants individually, experiencing their senses as if they were my own. The same magnetic current that moved the blocks through air also carried with it the sensory information of every person within it.

There were caveats to this, however. For the most part, sensory sharing was achievable only on the arena floor, where the air was dense with building blocks. In addition, sensory signals were usually only clearly detectable through the sensory-enhancing implants. Thus, those running the games were usually the only ones privy to this skill.

But Sweetly could never do things by halves.

I wasn't sure exactly when she had realized she could tap into the neural network, but it was likely earlier than when I first noticed it. As she stood motionless on her platform, eyes closed, I could sense not only the chill against her skin, the oily smell of the sea below, and the platform against her feet, but the other contestants as well. Sweetly reached out, her invisible strings growing and reaching.

The other three had all passed at least one challenge—some mental, some physical. Then, one of the Solar females fell, having overlooked a platform rigged to collapse. I felt her life snuff out through Sweetly, who gasped as if enduring the pain of death herself and began to cry. The irony of her unique mind was that though she felt such pain through others, without that sensitivity, she would not have lasted so long in the games. Her empathy was both a blessing and a curse.

So fascinated was I with her ability that I pushed forward harder, making her senses my own and feeling her delicate strings. I was lost in the sensation until she let out another gasp of pain, as if something had stung her.

I pulled back with a start.

I hurt her.

Had I pushed too hard? The sensation was new and strange, like holding someone's hand and suddenly realizing you'd been gripping hard enough to break bone.

I moved forward again, carefully this time. Her senses were delicate like webs. I tugged them, as gently as I could.

If I pulled them, could I steer her from within, like a puppet?

The Umbra male nearly failed a jump between two far-set platforms, but kept on course. The last remaining Solar female could barely hold steady in a series of platforms only a hair wider than her feet. Sweetly retracted her strings and opened her eyes. I quickly pulled out of her mind and focused on the arena. She eyed the choices before her and headed down the path taken by the Umbra male.

The first challenge she faced came in the form of oily black figures that slithered out of the dark sea and up to the platforms. She dispatched them with her usual efficiency, wincing and sobbing at every shot from her gun.

The second came in the form of a puzzle—listening intently to the tones played by a musical instrument and selecting the one that matched the tone used to remove the obstacle blocking the way to the next platform. For Sweetly and her sensitive hearing, it was an easy task.

Just as she passed the puzzle, the male fell. Her entire body tensed in alarm as she looked in the direction he went, reaching out with her feelers, but it was already too late. The competition was down to two. I watched her brace herself, swallow her fears, wipe her face, and move on.

The thought of this girl, unique and resilient, being poked and prodded by the gods burned me from the core. What would their tendrils feel like to her when the smallest sound and touch brought her to tears? Would they invade her mind, peeling her apart one layer at a time to get to her memories, while she sobbed in their invisible hands?

My hands trembled. One's hand around my wrist tightened and I forced myself to stay steady.

H'otto must be so excited to deliver her so he can secure his position as the one who brought the best offering.

Sweetly landed on a low platform. The next one was high. She paused to consider how best to make the high jump.

The Solar female moved fast. She had not encountered an obstacle for some time and was growing careless.

Sweetly gathered the air around her, moving it slowly, building pressure.

The Solar female gained momentum. I felt her confidence, but I also knew it would be shattered soon.

Sweetly tested her jump, lifting off the ground slightly, then timidly landing back down.

Her fate can be changed.

The Solar female landed heavily on a brittle platform. It crumbled like a pastry.

Sweetly jumped.

It's not too late.

The Solar female shot a chain and hook from her right hand. It caught the next column. Her horror was palpable as she swung, moving far faster than she anticipated.

Sweetly was airborne, heading for the next platform. My own body tensed in anticipation.

What will happen if they find out I did this?

The Solar female struck the side of the column face-first. I winced at the impact. She blacked out just long enough for her chain to lose form. Her legs and feet sank into tar. She tried to clear her head and manifest, but it was already too late.

Sweetly was almost on top of the next platform. I gritted my teeth.

The gods want "interesting."

I pushed forward.

I'll give them "interesting."

The Solar female sank below the surface.

Sweetly gasped as my consciousness invaded hers. I pulled her foot back just as it touched the edge of the platform. Instead of a solid landing, she landed half on, half off. The unexpected change threw her off guard, but she still had enough sense to try to balance herself.

I arched her head backward. The rest of her followed.

The sea swallowed her in an instant. She struggled as it filled her nose and mouth.

One's hand around my wrist was a steel vise.

Sweetly fought. I stiffened her limbs. Her mind was overwhelmed. Fear and pain blended together and I shared in that horrible sensation of drowning. Then, the fear became delirium, and her heart slowed.

I counted.

I heard H'otto's voice ordering me to end the game.

Not yet.

One's fingernails dug into my skin. She was trying to wake me, thinking I had fallen into a trance.

Not yet.

Her heart stopped. I held on.

Then, it was over. The black ocean disappeared, as did the platforms.

Four bodies lay on the arena floor.

"Oh, Seven," I heard One whisper. "What have you done?"

The tide of emotion receded all at once and I felt clarity return. Fear crept in as I kept my eyes on Sweetly. In the heat of the moment, I broke what was reserved for the gods. I . . .

"I saved her," I said softly.

THE SEED RACES of the Galaxy of the Starry River shared many common traits. Culturally, socially, and technologically, they were all compatible on some level. Smiling, gentle touching of the hands, or the kissing of mouth to mouth, for instance, were generally accepted as a show of affection and not likely to be misconstrued as an act of hostility from one planet to another. Of course, for this to happen, certain physiological similarities also had to exist. For example, one must possess at least one mouth to accomplish the act of kissing.

The existence of vital organs was similar as well. The lungs, in whatever shape or form, provided necessary gases to the blood and subsequently to the heart, which in all seed races was the main pump house of the body. The heart affected the brain, which shut down and degraded quickly without its supply of blood being pumped through. The heart could be started back up again in some circumstances, but depending on the amount of time that passed, the damage to the brain might be irreparable and permanent.

All that to say, the sound of a heartbeat in every sentient being in the galaxy was the same.

THUMP. Thump.

Slow and steady. I heard it, and I knew One did, too.

Thump. Thump.

Weak but steady.

"It seems we have a winner," came H'otto's booming voice. But there was a shred of uncertainty in it. He saw four black bodies, but didn't know which heart was beating.

I knew.

Thump. Thump.

My throat tightened.

Thump. Thump.

Three bodies disintegrated. One remained.

I had failed. She was alive.

One pulled the strings and the arena got to work. It read the last body, analyzed it, and began to attempt repair.

Thump. Thump.

I couldn't breathe.

Her blood pumped. Her body twitched. Her planet was saved by her victory, though that did not matter to me in the slightest.

If she were to be fixed, her life as a champion would begin. I'd failed to save her from her fate as a toy for the gods, and the rest of us were now in jeopardy from the addition of her presence.

And *I* was in jeopardy if the gods ever found out what I'd done to her.

Her fingers moved. Her head turned. Then, slowly, Sweetly sat up.

"H'otto will be disappointed," One said as she released the arena's strings. "We cannot do any more for her."

Below us, Sweetly moved. She did not stand. Instead, she crawled on all fours. The sea had dyed her skin an oily black.

I reached out.

Her brain function had been severely reduced. Her sensitive senses were dulled by at least half. The arena had struggled to make up its mind on whether to rebuild or break her as she straddled the line between living and dead, and had settled for something in the middle.

The creature that had once been Sweetly shook itself out like an animal. The arena had replaced her once-delicate features with a smooth, featureless black surface. She made a chittering sound and I felt a twinge of emotion come from her mind, which now functioned at a fraction of its original capacity.

Happiness.

For the first time since setting foot into the arena, Sweetly was happy.

H'OTTO WAS bitter in his disappointment.

I spent several days waiting for the ax to fall. While One did not appear to inform H'otto of my transgression, there was no way to keep it from the gods. When she inevitably attended worship, the gods would know every moment that had occurred during Sweetly's final game. I waited with bated breath for their wrath.

Nothing came.

Time passed and no punishment befell me. Everything within the orb went on the same as ever save for the heavy air that hung over H'otto whenever Sweetly crossed his path.

I was hesitant to let down my guard, and yet with every moment that passed without repercussion, I couldn't stop myself from wondering.

Perhaps a little risk can indeed keep me "interesting" in their eyes.

Like Mod, Sweetly did not receive surgical enhancements. I was glad—I liked them both as they were.

I sat in my room, Mod playing happily with his cubes on his cot. Sweetly curled up in my lap and chittered softly. She no longer spoke, but I could read her as clearly as the stars. Happiness. Relief. Gratitude. All present in her joyful sounds and the movement of her slender, graceful body. I stroked her head and sang an old Maedan song.

"Sweetly, so sweetly, the sunset birds sang . . ."

CHAPTER 19

I STARED AT THE BLOOD-COVERED PLAYING FIELD BELOW ME, hands still raised in the conductor's pose. One's hand was still around my wrist; she'd forgotten to remove it in her shock.

"W-what happened?"

One said nothing. Slowly, she released my wrist and stepped to the edge of the balcony. I dropped my hands and followed her.

Below us, a hundred contestants lay dead. I gently lowered the maze walls around them and retracted the giant metal spheres that rolled through them. The countdown above us had gone on for only a small fraction of the allotted time, nearly none at all. Bodies and viscera littered the floor. I stared at them, dumbfounded.

"They didn't move."

"They did not," One agreed grimly. "Not a single one."

"They didn't even try." I tore my eyes from a particularly small body—a child.

The arena was dead silent. Even H'otto had not spoken up since the final contestant fell. I had no idea if the broadcast was still running. Though I had seen plenty of death within the arena by this point, I still couldn't shake the unease from my bones.

"We will have to convene with H'otto," One said, and turned sharply from the scene.

I hurried after her through the innards of the orb. My mind spun trying to comprehend the events that had just taken place. I'd watched recordings of games past, and I'd heard One's accounts of every one. For contestants not to figure out the game in the trial round was not unusual, nor was it rare for all contestants to fail the round despite having figured out the game. But there was not a single instance of contestants who refused to play, or even to try to save themselves.

I hadn't noticed the lack of participation until at least half the contestants were mowed down. Even the ones who initially made an attempt to run eventually sat down, eyes closed and legs crossed, and waited for the end to come.

Did I do something wrong?

I wracked my brain. No. I ran the game as intended.

Should I have stopped it?

H'otto wouldn't have liked that. It wasn't my call to end a game and he had never given a signal for me to do so.

We found H'otto in the heart. Something about the way his back was silhouetted against the blue-green screens frightened me. He didn't turn around when One and I entered. I slowed my step and moved a little behind One.

"They refused to play," One said.

"I see that," H'otto said slowly, fixed on the glowing screens, where the bodies of a hundred contestants lay. "Was there a malfunction in the translation?"

"I have no reason to believe so," One replied. I saw her glance toward Axi. "Their attentiveness at the beginning indicated they understood the instructions. They simply . . . didn't follow."

The silence was thick. I was afraid to speak up for fear of drawing attention to myself. After a long moment, H'otto turned around.

"Who reported this planet ready for the games?"

He knew the answer to that question, but he wanted to hear it from our mouths.

"Two did," One replied.

"Two," H'otto repeated. "Axi."

"Yes, arena master?"

"Contact Two. Tell them to return immediately." He suddenly lifted his gaze toward me. I struggled not to cower before him. "Seven, please go out to the planet."

I glanced at One. "Me?"

"Yes," H'otto said, though his attention already appeared to be off me as he headed out of the heart. "Find out what went wrong and report back. And quickly. The gods are not forgiving of scheduling delays."

With that he was gone. One and I exchanged a look.

"You should get out there," One said, then added, "Do be careful."

"What will you do?"

She sighed. "Go over Two's notes, I suppose, and see what might've gone wrong."

It would be a fruitless endeavor—she and I both knew Two's notes were accurate and meticulous. I wondered, briefly, if she was doing the research only to prove she had done nothing wrong herself.

There may come a day when you have to decide what you need to do to survive, and let go of the ones who can't.

I waited for her to leave. "Axi. What will happen to Two if this planet isn't able to play the game?"

Axi gave a long pause. "Glory be," she said.

THE PLANET'S name was tremendously difficult to both pronounce and translate. After much discussion with Axi when preparing for the game, I had given up and begun to refer to it using a word from the common Maedan dialect—Yatam, which meant "to meditate."

I had chosen this word due to the planet's expansive, peaceful deserts, much like the region of Maeda that birthed me. The people of Yatam were reptilian in nature, covered head to toe in beautiful, iridescent scales. They built their structures with tan-colored sandstone and spent much of their time outdoors in the hot sun, socializing or simply sitting in meditation, soaking up its warm rays. Vast cities built in the shape of concentric circles dotted the deserts, and between them lay tiny settlements occupied by quiet families and nomads who preferred to live far from the hustle and bustle of the metropolis.

The chameleon suit irritated my skin. I resisted scratching my arms so as to not disturb the tens of thousands of sensors pricking my skin. It was a terribly awkward and restrictive thing to wear, despite being the most effective and efficient way to disguise oneself on an alien planet—if used correctly.

Trips to the surfaces of the planets were always risky business. The planets selected for games did not possess direct contact with races on other worlds, and thus to be discovered as a visitor from a world not their own would cause great disturbance. The chameleon suit read the motions and body structure of its wearer and projected a translated image using information extracted from the locals. However, the wearer must carefully plan every move to avoid distortion of the projected image, such as a misplaced limb or contorted skull. It was just as well that Mod and Sweetly could not accompany me on surface missions, as the application of this damned thing to their bodies would be nearly impossible. The process was so utterly complicated and miserable that the past five days had consisted of me returning to the orb only to eat and sleep without removing the suit and then heading right back out. If not for the translation function, I might've tried to disguise myself with clothing and makeup instead just to avoid the discomfort.

On Aukron, this mission would've proven terribly difficult

for me, as the chameleon suit would have struggled trying to mold the movements of my thin, petite body to that of the large, broad Aukronites. Thankfully, the people of Yatam were of similar stock to Maedans. They were taller and had large bones, but their bodies carried very little fat, resulting in overall slender forms.

Per Two's notes, the Yataman also had a penchant for language as well as a tendency towards omnilingualism, so much so that I could feel the chameleon suit struggling to translate at least five languages at once within my immediate vicinity, as the locals appeared to converse using multiple dialects simultaneously. If I had such a skill, I mused, perhaps I could dispense with the chameleon suit altogether.

A few locals strolled by. Young folks wearing the latest fashion, which seemed to largely consist of thick, light-colored material in patterned prints. Spotting me, they raised their arms and drew half circles in the air—the standard greeting for the region. I mimicked them, careful to make the motion large enough to imitate the natural movement of their bodies. The tedium of pretending to be a native was beginning to wear on me after five fruitless days.

As expected, Two's notes were immaculate. I had no idea if they'd returned to the orb yet to face H'otto's wrath, but so far I could not find a single reason for this misstep. By all accounts, the people of Yatam possessed the same instincts for self-preservation as all other races. I'd seen public records, watched logs from popular media, and observed the locals in various situations as well. Nothing provided a clue as to their refusal to participate in the arena.

"Hello, dear."

An unfamiliar voice made me jump. I turned to see a tall Yataman female bent over me, regarding me with concerned green eyes. An infant was strapped to her chest with a colorful cloth wrap.

"Are you lost?"

She had mistaken me for a child due to my small stature. I took a step back from them in case she tried to take my hand. Direct engagement with the locals was risky and highly discouraged.

"I'm fine," I said, and glanced around. I had been walking through a small park in the middle of a remote settlement, observing families frolicking leisurely. Now that I thought about it, I must've looked like a wandering child, the only one not recognized by the close-knit locals.

"Is your parent around?"

I had no answer for her. Suddenly, I realized why Two was the preferred person for field research—being mistaken for a child was troublesome among all seed races, and the chameleon suit could only compensate so much for my size. I glanced around. If I ran, I would only attract attention. If I returned to the orb via teleportation, I would cause an uproar, especially with the planet already on alert due to the start of the games a few days before.

"Why don't you come with me?" The Yataman pointed to a row of small, pod-shaped homes at the edge of the park. "I will call someone to help find your family."

I took another small step back and the Yataman took a small step forward. Her eyes took on a slightly lighter shade of green, which according to Two's research meant she was experiencing mild tension, perhaps in anticipation of me running away. No "parent" had come forth to claim me. If I tried to brush her off, she would likely report me as a missing child, and then I would have to go through the tedious process of having Axi program and fit a whole new chameleon suit skin for me.

Then, another thought occurred to me.

"Alright," I said in a small but friendly voice. "I will follow you."

Thankfully, she did not attempt to take my hand, but did make sure I walked in front of her. She ushered me to a small house at the end of the street and I went in. If she tried to harm me, I figured, I could still teleport out whenever I needed. If there were only one witness, she might be dismissed as insane.

Thankfully, this particular individual did not appear to mean any ill will. I walked into her modest home and kept my back to a wall. Once inside, she unstrapped her child.

"Let me put him down," she said, and set the baby in what looked like a round crib lined with soft netting. He sat and regarded me curiously, a stranger in their home. It was then that I got a good look at his face for the first time.

Unlike the rest of his kind, this child possessed very few of the iridescent scales his race was so proud of. What little he had grew in scattered patches over his green-blue skin. His face was almost entirely bare of it save for a crescent shape around one eye and a few smatterings on his skull and neck. As I stepped closer to the crib, I saw a dark, thin scar that extended from his chin to the base of his neck.

"He's had surgery for his vocal chords," his mother said, noticing my attention. "Pretty standard for Titen Syndrome." She gave me a sideways look. "You might be a little young to know that."

There was something in her voice. Defensiveness, perhaps. I recognized it as the same tone Mama Dorma used to use when someone asked if her grandchild was birthed by a Kol. I looked at the baby again. He was not much older than Tam had been when I left Maeda.

"He's adorable," I said with a smile.

His mother relaxed visibly. She removed her jacket and blouse and offered me a drink, which I politely declined—from what I understood of Two's notes, the Yataman took in fluids with tremendously high salt content. As she went to a display screen to find the contact she needed, I took in the details of her living space.

Since direct engagement with the locals was discouraged, all of Two's notes regarding the living spaces of the people of

Yatam came from popular media and academic sources. It was unlikely that I would find something they hadn't, but after five days I was willing to give it a try. At first glance, I saw nothing unexpected—the Yataman woman lived in a small home with a layout typical of most of the middle-class population of the planet, consisting of an open floor plan and a sleeping space elevated from the rest of the home. A variety of green, spherical plants covered in pointy thorns sat in pots made of blue stone along walls lined with oval windows. A piece of light gray paper lying on a low table caught my eye. On it was an image of the orb followed by a block of text in one of the most common Yataman dialects.

"Awful business, that," said the woman. Her baby babbled as if in agreement.

"Well, yes," I said, trying to keep my answer simple.

She shook her head and gathered up the paper. "Shame the things heathens will say these days."

The comment went over my head and circled back. "Heathens?"

"Oh, yes." She crumbled up the paper and tossed it into a waste receptacle, then went to a spot on the far wall I hadn't noticed before. I watched, fascinated, as she slid open a hidden compartment and pulled out what could only be described as a small altar. A tiny platform, no wider than my forearm, bore a small statue of what I guessed was a figure of a deity of some sort—it looked very much like a regular Yataman, which wasn't unusual as the seed races generally preferred their deities to look just like themselves. I regarded this display curiously. Two's notes did not include a thing about religious practices. I had assumed the Yataman were atheistic, as nothing pointed to the contrary.

I watched the Yataman retrieve from her kitchen what appeared to be a small bottle of oil, which she poured into a dish and used to anoint the small statue and herself. Then, she turned to me.

"Has your family taught you to worship yet?"

"No," I said after a moment of hesitation. "They said I am still too young."

"Well," the Yataman said thoughtfully, "I've known younger than you who are taught. But then, it is up to your family. After all, worship and prayer must only be done in the privacy of one's own home, so says Sala."

Sala.

I could not remember this name from Two's notes. I ventured forward carefully.

"My family has not taught me about Sala," I said, and caught a hint of surprise from the Yataman, which she quickly hid.

"When you return to your family, you should speak to them about teaching you," she said. I watched her rearrange a few adornments on the tiny altar—offerings, perhaps—before quickly pushing the altar back into its hiding place. "To speak of Sala or worship outside of one's home is inappropriate." She sighed. "Of course, now that terrible orb is here, spreading their sacrilege, who knows what will happen."

I left the moment she turned her back.

BACK IN THE ORB, I impatiently peeled away the sticky strips of the chameleon suit from my body. Mod came forward to help take away and lay out the pieces I shed. After a lengthy scrub to remove all of the substance left behind by the suit, I ventured to the heart.

"Axi."

"Yes, Seven?"

"Are you still connected to the planet's information network?"

"I am."

"Give me everything you can find about *Sala*."

"There are two hundred and ninety-eight relevant items. Shall I begin enumerating?"

I sighed. "Sure."

"*Saalah*, a dish made of fragrant fruits and dried meat. Popular among nomads in the east Yi-Tan region. *Saelack*, a pair of hard metal . . ."

I FINALLY FOUND what I was looking for on entry one hundred and eighty-five. Mod and Sweetly had fallen asleep, curled up together in a corner carefully cleared of wires by Mod's large, gentle hands. My head was aching and my eyes were bleary, but I held on.

Yatam, as it turned out, was as far from atheistic as possible. In fact, they had one of the most stringent religious systems I'd ever encountered. Every planet I'd seen so far, in person or via Axi's database, had at least two variations in their religious beliefs and practices. But the people of Yatam held a single, unwavering theistic belief, and a very simple one at that. So simple that there were no scriptures, no texts, no academia, and no relevant structural establishments. Their religious practices involved no holidays, no rituals, no celebrations, and no commandments. In fact, the one and only religion of Yatam, abided to strictly by nearly ninety-nine percent of the population, involved only two components:

First, *worship in privacy and silence*. The Yataman did not pray openly and spoke of the symbol of their worship, Sala, only in the privacy of their own homes. It was strictly the job of immediate family—or someone they deemed close and trustworthy—to teach their children the way of Sala. This resulted in the ways of worship differing from family to family. Even the idols and symbols used for worship were up to the interpretation of the individual. The Yataman who had taken me into her home had anointed herself with oil and kept a small statue, but it was likely that her way of worshipping was not shared by the rest of the planet. When she'd realized I had not been taught, she'd quickly hidden her altar and had avoided further discussion. Since discussing the topic with others outside the family was often considered taboo, there was very little shared practice. And because acts of worship were restricted to private residences and varied from household to household, it was only natural that not only had Two missed it, but even the billions of cameras around the planet had failed to capture meaningful information.

Second, *there is none besides Sala.*

This was the tricky one. I ran it through translation many times, as a whole and one word at a time. It was not phrased as "know no other god" or " there is only Sala." It was literal and specific—there was *none* besides Sala.

Whether the degree to which this statement was ingrained within the Yatam population was due to tradition, habit, or genetics was unclear. But now that I had a lead, I knew exactly what to look for. After much more extensive research with the help of Axi, I finally found the real, true reason the Yataman refused to defend themselves within the arena.

There was none besides Sala.

It didn't matter that each family or even individual saw Sala as a different symbol or image. There was only Sala—the idol, the deity, the ideal. There was no other and to recognize another meant . . .

Well, I couldn't find anything on what the consequences would be. Without scriptures or religious text, there was no set, shared rule on what would happen if one recognized another god. However, perhaps the fact that this was left up to the interpretation of the individual drove the belief even further.

Yataman did not accept other gods. Not only that, they could not seem to process that other gods could possibly exist, even when a black orb landed on their planet and spoke to the entire population in every existing dialect. I could conclude only one of two possibilities—either the Yataman were terrified of whatever consequences they created in their heads, more so than death; or, they simply could not accept the possibility of the existence of any other deity, so much so that they were frozen in hesitation and indecision.

Ultimately, it didn't matter which—the result was the same.

"Do you require anything else on the topic, Seven?" Axi asked.

I shook my head. I'd had far more than I could stand in one day. However, there was something else I needed to know.

"Tell me about Titen Syndrome."

"Interesting."

"They will not play," I said. I had found One on the arena floor testing out stages for future games on Yatam, stages that would likely never be used.

"And if we were to impersonate their sacred one, Sala, and order them to play? It's not to my taste, but it has been done before."

"It wouldn't work on this planet. Sala would never speak to them in a public congregation. The ones who believe Sala speaks to them hold the belief that it is an occurrence in privacy, for their ears only."

One sighed. "H'otto will want to try again regardless. Too much time and effort has been sunk into this game."

"He will fail."

"I know. But it won't stop him." She studied my face. I knew my agitation was showing. I couldn't stop picturing the children I saw in the park.

If this planet will not play, what will happen to them?

"I want to talk to him."

"You won't change his mind," One said.

"I know," I said softly. In my mind, I saw the infant without scales, whose life had barely begun.

And I can't change mine.

207

. . .

A̲x̲i̲ ̲i̲n̲f̲o̲r̲m̲e̲d̲ me that H'otto was in the heart and I headed straight there. Fear and dread mixed together and tried to slow my steps, but I forced myself on. I had no idea what I was going to say to him, only that I had to change his mind, absolutely had to, before he doomed a planet simply for following their nature.

Voices.

I paused midstep.

"I never miss *anything*."

Two. They were back. I hadn't expected them to come back from the blue planet they were scouting for at least another day or two. They must've pushed the capsule to the limit to return this quickly.

"You obviously did," came H'otto's voice. Though he didn't raise his volume, his tone chilled me. "I think you know better than most what a mistake of this magnitude means, Two."

"If I didn't find it, it was impossible to find."

"What you missed doesn't matter. The end result is the same. A game has failed before even starting. Time and resources wasted. You have neglected your holy duty."

"Reset the planet. Try again with different parameters. It doesn't have to fail."

A dry chuckle. I took a step closer, standing just outside the heart, listening over the sound of blood pounding in my ears.

"Reset the planet," H'otto mocked. "Do you think you're worth that? A hundred of you isn't worth one reset. Your one and only purpose is to ensure the games happen, and if you cannot do that, there is no use for you."

There was a pause. I could almost feel Two grasping at any sign of hope. Was the executioner about to become the executed? I felt sick, like I was watching my old nightmare unfold.

"But you're not without your use," H'otto went on. "I would

be hard-pressed to find a field researcher better than you. But mistakes do not go unpunished."

"What do you mean?" The fear in Two's voice was unmistakable, as if they already knew what H'otto was about to do.

"Axi, show me Four."

My entire body tensed up as I heard Viva's voice. I'd never forgotten about her. Once in a while I checked in on her and her ever-revolving room. It had become something of a comfort and familiarity to listen to her laugh and chatter, even knowing that her lover was never going to appear.

"Will you be home soon?"

"What are you doing?" I heard Two ask. There was a shakiness in their voice.

"I think I've humored you long enough."

I peered carefully over the edge of the door. On the only screen I could clearly see, Viva paced the same path she always did in her living room, smiling and holding the communication device.

"If you don't feel you deserve punishment, perhaps she should pay for your infraction."

"No!"

What I heard next was a scuffling sound, followed almost immediately by a heavy *thump* that made me jump. From where I stood, I just barely saw Two as they were thrown back, the back of their head striking Axi's obelisk with debilitating force. I pressed both hands over my mouth to stifle a gasp as their body lifted off the ground, as if pulled by invisible strings, until they were dangling high in the air above the obelisk. I watched in horror as their slender body folded backward more and more. I waited for the inevitable snap, but it stopped just short of it.

"Now *that* is an overstep I cannot overlook," I heard H'otto say in his usual calm tone. "Attacking an arena master in his own arena. You truly forget yourself. What did you think would happen?

"Don't do it," I heard Two croak. I didn't know how they could still talk with their body bent to the point of breaking. "Do whatever you want to me. Just don't—"

"*You* do not make decisions," H'otto say, cutting them off. "Here I thought I could spare you. But there is no place for a champion who does not know their place. Have patience. Your turn will come after hers." He lifted a hand and snapped his fingers.

On the screen, Viva's surroundings vanished. She looked around the empty room in confusion.

"Axi," H'otto said.

"Yes, arena master."

"Sever her."

FOR MANY NIGHTS THAT FOLLOWED, I feared silence. Because when there were no other sounds to occupy my ears, all I heard was Two's scream that day, a ghastly, haunting sound of despair, as Viva's body collapsed bonelessly onto the floor.

TEN

CHAPTER 20

NOT A SINGLE SURVIVOR FROM THE SECOND TRIAL ROUND.

Not a single manifestation.

Not a single attempt.

The people of Yatam stood in their places as they were mowed down. The grounds of the arena floor were littered with shiny, bloodied scales shed from the fallen bodies. Their countrymen watched, mourned, prayed, each in their own way, and moved on. Even the interest the planet showed in the orb waned fast despite the atrocities taking place inside it.

After the game came to an end, Axi informed us that eight other orbs had arrived within the vicinity of Yatam, parked several planets' distance away.

"Lurkers," One whispered to me. "They've come to learn what's causing our failure and entertain themselves in the process."

The third game went no better. By this time the number of orbs had tripled.

"Glory be," Axi whispered to herself. "Glory be."

"SEVEN."

His voice shook me. The screens before us displayed a

variety of scenes from Yatam, most of which were people conducting private prayers. Even after three deadly rounds, the faith of the people had not wavered in the slightest. After I'd filled H'otto in on the nature of Yatam's religious practices, Axi's drones had begun to monitor the interior of private residences with greater frequency. But he had been right when he'd told Two it made no difference. Knowing the Yataman's secret did not help progress the game.

Two.

I had scoured the orb. Their usual capsule sat empty in the parking bay. With every day that I failed to find them, my hands trembled harder.

H'otto turned slowly and I saw rage etched into every wrinkle on his face. It was a vast difference from his normal pleasant demeanor, and for a moment it was like seeing the real face behind a mask. I had never witnessed him so angry, so bitter, and so ugly.

"Head to the holy grounds," he said, gnawing on every word that came out. "Inform the gods that this planet is not worthy."

"Not worthy?"

"It will be burned. A planet that refuses to prove itself is a worthless planet. We will act on the gods' will."

"Gods' will," I repeated stiffly, but H'otto was already gone, stomping out of the heart without a look back. With his short legs, it would've almost been a comical sight if every step didn't spell doom for billions.

"So," One said. She had been standing in the far end of the heart, silenting watching the screens. "Looks like they really can't be shaken."

Neither One nor I had run the previous game. Instead, we had set up a simple sequence executed by Axi. The contestants merely needed to cross a field with minimal interference containing only the weakest of predators. Sweetly's people would've completed this task within minutes. The Yataman did nothing. They sat with their heads bowed, as if accepting their fate, as the predators advanced and took them out one by one. Even when given an easy win, they refused to play. In their own way, they were the toughest opponents the orb had ever faced.

"And now we must enact the gods' will," I said, half to myself.

"Yes. H'otto will not allow for a reset."

"Reset?"

I'd heard that word before. Two had spoken it to H'otto in the heart. One looked away as if having said something she shouldn't, but I couldn't let it go.

"What is a reset?"

I watched conflicting emotions play on her face, as if trying to decide whether what she had to say was worthwhile. I waited.

"I have never seen it done," she said finally. "Frankly, it sounds almost like a myth. But I've heard of it being performed in other galaxies."

"What does that mean?"

"Memory wipe. Planet-wide. Reset its people so that none of the events are remembered, and try again."

I gaped at her. "That's possible?"

"I inquired with H'otto once. He was dismissive of it."

"Why?"

"It's a troublesome process, reviving hundreds of bodies."

"Reviving?" I couldn't hide my shock. "The dead can be revived?"

"Organic beings are only flesh and memories, dear. The arena stores the memories of every contestant who enters. Manifestation can be used to create flesh and organs as well as circulate blood."

"How can manifested bodies function outside the arena?"

"By replacing the manifested tissue with harvested organic tissue once the frame is built."

"Harvested?"

One shook her head. "You should go. Chasing this dead end will do you no favors."

I SAT ALONE in the control room of the capsule, watching the stars drift by outside. Mod and Sweetly were sleeping, huddling against each other in the capsule's upper compartment under a blanket Mod had manifested.

My children were perfect. Unburdened by worry and fear, they marveled at everything that crossed their paths, unmarred by the horrors of the games and undisturbed by this way of life. If given eternity, they would take it head on, finding joy in every second. They were better than the seed races that had produced them, these precious children. They were better than the rest of us champions, so worried and fearful and yet continuing to bring our atrocities from planet to planet.

But in the eyes of H'otto, they would always be imperfect. They were not worthy of the implants because they would never be able to orchestrate a game. They would never conduct research or design the stage. And as far as H'otto was concerned, since they could never experience these things, they had nothing to offer the gods.

So what did that mean?

Two's scream echoed in my mind and I shook my head hard, trying to dislodge the sound. I had run from it then, but now I regretted having done so, because I hadn't seen them again since. My imagination and confusion were running wild and I felt itchy and unsettled both inside and out.

I couldn't make sense of the pieces. The puzzle had no solution.

An image bubbled up. A bright light and an alien with white skin and black stripes.

I turned away from it, as I always did.

It bubbled up again, drawing closer.

I pushed it down. Above me, I heard Mod and Sweetly stir, shifting in their sleep as they often did.

For their sakes, I needed answers, and the only clue I had was the dream I'd kept at arm's length. According to the Maedan clock, Tam was approaching young adulthood. Had I really kept it at bay for this long?

It rose up again. It wanted to be seen.

And I knew it couldn't be kept away any longer.

THE DOOR STOOD open a thin crack. Light poured through. It was white, and so bright I had to blink to focus. This time, I let it come as the scene became clearer.

The figure lay on a table tilted at a steep slant. Milky white skin covered in parallel black stripes. He was male. His head was on the large side, and he had thick forearms and thin legs. I had convinced myself he was bound, but now that I allowed myself to look, I saw that he wasn't tied down at all. Instead, he lay as if relaxing on a bed, four green slitted eyes looking upward, a dazed expression on his face.

Slowly, he held up one hand and studied it. He looked half asleep.

"I should be afraid," he said. There was a croak to his voice. "But I'm not. I suppose I ought to thank this thing in my neck."

He let out a laugh, as if someone had told a joke only he could hear. An ironic, cruel joke. But funny nonetheless.

"Will it hurt?" he asked. "Do you know?"

No answer, but I saw another figure step into view. A familiar figure with smooth, translucent skin.

"I don't blame you, you know," said the one on the table. He sounded as if he was falling asleep. "You're only doing as you're told. Quite a shit job H'otto stuck you with."

No response still. I watched as Two reached up and touched something out of sight. Medical equipment perhaps. They hadn't looked at the alien on the table once, as if avoiding their gaze on purpose.

"Anything for Viva, eh? I admire that."

Two said nothing.

"Hey," he said. "This was my own fault."

He grabbed Two's arm.

"So just answer me," he said. "Will it hurt?"

Two finally turned to him. They reached up and cradled his face gently. He smiled blearily and leaned into their touch.

"Of course not," they said, and I heard their words shake. And all at once I was back in the revolving room, stroking Tam's face as I said goodbye to him for the real, final last time.

"You're going to be fine. Just fine."

THE ORB HOUSING the temple appeared. I directed Axi to dock, navigated the walkways quickly, and paused before the fog wall to gather myself.

This can't go on.

My heart pounded and my mind raced.

How long before it's my turn? And when will my children follow, if I'm not around to protect them?

Things had to change. I wasn't sure how yet, but I was going to make damned sure they did.

"PLEASE," I said as I felt the tendrils come for me. "Allow me to speak."

The tendrils paused. The fog quivered. I sensed confusion, but thankfully no offense at my boldness. I took a step forward and forced my beating heart to relax.

"I apologize," I said sincerely—they would sense insincerity in a second. "I speak better out loud. I do not know if I can accurately convey what I am about to say otherwise."

The fog before me moved. It turned and spun, rolling like a cyclone. When it settled again, I saw shapes being formed—a face as tall as ten of me stacked end to end—though I used the word "face" loosely. The thing before me looked like a child's illustration at best. Two dots represented eyes, a single line that formed the mouth, and nothing more. It took me a moment to realize that this was how the gods saw the majority of the beings from the Galaxy of the Starry River.

Slowly, the line mouth curved into a smile. It was a rather unnerving sight.

"A planet has failed the trial rounds," I said. "Its people refused to participate."

The mouth flattened into a line, then curved slightly downward. A look of disappointment.

"It's a planet with massive potential," I went on quickly. "It is technologically advanced, socially complex, and rich in culture. Its people are strong and clever and possess a natural talent for language. And I believe I understand the reason they refused to play the games."

The face tilted slightly—curiosity.

"It is because they believe in no god but their own."

A light nod—go on.

"Their imagination in this aspect is limited. Whether it's cultural or genetic doesn't matter. They will accept no other voice speaking to them, claiming to be their ruler or creator or whatnot. They simply cannot accept it. They can discover and find use for every resource of their planet, as well as create medicine for every ailment that plagues them. Every problem that arises leads to ten thousand solutions. But their creativity and imagination ends when it comes to their theocratic system because it is rooted in their limited reality only.

"Even in their beliefs, they spin no tales and tell no stories. Their mothers do not tell their children of lessons from their god or tales of holy persons. They are told only to worship their god, in their own way, and that there exist no others. They are even forbidden to discuss the matter outside their own home.

"And thus, a 'voice of god' meant nothing but falsehood to them."

My head thumped. My hands shook. The face of the gods looked down at me, amused, waiting. I swallowed my fear.

"I want to ask for a reset."

The simple face tilted one way, then the other, thinking.

"The seed races of this galaxy are changing. You yourself created them, but you are not getting what you want from them, not the right way. There is a better way to do this, even for those who do not believe in you, whose disbelief is so strong that they cannot even imagine the concept of gods other than their own, or even gods at all. The demigods do not understand the seed races. We are far more complex than they know. Their judgment is imperfect because they have never been of a race themselves."

The face didn't change. For a moment I nearly lost my nerve, thinking they had had enough of me. But I steeled myself. I had said too much already. I thought of Mod and Sweetly, and the sound of Two screaming in despair. I couldn't back out now.

"Mod, for example. Eight of the Galaxy of the Starry River."

A small smile. They liked Mod.

"H'otto believed him to be unworthy. He did not think he had anything to offer you because he was made differently. But look at what he's brought you. How many others like him has H'otto passed up? How many have the other demigods passed up simply because they were different? And how many have been passed up because their spots in the games were taken by those who could not fully participate in the games, like children who died swift deaths? What could those children have grown up to offer?"

The face was thoughtful once again.

"The demigods do not utilize the seed races to their fullest potential. This game could be done better. Done differently. This planet does not have to be wasted. Reset it, and it can serve again in the future. It is worth the effort. It is worth a second chance."

I was talking faster and faster. If I paused, my nerves and knees would both give out.

"This planet won't be the last one to refuse the games. These people won't be the last ones who don't believe, but that doesn't matter. You can still reap what you sowed. You created these races to feed on their experiences, and you can do that tenfold. To worlds like this one, you don't have to be gods. Gods are abstract and unreal. You are real. The universe and the games exist because of you. You are ... you are ..."

My mind strained. Then the word came to me.

"You are producers."

CHAPTER 21

I RETURNED TO THE ORB, MOD AND SWEETLY CLOSE AT MY SIDE, as if sensing my unease. Even as I ventured into the heart, where they rarely went, neither went a single step farther from me. H'otto was there, pacing restlessly. Nix worked in the corner. One stood with Axi. All eyes were on me as I walked in. H'otto stopped his pacing.

"You have spoken to the gods." It was not a question.

"Yes," I said. My knees knocked. *What have I done?* The gods had given no response to my little rant. In the heat of the moment it had all felt so right, so logical, but playing it back in my head, it all sounded like nonsensical rambling. An image of my own face on the other side of Axi's obelisk flashed through my mind.

"Good," H'otto said shortly. He turned to Axi. "Begin procedure to raze the planet."

Silence.

"Axi," H'otto said, a little louder.

No response came.

"Axi?" H'otto stepped to the obelisk and reached up with one of his arms. He tapped Axi's chin with one finger. "I said to begin the razing process."

"That command can be given only by the arena master."

The shock and confusion playing on H'otto's face matched my own. I hoped he couldn't hear me swallow thickly.

"Have you lost your mind? I am the arena master."

"That is incorrect," Axi said.

It can't be.

"What is the matter with you?" H'otto shouted. I had never once heard him raise his voice until now. *"I am H'otto! I speak for the gods. I am the arena master! Raze the planet!"*

"I cannot perform razing without explicit command from the arena master," Axi said calmly. "Should I perform razing?"

They can't have.

"Yes!" H'otto exclaimed.

At the same time, I said, "No."

"Razing process not started."

H'otto's eyes bore into me, but I didn't dare meet his gaze. My mouth was dry. I'd never been so scared in my life. Even as I had cowered in that arena myself, my skin and flesh torn apart in the darkness, I had not felt fear like this. But there was something I had to do, as soon as possible, even before I fully processed the reality of the situation.

"Axi," I said. "Give me Two's location."

Axi hummed for a moment. It might've been my imagination, but I thought I detected a change in her tone, almost like happiness. "The second champion of the Galaxy of the Starry River is currently in subbasement three, accessible only to the arena master."

"Thank you," I said and turned around to head out of the heart. Two of H'otto's hands clamped around my arm and stopped me in my tracks. I finally dared to look at his face. The rage in his eyes could burn and sear.

"You," he said through gritted teeth. "What did you *do*?"

I steeled myself. "Let go."

"What did you *say* to them?" he growled. For the first time in a long time, I realized how much like an animal he truly was. His claws buried themselves into my arm and I hissed in pain.

223

Sweetly pounced over my shoulder, striking H'otto square in the chest and knocking him to the ground. I cried out as his claws left deep welts in my skin. Mod held his arms protectively over me as I willed the arena to stop the bleeding. Sweetly thrust her featureless face over H'otto's and let out a half growl, half hiss.

"Get off me, you filthy creature," H'otto snapped angrily.

Sweetly's face peeled back. The black layer pulled away like a spreading oil puddle in reverse and a new face appeared underneath. It was terrifying and bizarre in its simplicity—two dots for eyes, a line for a mouth. It looked like a child's drawing, but I shuddered as I recognized it.

The face of the gods, now on Sweetly, opened its mouth, revealing rows and rows of sharp teeth. The anger on H'otto's face was replaced by horror. I stared, unsure what to do as Sweetly leaned in, teeth bared to bite.

"Oh my!"

One's voice startled me out of my daze. I snapped my fingers. "Sweetly, stop!"

The eerie face of dots, line, and teeth swung toward me and for a moment I thought she might attack me instead. But the black layer oiled back over her new features, and soon she was back to her normal, expressionless self. She hopped off H'otto and sauntered over to me, chittering.

"What's happening?" I heard One ask, but I didn't have time to answer. She gave me a wide berth as I passed her.

I had to hurry. I could still save them.

THE SUBBASEMENT WAS DOWNRIGHT FRIGID. My breath blew out in white smoky puffs. I ventured through dark, narrow halls, following my instinct. I had no idea where I was going, but something in the air was guiding me. I could feel them, the way I felt the contestants in the arena.

The long hallway of the subbasement was lined with doors

on both sides. From each one, I heard humming. I walked until I reached one that was silent. I braced myself for what I might see, but it wasn't enough.

The sight that greeted me when I opened the door would haunt me for a long time to come. I forced my legs through the doorway, pushing them a step at a time though the rest of me wanted to turn and never look back. I stopped in front of Two.

"What are *you* doing here?" asked what was left of them.

The back of their head was gone, as was most of their beautiful translucent green skin. Their muscle fibers were intertwined with thousands of silver threads, so thin they were barely visible, and it was these threads that bore their weight, extending from all over their body to the walls and ceiling of the room, suspending them. Empty sockets gaped from where eyes used to be. Where their scalp once was, their brain—a deep purple mass—pulsated.

For a moment I was speechless, stuck between wanting to run and wanting to weep. Two lifted their head slightly. Eyes or no eyes, they knew exactly who I was.

"Did H'otto let you down here to see what might happen to you if you mess up a game?" they asked with amusement unbecoming of their condition. "Beware the wrath of the arena master, little Seven."

I swallowed. The words I was about to say didn't feel real.

"I am the arena master."

Two's lipless mouth froze. "What did you say?"

"I am the arena master now," I said. "I will fix this. I will fix you."

Two threw back their head so violently that I feared their brain might rattle loose and fall onto the floor in a soggy mess. Then, they laughed. It was a wild, jarring sound.

"Little Seven overthrew the demigod," they said in a singsong voice. "What do you know? Oh, you certainly are full of surprises, aren't you?" Empty eyes turned back to me. "You think you can fix me? You're too late."

My strings were already moving. I didn't know if it was privileges granted to me as arena master or because Two was hooked directly into the arena itself, but my strings entered their body effortlessly, like the instruments of a skilled surgeon.

"I can feel that, you know," Two said. Their tongue had certainly suffered no damage. I said nothing. "You must fancy yourself a healer. Well, you're going to be disappointed. I'm far beyond what you can do."

Perhaps. Or perhaps not. I focused my senses on their body, searching for what was beyond repair, which was a lot, and what wasn't.

"Just go back upstairs."

I found the hooks of the arena. They were numerous.

"Go back and leave me alone."

It would take time.

"Go—"

"Who's Viva?"

Two fell silent, just as I thought they would. I took the chance to slip my strings under the arena's tiny hooks within their flesh.

"How did you know about Viva?"

"I saw her on your screen, way back when we took that first trip."

"Snooping, were you?"

"You left your door open."

Two chuckled. I nearly slipped up in surprise. After all this time, equivalent to over twenty times around the Maedan sun, this was the first time I'd ever heard them make any sound that resembled true joy.

"Did I ever tell you about my world?"

I shook my head. Two knew perfectly well that they had never told me a thing about themselves.

"My people had a rule about mating. Not sex. Mating. I know to your people that's the same thing. We could do the deed with whomever we wanted, but to mate and commit, well, you had to stay in your own tier." They paused. I thought they might be waiting for me to ask questions, but they went on before I could. "You know, the more planets I've been on, the more idiotic this sounds. We had this caste system with four rungs—or maybe it was five; I don't remember. You could say a lot about what exactly defined the rungs, but it boiled down to net worth. Money. I was on the upper rung. Privileged, you could call it. Those on the upper rungs could mate only with those on their rung. If you tried to mate with a higher rung, you must be doing it to get to their wealth. If you mated lower, you must be desperate, or being taken advantage of. Those from the upper rung with a mate from a lower were called a name"—here they made a sound I could not replicate—"it meant one who likes to insert unsavory things into certain parts of their body. Oh, it was an ugly word."

"Were you one of them?" I asked as my strings carefully pried away the arena's hooks one at a time. "One of those . . . words you just said?"

Two didn't answer. Instead, they sighed. "You know," they said wistfully, "I've noticed something since joining this lot— the champions. We are supposedly the best of our worlds, the most worthy of the gods' love. But that's not true. I'm sure you've noticed."

I said nothing. It was something I'd considered for a long time, but never said out loud.

"We are the odd ones. The ones rejected by our worlds for one reason or another. We stand out, and not in good ways. We think the wrong way, talk the wrong way, act the wrong way, and choose the wrong way. That blue planet I just visited had a saying—*aim crooked to shoot straight*. That is what we are— people who can't aim but somehow find our target in this game."

They paused. I worked in silence.

"She was kind," they said softly after a long moment. I didn't have to ask who they meant. "I'd been raised to believe that most everyone was beneath me, but the moment I met her, I knew she was above me."

"Above you?"

"In every way, shape, and form. She was better. She was . . . more."

Most of their body was not going to be salvageable. "What happened to her?"

"She collapsed a stage." They chuckled sadly. "A simple mistake, really. She took on a game before she was ready. Orchestrating is hard and she rushed."

"She killed the contestants?"

"No. Not everyone's like you," they teased, then shook their head slightly. "Sorry; habit."

"It's fine." I found their nervous system and followed it. To my relief, it was mostly intact.

"She dropped the facade. Really dropped it. Everything fell away. The arena walls were exposed."

"You mean—"

"They saw the orchestrator's stand."

I shuddered. It had never occurred to me how to react if the balcony overlooking the arena floor became exposed.

"The contestants attacked them. Viva and One. A few even nearly made it into the innards of the orb. It was the closest we came to a mutiny from the contestants. But of course, H'otto was never going to let that happen."

"So he . . ."

"Annihilated them. In a blink. The orb acts on the arena master's will." They turned to me. "*Your* will."

Respiratory system. Circulatory system. All shot. I tried not to let disappointment show on my face.

"Is that what happened to the rest of them?"

"More or less. The worst thing you can do is interrupt a game. It ruins the crop."

"Crop?"

"We are 'seed races.' We were planted to be reaped."

I nodded grimly. The nervous system might be all I could salvage.

"I begged for her. I can be quite good at groveling when I want to be." They laughed as if telling a joke. "In the end, all I managed was to strike a deal."

"To lock her away?"

"And become his surgeon. Or perhaps butcher is a better word for it. The demigods hate to get their own hands dirty." They paused and sighed. "But I misstepped. We all do eventually. And when it happens, H'otto finds other ways for us to contribute to the games."

I swallowed. "The one I saw . . . in the other room . . ."

Two arched a brow, though there was no eye underneath it. "You remember that? Here I thought you were too drugged up. Six. He had a lovely name, though I never did learn to speak it."

"Where is he?"

"Ever wonder about what flows through those machines down in computing?" A shudder coursed down my spine, a cold tingle quite different from the one sent by the implant. "Or how the control consoles on the capsules work? Or what goes into those jelly cubes you eat? At its basest elements, an organic being can be used for many things, including growing more of itself."

I nearly lost my strings as my stomach lurched.

"In case you ever wondered why I never stick around this place long," Two went on, "well, I just can't stand looking at them. The ones who became part of the machines, and the ones who inevitably will."

I didn't need to ask who they meant.

"Nasmi."

I blinked. I had never known that Two knew my name. My old name. For a moment it was like a waterfall of memories poured into my mind. Maeda. Tam. The man I'd almost loved.

"Yes?"

"Do you really think you're making a difference?"

I shook my head, then realized they couldn't see me. "I don't know. But I'm trying."

"Maybe you should give up while you still can. We are champions. It is the will of the gods that we suffer in this manner."

"*No.*" I said, firmly, and pulled nearly a hundred microscopic hooks out of Two's body. They shivered at the sensation. "I won't accept that. Suffering cannot be our fate. It is a choice, and I'm done having that choice made for me."

MY KNEES MANAGED to stay stiff long enough for me to detail Two's repair to Axi, though my fingers shook the entire time. The implant in my neck tingled, but this was too far beyond what it could fix. I waited until I was out of the subbasement to collapse.

What have I done?

The enormity of it came crashing down on me like a meteor and for a moment I couldn't see straight. The weight of the situation pushed me to the ground and I forced myself to breathe, leaning against the nearest wall. The sea of building blocks around me began to spin and writhe like swarms of agitated insects. The arena's hum grew into a cacophony. It was responding to me, syncing itself to what it thought was the command of the arena master.

I was the arena master.

I breathed. In and out.

I'd had no idea what to expect when I'd pleaded my case to the gods. I'd thought at best, they might persuade H'otto to reset the planet and spare Two. Never once had I thought this would happen. I had committed mutiny, overthrown the one who took me in after my own world abandoned me.

The blocks around me slowly calmed. I waited for the heat and vibration in my chest to pass. Time ticked by.

Suffering is a choice.

I had made that declaration to Two. Now, I had to make sure I believed it.

A clamoring through the halls caught my attention. I turned to see Sweetly running toward me. She dove into my lap and rubbed her face on mine. I could only give her a weak smile. Seeing my state, she paused, nuzzled my chest softly, and stared at my face.

Then, she reached into me with her strings, feeling around my mind as she had felt the other contestants during her time in the game. The black of her face peeled back, just like it had for H'otto. But what appeared was not the face of the gods, but that of Two. Not the Two of the old days, but the one I had just seen—eyeless, missing patches of skin.

"Clever little Nasmi," she said in Two's voice. "It's our fate to suffer."

I pushed her away before I could stop myself and she let out a surprised yelp. She had skimmed my memories, not in accuracy but in a rough image, then reconstructed them with her own face. The sensation was invasive and disturbing. And familiar.

It felt too much like worship within the holy grounds.

Sweetly whimpered and I quickly embraced her. She purred when I told her she was a good girl.

There was still so much I didn't know about her. She was one of a kind, my daughter. The miraculous product of the orb and a member of the seed races. She was unique and she was more, and she wouldn't exist if I hadn't taken a chance.

I held her tightly. A moment later, Mod joined us, panting from his effort to keep up with his nimble sister. He knelt next to us and wrapped us both in his enormous arms.

All of this—sparing me after I interfered in the games, the existence of Sweetly's power, and putting me in the arena master's seat—was a sign. The gods were telling me what they wanted me to do loud and clear. Ironically, this was as close to true enlightenment as I'd ever received from them.

Take chances.

I FOUND One on the balcony overlooking the arena. She eyed me with unease as I approached, Sweetly and Mod at my heel.

"What did you do?" she asked. There was a level of caution in her voice, as if she was trying to decide how exactly to talk to me.

"I spoke to the gods," I replied. Sweetly nuzzled my hand and I patted her head. "I told them that things have to change. And it looks like they agreed with me."

"You asked to take over from H'otto?"

"No. I only pointed out that his way was flawed." I hated the way she wouldn't meet my eyes, like she was afraid. It wounded me to see her wary of me, after all she'd taught and done for me. "I never intended to usurp him."

"Well, it doesn't matter now, does it?"

"One."

She finally looked at me straight on.

I straightened myself as much as I could, hoping that I looked much more grown up and confident than I felt. I had come too far to doubt myself and I needed to believe this was the right thing to do. More than that, I needed *her* to believe.

"I did this for *all* of us. We are champions and we deserve better. We know the seed races better than H'otto and others like him. I can't do this alone." I reached out a hand toward her. "Will you stand with me?"

She looked down at my extended hand, and I feared, truly feared, that she wasn't going to take it. But a heart-wrenching moment later, she smiled and wrapped her warm fingers around mine.

"Yes," she said. "I will stand with you, arena master."

I rushed forward and embraced her. She hugged me back. Sweetly chittered happily.

"Well," One said after we parted. "What's next?"

I sighed. The truth was, I hadn't thought it through. "I'm not sure yet. Where is H'otto?"

"Keeping his distance after your pet here went wild on him. That was a neat little trick you taught her."

I glanced at Sweetly. "I didn't teach her anything."

"You didn't?"

"No." I knelt down in front of Sweetly. "I guess there's still a lot about her I don't know."

"You are full of surprises," One said. I couldn't tell if she was speaking to me or Sweetly. "But, arena master, there is one thing you must do."

I lifted my gaze to her. "What's that?"

"You must be certain."

"Certain?"

"Absolutely certain. From this point on, every step you take will be scrutinized. You must be confident and resolute in everything you do. Even if you are not, you must pretend to be. The gods will be watching, and they will be waiting. Win or lose, you're going to make a good show for them, so it is for your own sake that you must win this gamble you've taken on."

CHAPTER 22

I HAD NOT STOOD ON THE ACTUAL ARENA FLOOR FOR SOME TIME, having become so used to pulling the strings from the balcony above. Part of me expected it to trigger a flood of emotions, but it didn't. Perhaps because of the time that had passed, or perhaps because my memory had simply faded.

Or perhaps it was because of the drastic change to the arena itself.

I looked with satisfaction at the arena dome and floor. Once rust-colored with exposed metal innards, it was now a pristine, flawless white. The horizon line where floor met wall was barely visible, giving the space a surreal feeling, like floating in an endless white space. Axi had done an excellent job running the procedures to automatically cover the entire arena with pure white building blocks. The space looked larger, clean and almost majestic.

Sweetly and Mod chased each other, chittering and laughing in the newly modified space. I watched Sweetly as she leapt around on all fours. I still hadn't figured out much about the ability the arena appeared to have bestowed upon her, but I had a feeling it was going to be very useful. Abnormality was a gift.

"What do you think?"

Two stepped beside me. Their metal feet clicked delicately against the floor. I admired the new body Axi had created for them with input from One. Unlike Nix's clunky shell, Two's body was slender and light and moved with an oily grace and smoothness. What was salvageable of their brain was encased safely inside the chest cavity, protected from harm and cushioned against sudden impact. True to their skill, even with only a brain left, Two required almost no additional assistance to move the arena-constructed body. No physical connection was necessary between the brain and the body itself—with the right implants to the brain, Two could move its components completely on their own.

They swiveled in place, tapping into the arena's neural network to take in the space around them. Then, a fan of blue light emitted from their headless neckhole—a hologram displaying a simple face. Two dots for eyes, a line for mouth. The line curved itself into a thin smile. They approved.

Speech had proved to be the most difficult thing to salvage in attempting to transfer Two into a new body, far more than gross motor skills. In the effort it took to produce semiaccurate speech, Two often lost control of the rest of their body, leading to stumbling and falling while attempting to talk. If they needed to speak extensively, One or I often needed to assist in ensuring their body stayed upright. In the end, the speech functions had been left in, but the hologram had been added as a method to express simple emotions and responses when words weren't necessary.

And yet, despite their grace and expertise in moving their body, Two was a stark reminder of the consequences that awaited me—all of us—if I failed. I couldn't forget the sound of their scream as Viva had collapsed. Severed, which I'd later learned meant the breaking of the connection between her mind and body. It was not a process that could be easily reversed, even with the arena's technology. Two did not take this news well, though they made admirable effort to pretend they did. Being severed was a terrifying fate and a power reserved for the arena master.

Me.

I had still yet to become comfortable with that title. I was feeling my way as I went, trailed by the ghosts of champions past and visions of those who still stood in their own skin joining the ranks of the half living, half dead.

"What a change," One said, pacing the space slowly, hands behind her back.

"I thought it was time for a new look," I said, pulling myself out of my mind. "The more evolved seed races prefer a certain degree of luxury." I gestured at the white all around. "Or at least some semblance of it."

She nodded, though I couldn't tell if she agreed or not. It didn't matter. I remembered her words—confidence, certainty.

"So what is your next step?"

"Axi is preparing to begin the reset."

The reset process was indeed a difficult one. It had taken much research through the archives and conversing with Axi to understand the steps. Time could not simply be turned back. Even the gods did not have the power to accomplish such a feat. I had thought initially that the energy and precision it took to erase the memory of a planet was the difficult part, but as it turned out, that was an easy task compared to the preparation needed.

The first step was to restore those lost within the games. It was impossible to pretend a segment of time did not occur when several hundred people were missing. Their recreation took time. Memories were harvested from their time in the arena and bodies were created from material replicated from the organic source I tried hard not to think about. Not every single body would be perfect, however, as bodies were constructed from the seed race blueprint and persons containing genetic anomalies would have a higher risk of flaw in functionality upon recreation. This would affect their lifespan or ability to function on a day-to-day basis. Thankfully, genetic anomalies were rare and design flaws could be played off as naturally occurring illnesses.

Second, the brain did not appreciate holes in memories. If a person woke one day finding they could not remember a certain part of their life, their instinct would be to search for answers and attempt to fill in the gaps. A planet as scientifically advanced as Yatam would quickly notice if the memory of several weeks suddenly disappeared from its entire population. To pretend that this time did not occur was impossible—machines and instruments all over the globe tracked the passing of days, changing of seasons, planetary alignments, weather patterns, etc. Not only did the memory of the games need to be removed, but plausible memories needed to be generated using sampling from each individual, then fill the missing space. It might create a slight sense of déjà vu. But if we were lucky, the overall impact would be insignificant enough not to trigger a worldwide investigation.

Third, the time it all took to prepare needed to be accounted for. We could not take the time of the planet's whole cycle around its sun to prepare, for example, since the longer we waited, the more changes would occur and the more difficult it would be to rewrite history in the people's minds. And we could not simply erase the entire cycle, as it would cause the mystery of every citizen on the planet aging a year without explanation. This was a problem especially noticeable in young children, for whom one cycle led to massive developmental differences. Therefore, during preparations, energy was required to hold the planet in stasis.

"The others are arriving?" One asked.

I nodded. "Soon."

Holding the planet in stasis, I'd learned, meant creating a transitional space. In the words of the champions, a "jar." To turn an entire planet into a jar was a massive undertaking. In fact, the point when Axi explained this process to me was the first and only time I truly doubted whether I was ready for what I'd set in motion.

"Axi," I said to the space around me, "transparent display."

The white above us faded to black. The dome disappeared and was replaced by the dark of space. From Yatam's orbit, we had a clear view of the starry river the galaxy was named for—a thick cloud of stars that extended from one end of the visible space to the other. But what I wanted to see was not the stars. It was the orbs.

Hundreds of orbs had joined us in orbit. Soon it would be thousands, then tens of thousands. Then more. Games all over the universe had halted so that the energy of their orbs could be combined to hold Yatam in stasis.

"Requests are being made to open communication channels," came Axi's voice from above. It was strange to hear her voice replace H'otto's on the arena floor. "Shall I proceed?"

This was what I had anticipated with the most apprehension—my voice being heard by arena masters from all over the universe, undoubtedly wondering about the newcomer who had convinced the gods to reset a planet and unseat a demigod. Fortunately, I already knew what I would say to them.

"Proceed."

A green circle appeared around one of the orbs overhead. It was followed by another, then another, lighting up the domes like glowing insects. The channels were open. My voice would be the next one heard.

"Glory be to the gods," I said, loud and confident. "Glory be to Headspace."

There was a momentary pause. I waited with bated breath. Then came the voices, thousands of them, each in a different language, translated through the arena.

"Glory be."

"Glory be."

"Glory be."

. . .

SEEING H'otto locked away brought on an unexpected sense of guilt. Despite what he had done to the other champions, I couldn't deny the fact that he had taken all of us—the lost and outcast—under his wing when we needed it. He had given us a home and a purpose when our own planets rejected us. Truthfully, when I had wanted things to change, sealing away H'otto had never been my intention.

I preferred not to think of the holding space Axi created for him as a prison. It was spacious, and aside from the walls, which were set to override manifestation, he could create any creature comfort he wished inside it. However, he had done nothing to make it more livable for himself. When I arrived in the subbasement to see him, the space was just as bare as it had been upon creation. Axi lowered the transparency of the wall between us and we stood face to face.

"So," H'otto said. He smiled faintly and I suddenly had a clear memory of the very first time I'd laid eyes on him. Fresh out of the jar, I had seen him as small, warm, and harmless. But now, standing and facing me the exact same way, he looked completely different. Past that gentle facade was a coldness that came only with a lifetime spent inside this arena, serving the faceless gods. "Little Seven is all grown up."

"If I let you out," I said, "what would you do?"

"Kill you," he replied simply. His frankness and lack of malice made it all the more disturbing. "It would be fast, but not painless. Then you could join Six in the chemical vats."

"Then I can't let you out, can I?"

"No, you cannot." He paced back and forth in front of me slowly. "You know, the gods would punish me for killing you. They hate to be robbed of a good show. But I would kill you anyway." He tilted his head back and sighed. "Oh, Seven. You haven't a clue what you've gotten yourself into."

I ignored this. Nothing he said was going to convince me to turn back. "I am changing the way things are done. For myself, and for—"

"For your little family," he interrupted. "Did you think I hadn't noticed? Tell me, what's the name of your child?"

I almost said, "Mod"; then I realized that wasn't his question, and for a strange, unsettling moment the answer escaped me.

"You don't remember, do you?" H'otto cracked a wide grin, displaying his sharp, even teeth. "You've become so wrapped up in this fake family you've created for yourself that you're forgetting where you came from."

"So what?" I snapped back. "My planet had no use for me. My new family is of my own making and I will do whatever it takes to protect them."

"And risk them, too?" H'otto arched a brow. "Did you think when the consequences of your failure come crashing down, you would be the only one bearing the load?"

"It's better than leaving them be until you decide to make them part of the arena, like you did to the others."

"I showed them kindness. Those who fail to serve the games would meet far worse fate at the hands of the gods."

"Worse than what you subject them to?"

"This is your last chance," H'otto said, and I hated how fatherly and reasonable he sounded as he spoke. "Let me out, own up to the gods for overstepping your bounds, and I can still protect you and yours. You can still be a proper champion. The gods will forgive you for your transgression if you beg for mercy now."

You can still be a proper Kol.

"I need *nothing* from you," I said.

"Well then," H'otto said with a click of the tongue. "I won't waste your time. I'm sure you have plenty to do."

"I do." I turned away to leave.

"Just remember," I heard him say behind me as the wall regained its opacity. "You've been allowed to interrupt thousands of games for the sake of one. The gods will have high expectations. If you fail to deliver, what befalls you and yours will make you envy the ones you currently pity."

THE STASIS of Yatam lasted the equivalent of a hundred and seventy-six of the planet's day and night cycles. In that time, it would normally complete one and a half rotations around its sun. There was not a moment that passed that did not remind me of all the orbs around us, feeding their energy to the planet to hold it in place, sustaining the pocket space in which the Yataman lived the same day over and over. I left the arena dome on transparent display, watching the orbs in the sky as I worked. Once in a while a few would depart to search for an energy source, but most stayed in their place, unmoving, and I knew that each one held at least one set of eyes watching me.

I STOOD in the heart of the arena, watching the orbs leave Yatam's orbit on its many screens. With each one that departed, the planet moved a little farther forward. Soon, it would be ready to return to its normal track.

"Not all of them are leaving."

I looked down at Two, who was sitting on the floor against Axi's obelisk—the most convenient way to prevent falling while attempting to speak. Their voice had a buzzy, filtered quality as it emitted from the neckhole of their metal torso.

"I expected at least some to stay," I said. "It's only natural that they would want to see how this turns out."

"They want to see you fail." There was no malice in this statement. It was the truth.

"You're as pleasant as ever," I teased. "You don't think I can succeed?"

Two raised one of their slender limbs and examined it. "Don't think I'm not grateful," they said. "I am. But I have been in this place a lot longer than you. It's a difficult lot to be optimistic about. What you're about to do . . . it's never been done before."

"What *we* are going to do."

"We?" The holographic face appeared, with a small curved line over one eye—an arched brow. "Dragging the rest of us down with you, are you?"

"If you're up for the ride."

"Doesn't seem like I have a choice." Though their words were sarcastic, the holographic face changed to a smile.

I turned back to the screens. At least a hundred orbs remained just outside of Yatam's orbit. Two stood with some effort and stepped next to me.

"They're waiting for a show."

I nodded. "I know.

"So where are we headed?" They paused. "I must admit this is unreal. Seems like yesterday you were that shy, pitiful thing trying to hijack a capsule and fly back to a life that no longer existed."

I allowed myself a small smile. I had spent no small amount of time during the reset trying to figure out the next game. My *first* game, and possibly my last if it didn't turn out well. Two's comment was ironic, as the choice I made in the end was the first planet I had seen outside of my own. The first world that had made me realize the universe was far larger than I could ever imagine.

It was the world that had inspired me to live, and now it would be the world that would begin a whole new way of life for me and mine.

"Axi."

"Yes, arena master?"

"Set course for Harmony."

CHAPTER 23

Harmony had changed.

Quaint, modest dwellings spread out over vast, undeveloped landscapes had been replaced by dense, shiny skyscrapers. Train and monorail tracks cut through mountains and fields, connecting massive cities and bustling towns. The city of Prosper had tripled in size and added multiple arts and museum districts. Days were filled with fast-walking crowds and the clanking of machinery, and nights were lit by bright, colorful artificial lights.

And yet, the qualities I adored most about the Harmonians remained. Their atmosphere was clean and crisp, education was provided free for all, and since my last visit they had celebrated many more anniversaries marking their years of peace. It was just as beautiful as I remembered, and time had only blossomed its culture and civilization. Harmony plucked at my heartstrings.

But more importantly, it was ready.

"You're sure about this place?" Two asked me as we arrived within view of the planet.

I nodded. "I am. This is a world that is not only mature, but values reason and logic. I think they will perform well." Two drummed their fingers on their folded arms. "Is there a reason I shouldn't be?"

"I have spent much time on this planet. Culturally and technologically, I can't deny that they are certainly mature."

"You sound like you have reservations."

Their metal body clicked, but no face appeared over the empty neckhole—they were thinking. "Let me show you something."

They turned to Axi and said something I didn't catch. The screens pulled up a familiar structure that took me a moment to recognize.

"This is the Institute of Higher Learning. It is in Northeast Prosper."

I nodded. The building still largely looked the same, but had been repainted, and shiny metal adornments had been added around its motto.

Suffer be the idiots.

"I suggest you visit here," Two said. "If you still feel you can take on this planet after that, then I have nothing else to say."

THE INSTITUTE OF HIGHER LEARNING was even more magnificent and imposing in person. A sprawling campus filled with fragrant flowers and towering broad-leafed trees surrounded a main central building. The wide metal gate bearing the institute's name appeared to be new, as were the top two stories of the main structure. A large screen welcomed visitors and rotated through the day's announcements.

"It states that the new research facility on floor eight is open today for scheduled tours," Axi said in my ear. "And a guest lecturer will be presenting on the first floor, the only floor open to all visitors."

I had no idea what Two wanted me to see here, but I was glad to set foot on the surface of Harmony at last. This planet beckoned me like an old lover, its sights and sounds calling out to me from every direction and filling me with excitement and intrigue. I couldn't entirely place why I adored it the way I did. Perhaps because it was the first world I had seen outside of Maeda. Perhaps it was the way they valued unity and peace. Perhaps it was the hope that I had finally found a planet that could rally behind its champion beyond idle gossip.

Or maybe it was one of the first lessons One had taught me —*the gods abhor ignorance*. I couldn't help feeling like the hands of fate were pointing me to Harmony, with its love of knowledge and logic.

A body bumped into me from behind. I jumped, fearing the impact would damage the chameleon suit, and found myself face-to-face with a tall, smiling Harmonian.

"My apologies," he said. "I didn't see you." His skin was a warm red, set sharply against the velvet black of his mane. By the standards of the city, he also appeared to be well dressed. Brown eyes flickered and took me in from head to toe. Thankfully, I ran no risk of being mistaken for a child here, as I was of the proper stature to fit a short adult Harmonian female.

"It's alright," I said dismissively, and hoped that was the end of the conversation.

"Are you here for the tour?" He nodded toward a group gathering at the gate, led by a blue-skinned female.

"No," I replied simply.

His smile broadened. "Well, I hope you'll come by my lecture, then."

Then, with a wink, he was off. I turned back to the digital display.

"Axi," I whispered. "What is the topic of the lecture on the first floor?"

"The title translates to *The Influence of Media and Storytelling on Critical Thinking*."

"Interesting," I murmured to myself, and watched the retreating form of the man who bumped into me out of the corner of my eye.

. . .

I stood in the back of a vast, pristine lecture hall watching the red-skinned Harmonian address an audience of several hundred, most of which consisted of students and young academics. Having spent much time studying the features and body language of the race, I knew that he was just short of middle aged, and could be considered to be handsome. Harmonians favored certain color combinations of skin and hair, and his combination of black and red, whether artificial or natural, was a highly desired one.

And he was charming, especially when standing before an audience. I couldn't deny his eloquence and articulation. However, despite his best effort to draw their interest, the audience was bored. He was animated, energetic, and knowledgeable, but impressing a roomful of students who lived and breathed lessons and lectures was no easy task.

I, however, found his lecture enlightening.

He began by talking about lore and stories of childhood, and I immediately identified traits from Two's old notes. The Harmonians put very little stock in fiction. The minute amount of it that did exist was used strictly for educational purposes to impart social lessons to children. Their history books contained no speculation or conjecture, as no past figures of history ever recorded anything but accurate events without deception or exaggeration. Their elders told very little folklore. Their songwriters sang of no giants or angels. Their art showed only stunningly accurate portraits, figures, and events. Their holidays marked actual historic events. Every child knew of great figures of history and yet had no shared knowledge of a single storybook character. Indeed, the concept of "storybook character" was almost nonexistent.

Most primitive civilizations I'd encountered thus far held some degree of faith in holy entities and legends of greater beings. As technology inevitably took over, this notion tended to decrease, but still remained in some form or fashion, even if only as historical and anthropological studies. As far as I could tell in Two's research, Harmony had always been this way. This was possibly an evolutionary trait that had come about in which those with superior logic and reasoning skills were more desirable as mates early in the establishment of the seed race. It was not a matter of a race discarding myths and legends as they became more scientifically advanced—the Harmonians had never had a concept of myths and legends to begin with.

As he went on to elaborate on the influence of popular media, I began to understand Two's concern with this planet. Harmony functioned on facts. It wasn't that its people lacked imagination; it was simply not in their habit to use it. Media were taken as tools to communicate fact; what was stated could usually be proven, and if not, someone had better prove it soon or forever lose their credibility and be labeled an "idiot" in the eyes of the populace.

Suffer be the idiots. It suddenly made a lot more sense.

Listening to this man speak, I mulled over the points he made. Where Yatam functioned on absolute faith, Harmony functioned on absolute logic. Unless something was stated and proven as fact, it was assumed to be false. Once inside the orb, what would their reaction be if they were left to their own devices, told to please an invisible entity that they'd never seen? The risk of a repeat performance of Yatam was high, or they might reason that taking extensive militant measures made far more sense than harping on the games. The interest of this race must be carefully managed, as anything relating to an unseen "god" was unlikely to produce the desired reaction from the populace. And if this game that I had staked so much on were to fail on the trial round, then the consequences would extend far beyond simple death.

And yet I was undeterred. I stayed for the rest of the lecture and slipped out shortly before it wrapped up. I understood

Two's worries, but seeing the way the Harmonians worshipped fact and proof also bolstered my resolve.

Harmony was the right place. They would deliver the game I needed. While they had little imagination for the unproven, they also accepted anything heard in the media as fact, as their own media always, *always* reported facts, for fear of prosecution for "idiocy" if nothing else.

All I had to do was show them, from the get-go, that they were playing for something real, something solid and realistic. They might not play for an invisible god, but they might play for something more tangible. Rather than being a handicap, the Harmonians' obsession with facts could be used to my advantage.

HARMONY'S RESPONSE to the orb's arrival was almost exactly as I expected—military activation, monitoring through drones, and news reports around the clock. For a day, the planet stood on full alert, weapons loaded. Then, when we caused no immediate harm, the news reports slowed and people went about their business. They were nothing if not logical, the Harmonians. They stayed ready and alert, but spent no time speculating about things they did not know.

I waited two day cycles, ensuring the majority of the planet was aware of our presence, before beginning the first phase. Harmony's extensive communications network served its purpose and then some.

The video began with an image of an average Harmonian walking through a bustling street that was designed to look like one of their many major cities. He walked with his head down, white mane hanging over his face, downtrodden. A light rain fell, drops glistening against his smooth black skin. Then, suddenly, he stopped and lifted his face upward to the sky. A spot of light shone on him, and the video faded to black, followed by white words on the screen—customized to local dialect based on the region the video was being played in.

SOMETHING GREATER IS COMING

The video circulated rapidly. There were many reasons for its popularity beyond its mysterious message. For one, the character I had generated with Axi's help was based on the Harmonians' general standard for beauty. Though their skin and hair color varied greatly, I stuck to the preference of the population, which found steep juxtaposition between skin and hair color to be most attractive, the epitome of which being black skin and white hair or vise versa. There was also a slight bias towards males as leaders—unusual, as most planets I'd seen so far with binary genders appeared to lean toward matriarchal societies, like Maeda. The statement at the end was clean and simple. I had considered phrasing it as a question, but for a society with next to no creative imagination, a statement of fact spoke to them much more effectively. A question would only trigger confusion. As it was phrased as an inevitability, the Harmonians quickly spread the message amongst themselves that something great was indeed coming rather than puzzling uselessly over what exactly the word "greater" could mean.

Just as this video's novelty began to wear off, I circulated the next video. It was essentially the same, but this time featuring a white-skinned female with black hair. And after the message at the end, a digital code was given, directing the Harmonians to locate a particular form within their information network. And here the real tricky business began.

"YOU ARE ASKING THEM TO VOLUNTEER?" I could hear One's apprehension, but it did not matter to me. I had to believe this would work. "You realize that the games have always drafted participants. Never once has it relied on volunteers."

"And that is why the attempt failed," I said. "A game with willing and able participants is far more likely to succeed."

The form was simple—it enticed potential applicants to supply information in order to join a lottery to be selected for a competition guaranteed to end in fame and notoriety. Anyone could enter, with two specific caveats. One, only those over a certain age might enter—the age above the line indicated by Harmonian law to be the division between "child" and "adult." Two, those who entered must be of sound mind (though not necessarily of sound body).

"You are excluding a good part of the population."

"The gods have no need of unripe minds or those who cannot properly play the games."

One said nothing more, but I knew she was thinking I had once been one of those "unripe minds." I pretended not to see her doubt.

This was going to work. I believed in it. The gods wanted prize entertainment, to reap what they sowed, and this was going to bring what they desired and more.

"ARE YOU READY?"

Two's holographic face looked down at me, brow arched —*are you?*

The truth was no. I didn't think I could ever be truly ready for this. The irony of it all was too much. I had once been a different person, hadn't I? H'otto had proved that.

Tam. I had a son named Tam.

Did it matter now? The child I knew no longer existed. The baby I vaguely remembered in my mind was no longer there, and the person he'd grown up into was a stranger I never met.

I tried to remember that world, the world I had once shared with him, and found the memory distant and cold, like a dish of food shriveled and dried beyond recognition. I could not remember the good things anymore, the bright days and warm nights. Maeda was just another alien world, one that I'd thought I knew but never really understood.

I looked at the figures around me—Mod, whose world jeered and laughed at him for being a simpleton; Sweetly, whose people saw only her beauty and talent, pushing her to exceed her limits and refusing to recognize the illness that caused her endless distress; and Two, who embodied grace itself and had no flaws save for loving someone their people deemed beneath their caste.

One stood ready on the balcony above the contestants. She had finally stopped scratching at the implants in her wrists.

And me, the "Kol," born to serve, now master of the arena.

"Let's go," I said, and walked out of the heart of the arena without looking back. The others followed, falling into step with me as we headed toward the arena floor together.

The worlds that had birthed us were not good enough for us. They never had been.

From here, we pave our own paths, and we will never again choose to suffer.

CHAPTER 24

"*Welcome, gentlemen and ladies.*"

Two sauntered onto the arena floor. Even though we had gone over the script many times, I was still nervous. Though it appeared my worry was for nothing. Among their many talents, Two was an excellent actor.

The Harmonians turned toward this newcomer on the pristine white floor, and from my spot on the balcony, I could both see and sense their confusion. But there were twinges of excitement as well.

From the balcony, I watched. My words projected throughout the arena through Two, just like H'otto's did. Impartiality was important—I did not want the Harmonians to hear a distinct male or female voice and create assumptions based upon it. Instead, the voice they heard was a neutral one —the old voice of Two.

The tiny cameras flying about the arena flocked toward Two. The holographic face flickered on and Two winked at the entire world of Harmony, as well as the hundreds of arena masters and champions watching from just outside the orbit. *And hello to you, world. Welcome*"—as they said these words, they spread their arms wide, legs straight and together like a dancer, missing none of the grace they had had in their previous body thanks to One's assistance from the balcony—"*to Headspace.*"

The Harmonians watched them with curiosity. This crop was much different from the ones on Aukron and Duo. For one, there was not a single child in sight—I had made sure of this, despite the fact that hundreds of underaged contestants attempted to enter themselves. The group was also sharp, bright eyed, and alert. Some appeared apprehensive, but no one wept or panicked. They had, after all, chosen to put themselves forward. In fact, I had been shocked at how very many of them volunteered. I had originally feared that, left to their own devices, very few people would step forth. But the lure of possible fame and fortune was real and powerful, much more powerful than the prospect of pleasing some invisible godly figure.

The group was also a physically attractive one by Harmonian standards. This was intentional. Despite H'otto's insistence in the past that contestants must be random, I had been heavy-handed in my selection for the majority of them. At least seven out of every ten contestants were my choosing, picked based on their appearance, intelligence, social prowess, and in some cases, preestablished fame. Not only did these contestants have a high chance of success in the games, but they also offered endless potential for their interaction with each other. Already, I could see a small-time media personality taking her chance to primp her pink mane and mug to the cameras while several others pointed and gawked.

H'otto had never understood what the gods wanted. This was never about being worthy. It was about being entertaining.

"*First things first—yes, we are broadcasting from within the sphere. And no, this is not a hoax, or a joke, or a conspiracy. This is real. The games are about to start. Get comfortable, folks, because you are about to see something great.*"

The Harmonians enjoyed tight, form-fitting fashion, mostly to show off their sinewy limbs and the curves of their muscles.

Hair adornments were also common, along with the tinting of skin and hair. There was a limit to how Two's new body could be decorated, but I had been able to put together a look that worked well for them. Their body was covered by a thin film that mimicked skin-tight clothing, changing colors subtly as the light from the arena struck it from different angles. Reaching out into the arena, I could sense that the Harmonians regarded this as flashy and boastful, but undeniably fashionable.

"You might wonder what you're doing here," Two went on, gesturing grandly as they spoke. *"Fear not. You've all volunteered for something incredible. Let's start with the basics. The name of the game is Headspace. The rule of participation is simple, and there is only one—think, and you shall obtain. It's unfair that we should all be born with different bodies. But, we're all born with heads."* I heard a few chuckles and a murmur of agreement. *"Well, almost all of us."* Here, Two gave a well-timed shrug and the chuckling around them grew. *"In our heads, we are equal. And in this game, your head is all you will need. Your chances are as good as anyone else's. Think, and you shall obtain."*

"What do we win?" someone called.

This was a question I had anticipated. "Gods' love" meant nothing here. The Harmonians needed something real and concrete. I had debated through and through about what exactly to tell them. There were a number of lies I could tell—money, fame, fictitious treasures. Any of these would work to motivate the contestants. But in reality, for them to be driven and give their all to the game, nothing was superior to the simple truth. H'otto used to wrap it in layers of prose about worthiness, but I chose to be as straightforward as possible.

"You get to live." Two gave a flippant tilt of their holographic head. *"You see, incompetent planets are dull planets. If Harmony is not able to produce a winner of the game, the planet will be burned from one end to the other, until not a single life is left."*

They paused. This was it, the moment that would define

how the planet responded to this game. Failing to please invisible beings was too far outside of their imagination, but the image of their beautiful world burning out one life at a time was vivid, and the possibility of not winning a game that was right in front of them was real.

"You can't be serious."

I felt it. The stir. The struggle between belief and disbelief.

"I absolutely am."

The struggle grew. I decided to drive it home.

"Repeat after me," I whispered, and the arena carried my voice to Two's mechanical ears.

"We came from the stars. We possess technology and power far beyond yours. You can already see that. Win, and you will be the hero who saves the world. Lose, and you will die with your failure. Unless you prove your worth, your existence has no meaning." Two gave a dramatic pause, then leaned forward as if imparting a secret. *"This is a fact."*

I held my breath. It came down to this. How would they react?

Then, without warning, a short, strong Harmonian leapt out of the crowd. Her movement was fast and sharp. Had I not been connected to the arena, I would not have noticed the change in the shape of her legs and hand. Her leg bones had bent into the shapes of springs, propelling her over the heads of the others and toward Two. Two leapt out of her way as she landed, one rock-coated fist smashing into the arena floor and leaving a noticeable dent. Her expression was one of anger, but it quickly melted away when she looked down at herself and saw the changes to her body. Shock, confusion, and realization played on her face as her limbs slowly changed back to normal. She looked back at her fellow contestants, then at Two.

"Well," Two said, their holographic face split into a wide grin. *"Let the games begin."*

. . .

THE HARMONIANS' competence within the arena rivaled that of Duo. The spectacle before me was nothing short of stunning. Without terrified children, confused elders, or, in H'otto's words, the "addled," the game went forward at full swing. Once they accepted the reality of the game and saw the transformation of the first contestant, combined with the hints I'd provided, the Harmonians figured out the game very quickly. Unlike those on Duo, they divided into effective teams and watched each other's backs.

The stage I set was similar to the one that first introduced me to Sweetly—a wet and dreary city filled with quiet, prowling predators. The Harmonians were initially split up, but quickly found one another and began to set up a base of defense in a dead-end street, where they could be attacked from only one side. From there, they scaled the nearby buildings and split their team into groups that kept watch, attacked, or defended, further divided by long and short range depending on what each person was capable of manifesting.

But it wasn't enough.

I reached out into the arena. A well-designed game was only step one. A cast of competent players was step two. The entertainment provided by an intelligent race was more than just their ability to play. I needed more.

It didn't take me long to find that important third factor. My hand-picked contestants did not let me down.

An older contestant immediately leapt to protect a younger one, who, by "coincidence," possessed the same hair and skin color as his grandchildren.

Two females of similar age from the same region bonded quickly and moved around the arena together, close as sisters though they had never met outside the arena.

A pair of Harmonians, former lovers now living continents apart, regarded each other with shock at the strange circumstance of their reunion, then proceeded awkwardly together, uncomfortable with the situation but glad to have found a familiar face.

An athletic male, cool headed and organized, had formed his own group of young, competent players. Together, they systematically made their way through the arena.

So many possibilities. So many stories.

I pushed forward, syncing my own mind to the contestants'. I needed to know them, and know them *well*. In their minds lay their stories and secrets and what defined them as individuals. *This* was what the gods truly desired.

A businessperson.

A creative.

A performer.

A designer.

A loner.

A lover.

A mother.

I paused.

She had dark hair and light brown skin, a combination seen as common and plain by her people. I had little inkling of her background, which meant she was a filler not picked by me. She appeared to be just barely old enough for the game, and judging by the look on her face, she regretted completing the entry form immensely. But none of those things made her unique. What drew me to her was what I saw inside her mind.

She defined herself as a mother and little else, a rare choice for someone who had just departed her childhood. Though I had many contestants who offered complex and interesting stories, I had to take a second look at this girl who was barely a woman.

I ventured forward as far as I dared, careful not to disturb her as she found her way through the stage. Her mind was chaotic and it showed in her actions. She was frazzled, worried, and not just about living or dying in the game. She had bigger problems.

She was terrified. Not of the predators around her, but of not returning from the game.

She had a child. A very ill one.

I watched fragments of her memories bob up and down in her consciousness, like the lure of a fishing pole.

A tiny daughter born far too early, afflicted with a rare disorder. This child had never been inside her mother's home. Her entire short life to date had been spent inside the pristine, sterile walls of Harmony's expansive medical facilities. She'd had eight tubes connected to her when she was born. Now she was down to four. Her smile lit every room, though she could walk only a few steps on her spindly little legs before becoming tired. The doctors said there were two scenarios in which she could go home. The first was if she ever got down to two tubes —one to feed a nutrient mush directly into her bowels, and one to keep her heart beating.

The second was an extremely new, extremely experimental drug that could be used to manage her condition. But the chance of her being chosen for the exceedingly competitive trial was small. Her young mother, already overwhelmed, had no idea how to increase her daughter's chances.

Until, that was, a strange and unexpected opportunity had presented itself.

I followed her. She was full of fear and hope, a series of conflicting emotions. She was terrified of failing, so very afraid that her daughter would be without a mother. Her mind was filled with thoughts of her daughter calling for her and not understanding why mother was not coming. And yet, in the back of her mind was a beautiful fantasy, in which she walked out of here a winner and used her newfound fame to finally obtain the much-desired treatment for her child.

A phantom ache gnawed at my chest as I watched her.

A scream snapped me out of my trance. I had too much at stake to let myself become drawn in by a single contestant. I told myself I would check back on her and followed the sound of the scream.

In the far corner of the city, the pink-haired celebrity was alongside one of the other contestants—a fan who had fawned over her upon arrival. I directed several cameras to them. The actions of a contestant with some degree of fame, no matter how minute, enhanced the interest of the audience. If she weren't running for her life, this woman would probably be thrilled to know how large her audience was at the moment.

It's not about the game. It's about the players.

A predator growled around the corner. Pink Hair screamed again and slashed unproductively with the short knife she manifested. Her companion leapt in, eager to show off his skills and protect her. But his own manifestation—a clunky firearm with a long barrel—only succeeded in a misfire.

I reached out to him. Despite the danger before him, he was euphoric. Pink Hair's hands were on him, clinging to him for dear life. He was young, with a head full of heroic fantasy, dreaming that not only was he going to be the hero of this story, but he was going to walk out of this with Pink Hair on his arm, his perfect damsel in distress.

He fired, this time successfully, but missed. He rallied himself inside and recovered quickly, firing again. This time his shot finally found the target, buying himself and Pink Hair a moment to escape. He took her hand and dragged her around the nearest corner, where they paused to catch their breath. She leaned against him and he was intensely aware of the heat radiating from her soft hands and firm torso. I felt him flip back and forth between foolhardy bravado and his base, physical desires. He was reasonably skilled, and more than a little handsome by the standards of his people. Though unpolished, his boyish nature had potential to attract the support of the people.

And her.

I switched my focus to Pink Hair. She had a name given to

her at birth, but what she used as part of her media persona was a fanciful word that translated to Gala. I had chosen her due to her small corner of fame, but her skill in the arena had been subpar so far. She hadn't shown herself to be more than a pretty face, and at the first opportunity she had, she fled to the side of someone else to seek protection. Charming as she might be, she would never serve as a contestant of interest if she could not stand alone.

I reached into her.

She was as I expected. Under her fear lingered an obsession with her own appearance in the moment. She feared looking poorly just a little more than dying, and as I peeled back her memories and emotions layer by layer, I found little of value. That was, until I struck darkness.

It was buried under smiling faces, colorful hair, and beautifully posed photos, beneath her ambition and drive and desire to stand out. I had a feeling it was hidden from even herself most of the time. Lying to oneself about oneself was the talent of every seed race, and Harmonians were no different.

Gala saw those who worshipped her as beneath her.

On a planet of over ten billion, Gala's fans numbered just less than a hundred thousand. And yet, that comparatively small number was enough to feed her ego into sprouting the smallest black bud. I reached in, deeper and deeper.

Her fans were only fodder. Stepping stones to something bigger. She sought after them with desperation, growing the count at any cost. They weren't people. They were numbers.

Seeds to be sowed and reaped.

I watched her cling to her current protector. That black bud inside her bloomed a little at every sign of danger, pulsating, threatening to burst. A dark thought that she refused to acknowledge even to herself.

Underneath all the layers of makeup and smiles, she believed he should die for her.

Die for her life.

Die for her beauty.

Die for her safety.

Die so she could go on to entertain the masses.

A tingle coursed through me, one that was different from the one emitted by the implant in my neck. It was a tingle of excitement at having found a contestant who embraced the way of the gods before she even knew they existed. She would be an excellent addition to the first batch of survivors.

Unless . . .

I shivered at the thought that struck me.

There were other ways to elevate a good story to a great story. Whether she ultimately became the champion or not, Gala's story could start off with a bang.

Could I really do this?

Gala and her admirer had moved on. He took down another target as they made their way through the stage. The number of remaining contestants was dwindling.

I tensed my body. My teeth ground against each other.

The eyes of Harmony were on the contestants, but the eyes just outside its orbit were on me. With every moment that passed, more orbs gathered, waiting, watching. They needed to see that this game was unlike anything they'd ever seen before. Unlike anything the *gods* had ever seen before.

I tightened my fingers into fists.

For the sake of me and mine.

"Axi."

"Yes, arena master?"

"How many contestants are left?"

"Last count is forty-six." A pause. "Forty-five."

I focused on Gala and her companion. "Set a parameter around these two," I said.

"Complete."

"Kill the rest."

Those words came out of my mouth, but in a voice I didn't recognize. My knees trembled the moment they were spoken, but it was already done. I pushed all hints of hesitation out of my mind.

A single predator, a puppet on my strings, moved toward Gala and her companion. They heard it coming—I wanted them to. He turned, raising his weapon.

The predator charged.

The man cursed and tried to take aim.

Nothing holds more intrigue than relationships.

Pink Hair let out a small shriek and turned to run. Her foot tangled in his and for a brief moment it seemed he might fall.

Drama is what will win this for me.

I reached out, grabbed hold of his consciousness, and flung his body to the side before he could steady himself. He barely had time to let out a surprised cry before the predator was on him. She ran from the gruesome scene without looking back.

THE ENTIRE PLANET—PLUS hundreds of orbs filled with arena masters and former champions—watched, hearts in their throats, for the first round on Harmony to conclude.

One by one the Harmonians fell to the predators. They fought valiantly, and their manifestation skills, for a group of first timers, were truly impressive. I foresaw they would be excellent contenders, but the first round needed to be played out carefully. Too many survivors would lead the planet to relax and think they had an easy win. No survivors might lead to a loss of hope that would result in public panic and excess social unrest, which would distract from the game itself.

In this case, there would only be one—the perfect one.

The clock ran out.

The city dissipated.

The last survivor knelt, shaking, among the bodies of her fellow contestants. Sweating, weeping, she stood. Blood dripped from her pink mane where she had fallen and hit her head during her escape. She gagged at the sight of the bodies and I sent the camera to her despondent face. The entirety of Harmony could see her now, and I anticipated that the gods would more than enjoy the media frenzy that would soon follow.

It didn't matter how it had happened because all that counted was what the carefully placed cameras had caught. At this moment, it looked an awful lot like a minor celebrity with garish hair had pushed a fan risking his life to protect her into the way of harm, then run away as he died screaming.

Harmony had its first winner—one who had survived at the price of another's life. I allowed myself to feel a hint of pride at the dramatic conclusion of the first round.

Until my eyes landed on the young mother, who had died curled into herself on the ground, the way I had when the swarm fell on me through the leaves of the arena's fake forest.

CHAPTER 25

I STOOD AT THE RAILING IN THE COMPUTING ROOM WATCHING NIX go about his work and considered, not for the first time, leaping over the edge to strike my head on the hard ground below.

But I couldn't do that. Not anymore. I was no longer a lost child whose life was worth little to nothing. The gamble I had taken was far too great, and however much I wanted to, I could no longer selfishly think about taking my own life.

Funny, how I had once dreaded the thought that my life hinged on the whim of someone else and a turn of their wrist, and now I'd taken a life just like mine in that exact manner.

I had never learned her name. Knowing it might crush my already wavering resolve.

But irony never failed. Her death brought great attention and scrutiny to her life. The public was quickly made aware of her fragile, newly motherless child. Support poured in from all directions and the powers in charge acted quickly. She was enrolled in the drug trial program and early tests revealed great promise. A major hospital figurehead spoke at a press conference, extending his well wishes to her and offering high hopes that she could be released from the hospital before her next birthday. Given the Harmonians' obsession with facts and research, I knew he was far more likely to be right than wrong.

I watched this child on the screens in the heart, smiling and being held by her extended family. She was weak, but now she had a chance to grow up strong, one that wouldn't have been presented to her had her mother not taken a chance.

I steeled myself.

One might argue that all of this was fruitless. After all, I had put her entire planet in a precarious position as far as its continued existence was concerned. But this couldn't be further from the truth.

Harmony will win.

I would see to it. The best stories ended with a winner. If nothing else, I would see to it for the sake of this child that her world survived. The risks her mother took wouldn't be in vain. None of the deaths would be. They were all part of a greater plan. *My* plan.

There was freedom and exhilaration in resolve.

WHEN THE ORB WENT SILENT, Harmony lost its mind.

Rather than continue the games day after day, I directed my team to cease all outside communications and video campaigns for ten day cycles. Then, fully suited, I ventured out to the planet's surface once more.

The peaceful atmosphere surrounding the Institute of Higher Learning was all but gone. Students lounging around the garden and researchers casually engaging in discussions were replaced with clusters of people huddled together, talking and gesturing rapidly. A buzz of conversation covered the grounds and I couldn't turn my head without hearing something about the game. Distinguishing all the different conversations through the translations was difficult, but I was able to make out enough to know that they had latched onto exactly what I hoped they would.

A few people discussed the possibility of doomsday,

wondering whether their course of life was worth carrying on if the world was to end soon.

A pair of males whispered about certain supplies and goods that could be bought and sold for greater profit under the right circumstances, just in case the world didn't end.

I heard no speculation of conspiracy, nor anyone casting doubt on what they'd seen. They'd heard the claims and seen the proof, and they'd embraced the reality of the situation quicker than I'd seen any other seed race do. H'otto's rhetoric about the gods, I was sure, wouldn't have worked nearly as well.

But most importantly, the name on everyone's lips was the one I had let survive.

Gala had carved out a small slice of fame in Harmony's information network taking photos of herself dressed in the latest fashion trends. She had hoped to be famous, but the fame that befell her was undoubtedly different from what she had imagined. Within a day of stepping out of the orb, there were three attempts on her life.

Gala went into hiding while the planet went into overdrive talking about her. She was being praised as the symbol of hope for Harmony in one house and being burned in effigy in the next street over. Families and friends split apart due to differences in their opinions of Gala. Rallies were being held calling for her execution, followed by demonstrations to recognize her achievement in having saved the planet from destruction. I took these all in and knew that the gods would soon consume them with delight.

A cheer erupted from the far side of the campus, startling me. I raised my head toward the commotion and spotted a small but growing crowd gathered at the foot of the main building. Someone stood atop a short wall surrounding a large flower bed and loudly addressed the group. As I drew near, I spotted the familiar red skin and black mane.

"The government has failed us," I heard him say as I

approached. Rather than the even, smooth tone of an educator he had struck at the lecture, he was speaking with great passion, gesturing broadly and fiercely. Slipping into the crowd, I watched him with interest.

"They have taken no action on the invaders, nor have they given any answers on what plans they intend to make. In every nation, every state, they have chosen to sit back and watch while we live in fear for our way of life."

True, I thought. Though there was no action that the governments could reasonably take. They were out of their depth, unfamiliar with the enemy, and had no precedent to look to. As theirs was a society that relied on facts, they could not communicate with the population when they had no facts to give.

But that didn't matter.

"New leadership is in order," the man continued. I scanned the crowd to see more and more entranced faces looking up at him. He commanded their attention with absolute confidence as he listed out the faults of the current government and demanded that the people speak up and rise up for change and action.

And yet, I noticed, his little speech, charming as it was, had no substance at all. He stated obvious problems, offered no solutions, and called for action without saying once what those "actions" ought to be. He was riling up the crowd, making them cheer and jeer and shout. For what? They didn't know, and he didn't know either.

But I had a feeling he didn't care. As I observed this man move the masses with his words, I couldn't help but notice that he looked completely different compared to the last time I had seen him, behind a podium reading from a screen. Though he was articulate and charming in both scenarios, today he looked alive.

"The enemy is not Gala."

I pursed my lips.

"She is a victim, like the rest of us."

His tone had changed to one of sadness. It was a rather quick switch, and I watched his entire being—expression, body language, tone—suddenly and expertly shift from the very image of a rebel leader to a broken man in mourning.

"The enemy is the orb, and our so-called leaders who failed us. They, not Gala, are the ones who have made my brother's death a true tragedy."

THE GODS WERE PLEASED.

In addition to my visit to the planet, I took in hours and hours of recordings prior to worship. Gossip media, newsreels, speculations and discussions. The gods relished them.

H'otto ran the games quickly and efficiently, but I had come to realize that this was not what the gods wanted.

They reached the end of my recent memories. I felt their desire for more.

No more.

Clear disappointment.

Patience.

Curiosity. I knew they would not balk at the idea of waiting. After all, they'd waited for millions of races to mature one at a time, all for the purpose of good entertainment.

There will be more.

I needed time. More importantly, Harmony needed time. Following the rounds one after another created a faster game and kept the planet on its toes, but given a little time, the people became restless. They needed time to stew, to talk, to turn on each other, to form factions and cause chaos.

There is more to the game than the game itself.

More curiosity.

The world and its people are far more entertaining.

I felt a pause. Then, I saw my own memories, along with the hundreds of recordings I'd consumed, rewind before me.

The gods searched through my memories. The millions of images crossing my sight at light speed made me dizzy until they suddenly froze on one. I couldn't say I was surprised.

"... the value of being Harmonians hold each other in high regard ... my brother's life is worth no more than any other's, and his sacrifice allowed another to live ..."

You like this one.

Agreement. I felt a stir—excitement, perhaps mine, perhaps theirs.

He appears competent.

Agreement again. The flutter of excitement grew, pounding a steady beat like a heart. Nothing got past the gods—they had noticed my attention to him, and through that dubbed him to be "interesting."

I'll see what I can do.

His name translated to Able.

Something about that name intrigued me, as if his family had high expectations of his life in general. Names with meaning were common for most races, and the most common themes were usually along the lines of beauty, strength, intelligence, and grace. But "Able" was a name that stood out. It was strangely unspecific, and yet somehow spoke volumes.

A mere ten days had passed since the first round had ended, and Able had already gone from a humble educator, virtually unknown, to one of the most well-recognized voices on Harmony. He loudly and proudly called out the incompetencies of the planet's leadership, urged forgiveness for Gala with emotive speeches, and moved millions as he spoke softly and sadly of his younger brother. He was physically fit, articulate, and extremely intelligent. The more I delved into his background, the more aptly named he seemed. He was well educated, well traveled, well spoken, and well liked. His successes in life were many and his failures were few. Able, he certainly was.

But to be noticed by the gods took a little something more. As I watched this man speak passionately to his people, I felt a need to squint, almost like trying to see through murky waters to something underneath. Aside from his unique position in this turn of events, there was something else about Able that lurked beneath the surface—a glint that I wouldn't have recognized had I not spent a lifetime's worth of years observing so many worlds and races. I heard it in the slight quiver of his voice and saw it in the slight upward twitch of his mouth every time he mentioned the "tragedy" of the first game.

Under his supposed rage and sorrow, there in the middle of all the chaos and drama, Able was happy.

CHAPTER 26

I brought Able into the arena first on purpose. He had not volunteered for the games, so his selection should be a total surprise. I wanted to see his reaction to this sudden change in fortune. He was alone for fewer than ten seconds before the others began to teleport in, but those few precious seconds told me volumes.

I had expected shock, perhaps a little fear—he had to be aware after the first game that stepping into the arena could lead to death. As the cameras zoomed in on him after his teleportation was complete, the world saw terror and apprehension on his face.

I, however, saw the half second of calculated calm that came before.

Now that he was within the arena, I could read him much more clearly. Upon arrival, he immediately sized up the arena, examining the space all around him. Then, as the other contestants began to appear, he turned his palm and manifested a simple coin. He weighed the coin in his hand before allowing it to vanish. Next, he pushed two of his fingers together, willed them to merge into one, then separated them again, never once looking away from the arena floor or dropping his wary mask.

This was all done before the next contestant gained their footing.

Probing his mind, I felt a strange indecision. Able was watching as the next contestant was brought in, holding his face neutral and emotions in check. The degree of control he exhibited was astounding given the situation. I found no fear at all, despite the fact that he had just arrived in the exact situation where his own brother and ninety-eight others had lost their lives. Instead, there was something else there.

While Gala hid her darkness under layers of color and denial, Able wore his like a treasured pendant, close to his heart.

The next contestant was an older male. Able's mind shifted and clicked. A decision was made. His expression changed into one of worry and concern. He approached the newcomer and offered a sincere show of friendship. They embraced briefly and exchanged encouragement. I heard shaky courage in his voice, and at the same time felt the calculation in his mind as he checked exactly how much his voice and hands ought to quiver. I watched with fascination as the next contestant appeared. This one was a trembling young woman. Able sized her up quickly and I sensed him shift again, this time taking on a strong, more authoritative voice, one that immediately reassured her and made her feel protected.

And he shifted again with the next, and the next. He introduced himself to every contestant, but never forcefully. He read the body language and posture of each individual and only brought up his brother—always shyly and with unmistakable but subtle sadness—when prompted by another. Every interaction elicited kindness and sympathy and was very, very calculated. Able was in control, absolutely and completely.

"Axi," I said, "bring in Gala last."

I heard no response, but Axi was reliable. Sure enough, after the ninety-ninth contestant completed teleportation, there was a slight pause, just long enough for the contestants to look each other over and wonder, before the final one was brought in.

Every eye was on Gala as she appeared inside the arena. For the first time since his arrival, I saw a true change in Able. But it was not anger at the one responsible for his brother's death, nor sorrow at his loss. It was a stirring in his body, perhaps excitement for what was about to come. The tension was palpable as all other contestants in the arena looked from him to her, waiting to see what he would do to this woman who could be regarded as his brother's murderer.

He took a decisive step toward her. She flinched, almost shrinking within herself. There were audible gasps as he reached out to her as if to grab her, then looks of shock as he wrapped her in a tight hug. Through the arena, I felt her surprise, then the wave of emotion that came after. Sadness, remorse, apprehension, and most of all, relief.

"I know it hasn't been easy for you," I heard him say to her, just loud enough for the people in their immediate vicinity to hear. Though his voice shook, as if just on the edge of tears, there was no such turmoil of emotions in him. Every word he said, every action he took, served a purpose. "We will get through this together."

Then, releasing her but leaving one arm around her shoulders, he turned to the others. Here his voice changed again, this time to a tone of strength and authority.

"They will not break us," he said firmly. "One life does not compare to the survival of our world. We must proceed together, combine our strength, and show these invaders that they will *not* break Harmony!"

Thunderous cheers erupted through the arena. I smiled. Within minutes of his arrival, Able had set himself as the hero within the eyes of the people.

The gods would enjoy his time in the arena like no other.

. . .

THE SECOND GAME was a rather different sort from the first.

The Harmonians made their way through a field filled with hills and caves, protecting themselves and attacking the creatures that came at them. Their targets varied in size, shape, and speed, but all shared one common aspect—the jewel atop their heads. Those who took down a target must also collect the jewel, and a minimum of ten jewels was required to pass the round.

Designing the games, I'd found, required a certain finesse of balance. Most cultures tended to avert their gaze from certain sensitive matters such as sexual assault, the demise of children, and extreme gore and violence. It wasn't unusual for the people of the planets we had previously landed on to turn a blind eye to the broadcasts or avoid discussing them, as my distaste for dead children was shared by most. Games that emphasized fair competition—and a good bit of fun—instead of senseless suffering attracted far more attention. My games, simple, exciting, and filled with competent players, were watched closely by every eye on Harmony.

I took note of the groups that had formed. Able held sway over more than half of the contestants. He directed them like a general in battle, quick on his feet and efficient in his actions. More than a few within his group found him charming and admirable and were already in the backs of their minds ready to lay down their lives for him if he so requested. On every planet, there existed those who desired to follow.

A few of the contestants did not quite buy into his act and kept their distance. They were fewer in number, but shrewd and competent. Among these were also the ones who had not fully decided if they forgave Gala for her apparent selfishness in the first round.

Able led his group through the field. I watched him take down the targets left and right, but the jewels he collected did not end up in his pockets. Instead, he divided them among his group, ensuring anyone who was not able to earn their own received at least a few. Altruism at its finest, though I felt the calculations that ticked off in his head with every generous act. He paid special attention to Gala, whom he kept close to him. She had not yet successfully taken down a single target, but he made sure she got a share of the jewels.

Forty-six Harmonians survived the round. Among the survivors were Able and Gala. At the end of the game, almost all of the remaining contestants had joined up with Able.

But, I noted, Able himself did not possess enough jewels to pass the round.

"Well, well, well," Two said to the remaining contestants. The Harmonians, battered and exhausted, eyed their robotic host with disdain. *"It seems we have quite a group, do we not?"*

Their seething anger filled the arena. The more I provoked them, the stronger their emotions, and the more I had to feed to the gods in prayer. Two sauntered amongst them, leaning far too close for their comfort and flicking hairs and shoulders with their long metal fingers.

"But do you all have enough to pass the round? That's the real question."

Here Two took several steps away and turned to face the group. They stuck out one hand and pointed at Gala, then curled and uncurled their finger several times. Gala stepped forward, looking like she felt the weight of the eyes on her with every step.

"Beautiful little lady. Harmony's first winner," Two purred, then reached out and touched her chin. Her mouth quivered. *"Did you collect enough stones for me?"*

Gala reached out shakily and dropped a handful of jewels into Two's hand. She had not collected most of them on her own, but the rules did not state whether sharing was allowed. She feared being caught doing something wrong when her reputation was already on shaky ground. Two took her jewels, disintegrated them, and gestured for her to step aside. She let out a breath of relief.

They pointed to another person, an older male standing just behind Gala. He stepped forward and handed over his jewels—eight, not enough. Two took his jewels, rolled them around in their hand, and disintegrated them.

"*Well,*" they said, "*that's unfortunate,*" then raised their hand, one finger pointed at the old man's head. "*Bang.*"

His head popped like a soap bubble. Gala screamed as his blood splashed all over her, staining her mane. Able quickly pulled her away from the collapsing body. Gasps and shocked screams ran through the remaining contestants. Two's smiling holographic face turned to them.

"*Oh, don't look so surprised. You already knew that failing to collect enough stones means you don't pass the round. You didn't think you would get to go home, did you?*" The smile broadened as a red circle appeared in the dome. The contestants looked up, panicked. "*You have until time runs out to decide who gets the stones. Figure out if you want to be generous and let someone else live, or take the stones for yourself. Go.*"

The commotion that followed rivaled the game itself. From the balcony I spotted tearful exchanges as a few people who had barely scraped through handed their stones over to more promising contestants. A fight broke out between two males who both believed they had the right to be the survivor. Gala stood awkwardly to one side, the only one absolved of this dilemma. I'd had Two single her out on purpose, knowing this would add to the controversy around her.

Able was being the gallant gentleman I expected him to be. I watched him give the five jewels in his hand to a young female, the same one he'd greeted upon her entry to the arena shortly after him. He was touching her affectionately, like a father would, and telling her she was going to be alright. She sobbed so hard her entire body shook. The red circle above counted down.

Three . . . two . . . one . . .

Then, at the last possible moment, the girl suddenly

grabbed Able's hands and shoved all of her jewels into his palms. I saw the surprise on his face, though I did not feel it in his mind. He had only a moment before her head exploded in a splatter of blood and bone, along with twelve others. Able fell to his knees, jewels falling from his hands, as if shaken to the core. The others comforted him, telling him that she had done the right thing—he needed to be around to protect and lead others. I watched him break down as he mourned her and told others they must remember her name.

But what I felt from him, undeniably, was mild relief. He had picked the correct person to give his final grand gesture to, one who would feel too guilty to let him die.

It was quite a gamble, I mused. The girl could easily have accepted his offer and decided to live. His generosity had nearly led him to death, but in the end it had paid off. I reached out to him, delving further, searching for remnants of fear and apprehension from having taken such a large risk.

I found nothing. Despite what he had just gone through, Able was as calm inside as the Crystal Lake of Aukron.

THE IMAGE that graced every screen on Harmony for the ten days that followed the second game was one of hope, unity, and forgiveness—Able embracing Gala, who wore a shocked, teary look on her delicate face. It was the perfect picture, a spontaneous and unexpected moment of emotion from them both that tied the people of Harmony together in one fell swoop.

And yet, it had not been spontaneous at all. Looking at this picture before me, I could remember everything that had gone into that moment on Able's part. The calculated movements, the anticipation of the others' reaction, the turn of his mouth and eyes just right to sculpt that careful display of emotion.

Able was playing a bigger game than just the survival of his planet.

. . .

I WATCHED him survive a second game, then a third, always playing the kind leader, always protecting Gala. Under his guidance, she grew more confident and bold, and whenever she did well, she looked to him with light in her eyes and he beamed back with pride.

Outside of the arena, he was a darling of the media through and through. His meteoric rise to fame was unparalleled. For a population that relied heavily on facts and logic, the people of Harmony were very eager to convince themselves that he and Gala were linked in a romance for the ages based on their inter-action within the orb, which spoke volumes to Able's acting skills whenever a camera was pointed at him. If he became the champion of Harmony, he would likely be set for life, making rounds around the globe, banking on his legacy as a hero.

And yet, I wondered if this was what he was truly after. More than once, I caught him scanning the arena walls, looking past the other contestants, past the game, even past Two, as if searching for something on the flawless white walls. When his gaze raked over the balcony where One and I stood, I could almost believe that he could see me.

"AXI," I said as Able cut his way through a maze of toxic plants, his loyal team at his heels. "I need a chameleon suit."

CHAPTER 27

Standing on the arena floor amidst other contestants was nothing short of surreal. I had never once imagined that I might stand in the middle of a game once more. Proximity made connecting with the contestants much easier. I navigated their ripples of emotions like wading through a gentle current. Fear, panic, worry, paranoia . . .

Calm.

I followed that trace of calm and it led, as expected, to Able. He looked up as I approached him and for a split second I saw the calculations in his eyes as he sized me up and decided on the appropriate response. Once he took in my small stature and the shy, timid eyes I had perfected through watching clips of the previous rounds, his face softened into that warm, fatherly expression.

"No need to be afraid," he said, smiling encouragingly. At his words, several other older contestants came up to me offering kind words. I said nothing. Instead, I kept my head down, feigning fear and apprehension.

"Well, well, well."

The group parted immediately, making way for Two. After they took out the old man in cold blood, there was next to no desire to rebel left among the Harmonians. Logic dictated that going against the robot was not a fight worth attempting.

"I hope you're all ready for something"—they spotted me in the group and gave a slight pause, but recovered almost immediately—*"extra exciting today."*

Gala stuck to Able's side, and he reached out and squeezed her hand gently. Gallant, as always. As Two laid out the rules of the game, I zoned in on Able. He was listening intently, focused, planning. His concentration was impressive. He turned slightly in my direction and I looked away, keeping my face passive and meek.

Then, the arena floor dropped out from under us.

I already knew the rules of this game—it was, after all, my design. But I gave a few panicked flails for good measure as my body struck water and sank down. The seas of Harmony were dark and dense. Moving through them proved difficult with the chameleon suit on. I manifested an air bubble around my head and gained my bearings before looking for the others.

Several contestants struggled. Able had already made his way to one of them and was pushing them upward out of the water. Others followed his example. Without him around, would they feel so generous? I doubted it.

I started down toward the large, shadowy structure in the depths below. The sunken ship was modeled after a Harmonian military freighter. On the outside, several entrances were lit with white lights. The contestants who had a good grasp of manifestation were already making their way inside. I maneuvered myself underneath one of its enormous fins and waited.

After a while, the contestants who had initially struggled began to make their way under the water. I kept my eyes on Able. When he selected his point of entry, I stealthily propelled myself toward him.

He spotted me. I gave him my best lost baby animal expression and he waved me over. I joined his group as we ventured together into the massive ship.

The innard of the ship was silent and dark like a tomb. Able clutched my hand and I saw him gesture toward Gala, who swam ahead and lit a light dangling from a new growth on her head, similar to certain kinds of deep sea fish common to watery planets. She moved on ahead, leading the group. I marveled at how Able had instilled this confidence in her.

Suddenly, the light went out. The waters around us bubbled with movement and I felt the panic of the others at suddenly being plunged into darkness. I grasped at Able frantically, feigning panic myself.

Someone else lit a light and I dodged just in time to avoid the sharp-toothed fish that came at me, slicing through the water like a knife with its paper-thin body and slick silvery scales. There was blood in the water. Someone had been cut already. Unable to make himself heard underwater, Able grabbed the nearest person, shook them, and gestured toward the deeper parts of the ship. They nodded and grabbed the next person while fending off the fish, and the message was passed on. Able's hand wrapped around my arm and he propelled both of us through the water, deeper and deeper into the ship.

The others followed. Every now and then, Able left my side and went back to his group, helping guard them from behind by condensing the water into a near-solid state to slow down the fish in their pursuit. I was not the least bit surprised that he had already learned how to manipulate the environment of the arena. As he returned to escort me once more, I searched him again for fear, panic, and urge to survive. And again found nothing.

Suddenly, the tunnel collapsed. I spun around in genuine surprise but could see no one behind us. I wondered if this was One's doing, as I had not designed any part of the ship to spontaneously collapse. Able turned also, his face hidden in the dark water. He looked toward the collapsed tunnel, then tightened his grasp on my arm and pulled me forward.

The long tunnel ended within the center of the ship at a raised platform inside the only compartment with breathable air. Able pushed me onto the platform. In the center was a basket of tokens—proof of having completed the challenge. I broke the air bubble around my face and heard Able climb up behind me, shuffling to remove the diving mask on his face. I allowed myself a breather to shake off the water, and he was on me.

For a split second as his arm slipped around my neck, I thought he was giving me a hug out of relief. Then he tightened and squeezed and I knew something was off. And yet once again, his mind betrayed no emotions at all.

"Who are you?" he whispered in my ear.

I did not fear him, but for a moment I was too shocked to respond. His arm tightened around my neck.

"Don't lie," he said flatly, his warm breath puffing against my ear. "I remember you from the Institute, and you were there again when I spoke in the courtyard. You change your skin and hair, but your face is the same. I saw that robot notice you, too." His other hand slid down the side of my body, searching for something out of place. Could he feel the layers of the chameleon suit over my skin? "And did you think I didn't see you swim? Funny how you can move through the water like that, and then as soon as I'm around, you're practically lame." He gestured around us. "And the cameras—you don't like them in your face, do you? That's why they're not here."

I was truly impressed. He had learned how to manipulate the water by watching me propel myself around the ship. And . . .

"The tunnel," I said, whispering with his arm choking me. I could remove him any time I wanted, but I wanted to see his intention first.

"I collapsed it. Pulled it in with the water while I was trying to stop the fish."

"Interesting."

"I didn't sign up for this game."

"I know."

"Someone wanted me here."

"Yes, they did."

His mouth brushed against my face. I could hear his breathing speed up just a little. "You make a terrible Harmonian."

"Do I?"

"Even in the darkest tunnel, you never opened your middle eye. I'll ask you again—*who* are you?"

I lifted one hand and snapped my fingers, and finally felt a hint of surprise from Able as gravity suddenly shifted for him. He dropped to his knees heavily and caught himself with his hands. But when he lifted his face to me, there was no malice or fear. Instead, I saw a hint of something else, a combination of curiosity, excitement, and arousal. I grabbed one of the tokens out of the basket and tossed it on the ground in front of him.

"Keep winning; you might find out," I said, and stepped on his fingers as I walked past him.

"Did you accomplish what you hoped for?" One asked.

"I did," I said simply, trying to keep my voice even and calm. My heart pounded. I stepped next to her on the balcony, the chameleon suit still clinging uncomfortably to me.

"I have to hand it to you. I've never seen or heard of an arena master stepping into the games the way you did."

"There's more than one way to play this game," I told her. Beneath us, the waters of the arena receded. The sunken ship crumbled into building blocks. The remaining twenty or so contestants regarded each other, relieved to be alive.

Save for one.

Able's eyes scanned the arena walls, the token clutched tightly in one hand. Gala went to him. She had managed to complete the stage thanks to the confidence he'd instilled in her and a little help One had lent her at my behest. For a brief moment, when she touched his arm, he turned to her with a blank look, as if unsure what to make of her. Then he quickly snapped back to his senses and gave her a hug.

But for the first time, his performance slipped. The world could reason it away as exhaustion or momentary confusion, but I saw it. His eyes were not on her, nor closed in the pretend bliss he wanted the world to see whenever she was in his arms. Even hugging her, he kept searching the arena, looking for me. One of his hands roamed around the base of her scalp and, reaching out to him through the arena, I detected an annoyance, a sense of impatience, a *desire* to snap her neck just to have her out of his way.

"If you don't mind me asking," One said beside me, "what's your interest in that one?"

"He's not playing the game," I said, watching Able turn on his diplomatic leader persona as others gathered around him. "He's playing *me*."

CHAPTER 28

His audience had grown since I had last watched him speak.

The stadium was surrounded by security personnel. Every person who entered was searched from head to toe, though I couldn't imagine anyone would see value in committing violence against the man saving their world. To avoid the frisking, I teleported directly into the stadium, into a small enclosed corridor hidden from security cameras, and melded seamlessly into the audience.

They chanted his name.

They buzzed about his looks and charm and supposed unexpected romance.

They awaited him with stars in their eyes, idolizing and worshipping him, holding pictures of him as if they were the greatest treasures to ever grace the surface of Harmony. It was probably the closest most Harmonians had ever come to a religious experience.

Only a handful of days ago, he had been a simple educator standing before a bored audience trying to teach them about media and culture. Now he was making use of everything he knew, on top of the fame the games provided him, to hype himself into the biggest celebrity the planet had ever known.

The crowd let out a deafening cheer as Able appeared on stage. He was dressed to the nines, his mane sleek and shiny. Gala followed him, meek but beaming. Her pink mane had been colored a modest brown and her formerly trendy fashion had been replaced with regal robes and expensive but tasteful jewelry. This was not the fame she had initially sought, but I had a feeling she was perfectly glad to trade one type of celebrity for another. Able leaned down and nuzzled her cheek —a deliberate display of affection for the audience.

It worked. I heard multiple people around me sigh with fondness at their closeness.

Then, he took the stage.

"People of Harmony," he started. "Thank you for—"

His eyes landed on me. I had changed the color of my mane, but I knew he would recognize me. I could almost see him lose his grasp on his thoughts, but he recovered in the space of a blink.

"—gracing me with your presence. We are here today to memorialize those lost in the cruel games within the orb. But more importantly, we must remember the games are not yet over . . ."

Every civilization had its own titles for its designated leaders. King, emperor, prime minister, president, etc. Harmony as a whole was governed by a council of leaders from around the globe, each of whom was selected through democratic election. In order to be considered for election, however, a candidate had to first prove their competencies in a number of areas, including academics, physical health, social graces, and experience in governance.

Or, in rare cases, a candidate could be elected based on sheer popularity. An exceedingly rare and difficult feat, but documented multiple times in the meticulous historic records of Harmony.

"Will you join me in looking forward to the future?"

I scanned the crowd. Every pair of eyes was entranced.

"Time will not stop, nor will progress. This is just a stumble in the long and proud history of Harmony."

Was that what he was angling for? The next time he spoke, it might be on the steps of Prosper's gleaming capitol.

"We must embrace tomorrow, next year, and all that follows. This is not a time for fear, but one for change."

Change in leadership? In government policy? In social culture? I could tell it didn't matter. Whatever that change was, it was going to be carried out by him, with the lovely and beaming Gala at his side, the best and unending evidence of his kindness and heroism.

I waited in the crowd for him to finish his speech, musing inwardly that unlike the very first time I heard him speak, when he had lectured expertly on a practical subject to a disinterested audience, he now gave a glitzy speech with no substance and captured the undivided attention of tens of thousands, and probably a hundredfold that, all viewing on digital screens. Amazing that even on a planet that worshipped fact and logic, one extraordinary event plus a silver tongue could turn reason and common sense on its head.

When the speech wrapped up, security personnel stepped forward and parted the crowd. Able, with Gala close behind, made his way through the forest of bodies, shaking hands and hugging his fans. I made my way to the front of the crowd and without a pause he grabbed me and gave me a quick hug. I heard his voice in my ear, rapidly whispering a string of incoherent numbers and words, and then he was gone, without a look back at me.

"Did you get that, Axi?" I said as I retreated from the loudest part of the crowd.

"Yes."

"What did he say?"

"It appears to be a physical address."

. . .

HE LIVED ALONE, just as I expected. But I could see through the creature comforts of his home. His simple, comfortable furniture told the story of a prudent, reserved man who valued simple things. Two entire walls were lined with academic texts and I had no doubt that he had read every last one at least once and could probably talk at length about any number of topics in casual conversation. Art pieces depicting mountains and trees hung from the walls—images of nature appeared to be a common preference for interior decorating across the galaxy, especially in more advanced civilizations where people rarely ventured outside of their concrete jungles. I was examining a painting of a large yellow flower when he walked in. He didn't look the least bit surprised that I was already inside his house.

"So," I said. "I'm here."

He was in front of me in two steps and actually managed to catch me off guard, and before I could react his mouth was on mine. His arms slipped around me and pulled me in against him. Certain areas of the chameleon suit contracted and pulled in reaction to his close proximity, struggling to simulate the proper sensation of skin and friction. I mentally thanked the gods that Able was of a similar stature to the average Maedan rather than of a more difficult physiology like Mod.

He kissed me long and deep, and though it had been a very long time since I'd been kissed, I couldn't help but admit that he was excellent at the act of it. Far from the awkward, sloppy kisses and meaty gropes of my Maedan husband, Able played my body and tongue like a musical instrument. As his fingers traveled up and down my skin, I thought back to one of the very first things One had said to me—*we all eat with one end of our body and mate with the other*.

"Do you kiss her that way?" I teased as he finally pulled back.

He smirked and kissed me again. "This isn't about her," he whispered, and scooped me into his arms. I let him carry me into his bedroom and for a moment allowed myself to enjoy his touch.

Able was strong and firm. As he laid me down I slid my fingers over his sinewy muscles. He made a deep sound in his throat, like something between growl and purr, a biological sign of arousal in his race. I had no doubt that he would be a most competent and efficient lover.

"You excite me," he whispered into my ear. I chuckled.

"Is that so?" I whispered back, allowing him to caress my neck and torso. "What do you know about me?"

"Nothing," he replied, a hungry look in his eyes. "That's what makes it exciting."

"That's what you want, isn't it?" I pulled him in, his eyes a finger's length from mine. "Excitement."

"Oh yes," he replied breathlessly. His body language read desire and need. "You make me lose control."

"Do I?"

He kissed me again, a long, desperate kiss that lingered and lingered. I allowed myself to savor it. Then, when he pulled away, I smiled.

"Good try."

The lust and desire disappeared from his face. It was rather interesting to watch, almost like a machine retracting its tools and arms. He sat up and rolled off me. I would be lying if I said I didn't miss the feel of his skin just a little.

"What gave it away?" he asked, the heat from just moments ago already evaporating.

"Nothing," I said. Even lacking the connection of the arena, I'd become accustomed to reading Able. At this moment, he was probably gathering up his disappointment, letting it pass, and already moving on to plan the next step. "I'm just a little harder to fool than most."

I gave him a second to think out his next move. Every race had their own name for a universal game of strategy. For Able,

I'd come to realize, every day and every encounter was just another round of chess, and that was how he liked it.

"DRINK?" he said after we made our way to the main living area of his home.

"No, thank you." I also had no interest in the sour liquors of this planet. "You know, it's funny. Every civilization I've encountered has its own way of achieving inebriation."

"Everyone drinks, eh?"

"Liquid is the preferred method, yes."

Able poured himself a drink and walked to the window of his living room, which faced a rather pretty view of the city. He looked relaxed, but I had been in his head enough to know that his guard was never down.

"Maybe it was for the better," he said after taking a sip. "After all, I don't know what you really look like."

"And yet you were willing to take the chance," I said. "For what it's worth, we are perfectly compatible. I'll have sex with you if you like, but it wouldn't change a thing. I will not be swooning over you like the rest of the planet seems to be."

"You're obviously not Harmonian. I don't suppose you would show me what's under that disguise if I asked?"

"That's the privilege of a champion. Win the game, and you will see."

"I will."

"Confident, aren't you?" I took a slow stroll around his space. "You know, for someone who claims to mourn his brother with such deep and unending sorrow, I don't see much memorabilia of him. Or any, for that matter."

"Maybe my people don't like to keep memorabilia of our deceased families."

"I've researched your race enough to know that's not true."

Able chuckled. He turned and set his drink down on the nearest surface. "You know, you have a lot of nerve," he said.

"You invade my planet, force my people to play your ridiculous game, then you come to my home and accuse me of not missing my brother? What's your purpose? Or do I have to win before I get an answer to that, too?"

I laughed, and I could tell it irritated him. To be laughed at was a major offense to Able, who probably spent his life laughing inwardly at everyone else.

"Don't act like you care about your people *or* your brother. I've been inside your head. I know how you think. You're not playing this game for anyone but yourself. All that stuff you tell them about your sorrow and your willingness to die for them is for show. You like their attention." I tilted my head. "Although not that much. They just amuse you, isn't that right?"

Able cracked a thin smile. "And what of you? Is that why *you're* here? Because we amuse you?"

"Well, you amuse *someone*."

"Do I amuse *you*?"

"Maybe."

He stepped toward me. He was quite a bit taller than me, but I did not think he would be foolish enough to think his height would intimidate me in any way. He stopped a step's distance away from me and leaned down. We were face to face, a mere breath away.

"So," he said. "What is it you want?"

I smirked. "Someone entertaining."

"And that's me?"

"I don't see many contestants who challenge me directly."

"And who *are* you, exactly?"

"The one in charge. That's all you need to know."

"Fair." He straightened and stepped back. "If you think I'm impressed by you, you're wrong. You're just another challenge to me."

"I know," I said. "But you haven't had a lot of challenges in your life, have you? In fact, you haven't ever had a lot of things to care about in your life. Your brother included."

Able chuckled. "My brother was a foolish little boy. He thought he was a hero, sticking his neck out for that woman. Frankly, I'm a little relieved. I was getting tired of looking out for him. Still, he was useful. If I win this game, I can ride this 'tragic story' to fame and fortune and be set for life."

"And power?" I nodded toward the city outside his window. "I know how your elections work. Your little speech earlier sounded like you were angling for a position in leadership."

He shrugged. "Power is a tricky thing. I have some thoughts on how Prosper should be run, but I have no delusions about what it takes to get things done. Do other planets suffer from this much bureaucracy?"

"Most of them, yes. It's an unfortunate byproduct of social advancement."

"Precisely. Which is why I don't imagine changing the world. I will take it as far as I can take it. However long that ride lasts, it'll at least be entertaining." He paused to take a sip of his drink. "Of course, all of that is moot if I can grab the real prize of the game."

I arched a brow. "Prize? Last I checked the prize was getting to live."

"For the rest of them, yes."

"And for you?"

"You."

"Me?"

"Or rather, what you have."

"Which is what?"

"I don't know yet. But something more than this." He gestured around himself.

"You're too far ahead of yourself."

"Am I? The fact that you're here tells me you're taking me seriously. And whoever it is that finds me amusing enough to pick me for the game before I even volunteered will definitely find me even more so after I win." He winked. "You watch. I'll beat them all. And you, too. Whatever you throw at me, I'll take it."

I smirked. "Alright. I'll be waiting." He raised his cup to me in a mock toast. "Tell me, did you ever intend to volunteer for the game?"

He shook his head. "No."

"Why not? I would've thought you'd find it a fun little challenge."

"Maybe," he said thoughtfully. "But usually I'm not a fan of chance, waiting to be picked or not picked by someone else. In all matters, I prefer to be the one in control."

I FELL to my knees and retched. The sheer cliff and dizzying height we had just scaled played before my eyes. Every time I closed my eyes—or even blinked—I saw that bottomless drop again. My lungs burned from exertion. Every one of my fingers bled from the climb. I had crawled up that cliff with sheer will and at the cost of most of my fingernails—manifested into shapes of claws that could barely hold my weight as I clung trembling to the tiny gaps in the stones.

Why was this happening? Had I really just seen nearly a hundred Maedans fall screaming to their deaths? Out of the corner of my eye I could see the only other survivors. A man and a woman. Three of us out of a hundred lived. My mind echoed with the sound of screams—loudly at first, then fading as they disappeared farther and farther below.

"Well done," boomed the voice from above. The speaker for the gods, as he called himself. I cradled my bleeding hands. "Rejoice, champions of Maeda. You are the first three to step on this new journey."

Champions. Is that what we were? I didn't feel like I'd won anything. I had only survived.

"The gods smile upon your fortune. But don't let your guard down. The next game will not be so easy."

Next game?

I shuddered. I couldn't do this again. I couldn't. I tried to uncurl my fingers and whimpered at the pain. My entire body was numb.

Why?

Why?

Why was this happening?

I hugged myself, smearing streaks of blood on both arms.

How many more games would I have to play? How many could I survive? Was my only path forward to play or die?

The world was watching me, but I had never felt so alone. What was my family going to say when I got out of here? I, a Kol, had lived, when others without the mark had died. Would they welcome me and be relieved at my survival, or would I face punishment?

Tam's face floated to my mind and I took a deep breath. My heart gradually slowed. I unraveled myself and looked down at my filthy, blood-soaked fingers.

I would do it for him.

This was not my world. It was his. Even if it continued to deny and belittle me, I would fight so he could have his place in it.

"Brace yourselves, champions. Your journey is only starting."

I wanted to laugh. My journey? No part of this was mine. It was not my world, or my journey, or my game. I was born to serve others, and I would spend my last breath serving the only one who mattered—my son.

And if that meant tearing myself apart in this game, then so be it.

"Dream?"

I snapped out of my trance. Mod looked at me with concern. I gave him a smile and patted his hand.

"Yes. Just dreaming," I told him as the holy ground drew near. I had plenty to offer the gods, but for the first time in a long while, I wasn't preoccupied with wondering if my recent memories would please them. Instead, I thought about Able.

He desired me, though at the core of his desire was conquest. Should he really win me over and wrap me around his finger like the rest of his planet, he would quickly lose interest. I, along with the game, was a challenge unlike anything Harmony had to offer, and it fed a deep, greedy part of him. Should he win, he would be a very different sort of champion than the rest of us, and the gods would surely find him fascinating. I shuddered at the thought of him working under H'otto, systematically undermining the rest of us until there was no one left.

But H'otto wasn't in charge anymore.

I opened my right palm. Seven strokes forming the winner's laurel stared back at me. I was the master of the arena now, and the game that had once made me feel so lonely and lost was under *my* control. Should Able become Ten, he would be a difficult one to manage. I would have to stay one step ahead of him at every turn and challenge him at every chance. *But if I manage to do that . . .*

I lifted my gaze to the approaching silver orb.

If I could keep Able in line, he could be a most useful person to have on my side. With every passing day, more orbs gathered to bear witness to my feat or failure, and I had begun to realize that even when this was over, I would need anyone I could get on my side.

I was not who I used to be, but my goal of protecting my child had never changed. I wasn't powerless anymore, and I never intended to be again.

I could build Able into a powerful ally.

After I broke him first.

CHAPTER 29

"*Welcome, welcome.*"

Two sauntered onto the field. I watched from the balcony. Able scanned the arena walls as usual. Though he could never quite figure out where I was, I had to admit he came close more often than not.

"*Today we have a truly special treat for you.*"

There were eight contestants remaining, made up of Able, Gala, and six of Able's most faithful supporters. Ironically, I'd found through connecting with them that none of these supporters followed him out of their desire to help him win and save Harmony. Rather, they believed that Able could somehow find a way around the rules and save them from certain death. So strong was Able's hold on them that they actually showed signs of faith over facts, a tremendous feat for this logic-obsessed planet. If they survived the game, I wondered, perhaps they would progress toward some form of organized religious system for the first time in their history.

"*How do you like the city?*"

The scene before them was a dark and eerie cityscape modeled after a major capital city on Harmony. Specifically, the one Able lived in. I saw him smirk ever so slightly, as if smug in the knowledge that this whole arrangement was made with him in mind.

"The rules are simple—take out the target before the target takes out you. But there's a special award for this round."

I sensed restless stirring. The word "special" rarely failed to capture attention. Two let the heavy silence hang for a moment before continuing.

"Whoever takes down the target first will earn a one-way ticket out of the game."

I felt hearts beat and emotions stir. Gala drew a shuddering breath and I knew she wasn't daring to hope. Every contestant in the arena perked up save for one, whose heartbeat remained as steady as ever.

"Do you have what it takes?"

He already knew he did, and I could see the gears spinning in his head. Did he intend to win the ticket out and offer it to Gala? It would certainly boost him one step further in the eyes of his people, not to mention ensure her safety so she could fulfill her role in his longer-term plans.

"Let's play the game."

With a snap of Two's fingers, the contestants were sent to random spots within the city—separated from each other. I needed them apart, particularly two of them. I reached down and laid a gentle hand on Sweetly. She sat patiently at my feet, chittering happily. I stroked her head.

"Go get 'em, beautiful."

I FOLLOWED SWEETLY, seeing the city through her eyes. She was joyful, my Sweetly. She loved to be useful. Delicately, soundlessly she ran through the city, scaling the walls and keeping to the shadows.

Able thought this entire setup was a nod to him, but it actually served a double purpose—Sweetly moved best in a silent concrete jungle. Without excessive lights and sounds to distract her, she was razor focused on her task. She took my eyes through a quiet street, then up a high wall, where she perched against the flat surface and peered out.

A movement. She looked down. It was not the one she sought. She moved on, undetected.

A hop and a skip onto another wall. She went around the building to check the other side. Someone spotted her and took a shot. She dodged easily and kept going. This was also not her target. However, the one she sought would not be hard to find.

Sure enough, he appeared. She spotted him under a street lamp, talking with two other contestants he had managed to locate. Carefully, silently, she crept onto the building across from him. His companions did not notice her, as she was behind their backs. He did—she knew this though he gave no indication of it. She watched him until he gave instructions for his companions to split up into different directions, then waited until they were out of sight before lifting his gaze in her direction.

She turned. He followed.

She led him through the city, avoiding the other contestants whenever they were near. I ran along with her, occasionally casting a glance back at Able. There was something exciting about being chased by him, though in a way he had been chasing me since he stepped into the arena. He took a few shots but missed. Sweetly darted in and out of his sight and he picked up his step, staying close on her tail. They played this game of hide-and-seek as she led him farther and farther away from the city center toward a certain other contestant.

Gala had no chance as Sweetly pounced on her from behind. She let out a shrill scream as Sweetly forced her down onto her back and stood atop her on all fours, keeping her in place just as Able rounded the corner. He stopped in his tracks and I felt him waver for a brief moment, weighing his options.

Calculating, I was sure, whether it would serve his reputation better to be a hero or a mourning lover.

Sweetly turned her blank black face to Able and hissed, then turned back to Gala. The oily skin on her face peeled back to reveal another face underneath. I felt a twinge of pleasure at the shock that radiated from Able as he saw his brother's face. Gala's scream was cut short as Sweetly's sharp teeth sank into her throat.

Able snapped out of his trance and in a moment he was on Sweetly, barrling full force into her and knocking her off of Gala. I did notice, however, that he waited an extra split second longer than he had to, just long enough for Sweetly's teeth to sink into that extra-vulnerable vein in Gala's throat. As the poor girl bled out, he held Sweetly down and manifested his weapon in his other hand.

Underneath him, Sweetly's face changed once more. The blade in his hand came down but halted a hair's breadth away from her face—*my* face. I felt his struggle—and his own unhappiness at having felt that struggle at all. His mouth gave an unwilling twitch at the sight of the only "Harmonian" who had bested him.

"Win," said Sweetly in my voice, "and come find me."

His hand moved back and Sweetly swiped him across the face. He let out a cry of surprise and she was gone. I watched him get to his knees, still holding his face where she had left deep welts. He looked calm as ever, though I could feel the turmoil inside him. For the first time since stepping in the arena, maybe the first time in his life, he was shaken, and he didn't like it.

He was shocked at Sweetly's ability.

He was surprised there was still so much about the arena that he didn't know.

He was worried the game might not be as easy as he'd thought.

He was afraid of being beaten.

He was excited to have found a true challenge.

He was aroused at the thought of me.

And above all, he was angry. Angry that he was feeling all of these things at all. Angry that there was someone capable of getting a rise out of him this way.

I didn't let the cameras catch him in this state, as ruining his good reputation would take a lot of fun out of the game. I waited for Able to gather himself and remember that Gala was bleeding to death less than a handful of steps from him. As he rushed to her aid, I sent the cameras to him finally. His people would see him selflessly trying to help the woman whom he supposedly loved, which was exactly what he wanted.

For a moment, I almost forgot about the tremendous pressure on me to run this game. For the first time since entering this arena as Nasmi, I was enjoying myself.

HE TRACKED SWEETLY DOWN at last, and when he finally did, she was hunched over, gnawing at the open throat of another contestant. Unlike Gala, it was too late to save this one.

She turned to him and hissed. He raised his hand in the shape of a gun and she was on him in an instant. He managed two shots in that short space of time and both struck. But Sweetly, bless her, did not slow in the least. The bullets melded into the black tar-skin given to her by the arena. Able started in surprise once more at the realization that taking her down was going to take more than his usual tricks.

He manifested armor over his arms to shield himself from her teeth and claws. She knocked him off his feet and he landed heavily on his back. He was struggling, trying to think outside his usual arsenal. Her claws swiped at his face. He manifested his own claws and raked her flank. She yelped in pain and he took the chance to shove her off and roll on top, pushing her down with his weight. Then, wrapping both hands around her neck, he squeezed.

She clawed at his face and arms. In his concentration, all his manifestation fell away. Blood streaked down his face, neck, and forearms, but he never let up.

Sweetly's face peeled away.

"Able," she gasped in his brother's voice. "Able, please . . ."

He squeezed harder, cutting off the voice. I felt not a waver from him as he slowly choked the life from the creature wearing his brother's face. In fact, I thought I sensed pleasure, as if he'd waited all his life to have his hands around his brother's throat.

Truly complex, this one was.

I reached out to Sweetly. *Well done. Now sleep.*

Sweetly went limp, then lay still. Slowly, hesitantly, Able loosened his grip around her throat. When she didn't move, he wiped the blood from his face and stood. Cameras swarmed him from every direction—the victorious hero.

"Well, well, well."

He turned at the sound of Two's voice as they sauntered from the shadows of the dark city.

"Looks like we have a winner," they said, eyeing Sweetly's "dead" body with their holographic eyes. One mechanical hand raised up, and with a snap of metal fingers a shining object appeared, floating in midair above their palm. Able regarded this strange token, a small golden model of the planet Harmony, with curiosity. *"This is your ticket out."*

He reached out, but Two pulled it away. *"Not so fast. Unfortunately, given the circumstances, we can't give this to you."*

"Why?" Able looked in the direction of where he'd left Gala after stopping her bleeding. "If you want to keep me in the game, you're in luck. I don't want it. Give it to Gala."

"Tsk, so gallant," Two said. They tossed the token up and down nonchalantly. *"You see, contestant, a champion's title must be earned. And to earn it, they must compete. To compete, they need a competitor. So we can't let either of the last two contestants leave, can we?"*

I truly relished being able to surprise Able. "Last two?"

"Oh, yes." Two tossed the token high up into the air and it disintegrated into a cloud of golden dust. *"Our little pet took out all but the two of you. Funny, isn't it? If you'd just let that pretty girl die, you would've walked away the winner and saved your world already. But such a hero you are."* Then, they leaned toward Able and whispered out of the range of the cameras, *"Of course, if you won that way, the arena master would be sorely disappointed."*

Able's expression betrayed nothing, but I felt the calculation tick away within him—the prospect of Gala dying and him beginning his path of fame and prosperity, or the chance to face me one more time.

I sensed no regrets.

I GAVE Gala ample time to rest, putting the game on hold and letting the planet stew in its speculations and work itself up into a frenzy. There was much discussion of whether Able had made the right call to save Gala, but most people latched onto the romantic story that he valued the life of his love much more than the fate of the planet—illogical, but understandable, and even the logical people of Harmony knew that sometimes love outweighed reason.

While Gala recovered, I prayed.

The gods were pleased. They drank in my memories and Sweetly's, relishing every last bit. They wanted more, and I knew I had more to offer.

The last round was within sight, and I had long lost count of the number of orbs near Harmony's orbit, watching and waiting.

I HADN'T SEEN H'otto since kicking off the game on Harmony. Truthfully, there were times that I could almost forget that the old game master was locked away in the orb's underbelly. But he was an undeniable presence in the back of my mind, and I couldn't help feeling that little twinge of guilt every now and then at the position he had been reduced to.

Besides, I had to admit, I wanted to gloat.

The games were nearly over and the gods had been pleased with every step, not just inside the arena but outside it as well. The games, Able's rise to fame, his feigned romance with Gala and political ambitions, and the social and cultural unrest that resulted from it all fed directly to the gods' pleasures. I was one game away from taking my place as the permanent master of this arena. Altogether, it finally gave me enough confidence to face H'otto once more with my victory within grasp.

I imagined he would be angry or disappointed that I was pulling this off. Or maybe sad or frightened, though I had no intention to do him harm. There was the smallest bounce in my step as I made my way to his holding cell. Axi lowered the transparency of the wall as I approached.

"Hello, H'otto."

He sat on a bench against the far wall, head dipped, face cupped in two of his hands. The other two hands dangled limply over his legs. He didn't look up.

"Hello, H'otto," I said again, a little louder this time. He looked up and I was taken off guard by his eyes. His pupils had turned a sickly gray, and now that I took a closer look, his fur, once thick and brown, looked mottled and discolored. He looked not at me but past me, at a point in infinity.

He whispered something, but I couldn't quite hear. I waved a hand in his line of sight and he did not follow my movement.

"H'otto?" I ventured cautiously, wary that it was a trick.

"I tried to protect them."

"I beg your pardon?"

He didn't answer. Instead, he blinked. A strangely slow blink as his eyes moved out of phase with one another. I thought I could hear the sound of his eyelids scraping against his pupils. "They were made as children; they were grown like a garden. They were to be offered up until they withered and died, then they were to be scattered among the stars."

I raised my hand and tapped on the invisible barrier separating us. "I'm not interested in watching you act like a lunatic," I said.

"We are gardeners."

"H'otto?"

"We are caretakers."

"H'otto!"

At last he seemed to notice me. Dark, empty eyes focused for a moment, as if just realizing I was there. Then, as quickly as that recognition came, it was gone again.

"We tend the garden of the gods," he went on. "We were made to grow their crops. We farm until we are no more and the universe crumbles to dust. We carry the fruit of joy and anger and sadness to the plate of the gods. For it is our place as the tenders and their place as the tended. This is as it always has been. This is as it always shall be."

I opened my mouth to interrupt him again, but something stopped me and I stepped slowly away from the barrier instead.

"Close it, Axi."

The barrier grew opaque and soon H'otto's face was hidden from me. But I could still hear him. He was pretending. He was feigning madness to throw me off guard or garner sympathy for himself. He wanted me to approach him so he could attack me or try to escape when I lowered the barrier.

I told myself all of these things over and over as I returned to the heart. From there I watched him on the screens, and long after I left, he sat, unmoving, talking to the same spot where I had stood. Chills, followed by the tingles of my neck implant, ran down my back as I listened.

"They have no purpose if they cannot feed the godly desires. They have no purpose if they cannot pay tribute to the games, with their skills or their bodies. They were created to be tended and nurtured and grown, then plucked so they can help grow others. The work of the gardener is to tend and grow, not to collect and hoard the fruit of their labor, for to do so is to take from the gods."

Here he lowered his head again. "I wanted to *protect* them."

CHAPTER 30

IT CAME DOWN TO THIS.

I stood alone in the holy ground. Above and below me, countless walkways stretched from the worshipping grounds in the center. It was quiet today. Very few worshippers could be seen, thanks in no small part to the fact many of them were hovering around Harmony, waiting.

Gala's injury served multiple purposes. Aside from driving the drama of the games, it bought me time to think about the final round. Everything culminated at this point and I had to deliver. I had no doubt that even Able was driving himself to antsy fidgets, wondering what I had in store.

If only I knew.

I had a number of scenarios devised for every possible outcome. Now, with the final two contestants before me, I found myself at a loss. The games I had previously designed for them all seemed trivial and dull. The gods would desire a climax for the ages, something unlike anything they'd seen before. I'd set the bar high. Now I had to meet it.

The dense fog reached out for me, but I took a step back. I couldn't go inside to face the gods just yet. I didn't want them to sense my indecision. I'd left Mod and Sweetly in the capsule for this visit because I couldn't afford any distraction.

The old games weren't enough anymore.

I had seen to that. I had taken away the old virtues and replaced them with glam and glitz, drama and intrigue. This was no longer a simple game but a story, and it needed an ending.

The fog reached out again. It sensed me, knowing I always brought with me the most enjoyable treats. My memories were the best it had ever had under the demigods. It was colorful and fresh.

Fresh.

I stepped into the fog. The gods seized me immediately and drank me in. I relaxed and leaned into it, allowing them to pull the strings of my memory from my mind. They devoured it, savored it. I could almost see them lick their metaphorical fingers and compliment the chef. As I couldn't decide between pride and disgust, I chose neither.

Fresh is what they want.

The champions and demigods had once rarely prayed during the games. They consulted this place for enlightenment if needed. They filled themselves with knowledge and experiences to the brim, then carried it back here, hoping that their offering would be large and varied enough to please the gods.

But the gods wanted the morsels. They wanted to taste the bits and pieces, the details and crumbs. Every last bit. I waited for them to finish.

To say H'otto did not unnerve me would be a lie, but I still believed staunchly that I, a member of the seed races, knew what the gods wanted better than he did. The demigods always overthought everything. They made it all so much more complicated than it needed to be. There was no glory in this. Only entertainment. And in that moment, as the gods drew the last of my memories from the previous game, everything became simple and clear.

Would you like to see?

They paused, curious.

Come with me. See for yourself.

Intrigue. Excitement.

Memories are stale. They're what's already passed. Watch the last game through my eyes. See it new.

The sensation that followed could only be described as a balloon being inflated in a single breath. I gasped as they flowed into me, filling my veins to every extremity. Then, as suddenly as it came, it was gone.

I was standing. I didn't remember being brought down to the ground. I blinked and saw double, then triple. I turned my head and something inside shifted, as if someone was peering out of my eyes like they were binoculars.

The fog receded. I stood on the walkway alone. Though my feet stood flat, I teetered as if walking on a tightrope. Everything had an extra layer. I was intensely aware of my body, my muscles and tendons and veins.

Then, excitement. *Their* excitement. I could feel them dialing into my senses like tuning a radio. Yet I sensed that they had purposefully stayed out of my mind. They were riding along, clinging on eagerly but allowing me to remain in the pilot's seat.

Even now, they wanted nothing spoiled. I had, after all, promised them something fresh and new.

And that was what I intended to deliver. It was all so simple.

IT CAME DOWN to the last round.

Two contestants arrived in the arena—the last two. Harmony held its collective breath as they appeared. I had no doubt that books would be written about them and films and art inspired by them, the golden couple of Harmony.

Able.

And Gala.

Gala had become a fair player. However, her survival up to this point had a good amount to do with my hand in the game as well as Able's. They arrived in the arena and immediately embraced one another, though I saw the calculated look of emotion on Able's face as he scanned the arena walls as usual, searching for me.

At best, only one of them was going to walk out of here, and they knew that. The entirety of Harmony held its breath, wondering what awaited these unlikely lovebirds. Talk shows speculating on the outcome of the round received millions upon millions of views. Bets were being placed in underground casinos and millions were putting down money that Able would sacrifice himself for Gala, or at least try to. A high payout was offered for an unlikely outcome—that both would somehow survive and manage to save the planet in the process. The possibility that both would die was offered, but the Harmonians, ever logical, placed no bets on this. In a more faith-based world, there might've been at least a few who believed they could cash out even if the planet burned.

Two sauntered onto the arena floor. The holographic face looked the two contestants up and down and smirked.

"You're sure about this," One said from next to me.

I shivered.

Her voice traveled through my entire body, vibrating every cell from the inside out. Was this what Sweetly had felt every day before setting foot into the arena? The gods magnified my senses a hundredfold. Everything was in painful, crystal clarity. Even the movement of the building blocks in the arena was a distraction.

Pull back, I reminded them. Like children, they often became far too eager to experience the moment.

The movement and sounds around me slowed and quieted, at least for now. I let out a small breath of relief.

"I am," I said to One.

"Alright," One said slowly. "But this seems somehow . . ."

I turned to her, keeping my expression neutral, almost daring her to finish her thought.

309

"Barbaric," she said softly.

My skull was vibrating. The fear that my body was never meant to contain the senses of the gods was never far from my mind. "And the rest of this game isn't?"

"I suppose that's true," she said, peering over the railing of the balcony. "It's simply never been done before, and I don't know how the gods will feel about such a deviation from—"

"*I* know what the gods want," I snapped, cutting her off. The gods were pushing forward again and it took all I had to keep them at bay, like a parent trying to keep their hyperactive child from diving headfirst into an animal's cage.

Patience, I told them. *You must be patient.*

"This is a gamble I am taking," I said to One, struggling to keep my voice even. "We are here now because of every risk I chose to take. You are the one who told me to be certain, so do your part and follow my plan."

She nodded. If I weren't already busy trying to keep my senses aligned, I might've worried I'd crossed a line. But out of the corner of my eye, I saw a twitch of her lip, almost a smile, as she readied herself.

It's starting.

All at once they pulled back. My mind cleared. I let out a breath of relief. They wanted to see, and they wanted me at my best to give them their show. I knew exactly what to do. The answer had been in front of me all this time.

Able's story would end how mine had begun.

I reached out to Two, projecting my voice to their metal ears. "Repeat what I say."

Gala and Able clung to each other. I sensed a desperate faith in Gala, a staunch belief that Able would somehow get them out of this and that a happy ending awaited them. He had gotten her this far. What would she do if she knew what he really thought of her?

"*Our last two. Well, well.*"

Able kept his face blank. Gala trembled but tried to look brave.

"*This last challenge is going to be a fun one. I hope you're ready.*" Two ran a hand through Gala's and Able's manes in turn as they strolled behind them, repeating the lines I fed them. "*So many eyes on you two. So much hope. You wouldn't want to disappoint the ones who matter, would you?*"

Able's hand twitched. No one saw but me.

"*Now then.*" Two turned their back to the contestants dramatically. "*I will explain the rules. For the final game, you will be going up against only those worthy of you, the finest of the finest. And who best matches the final two but yourselves?*"

I saw Two freeze in their movement for a brief moment. They turned on their heels and glanced up in my direction, playing it off as an exaggerated turn of the head. They were wondering if there was some sort of mistake. I continued.

"*You are probably wondering what that means. Well, contestants —it means exactly what it sounds like.*" They gestured at the two contestants and tilted their head mockingly. "*The only ones worthy of taking you on are yourselves. So, let's see what you're really capable of. Kill each other.*"

There was a long, stunned silence. Not only from Able and Gala, but Two as well. I respected Two for keeping their composure, as I could feel the shock they were struggling not to show. Perhaps the lack of a proper face was a blessing in this case. The holographic face held its steady smile. Two folded their hands and waited. I held silent, listening for their response.

"Um," Gala spoke up. "I'm sorry?"

"*Kill each other,*" I said, watching Able, who was looking shocked, but calm as ever inside.

"You can't ask us to do that," he said, a little too loudly, with that perfect nervous tremor in his voice.

"*Can't I?*" Two tilted their head one way, then the other, metal fingers tented. "*I think you're forgetting your positions.*" I gave them a mental prompt and they snapped their fingers. The familiar red circle appeared on the ceiling of the arena dome. *"You have until time runs out. If there's not exactly one of you —not two, not zero, one—standing at the end of the round, you can kiss your planet goodbye."*

Now leave.

Two turned on their heels dramatically and walked away from the two contestants. They raised one hand, snapped their fingers, and the countdown began. Able and Gala stood side by side, unable to look at each other. Neither made a move. The stalemate lasted only a few brief seconds, but it was enough for me to reach forward, grab hold of Gala's fragile consciousness, and twist. Her face showed nothing, but her mind screamed at the invasion before I severed it from her body.

I slid into her, fitting her body around me like a glove, then lifted her gaze to Able and smiled. Axi pasted my Harmonian face over Gala's, and the look on Able's face was priceless as our eyes met.

"Come at me," I purred, and the gods cheered with their silent voices in the back of my mind.

For a fraction of a second, he struggled. Logic dictated that this might be a mistake, but something inside him was boiling over, burying his reason, overriding his common sense. This chance before him was too much to pass over. I felt his excitement and arousal, bubbling over further with every moment that passed.

He struck.

I RAN and Able chased me.

The landscape around us changed. Mountains and hills appeared, covered in lush blue-green grass. Able stumbled as the ground beneath him suddenly fell away into a steep slope. He recovered fast and the next thing I saw was him sliding down the slope, his feet replaced by flat, smooth shapes that aided in the motion.

The landscape switched again. Able was halfway down the slope when the field below it changed to water. He wobbled but stayed collected. One hand changed into claws and grasped the ground, slowing his descent. His right foot dipped into the liquid and he hissed in pain as the harsh waters of Aukron's Crystal Lake immediately shredded his skin. He pulled his bloodied foot out, climbed back up the slope, and pressed a hand over his wounds. Moments later the cuts healed without a trace. He looked up at me and smirked.

"You've been studying," I said from the top of the hill.

"Simple medical knowledge, constructs of the bone and flesh."

I jumped over him and into the water, trusting One to change its properties. Able immediately followed, knowing that if it was safe for me, it was safe for him. His legs changed to flippers. I dove underwater. He gave chase and I led him down. Deeper. Deeper.

The underwater city came into view. High, decrepit skyscrapers reached up towards us. I turned around and gave him a wink just in time to see him push a jet of water toward me. I ducked. It struck concrete and took a chunk off the highest building. I laughed and made my way between the buildings, out of his sight.

Then, the water vanished, as suddenly as it had appeared. I moved the blocks around me to slow my fall just enough to watch Able plummet past me toward the skyscrapers beneath. He flailed, but only for a moment. I sensed him concentrate as long, leathery wings sprouted from his back. He cringed at the strange and foreign pain of growing extra limbs. They were strong, well-formed wings, but he wasn't terribly good at using them. He flapped them as hard as he could, but not in a synchronized motion. They managed to slow the momentum just enough to save him from hitting the ground with deadly impact.

He stood, brushed himself off, and winced at his scraped skin and bruised joints. I lowered myself gracefully in front of him as he healed his new injuries.

"Did you expect me to crash?" he asked in an almost flirtatious manner.

"I expected you to die," I replied, equally flirtatious.

He dashed toward me, propelling himself by contracting the air around him. I dodged just in time and we were off again.

I leapt onto the wall of the nearest building, perched much in the manner Sweetly would. I hadn't stayed for more than a second before the air around me constricted. I leapt off just as the entire building collapsed onto itself. Before I could even fully settle on the next one over, it started to crumble, too.

Moving the blocks around me, I boosted my speed and made my way through the city, dodging his attacks. His ability in the arena was truly impressive. But compared to me, he was still an amateur. I led him to the city center.

Then, the arena went dark.

I sensed his surprise as his surroundings suddenly plunged into complete darkness. I took the chance and struck at him, just enough to graze his neck and ego. Even with his third eye open, he barely saw me coming. The absolute darkness of the Umbra Collective's capital city was difficult to navigate.

I blinked. My eyes changed. I had spent enough time studying Sweetly to know how to replicate her unique pupils. Able manifested an electronic light source, but it paled in comparison to my Umbra eyes. I led him on a chase through the dark city. Despite his obvious disadvantage, he never lost sight of me for long. Then, just as he changed his two main eyes to match the third eye—the night vision eye—the light returned. I delighted in his gasp of pain as he covered all three eyes with his hands, losing his manifested light and weapon in the process.

"Bitch," he muttered.

"Do better," I said.

He came at me and the entire city crumbled. Buildings and bridges fell apart like so many brittle crackers. He stopped short just in time to avoid being crushed under the debris. When the dust cleared, I stood on the front steps of the Institute of Higher Learning.

"Are you going to keep running?" he asked, approaching the bottom of the stairs. "Here I thought you wanted to face me one-on-one."

I smirked. "You're hardly worth facing if you can't even catch me."

He moved, but I was faster. We crashed into the pristine lobby of the Institute and he came within a hand's length of striking me. I changed course midair, landing gracefully on the ceiling. He hit the ground and propelled himself upward. I leapt out the way and broken stones rained down where he struck. I kept my distance from him easily, but he was getting faster at every turn, learning at every chance.

This game was not going to continue much longer.

I made for the nearest room just as he shifted gravity and dropped right between the door and me. He drew his weapon and charged toward me. It changed shape as he moved—a stick, a sword, a gun, a knife. He was trying to confuse me, take me off guard and force me to decide how to protect myself from an ever-changing threat.

I pulled a wall out of the floor. He smashed through it, but not before I leapt over his head toward the door. He spun around and followed me.

We were inside the auditorium where I had heard him speak the very first time. I raised a hand and every chair in the room, five hundred at least, rose into the air and flew toward him. He looked surprised for a moment. Then a smile split his face before they crushed him, burying him in a mountain of metal legs.

I waited.

Silence.

The last of the chairs clattered to the floor.

I waited a moment. Then another.

I reached out, searching for his presence, and found it. Strangely, it was difficult to pinpoint, as if his mind and body had become disjointed. It was a familiar sensation.

The image of Mod pulling himself, half-formed, out of lava came to mind just as Able's presence solidified behind me. I spun around and he was on me, knocking me to the ground. I hit him across the face. His cheekbone cracked from the impact, but he held tight.

"This is where we met," he said, blood streaking down his face.

"Yes, it is."

"Fitting."

"Isn't it?"

He raised his weapon. I felt his mind. He was relishing this fight, lost in it, aroused in every fiber of his being. He was waiting to see what other tricks I had left, eager to find out what I was going to do to stop him.

So I did the only thing he didn't expect—I didn't.

His blade thrust straight through my rib cage. He faltered a little, surprised at having received no resistance.

I reached up, grabbed his wrist, and pulled him closer, driving the weapon deeper through me—through Gala's body.

I smiled at him.

"Well," I said. "You got me."

He hesitated. Then, hesitation because pride and triumph. "I won," he said. "Looks like you lost, arena master."

"Did I?" I brought my head close to his and lowered my voice to a whisper. "Because I think your entire world just saw you chase this sweet girl, whom you swore to forgive and protect, who trusted you with her heart and her life, all around this arena. Then, just as she tried to defend herself, you killed her."

The mask Axi had imposed over Gala's face melted away. I watched confusion and realization dawn on Able. For a moment, in his desire to best me, he had forgotten whose body I occupied. Not that it mattered—thanks to Axi and One, the only one who had seen my face was him. The rest of Harmony saw only what I wanted them to see from beginning to end— the terrified face of Gala.

Able's weapon vanished. I laid Gala's head down on the ground. Then, as the cameras gathered around us, I gave my best impression of Gala, loud enough for each and every one to hear.

"I love you."

And then I pulled back. From the balcony, I watched him clench and unclench his fists, emotions playing across his face. Gala's head fell to one side, still.

I chuckled to myself and the gods joined me, laughing at this foolish boy who thought he could best me at my own game.

CHAPTER 31

THEY CHEERED.

Axi opened all communication channels and I heard the voices of the champions from across the universe. They cheered for my victory. Not my victory over Able, but my victory at having changed every rule they'd ever been held to.

The arena enclosed him in his jar. I hurried down to the heart. I wanted to address the champions—future masters of their arenas. I'd shown them the path to freedom, a path to being more than just slaves to the demigods or food for the gods. I wanted to speak to them and have them hear my story and tell them they could break free, just like I had. The other arena masters would undoubtedly hear my voice as well, but I didn't care. They should know that change was coming. It was time for the other champions to rally in this victory. *Our* victory.

However, when I arrived, I saw only one person—the last person I expected to see.

Every screen in the heart was off. Axi said nothing as I entered. The space suddenly felt very dark and cramped without the glow of the screens, which made H'otto's presence all the more menacing.

"Well, well," he said slowly. "The rebel child succeeds."

I stood my ground, though I was quite afraid. I reached out to the arena but could find no sign of Mod or Sweetly, nor One or Two for that matter.

"This room is isolated." He lifted his gaze to me, four hands linked behind his back. A drop of dark liquid rolled from his right eye. It slid over his fur and fell to the floor, where small puddles had already formed. "I saw to that."

"How did you get out?" I shot a quick glance at Axi, fearing taking my eyes off H'otto for too long.

One furry arm reached up and wiped away another black, tar-like tear. H'otto studied the black substance on his finger. It resembled Sweetly's oily second skin.

"It seems overriding Axi took a little more out of me than I expected." He shook the black drop away nonchalantly, then reached up and caressed Axi's silent face. "She took a bit of a blow from it as well. But don't worry; it'll take a lot more than that to break her." He turned to me. Traces of the black stuff stuck to his fur.

"You can't do anything to me," I said. Though I wasn't quite convinced of that. He took a step toward me and I took one back.

"Oh, I won't," he said. "Not just yet, anyway. But you've started down a dangerous path."

"I'm not afraid of you."

"You don't need to be. There is plenty for you to be scared of, *arena master*. Do you think the gods will favor and protect you now, with your little victory? Do you think what you've done is in favor of those around you?"

I whipped an arm in front of me, manifesting a hundred tiny projectiles that shot toward him. H'otto snapped his fingers and they dissipated into blocks.

"Calm down, child," he said. "That won't get you anywhere."

I looked behind me. Could I run? He had said this room

was isolated. Could the others come to me? I'd been cut off from everyone.

"You're wondering how I could do this."

I nodded. There was no reason to lie.

"I am a very different sort of being from you." Large drops of black tears fell from his eyes. A few began to drop from his nose as well. He looked as if he was melting from within. "You lot are merely seeds, planted by the gods for harvest. The masters of the arena are the gardeners. We can be kind, rear you with a gentle hand and water you with our love, then pluck you to be prized offerings for the gods. But we must pluck the weak saplings and bad fruits as well. Such is the natural order. Such is the way of the universe as created by the gods. A mere little plant like you cannot ascend from the dirt that grows you."

"I already have," I bit back. "I've played this game far better than you, and they've all seen it. The age of the demigods is over. We will not serve you anymore. I've shown the champions they can take control of the orbs and do it better than your kind ever has."

"And in that, you've doomed them all."

"Well, now that's just *enough*," said a new voice.

I started and spun around to see One. She strolled past me in her usual unhurried way toward H'otto. The look on his face changed and I could almost swear it was fear.

"No," he said.

"I think you've said all you need," One said. Her voice was even, but there was something different. An echo.

"Please, I can still be useful," H'otto stammered. His back struck Axi's obelisk. One advanced on him. I stared, unable to comprehend what was taking place.

"You've had plenty of chances to prove yourself," One said, and I heard that echo again. Layers and layers of echo, as if she were speaking with many voices at once. She raised a hand and placed it on H'otto's forehead. His eyes rolled back and black sludge suddenly poured forth from every orifice on his face. Thick black tar pooled on the ground.

"This is what will happen to you!" I heard him scream around the tar pouring from his mouth. *"This is what you asked for!"*

Then, silence.

One stepped back. What was left of H'otto crumpled to the ground like an empty sack. I couldn't stop shaking at the sight of the former arena master, now nothing more than a boneless mess. The holes where his eyes had once been stared through me.

"Well," One said. Her voice slowly returned to normal, the eerie layers of echo fading away. "I suppose Nix can move our former arena master to the subbasement. There's no reason we can't make use of what's left."

I was holding my breath, I suddenly realized. I forced air in and out of my lungs. One faced me. I opened my mouth but couldn't make a word come out. I couldn't stop staring at H'otto, now motionless on the floor.

"A rather odd feeling, isn't it?" she asked. "Having them ride inside your head. I don't think I'll ever get used to it."

"Who ... what ..."

"I am the first champion of the Galaxy of the Starry River," One said. "And I speak for the gods." She came over to me and slid one arm around mine. "Come, let's take a walk."

"YOU'RE WONDERING how long I've been doing this."

I nodded. I still couldn't figure out how to form a proper question. What I had witnessed was too difficult for me to understand, and my victory just moments before suddenly felt far away and insignificant. I didn't want One to touch me, but her arm around mine was tight. I followed her helplessly.

"You see, Seven, we all have to find our use around here. You've seen it already—those who either do not prove themselves useful or cannot be entertaining to the gods must serve their purpose in another way. Still, all of those are better than poor H'otto, I suppose."

I swallowed. "What happened to H'otto?"

"His body is no longer needed. It was already breaking down. I merely hurried the process. His consciousness, as are those of all demigods, is tied directly to the gods. Without the anchor of a physical body, he has returned to them."

"What does that mean?"

One cracked a strange smile. Her mouth curved but her eyes remained impassive. "In spiritual terms, it means he's in a better place."

"In real terms?"

"His consciousness has been melded into theirs. He will remain in a semiconscious state as they digest his memories, little by little."

"For how long?"

"For a little while, at least as far as they're concerned. For those like us, we could call it eternity. An eternity of drifting in and out of consciousness, sleeping and only waking to be probed of your memories and relive those moments. A worship that goes on forever. There are words for it in various languages. Limbo. Purgatory."

"Hell," I muttered.

"Let's not be pessimistic." One patted my hand and I struggled not to shirk away. "You see, in the beginning, there were the universe and the first beings who lived in it—what we've come to know as the gods. The gods, when they'd exhausted all there was to do and know in the universe, created other living things and fed off of their experiences and memories to alleviate their own boredom."

"H'otto called us seeds."

"That is one way to look at it, yes."

"Is that all we are? Livestock for the gods?"

"Perhaps, but *you*." She chuckled. "You've proven yourself to be more, shown them that we could all be more. You did very well. Much better than H'otto ever did. Perhaps even better than I hoped you would."

"*You* hoped?"

She smiled. My mind reeled as it played back the years that had passed, from the day she had given me that first warm smile to now. Every subtle reference to the other champions. Every little prompt for me to search and dig deeper, to talk to Nix and spend time with Axi. Even the little movements out of the corner of my eye.

"The implants."

"They don't bother me, but I knew you had doubts about them."

"You let me see you pick at them."

"I only needed you to think about the imperfection of the situation."

"You knew I would do something about it."

"I hoped you would." She shrugged. "I hoped they all would. I trained them all, you know. They all had their strengths. Three, so smart. Five, so young and teachable. But when I pushed them, they faltered. Missteps unfortunately are not tolerated, as you know well."

"You pushed them?"

"I had to. If they were to challenge H'otto's position, they had to get out of their comfort zone. I taught each of them and put them to the test."

I shivered. "I thought they fell into their fate because they could not entertain the gods."

"We all inevitably become uninteresting to the gods. At least this way they had a shot at a different fate."

"You pushed them into failure."

"I didn't wish for them to end up where they are, but alas, that is H'otto's way and a risk I had to take." One winked at me. "And you know *all* about taking risks."

I nodded, as I had no idea what else to do.

"To be honest, until you took things into your own hands, I

was still hoping Two would step up. They had every reason. After all, taking over from H'otto was the only way to guarantee Four's freedom. They were the optimal candidate. So gorgeous and clever. But being H'otto's butcher is not for the faint of heart, and they ended up escaping the arena every chance they had. Pity; they had such potential."

"Why? Why were you pushing us to go against H'otto?"

"I told you, didn't I? We must all find our own way to be useful to the gods. I saw quickly after entering the arena that the gods were growing bored with the existing way of the games. I wasn't certain I could go against H'otto myself, being the only champion in the galaxy at the time, so I made them a promise."

"That you would find a new arena master."

"I was beginning to grow wary of their patience running out."

"This is why you didn't want me to leave. You told me I had nowhere to go so I would stay."

One smiled, ever so slightly. "What I said was true—you have nowhere to go. It is the lot of the champions. But really, did you think H'otto was going to let you leave?" She reached out and pinched the base of my neck. I flinched. "*Zap*. Your head would've come clean off, wherever you happened to be in the universe. You didn't think the little chip was there just to keep you happy, did you? It is your collar and leash, and the arena master holds the other end. Had H'otto found out about your intention to undermine him before you managed to do so, you wouldn't have made it two steps into the holy ground. We are merely snacks to the gods, each bite by itself insignificant and inconsequential. It is the arena masters, the demigods, who depend on us to justify their existence."

I stopped. One did the same. The gods in my mind were silent, uncaring. They were growing bored again now that the game had ended. They had known what had been happening all this time. But if they had revealed the truth to me, well, where was the entertainment in that? We had reached the computing room. The lights below blinked off and on and I could see Nix going about his work below.

"So what now? You've pushed me to get to this point; you've given H'otto to the gods. What do I do now?"

"Why, you run the games, dear. Isn't that what you wanted?"

Is it? I had thought that by supplanting H'otto, I could protect Mod and Sweetly from the ghastly fate of our predecessors, but now everything suddenly seemed uncertain again.

"What happens," I asked cautiously, "when they grow bored of me, too?"

"Once upon a time, the champions who could not please the gods, either through missteps in the games or simply by being 'dull,' found their use in other ways. They became fodder, much like H'otto is now. They walked into the fog to worship and never returned. But once in a while there's one like H'otto, who grew far too attached to his 'children.' I don't think you can judge him for it, can you? Not after those children you've adopted under your own care." She sighed. "Poor H'otto. Rather tear his children apart and weave their fibers into the arena than hand them over to the gods. We could argue all day over which fate is worse."

"You didn't answer my question."

"Because you already know the answer, love." One reached out and touched my cheek, sending a chill down my spine. "You've changed the rules. You opened yourself up. A champion has never become an arena master before. You are the first, and with that, you've opened up all champions to their potential. There are going to be changes. You won't be the last champion to take power, nor the last one to put themselves directly in the attention of the gods. And if you fail, they will eat you like they ate H'otto. And your children, too. There will be no protecting them. Then, I will be on the hunt for a new arena master to entertain them, because that's the deal I've made for myself. In the end, it's all about how to stay in their favor." She flicked my chin. "But don't worry; the gods anticipate great things from you. I'm sure—or rather, I hope—you can deliver."

I DIDN'T KNOW exactly how I got back to my quarters. Mod and Sweetly were waiting for me, and they were confused and concerned by the dazed look on my face. I pulled them close and held them tightly.

I will protect them, I vowed.

Nothing had changed. I had been a slave once and I could be a slave again. The new champions of this galaxy would know freedom. They would know the truth. They would not be altered and controlled by implants. They would be kept in the shadows no longer.

And they would fight this fight alongside me.

I understood, now more than ever, that my life was never meant to be mine, whether as a Maedan, as a champion, or as master of this arena. I would gladly give it, just as I had before, for my children.

Gods or seeds or whatever else, they will live on.

ABLE—TEN—EYED me with interest as he stepped out of his jar onto the pristine white arena floor.

"So this is what you look like," he said.

"Are you disappointed?"

"I'm not," he said, and walked a slow circle around me, taking me in.

"Do I look strange to you?"

"No more than I was to you in the beginning, I'm sure." He stopped and we faced each other. "So there's a world of people out there like you."

"And many others. Should you choose to join us, you'll have the chance to see them."

"I have a choice?"

"I'm giving you one."

He laughed. "Actually, you aren't, and I salute you for it. You just baited me into killing the woman I supposedly love in front of the whole world. I can't imagine what awaits me if I were to go back."

"Fame. Or infamy. You will spend the rest of your natural life listening to the entire planet gossip about what you've done. If you attain your political goals, they will be forever marred by that one event. Even your victory will be tainted by how you came about it. You'll never again be able to set foot outside your home without hearing whispers debating whether you're a hero or a villain."

"You sound as if you know this firsthand."

"I do." I met his eyes. "I am Seven, the seventh champion of the Galaxy of the Starry River and the master of this arena."

"Starry River. Is that what you call it? On Harmony we call it the Path of Snow Birds." Able glanced around the arena. Then, he lifted his right hand and looked at his palm. "I guess that makes me—"

"Ten."

"Am I to abandon my name for this number?"

I hesitated at this question. Images of Maeda came to me. Hazy, blurry images of who I used to be on a planet where I had a name that I no longer used.

"Yes," I said. "Should you stay, the name your world gave you would be no more."

Able closed his hand into a fist, grasping the winner's laurel tightly. "I can live with that," he said. "And I suppose part of me is grateful. I would've gotten bored on that planet. Fame and fortune can be dull when there's nothing else to be had."

"I expected no less."

"So," he said. I could already see him jumping three steps

ahead. Never one to be satisfied with the present, this one. "When do I get *my* arena?"

I burst out laughing. I could tell Ten was offended, but I couldn't help it. I had been worried that he would be a difficult one to handle, but with one naive question he reminded me how green and young he truly was. I reached out and took his hand in mine.

"Take a walk with me. I'll tell you a story."

He looked confused, but followed. I snapped my fingers and the white faded away. We strolled in the black of space. Distant stars blinked all around us.

"In the beginning, there was the universe and the first beings who lived in it."

CHAPTER 32

I STOOD ON THE BALCONY OVERLOOKING THE ARENA FLOOR.

I had stood upon that floor many times, both feet planted upon that cold, grayish-brown metal, legs shaking. Nasmi, the contestant from Maeda. Then the student, fingers wrapped around the strings of the arena, unaware that it was actually the strings pulling me rather than the other way around. Then as the game runner, holding the fate of others who trod upon the floor, uncertain of what lay ahead, running toward destinations just out of their reach.

And now, as master of the arena.

Mod and Sweetly ran in playful circles upon the slippery white floor, laughing and chasing each other. Every now and then, Mod would pause to manifest white cubes that floated in the air. Sweetly pounced after them, chittering happily. The gods laughed in my mind, a soundless expression of joy that seeped through my consciousness.

I had thought they'd sever their connection to me after the last game. To my surprise, they chose to remain. When I'd inquired when they were going to back out of my mind and go back to the norm, they'd given me no clear answer save for a quiet chuckle.

"So they're the ones who came before me," Ten said from

my side. "I find it rather difficult to believe that they managed to win the games as they are."

I ignored his derisive tone. Ten liked to bait, and nothing irritated him more than people who chose not to bite. The gods perked up. They found him amusing. "As it happens," I said mildly, "they played far better than you did."

"Is that so?"

"Don't you have something else to do?"

Ten smirked and gave an exaggerated, almost comical bow. "Yes. At your service, arena master," he said, and walked away.

I traced my fingers against the balcony railing. Sweetly jumped into Mod's arms. He swung her around, laughing merrily. The gods watched them.

I can bring them to worship, I reminded them. *You can see them often.*

Laughter. Then, nothing.

"We need to reset the stage."

I nodded. Two never wasted time with pleasantries, and while there had been a time I'd found that particular trait of theirs off-putting and cold, these days I'd learned to appreciate it as a much-needed efficiency around the arena. "I know. Just give them a little longer."

"Just make sure to tell them to clear the floor before it starts shifting," Two said. They were headless today. Though I'd long become used to their mechanical body, I still preferred to be able to see an expression when they spoke, whether it was on an organic face or not. "Nine doesn't do anything unless *you* tell her to."

"She knows what needs to be done."

"Sure she does," Two replied. I felt like they had more to say, but whatever it was, they took it with them as they retreated toward the orb's interior.

Mod and Sweetly had sat down. Mod spun a cube on the floor and Sweetly batted it. I watched her movement. Once, she had been among the most clever and agile of her race. When inside the arena, I had been able to feel the amazing, indescribable complexities of her mind, like a detailed map of a massive mountain that showed every leaf on every tree. Now, her mind was a simple, smooth plane. Undisturbed, uncomplicated.

Perfect.

I gripped the railing. Mod looked up and smiled at me. He waved. The gods acknowledge his greeting, though I was the only one who felt it.

Perfect.

My children were perfect. They came from worlds that didn't appreciate them. Imperfect worlds that didn't deserve them to begin with. Here, they were loved, protected. Here, they were where they were meant to be, where they could be happy.

My fingers tightened. Mod appeared to notice the change on my face. He tilted his head quizzically. I forced a smile and he seemed satisfied, but I couldn't maintain it the moment he turned away.

Sweetly chittered. She glanced up at me. But unlike Mod, she couldn't distinguish anything abnormal about my expression at the moment. I could smile or frown or bare my teeth at her, and she would give me the same happy purr and try to pounce into my lap. Her cognition and intelligence, once razor sharp, were now a mystery. Sometimes she tapped into the arena at a level deeper than anyone; other times she seemed little more than an animal.

Small price to pay for her happiness. On her world, she had been miserable. Now, she was perfect.

She was perfect before.

My knuckles were turning white. Was I shaking? Mod looked at me again, that confused look back on his face. What would he have been if he had stayed on his world? Would his people have recognized how special he was and realized they were wrong all along? Could he have changed his world for others like him?

Sweetly leaned against Mod, rubbing her face against his body affectionately.

Could she have found peace here if I hadn't interfered? Could I have protected and guided her, and taught her how to guard herself against H'otto and the gods?

Mod looked increasingly concerned, but I couldn't fake a smile for him. The arena rotated rapidly around me and I couldn't pull myself out of the tailspin. The gods ignored me. They had no interest in my moral dilemmas.

I did right by my children.

Tam. I could remember Tam.

I did right by them.

I had left him behind because taking him from the world and family he knew would've been selfish. It was what he would've wanted.

I did right.

Had I ever questioned what Mod and Sweetly might've wanted?

I did right.

Had I once thought about whether they were happy where they were, or how they wanted to be?

I—

"Seven."

I snapped out of my trance. One approached me, unhurried as usual. I quickly replaced my harried expression with a neutral one.

"Are you certain about this?"

I cleared my throat. "About what?"

"The location for the next game," One said.

The gods echoed her question. Now that my focus was on the games, they were suddenly alert and aware.

Yatam.

Yes, Yatam, I replied, trying to temper my roiling emotions inside and out.

"What about it?"

"Are you certain?"

Are you certain?

Certain? I wasn't certain of anything anymore. The gods pushed and prodded at me. Mod waved eagerly at me, trying to get my attention as Sweetly chittered and ran in circles. One's question echoed in layers through my mind, like a voice shouting through distant mountains.

You brought me here. Let me do this.

"Alright," I heard One say.

Had I spoken out loud? I didn't even realize. I turned to One.

"Shall we move forward?"

I took my head, clearing it of the gods' presence. They backed off, but I knew they were never far away. "Not yet. I need time."

The gods voiced their impatience. If it were up to them, I would already be clearing a bunk for the next champion.

Anticipation makes it sweeter.

Reluctance.

Wait.

They pushed forward, wanting more.

Wait!

They backed off. For a moment I wasn't sure they would. One's expression was unreadable, but I had a feeling she could sense my struggle.

You put me in charge for a reason. Let me run things as I see fit. You will see.

I had to be certain.

It will all be worth the wait.

I had gotten this far by taking risks, and the risk of offending the gods was just another step forward.

Wait.

They relented. I let out a breath of relief as they pulled back, retreating to a distant corner of my mind. It was the closest I'd come to being alone with my thoughts since they'd hooked their consciousness into mine.

"Trash the old notes," I said to One. "Start cultural exploration anew."

One nodded. "Very good," she said. "I will proceed with the preparations."

I watched her back grow smaller as she walked away. That hunched form, which I'd spent so much time trailing behind during those early days in the arena. She had guided me from day one, and though I'd wondered whether I ought to feel more resentful of the role she had groomed me for, I couldn't deny that One had never once failed to keep me focused on what was important.

Mod was still looking up. I gave him a smile—genuine this time. My mind cleared, like a fog pulling away from the rays of the sun.

I must be certain.

Certainty had brought me here—no longer afraid, no longer cowering, but protecting those who came under my wing. I'd had my turn to be saved. Now, it was my job to save them.

My precious children.

I must be certain for their sakes.

I must be the one who determined what was best for them, today and tomorrow and in the endless future that lay ahead. There was no room for doubt, not for the master of the arena. To doubt was to put their fragile lives in danger once more, and I was never, ever going to allow that to happen, no matter the price.

I am certain.

ELEVEN

CHAPTER 33

"KILL HIM."

One's wrist flicked with the most graceful of movements. The splintered contestant on the arena floor died instantly, crushed under his own weight as the gravity around him suddenly increased a thousandfold. His opponent, the new champion, stood dumbfounded, unaware that he himself was bleeding liberally from several places on his body.

One dropped the strings and turned to me. "Looks like Yatam has succeeded in producing a champion. Well done, arena master."

I nodded, peering over the balcony at the new one to our ranks. Eleven, a champion by default.

Waiting for him had been the right choice. Stalling the gods time and again, waiting for Yatam to slowly circle its sun, had not been easy. But I had been patient. Ever since I had seen him that first time on Yatam, a mere infant in the arms of his mother, I had known he was destined to become one of us.

His name translated to Solace and he had grown into a fine Yataman male. He was tall and strong, and I supposed by the standards of some planets he might even be handsome. I'd followed his life closely, watching over him, a privilege I'd never had with Mod and Sweetly. He had been the center of much media attention on his planet since I'd plucked him out of the masses to participate in the game—after the trial rounds to ensure he was aware of the mechanics of the arena. Though the interest of the public was not due to his skills in the game, which were average at best. Nor was it due to his personality— he was awkward and reserved and attempted to stay out of the center of attention whenever he could.

Though he'd led a mostly quiet life, the Titen Syndrome he was born with had not been kind to him, just as I expected. Despite his own efforts to excel beyond average in life, his peers had constantly and persistently underestimated and isolated him. The fact that he wore his cosmetic differences so blatantly didn't help—the missing scales and unusual vibrato in his voice were difficult to hide. But this had ended up working to his advantage, as few of the other contestants had targeted him as a threat. Despite the fact his skills were far from outstanding, he had faced little direct sabotage, and with that, combined with his self-preservation instincts, he'd managed to eke out a victory, even if it was by default when his final opponent splintered. A close call, but I took it. The fact that he'd won despite the odds, even if it had been dumb luck, was proof that he was meant to bear the winner's laurel.

He knew alienation and struggle, and he was about to be rewarded for it. Eleven would not know the hardships of the rest of us. As the first champion in the true new age of the arena, he would be welcomed as a member of a new family, one that would not judge him for what he was but embrace his differences. He would be allowed to grow and find his place, away from the cold, prying eyes of his people.

And his place was with us.

"Hold the jar," I told One. "I want to talk to this one directly."

· · ·

JUST OUTSIDE THE ARENA FLOOR, Ten waited for me, arms folded and looking cocky as always.

"This was fun," he said simply as I approached.

"Tricky, is what this was," I said pointedly. "In case you haven't noticed, the point system didn't quite go as planned."

Ten chuckled. "Well, I stand by it being a great idea. It's not our fault the new champ didn't hit his goal, is it? What'll it be, arena master?"

I looked past him toward the arena floor. Even though Solace had not amassed the required points to save his world, I had a feeling that wouldn't matter. I'd seen how his world mistreated him and belittled him. He didn't need them. As a child of the arena, he would soon be freed from the restraints of a society that did not appreciate him. Looking at him, I felt my heart swell. Yatam had been the right choice through and through.

"He will join us willingly," I said. "He is one of us."

"And if he won't?"

I gave Able a hard look. He stopped talking and instead leaned down, took my hand, and kissed it. I went past him to the arena floor, where Solace knelt over the place where the other contestant had disintegrated. I did not want him locked in transition. I wanted to talk to this outcast first, to welcome him and let him know he was finally among those who accepted him.

I approached him gently and laid a hand on his shoulder. He looked up.

"Welcome," I said. "Eleven."

His face was wet with tears and he seemed to look right through me, unable to understand where I had come from. I waited for him to gather himself and realize the reality of things.

"I don't have enough points," he said stiffly, as if speaking to himself. "He was supposed to win. I don't have enough points."

I patted his shoulder. "That's OK. You don't have to worry

about that. Your world didn't deserve you. It never did. You can move on to bigger and better things now. With us."

He pushed me off. "What are you talking about?" he said, his voice trembling. "You said you would destroy my world if we didn't have the points."

"Your world?" I shook my head. "I hardly think a world that treats you like that is worth calling 'your' world."

"It is my world!" he shouted, taking me off guard. I had never heard him so much as raise his voice the entire time he was in the arena. *"I don't care how they treated me. They're innocent! We didn't ask to be part of this! You can't destroy an entire world for one stupid game!"*

Anger bubbled in me. I saw a weapon begin to form in his hand—a curved blade common to game hunters on his world. I doubted that he actually had the nerve to attack me, but my frustration was growing quickly. I snapped my fingers and he fell face-first to the ground, pulled down by gravity.

"You should feel privileged," I said through tightly bound lips. "You are about to join the ranks of the true elites. Your world that never accepted you will pay for not seeing your true worth."

"I'll never join *you*," he spat, followed by a string of curses that even Axi's translations could not make sense of. I reached into him and nothing but bitterness and hate jabbed back at me. I felt his heart, a wounded and damaged heart, but one that belonged to his world utterly and completely. No matter how his people cheapened and derided his existence, so long as they still existed, he was theirs—body, mind, and soul.

I had saved his precious world from being burned. If not for me striving to save those like him—to save *him*—his planet wouldn't even exist right now. *He* wouldn't exist.

Ungrateful child, a voice inside me whispered.

"Axi," I said, "transparent display."

The white of the dome faded away. Above us, Yatam looked back, beautiful and green.

"Begin the raze."

It was an amazing sight, truly, as a single beam of energy shot from the orb—the energy gathered from a new sun. For a moment there was nothing. Then, the planet began to burn. Fire radiated from that single point and grew and grew. The heat of the sun could not be stopped. It would burn, engulfing every life on the planet and boiling the seas, until nothing remained.

"No!" Solace cried. But it was too late. This fire would go on and on and there was nothing he could do. He averted his eyes from the sight, and I stepped behind him, grabbed him by the scalp, and pulled him up, holding him so he couldn't look away from the flames swallowing his home. He had no home left. He needed to learn this. He needed to abandon the world that did not appreciate him and become more.

One day, he will thank me for this lesson.

"Watch it burn," I said. "You will be stronger for it."

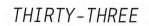

THIRTY-THREE

CHAPTER 34

"Axi," I heard him say as I stood just outside the heart. "Zoom in on that image."

He didn't know I was here. Without implants, the new champions were not quite as connected to the arena as I was or those who came before me.

I preferred this. Not only did it mean they were allowed to experience their emotions and thoughts unhindered by the arena, but it also gave me a slight advantage in moments such as this. I watched Eleven from the shadows as he directed Axi.

"What does the text say?" he asked. The image before him was one of the contestants—a thin female with dark, uneven hair and defiant eyes. On her wrist in black ink was a string of symbols that reminded me of the free Kols on Maeda who inked delicate patterns over their marks.

"*Kintsukuroi*," Axi replied. "A term that originated from an island nation, meaning 'repaired in gold.'"

Eleven stood in silence for a moment. I could see only his back, but I knew he was studying the features of the woman on the screen. I cleared my throat and he turned.

"Find something that interests you?"

I felt him struggle for a moment, but his face betrayed nothing.

"No," he said shortly, and walked past me out of the heart without looking back. He had little to say to me on the best of days.

I stepped into the heart and gazed up at the face on the screens.

Donna Astra.

Her name translated to Lady of the Stars, though she went by the second part of that name. There was very little outstanding about her, though I could see in those dark eyes the stubborn streak she pretended so hard not to have. She liked to think of herself as reserved and meek, preferring not to stand out or get into other people's troubles. And yet when trouble found her, she couldn't help sticking her neck out. I had no doubt she would continue to do so, over and over again.

Her competition was stiff. Ten had already claimed his own protégé in the game, and he had a talent for backing winners or near-winners. If groomed properly, the actor could certainly win this game, though I couldn't say I was a fan of the man—he was too full of grandiose delusions for my taste. Thirty-One appeared to like this one, but she was still green and her judgment was questionable.

But more than anything, this woman had caught the eye of the outcast.

After all this time, several lifetimes within the orb, Eleven was still a difficult one. Much like the champions before and after him, he had long abandoned the notions of theism that Yatam had imbued in him, though to say he had embraced the way of the producers would be a stretch. His resourcefulness and the omnilingualism that came with the nature of his race made him a most efficient and useful researcher, and he was even able to avoid using the chameleon suit most of the time. But while he did his work without complaint, Eleven still sought to empathize with the contestants rather than his fellow champions.

At least the producers found him amusing. I felt myself

fuming ever so slightly at the thought. The producers had become far too involved in the games, and perhaps that was my own fault. After all, I was the one who had shown them that there were far more entertaining ways to manipulate the games beyond sitting back and watching from the holy grounds. I hadn't minded too much until they prodded me to allow Eleven to push himself onto the arena floor, and that petulant child had been a thorn in my side ever since.

I turned my attention back to the screens again.

Eleven, despite his rebellious tendencies, knew better than to become overly attached to contestants. But this one was different. He had picked her out of millions of volunteers from the blue planet. A subconscious choice though it was, I had noticed the stirrings in him when they had encountered each other in the sewer. He often seemed to be researching her, though I had doubts she would tear her eyes away from Ten's protégé long enough to give Eleven the time of day.

If by some miracle she does, it will be a heck of a scandal for the producers to eat up.

It was only appropriate that Eleven would hand his heart over to a woman as willful as he was from a planet that called itself Dirt. But if he got too close ... well, it wouldn't be the first time he was made an example of, and it likely wouldn't be the last. Stubborn to the end, that one.

I had my own preference in this game—the most competent player, who kept her skills hidden better than all the others. Her name was Evangeline, which translated to Good News. It was a most appropriate name, and she reminded me of Mod—simple, yet exceptional. Her instinct for the game had also been outstanding, having managed to maintain her position with only the slightest tips of the scales in her favor by my hand. I hoped to welcome her into our midst with open arms.

Still, I didn't dislike Eleven's pick. Looking into those dark eyes, I tried to imagine this woman as the champion. Thirty-Three. Her chances were slim but not nil. She was strong, despite having only one solid trick up her sleeve. And she was resilient, enough to survive a splinter and continue on her way. She would not align with me so easily, as so many others had. She might be another difficult one like Eleven. But handled with care, she might be a worthy and entertaining one to keep around. The producers had begun to develop a passing interest in her as well. I wondered what she would think if she knew the incredibly high bar she was already setting for herself.

Under the right circumstances, she could move mountains.

Thirty-three.

Astra.

Of the stars.

THANK YOU

Hey reader,

We hope you enjoyed *Master of the Arena*.

Authors live off reviews. If you enjoyed this book, please leave a review on the site of your choice (e.g. Amazon, Goodreads, Barnes & Noble).

Also, want a free book? Get one when you sign up for J. D. Edwin's newsletter. Sign up at jdedwin.com.

ALSO BY J. D. EDWIN

Made in the USA
Coppell, TX
05 April 2023

15258907R00215